FOR A WARRIOR'S HEART

Ancient Songs
Book 1

LAURA STRICKLAND

ARE YOU SIGNED UP FOR DRAGONBLADE'S BLOG?

You'll get the latest news and information on exclusive giveaways, exclusive excerpts, coming releases, sales, free books, cover reveals and more.

Check out our complete list of authors, too!

No spam, no junk. That's a promise!

Sign Up Here

www.dragonbladepublishing.com

Dearest Reader;

Thank you for your support of a small press. At Dragonblade Publishing, we strive to bring you the highest quality Historical Romance from some of the best authors in the business. Without your support, there is no 'us', so we sincerely hope you adore these stories and find some new favorite authors along the way.

Happy Reading!

CEO, Dragonblade Publishing

ADDITIONAL DRAGONBLADE BOOKS BY AUTHOR LAURA STRICKLAND

Ancient Songs Series
For a Warrior's Heart (Book 1)

The Three Sisters MacBeith Series
Keeper of the Gate (Book 1)
Keeper of the Hearth (Book 2)
Keeper of the Light (Book 3)

Do our ancestors journey with us
In the color of our eyes?
In the strength of our limbs,
A fiery mane of hair.
Or does the connection reach far deeper?
Is there a better way for spirit to travel
Than via the blood of family?

~ Finlay the Bard

A T THE HALL *of a Scottish chief deep in the western Highlands, a bard entertains those gathered, singing and telling tales while accompanying himself on the harp. He weaves his tales in praise of his host's ancestors, with a rare talent that keeps his listeners enthralled from the highest to the lowest. Amid the leaping torches and the flickering candles, there is magic encircling the great chamber this night.*

Finlay the Bard gives a smile, knowing he holds his audience by the ears and by the heart. Slim fingers dance over gut strings and green eyes glimmer.

The tale he weaves is this:

Once, in Erin, the land of our ancestors, there lived a great warrior. Before ever Chief Airlee's forefathers came across the water to Scotland, this was, before he or any of us was so much as a thought in the minds of the gods. In a kingdom called Armagh, that fair land which on a clear day can be glimpsed still from the braes of our purple mountains, did this young warrior work and train. 'Twas a place of magic, of song, and laws so ancient we now hear only the echoes of them. Many are the tales of men who hold greed in their minds and those with a firm grip on justice. Songs such as this one I sing ye, for a warrior's heart.

CHAPTER ONE

Armagh, Erin, the first century AD

ARDAHL MACCORMAC STRUGGLED up from the green turf of the training field and stared at the blood on his hands. Quick and clever hands they were, well used to holding a sword or a dirk. Skilled at fashioning a curragh or carving trinkets out of wood to please the children of the clan. Now stained red, slick with the life's blood of his best friend.

Around him, the field teemed with other warriors working. At the far edge of the field, Chief Fearghal's war advisor, Dornach, directed half a score of lads tossing spears at wicker men. Across the way, a group at practice with the chariots made a rattling din.

Ardahl looked from his hands to the figure at his feet. Yellow haired, limp, slumped forward with a spreading stain across his tunic.

This could not be. It could not, it could not. *By all the holy gods—*

Someone shouted at him. With his pulse pounding violently in his ears, Ardahl barely noticed. Such shouting, common here on the practice field, did not penetrate his horror or break the paralysis that gripped him like a hard pair of hands.

"Conall?"

If he called to his friend, Conall would most assuredly get to his feet, give Ardahl that crooked grin of his, the one he'd known from their earliest days together. Prove this was a prank of some sort, the kind Conall loved to play. That the whole of this encounter had been but a prank from beginning to end. A poor sort of jest to be sure, for only moments ago Conall had seemed to be angry with him. So very angry.

He had changed lately, no denying that, had become harsh and all too ready to kindle, quick to pick a quarrel as he had just moments ago while they sparred with one another. Here, where they were supposed to be practicing together to face not one another, but their tribe's enemies.

"Ardahl!" Someone bellowed his name repeatedly, coming closer and still closer. "What has happened?"

The way such things often seemed to occur among men who trained together, warriors were flocking in. They had a sense for trouble. Disaster, betrayal. *Death.*

Ardahl turned uncomprehending eyes on the first of those to reach him.

Cathair. *It would be him.*

If Ardahl had an enemy here in Armagh, this land he so loved, it would be this man. A few years Ardahl's elder, Cathair considered himself foremost among the young warriors and carried his arrogance just as naturally as his mane of white-blond hair. As assistant to Dornach, he tended to make a habit of denigrating Ardahl's deeds and making him seem lesser, presumably so he could himself feel greater.

Now Cathair's broad face held an expression such as Ardahl had never seen. He looked from Conall, hunched over on the ground, to Ardahl and back again rapidly. "What is this? What has happened?" He stopped so fast in the turf beside Ardahl that his deerskin-clad feet skidded, and he blinked at the blood on Ardahl's hands. "What?"

Ardahl found himself unable to answer. He did not know what had happened.

Cathair bent down and touched Conall gently, turning him onto his back. Everyone favored Conall, even men who would admit to liking no one else. It would be nearly impossible to dislike him, with his cheerful nature and love of nonsense. Even though lately something had been eating at him like a sickness, culminating in—

This.

"I do not know what happened." Ardahl forced the words through a dry throat. Others were hurrying up now, looks of concern and then disbelief on their faces. They made a circle around the three of them—Ardahl, Cathair, and Conall there on the ground. The warriors stared as if they could not believe their eyes.

Nor, it seemed, could Cathair. He raked Ardahl with a pale blue stare before going down beside Conall in the grass.

"What's happened?"

What happened? What happened? What—

The query echoed all around. Ardahl, finding himself at the center of a ring of onlookers, also dropped to his knees beside his friend.

"Conall," he croaked. "Conall, get up. 'Tis not funny, this."

Cathair's big hands moved, reached out and touched Conall's head almost tenderly before searching out the pulse at his neck. When Conall's fair hair flopped back, revealing a quiet face, Ardahl was certain he was alive. Playing yet at some horrible game.

But the blood. So much blood. And the dagger embedded in Conall's chest.

For an instant the world blurred around Ardahl, and even though he knelt, he went dizzy. A grim silence now settled around him. These men, warriors all, had seen grievous wounds before.

Perhaps not so grievous as this.

Cathair's fingers fluttered from Conall's neck to hover above the hilt of the dagger, which he did not touch. He raised his face and stared into Ardahl's eyes.

"He is dead."

"Nay." Ardahl huffed the word. "It cannot be."

But the warriors standing around them had heard. A shiver of a whisper did go up then, like a cold wind in the barley.

Cathair, ignoring them, fixed Ardahl with a stern look, the sort he gave his companions when they proved careless on the practice field, or uncertain before a battle.

"How could it be otherwise, wi' all that blood? Ardahl, is this your dagger in his chest?"

"His. He drew it on me. He began a quarrel—"

"He drew upon you? His closest friend?"

"Aye."

Conall had many friends, and, aye, Ardahl held that honored place of the dearest. That much, no one could deny.

"I do not believe it." Ardahl stared again at the blood on his hands. Conall's blood? Another whisper rippled through the air around him, sounding like an echo of the word.

Believe.

Believe.

Believe.

"Get up. Ardahl, get up." Suddenly Cathair was on his feet, and Ardahl climbed to meet him, nose to nose. For aye, they were nearly of a height, even if Ardahl did not have Cathair's girth. Pale blue eyes gazed fiercely into Ardahl's hazel ones.

"Conall would not draw a weapon on ye. You be closest to him o' all the men. Tell me what truly happened. I will have to call the chief. The druids."

Ardahl went hot and cold in turns. He saw no mercy in that stare. A quick look about, as he turned in a circle with his bloodied hands hanging at his sides, showed him none anywhere.

Dornach, their war chief, came bulling up, clearly summoned from the far side of the field. He took in the scene, almost stumbling over his own feet when he saw Conall, now stretched on his back upon the ground.

"What has happened?" Swiftly he turned on Cathair. "Cathair?"

"Conall lies there dead. 'Twas no' me, but Conall's best friend who took him down."

Dornach, a stout and hardened man of middle years with black hair and dark eyes, swayed where he stood. As had Cathair, he bent to touch Conall at the throat before sweeping Ardahl with a look that took in his reddened hands. "I do no' believe it."

Nor do I.

"Ardahl," pronounced Cathair with ponderous scorn, "claims Conall drew the weapon on him."

"Nay!" Dornach said before bending and touching Conall once more, as if hoping he was mistaken.

"He did, Master Dornach," Ardahl ground out. "He's lately been changed. Quarrelsome and angry—"

A high-pitched, keening sound pierced the air. Someone came running, pushing at the barrier of gathered warriors. Her terrible cry preceded her like that of a gull wheeling above the water.

Dornach stepped away. Horror clawed its way up from Ardahl's belly when he saw Conall's mother, Beath. Face white as bone, eyes burning blue, she threw herself upon the figure in the grass.

"Nay. Nay! My son, my son, my son!"

The world once more spun around Ardahl. Light and darkness flickered before his eyes. He saw faces, those in the gathered crowd and Beatha MacAert's, as she lifted it to him, all grief. All pain.

"By all that is holy, I have lost my only son."

CHIEF FEARGHAL SOON came at a run, his druids following at a more dignified pace in a group of three, their expressions grave. Ardahl had by then gone numb with disbelief and dismay. Had it not been for the blood on his hands and the faint breath of a breeze on his cheek, he would have thought it a dream. Some dark imagining come in the night.

They took him to the chief's hall, Dornach walking behind him as if he were a prisoner and thence to the chief's private rooms beyond, where his lady wife stared like all the others before fleeing. Leaving the six of them, the chief, Ardahl, Dornach, and the three priests, alone.

"Tell us what happened."

The same question over again. Different expressions. The chief's had turned hard as flint. Dornach's blank as stone. The three holy men appeared to be reserving judgment, but Ardahl saw no leniency in their eyes.

"I do not know what happened."

"How can that be? You were there, were ye not?"

Ardahl searched his mind, which contained a jumble of thoughts and images. He shook his head. Even now he had no clear understanding of how Conall came to be dead at his feet.

Dead!

Chief Fearghal looked at Dornach. "What did ye see?"

"Very little. The men were at practice. I was on the far side of the field instructing the younger lads. All seemed well. Then there was a flurry. Cathair cried out—"

"Cathair?" Chief Fearghal interrupted. "He was there?"

"'Tis my understanding he was close by."

"May I please wipe my hands?" Was that Ardahl's own voice, sounding faint and far away? "They are covered in blood."

"That blood is the proof o' your crime," said one of the holy men, speaking for the first time. "It stays where it is."

Ardahl's stomach heaved over in a slow roll. They believed he had done this terrible thing. To Conall, of all men.

Believe.

"Send for Cathair," Chief Fearghal snapped. "We will hear what he saw."

Cathair, who detested Ardahl. Cathair, who would not mind seeing him out of the way, that he might be first among the warriors.

"I did no' mean to hurt Conall," he said quickly, knowing he had best say something before Cathair arrived. "I would never harm him. He is my best—"

Was. *Was.*

The pain of it hit Ardahl then like a crashing wave. He swayed where he stood.

"Stand," Chief Fearghal ordered him. "Ye will at least ha' the courage, the decency, for that. Ye will keep to your feet until the truth o' this is found and a punishment determined."

Punishment. Was it not enough that Conall must be gone from the world? He who had brought at least half the sunlight to it. The first person Ardahl went to with a trouble or a joke to be shared. The one he stood beside in battle. A touchstone of his life.

But Conall had been different lately. Less confiding. Angry more often. Ardahl had thought it the pressures of training, which had increased. They would face many battles this summer against Chief Fearghal's rivals to the west. A man like Conall, who refused to show fear, who dared not do so in the chief's hall for dread of losing face, often demonstrated it in other ways. Not till the knife was in Conall's hands had Ardahl looked into his eyes and seen the threatening intent.

"Stand there," Fearghal said, the very voice of command, "and speak your truth."

CHAPTER TWO

Light danced like bright raindrops, making the air shimmer and bounce as Liadan ran. It jittered all around her as sun does on water and dazzled her eyes. She did not feel the stones beneath her feet as she left the house, or the grass as she crossed the practice field. She could still hear Mam's wail in her mind.

It could not be so. It could not be so, what the messenger had said. Her brother, her beloved brother Conall, so strong and bright with laughter always in his heart.

Dead.

She had dreaded this. On some terrible, deep-seated level, she had. Ever since he'd gone off to battle when she was very young—for nearly six winters separated them in age—she'd feared losing him. She'd thought the news would come following some distant campaign, a fight over territory off to the west. Not here on their own turf.

She stumbled in the grass and nearly went down. Ahead of her in the green field she could see—

A great crowd of warriors. Liadan could see them standing all around Mam, who knelt in the rough grass, bent over something else. *Someone* else. Keening, keening.

The messenger, who had brought the dread news, turned back to look at her. Liadan's younger sister, Flanna, came after her, calling out.

Time slowed and then stopped, just like Liadan's feet, which dragged to a halt. She had reached her mother's huddled form.

The air around her grew bright. Too bright.

Her mam's yellow hair had come loose in the run and tumbled messily down her back. The pale-gray fabric of her tunic dress looked dull against grass so green it hurt the eyes, and there—there—

Red. Rich and full, not rusty like that dried on the bandages she sometimes helped to wash. All over the tunic she had herself helped to weave for her brother. Thick and padded the garment was, so it might afford him some protection if he entered battle.

It had done nothing to stop the blade of the knife that protruded from his heart.

She fell to her knees beside her mother and stared into her brother's face.

Untouched, it appeared calm and peaceful as he did when sleeping. Perhaps he merely slept, withal.

But nay. So much blood. Too much.

Conall's yellow hair made another bright patch against the sod. His eyes, blue as her own, lay closed.

A sob rose to her throat and fought for release. Mam wailed and wailed. Flanna came down into the grass beside Liadan. Only twelve years old, would Flanna understand?

"My son! My son! I ha' lost my only son!"

The warriors stood silent in a respectful circle. One of them stooped—it was Cathair, foremost among their young men. That was, unless Ardahl could be considered foremost. Ardahl. Where was he? Surely he above all others should be here at Conall's side.

Cathair bent close over Mam. He touched her shoulder gently and spoke in her ear so Liadan could hear.

"'Twas Ardahl who did this. Ardahl took your son's life."

Mam lifted her face and stared at him. Eyes awash with tears, cheeks blotched and reddened, she looked nothing like herself.

"Nay. Ardahl is nearest to him in all the world."

"They quarreled. I saw it all."

Another warrior stepped across from the clot of men not far away and called Cathair by name. The young man straightened with a last pat for Mam's shoulder. His pale eyes slid over Liadan and Flanna before he turned away.

"Cathair, the chief requires ye."

"Ardahl," Mam whispered in a voice such as Liadan had never heard. "Ye have taken my son. I will ne'er forgive ye. Ne'er. *Ne'er*."

She broke down then into wild sobs. Liadan and Flanna clung to her even as the pain and disbelief warred in Liadan's heart.

Ardahl. Nay. From as far back as she could remember, Conall and Ardahl had run together, laughed together, trained together. Could such a bond be severed even by a knife's blade?

Someone helped her up, strong arms lifting her. The same arms lifted Mam and Flanna in turn. Ferghan, one of the senior warriors, stood there.

"Come, mistress. We must take him. Carry him to the healers."

Mam raised a devastated face. "He is alive? They can save him?"

"Nay, mistress, nay. They will care for him, wash him. Prepare him for his cairn. We who loved him will carry him. Ye may follow behind."

But the dagger is still in his heart. His very own dagger.

Liadan wanted to spit that out. She could see the hilt of the dagger quite clearly as the men tenderly, so tenderly, lifted her brother. The pattern on the handle, showing through the slick coating of blood. That very dirk Chief Fearghal had given Conall when he entered the chief's service.

Dead by his own dirk? By Ardahl's hand? She could believe none of it.

But she followed. Mam went first after the men carrying Conall, and then Liadan, clasping Flanna's hand.

Liadan glanced into her young sister's face. It wore a look that must reflect her own. Pale with shock. Wide-eyed with disbelief.

Remember this moment, said a voice in Liadan's mind. *Remember your mam's grief and your own. The look in your sister's eyes. Store it in anger. If 'tis Ardahl who has done this, he must pay.*

He must pay in kind, however she felt about him.

HE HAD BECOME her enemy, had Ardahl. No matter how long she had followed after him with wistful eyes. Her brother's friend, who seldom seemed to notice her and who, when he did, clearly still thought of her as a child. No matter how she wanted to catch his smile, which was a singular thing, lighting and transforming a face ordinarily all lines and angles, wreathing it in joy. No matter how the glint of sunlight on auburn hair could turn her head. Or how she tried—in vain—to guess at the thoughts teeming in his hazel eyes.

A woman, however youthful, should not follow after a man that way. Especially one who was so plainly uninterested in her.

Now she followed her brother's body instead, borne by four strong warriors. Hearing Mam's wails all the while, watching her stumble and nearly go down once, twice.

Before they reached the healers' roundhouse, she let go of Flanna's hand and hurried forward to support Mam. They entered the hut together.

Somehow, so swiftly, word had gone ahead of them. The healers were waiting and ready when the little group arrived.

They stretched Conall's body on a pallet and gathered around him. Sunlight streamed in through the smoke hole in the roof— so bright and beautiful was the day—and the three healers, three being a sacred number, bent close to him.

One of the men, Master Dathi, was aged, the other two younger, his assistants. Dathi's veined hands trembled as he reached to hover above the handle of the knife, as if afraid to touch.

One of the younger men fluttered careful fingers at Conall's neck. "Dead, master."

"Aye. Och, aye." Dathi closed his eyes and whispered a prayer. For Conall's spirit? That it might wing swiftly westward to *Tír na nÓg*, the land of the blessed?

They all should have done that. She should. In her horror, she'd forgotten.

Had she imperiled her brother? Would his spirit now fail to reach the place of rest?

With an arm about her mother, who trembled violently, she eyed Conall's face. He looked so very peaceful. No hint that his best friend had just stabbed him to the heart. No anger, no fear, only the beautiful face of a youthful man at rest.

Gone from them so swiftly. How could that be? Whether Conall's spirit had winged to the west or otherwise, he had departed their lives.

No more early mornings spent with him when he got up for training and she rose also, being of a sort unable to keep to her bed once the sun was up. No making a meal so he could break his fast while he teased her and they laughed together. No more going to him with her troubles, the wise older brother—for Mam had lost two babes between her son and her elder daughter—seeking his strength and caring. Knowing he would mend things for her if he could.

Where be ye? she asked his quiet face. No answer, save a flicker of the sunlight coming down through the roof above him.

Flanna began to sob. Master Dathi looked at her kindly. "Why d'ye no' take your sister away?" he suggested to Liadan. "Before we prepare the body." His old hands again hovered over the handle of the dirk. Did she want to see that drawn from her brother's breast?

But she shook her head. "I will stay and support my mam."

Mam lifted her head. "Go, Liadan. Comfort your sister. If I faced watching your da go to his grave, I can face this."

But could she? Da's death had near leveled her. Changed the bright, cheerful woman she was. As would this. It would change all of them.

Liadan clothed her sister's hand with her own, and went.

CHAPTER THREE

THRICE HAD THE head priest, whose name was Aodh, asked Ardahl what happened. Thrice had he told them fairly he did not know.

Finally, Chief Fearghal spoke up. "How can ye fail to know how this happened, when ye stood right there?"

Before Ardahl could answer again, a clatter at the door of Fearghal's quarters, where they remained, heralded an arrival.

"Ah, here is one who will know."

Cathair burst in, looking overly large in his leather armor, fair hair gleaming in the gloom. His pale gaze went first to his chief, holding an odd gleam, then to the priests, and lastly to Ardahl's face, openly hostile.

"My chief," he gasped, breathless with his hurry.

"Cathair. You saw what happened to Conall MacAert, there on the field?"

"I saw some of it, my chief. Most of it."

"Tell us as clearly as you can what you did see, as Ardahl seems unable."

"Aye, chief."

"Ye were nearby?"

"I was. We had all been at practice since just after dawn. Preparing for the battles to come wi'—"

Chief Fearghal said dryly, "I know wi' whom we are at war."

"To be sure. Forgive me." Cathair wagged his head in sorrow. False sorrow? "Conall and Ardahl were sparring, across the field from Master Dornach." He cast a glance at the war chief. "As they often do. I was no' paying strict attention, not until I heard raised voices. They were quarreling."

He shot a sharper look at Ardahl.

"Were they?" asked Dornach in surprise, as if Ardahl did not stand there.

"Aye. 'Tis what caught my attention. The shouting and a sudden flurry. I realized 'twas not sparring anymore but a true quarrel. Even as I turned my eyes that way, they struggled together. Over—over the knife, so it appeared. Before I could so much as take a step toward them, the blade was in Conall's heart."

"I had no hold of it," Ardahl said. He must speak up or he would not have an opportunity. "I did not attack him."

"Nay?" Chief Fearghal lifted a brow. "Then why are both your hands red with his blood?"

"I tried—I tried to pull the knife out, then remembered 'tis often fatal—" The horror of seeing Conall's eyes go wide, of watching him begin to crumple, swamped him anew. "I swear to ye, I do not know how the knife got in his heart."

"But ye did quarrel with him?"

"Nay."

Cathair sneered. "I heard ye shouting."

Ardahl shook his head. "I did not shout. Conall did. He took a sudden anger with me. He began to accuse me of—"

Of what, Ardahl truly could not say. It had happened so suddenly. Conall's rage had been unprovoked, and his words unclear. Conall grew angry with him so seldom, though lately, aye, he had been much quicker to find fault.

"I do not know why he was angered or how—how—"

Steadily, Chief Fearghal asked of Cathair, "Was anyone else there with Conall and Ardahl? Another who could have committed this deed?"

"Nay, my chief. There was no one."

"No one else who could have heard or seen what happened?"

"Nay."

"Then"—Chief Fearghal's gaze glinted—"we can but draw a single conclusion. Two young warriors. One still stands, and one lies dead."

Was that a gleam of satisfaction Ardahl saw in Cathair's eyes? In no fit condition to employ discernment, he could not tell.

"Chief Fearghal," he said as steadily as he could manage, "Conall was as close to me as anyone in the world. I would never harm him."

"Even though it appears you have?"

Another step sounded at the door and Ardahl's mother hurried in. She had clearly come running from her weaving, with the bits of fluff all stuck to her clothing and her hair—auburn like his own—tumbling down. A face stark white with disbelief turned to Ardahl.

"Chief Fearghal. What has happened? My son—"

She reached to clasp Ardahl's hands but stopped when she saw the blood.

"Ardahl! What?"

"That, Mistress Maeve, is what we are trying to determine. A treacherous and terrible deed has been committed."

"Those outside, chief, those who ran to me said—they said Conall MacAert lies dead."

"So he does. Slain by the hand of his friend."

"Nay, nay, that cannot be. That cannot. My son would not do such a thing. My son—"

"Your son, mistress, will be held until justice can be pronounced."

"Nay."

"Our priests need time to ponder the occurrence, and the law."

"I cannot lose my son. I cannot! He is all I have."

"Mistress," the head druid said in a voice like the knelling of a bell, "it is as the chief says. We must ponder. We must study the laws and determine what is right in this matter."

"I cannot lose him," Mam said almost madly. "I cannot!" She drew a breath. "Let me take him home until you determine your justice."

"A man lies dead," said Chief Fearghal. "Ardahl will remain in our custody until he receives his determination."

Ardahl lifted his eyes to his mother's in agony. Since his father's death when he was but eleven, they had held each other. Been a family of two. He had done everything he could—including working to become foremost among Fearghal's warriors—for her sake.

Now he must abandon her. She looked as terrified by that prospect as he felt.

"Mam. Mam, I did not do this thing. I did not harm him."

She nodded.

But Chief Fearghal said, "Then who did? He has no answers, mistress. Go home and pray. Pray for justice."

NOT UNTIL NIGHTFALL, when they had fitted out a stout pen for him, did they let him clean his hands. By then it was near impossible. Conall's blood had dried hard, had become part of him, settled into the cracks and folds of his skin. He asked for a bucket of water, but the smell of the loosened blood sickened him, so he retched into the slop pan.

Good thing he hadn't eaten anything since dawn. Little came up but sorrow.

They had given him nothing besides the slop bucket and a blanket, so he sat on that and tried in vain to determine what had befallen him.

What he wanted—the one person with whom he needed to talk—was Conall. To him had Ardahl always turned with any trouble. They would walk or sit together and work things out. Make sense of any difficulty.

Although, indeed, lately Conall had seemed less ready to come to him. A bit short with him from time to time. There was something in it. Ardahl's tired mind could not figure what.

There had been much pressure upon all of them. Knowledge of the battles that would come this summer, and must be won if Chief Fearghal meant to hold his lands. The effort to remain at or near the best of Dornach's young warriors.

Such pressure—to be the best, to display courage in any situation—would plague anyone. Play upon the spirit.

But if troubled in that way, why had Conall not come to him? Since the very first battle they had entered together as young warriors, Conall had confided each doubt, every fear.

Had not Ardahl done the same?

He bent his head and pressed it against his upraised knees. Only months ago, Conall had confided that he had feelings, true feelings, for Brasha, the young woman he'd been seeing for the past half year. Not passing pricks of attraction or titillation as they all felt toward young women from time to time. This had become a matter of the heart.

"I do not know if I should tell her," Conall had said. Ardahl could still hear the hesitancy in his voice and see the wonder in his eyes. "I have never spoken those words to anyone." He'd grinned suddenly. "Save to my mam and our old hound, Blooney."

Ardahl hadn't known how to advise him. Women were dubious creatures, often harder to face than a screaming enemy warrior. And such words, once spoken, could not be recalled.

Now, huddled there on the floor of his cell, he wished he'd asked Conall for more. Had he spoken to Brasha of what was in his heart? Had she returned his feelings? Would she, too, be grieving him this night?

What would happen come morning? He lifted his head from his knees and looked at the remnants of Conall's blood on his hands. The druids would deliberate. The entire tribe, and Chief Fearghal in particular, relied upon their wisdom.

Whatever sentence they handed down as justice would be carried out. Should that be a sentence of death—

Ardahl drew a painful, jerky breath into his lungs. He had not expected his life to end so soon. Of course, any warrior, and one so often sent in at the head of his fellows, faced the possibility of death. That, though, was a matter that lay in the hands of the gods. Swift and fierce, it would come in a flurry.

As had Conall's death. A flurry so unexpected, he could not say how it had occurred.

If the druid Aodh came forth with a sentence of death for him, he would be hauled out to face it before all the tribe. His friends. His mam. Och, poor Mam. She, along with everyone he knew, would watch him die.

Had he the courage to face such a fate?

CHAPTER FOUR

L IADAN SAT UP all night with her mother, who sobbed and grieved without relent. Though she sent Flanna off to her bed, she doubted the poor lass got much rest. Mam's lamenting filled the small roundhouse.

By first light, which came early at this time of year, she was worried enough by her mother's state that she sent Flanna running for the healer.

Dathi himself arrived not much later, limping along after Flanna, for he was an aged man. Liadan met him at the door.

"Master Dathi, I am that grateful for your presence. I do not know what to do with my mam. She cries so hard I fear she will do herself a harm."

In truth, Mam had thrown herself down upon Conall's bed, the very place he had for most of his life laid his head, and refused to come away.

Dathi looked at Liadan with faded blue eyes. "Grief is grief, my lass, and in my experience the best remedy is to let it run its course."

"Aye, Master Dathi, yet I have never seen grief like this. Not even when my da died." He had perished from a wound got in battle that had taken poisoning.

Dathi lifted a brow. "If I recall correctly, your father's death was long and slow."

"Aye, so." Hideously slow.

"Your mother had time to prepare herself. What happened

yesterday—" He shook his head.

Liadan still could not believe what had happened yesterday. Conall and Ardahl, best of friends. But everyone said Conall's blood had covered Ardahl's hands.

"I will speak with her."

Dathi did, at length and with kindness. Liadan, hovering nearby, listened. Her respect for the aged healer, already lofty, soared.

"Mistress MacAert, ye must take hold o' yourself. Ye be frightening your daughters."

"I have lost my son! My strong and bonny Conall. The pride o' his father's eye and the very spit o' him. The lad I have loved since the first I took him to my breast. I have lost him!"

"Aye, and a heavy thing it is to bear. But ye will do no good lying here weeping yourself into a sickness."

"He is gone from me."

"Ye must remember he has gone in all his glory to the land of the ever-young, to live on in strength and beauty."

"I want him here with me."

Flanna came up and slipped her hand into Liadan's. Liadan could feel her trembling.

"When I lie here, I am near him. I can still catch his scent."

"Aye, and ye have spent the night so, but now ye will arise. There are duties to which ye must attend."

Mam broke into sobs anew. Dathi got up from her side and spoke softly to Liadan.

"I will mix her a draught. It will soothe her enough to get her through this day."

This day. "Aye." Already, daylight streamed through the door. "But, Master Dathi, what o' the days to come? The—the wake. The tributes." For there would be many. Her brother had been well loved. "The b burial."

Dathi gave her a sympathetic look. "'Twill not be easy, lass. Can ye be her strength?"

"I do not know." Could she? But who would be hers?

"I can leave more mixtures, if ye need to dose her again. Or call me back anytime." He laid his fingers lightly on Liadan's shoulder. "Day or night, I will come."

They watched him mix the draught from the goods in the bundle he had brought. Watched him dose Mam and help her stretch out on Conall's bed.

"She may sleep, or may not. Let her grieve as she might, for now."

"Aye, Master Dathi. Thank ye."

He eyed both of them. "And ye? Can I leave any potions for either o' ye?"

"I am all right." A blatant lie, but Liadan must be strong. For Mam. For Flanna. "Sister?"

Flanna merely shook her head, but after the aged healer had gone, she turned to Liadan with a look of panic in her eyes.

"Sister, what are we to do? Conall kept us in the chief's regard and in our place here. With him gone, who will care for us? Hunt for us. Provide for us."

Fancy Flanna, at her tender age, considering such matters. But aye, they had lost their provider as well as a light of their lives.

Fierce with belief, she said, "Chief Fearghal will not let us starve." Yet well did she know a huge difference existed between being a family of status, which Da before his death and Conall had in turn earned for them, and mere hangers-on with the tribe. She had known a few such, considered little better than the slaves captured from enemy tribes.

She would never gain a husband so—if indeed that was what she wanted. Most women her age did desire a man and a home of her own.

She had ever desired but one man.

Turning her thoughts strictly away from that, she focused on her young sister. Would Flanna's chances of a good marriage be ruined also, when she came of age?

So much rested upon a family's status, which in turn pivoted on the standing of its warriors. Where a fighting man sat during feasting in the chief's hall. What goods he claimed in spoils. Even how the shanachies praised him.

"Do not worry about that now," she bade the pale-faced Flanna. "The chief will decide on it—or the priests will. We must try to trust them."

Flanna appeared to find that as difficult as Liadan herself did.

"We must prepare for this day," she told her sister, "difficult as that may be. Do you want anything to eat?"

"I cannot."

"Nay." If Liadan tried to take any food, she would choke on it. "Then wash and dress yourself in your finest clothing. Braid up your hair. We must look our best when the others come to honor Conall."

Flanna's eyes abruptly pooled with tears.

"I cannot," she said again.

"You must. We must be strong for Mam."

Much to ask of a lass with only eleven winters to her name. But Flanna straightened and blinked the tears away.

She whispered, "Sister, what will happen to us?"

Cursed if Liadan knew.

DAYLIGHT CAME THROUGH the gaps in the walls of Ardahl's prison, flickering just as his courage had flickered all the night long. Sleep had not found him, and by morning dread lay in the pit of his stomach like a block of ice.

He suspected the chief—or possibly Dornach—had stationed guards outside the hut where he was being held, because he could hear them whispering from time to time. Talking about him, no doubt.

He wondered who they were. Whomever, he undoubtedly had trained and fought beside them. Feasted and drank—laughed with them.

Now they guarded him, in his dishonor.

As it had all night, his mind poked and prodded at what had happened yesterday afternoon. The sudden anger in Conall's clear blue eyes, coming seemingly from nowhere. The dagger. The rush of horror as Ardahl realized his best friend intended to attack him. The brief, violent struggle.

The blade in Conall's heart.

He still could not tell how it had ended there. The very question made him pace and sweat.

It could not be. None of this could be occurring. All a dream, mayhap. Or a horrible joke. Conall would appear at the door of the pen and give him a wide, mischievous smile, his eyes as bright as the morning.

All would be as ever, right between them. Because none of what had happened yesterday could have happened at all. An evil dream. Naught more.

But then, what about the traces of blood still on his hands? That which he had not been able to wash away, caught deep in the lines and creases. Conall's blood.

Voices sounded outside—a query and an answer. The bar lifted and the door swung open on its leather hinges.

Daylight outlined a large figure. Blinking against the brightness, Ardahl identified him.

Dornach, with his woolen plaid slung over his shoulder. Wearing his sword.

"Ardahl MacCormac," he called, "ye are to come wi' me."

"Where?"

"To the chief's hall. To receive your sentence."

Suddenly, Ardahl's legs threatened to fail him. He'd not experienced the like since before his first battle.

None o' that, lad, he bade himself. *Ye will keep face and conduct yourself like a man.*

That determination nearly deserted him when he stepped forward and got a look at Dornach's expression. Bleak as winter it was, and twice as cold.

This man who had trained him, laughed with him, been like a second father to him, could not now look him in the eyes.

Och, by the gods, he was doomed.

CHAPTER FIVE

CHIEF FEARGHAL SAT in the great chair at the head of his hall with his druid priests gathered in a group beside him. If Dornach appeared grim, the chief looked forbidding. His gaze fastened to Ardahl the moment he entered and did not waver.

Others were present. Seniors of the chief's council and, as Ardahl saw to his horror, Conall's family. His two sisters stood supporting his mother as if holding her upright. All three stared as if they had never seen him before. Had not given him countless meals. Had him in their hut and treated him fondly.

And there—the elite among the warriors, including Cathair. They gazed at Ardahl with a variety of expressions. Protest. Disbelief. And interest. Cathair—but nay, Ardahl could not quite name what he saw in Cathair's eyes.

More people came flooding in behind, just like the sunlight. Ordinary clansfolk, these, come out of curiosity. And with them, escorted by a guard—

Ardahl's own mother.

His heart fell to his feet when he saw her. Even though she, among them all, seemed to reach for him with her eyes. Speak to him with her gaze. Seek to comfort him. Suddenly he wanted nothing so much as to be at home with her beside their own fire, in simple harmony.

Her escort led her to stand at Fearghal's left hand, opposite Conall's family.

The two women—Conall's mother and Ardahl's—had long

been companions of a sort. Both had lost their husbands, and their sons were fast friends. They had worked and laughed together.

Now they stood opposed as enemies.

Once more, Ardahl's legs threatened to fail him. He straightened them along with his spine. All he had at this moment was his dignity. His status, hard earned. Naught but his pride. His heart might be in shreds; he must keep his head high.

But if they sentenced him to death, these druids, these learned men who knew so much, what would happen to his mam?

Sentenced to death. No more to see the sunlight on the water. The green grass covering the hills. The wild deer and the raw beauty of this land he loved.

Chief Fearghal cleared his throat, and the room went silent. From outside, Ardahl heard a lark on the wing, trilling her song from a full heart.

Fearghal did not rise. Instead, he lifted his hand to indicate the head druid, Aodh.

That man stepped forward directly into the beam of light streaming down through the smoke hole at the center of the round chamber's roof. He made an impressive sight all clad in white with his long hair, equally white, hanging down. He wore the sigils of his office, a golden medallion and brooch of amber. He wore also the gold scythe at his belt that declared his standing as high priest.

He looked like a man about to deliver a sentence of death.

If that be so, Ardahl thought, *then so be it.* He need only summon the strength to meet that death bravely, so as not to dishonor himself. His father's name. His mother. Then he would be free to fly away and follow Conall to *Tír na nÓg,* where they might be together again.

But ah, what would happen to Mam with him gone?

Aodh spoke in his sonorous voice, into the silence.

"Yesterday upon the field of practice, a dire deed did occur.

One young warrior in the fullness of his life was cut down by another. Here stands the accused." He pointed a long finger at Ardahl. "And here, the witness." Cathair.

"My fellows and I have deliberated all night over the fit punishment. Considered the laws. Studied what the Brehon tradition tells to us, searched for wisdom and an outcome that is just.

"A family"—he waved at Conall's mother and sisters—"has lost their son. Their provider, even as a young man has lost his life."

He will commit me to death. In that moment, Ardahl believed it. The sunlit face of the priest wavered before him.

"A chief," Aodh went on, "has lost his warrior. Should he lose another?"

Everyone there stared. Just like Ardahl, they had expected a swift sentence of death. Still, they made not a sound. To interrupt the druid priest would be beyond reproach.

"If a family has lost its provider," Aodh said weightily, "the law says they should have another in his place. Who better than he who cost them their own? Ardahl McCormac, step forward."

He did, though he could no longer feel his feet on the floor.

"Having slain Conall MacAert, have you anything to say?"

"I did not mean to harm him. He was my closest friend."

Gravely, Aodh shook his head. "It does not matter. For does he not still lie dead? You will henceforth take Conall MacAert's place in his household. Be a son to his mother and a brother to his sisters. Ye will support them, provide for them in all they need. Ye will take Conall's place in service to your chief and fulfill his vow of fealty. This is justice, and this the gods do decree."

A murmur rustled through the chamber, among those gathered. Gasps and whispers. Ardahl distinctly heard his own mother gasp and turned his eyes to her.

He asked, "What of my own mother?"

"She is henceforth without her son."

It was not death—at least it was not death, and he saw Mam's relief in her eyes. Not much better than a sentence of death, though, for did they not decree that he should lose himself? All that he was?

To take Conall's place.

He spoke again, in a croak. "For how long? How long must I serve this sentence?"

"It is a life sentence," Aodh said. "So do the gods decree."

Ardahl turned his gaze upon Conall's family, not sure what reaction he expected. Certainly not the horror he saw. Dismay so wide and deep it surpassed comprehension.

They did not want him. To be sure, they did not. They wanted their own lad, who brought laughter and sunlight into their lives.

Chief Fearghal spoke in a rumble. "When, Master Aodh, does this sentence commence?"

"Directly after young Conall's funeral."

"That will take place this afternoon. We shall all go up on the rise where our honored dead are laid." He fixed a burning gaze upon Ardahl. "When we come back down, ye will become Conall MacAert, for the duration o' your life."

Nay. But Ardahl could not speak that word. Not to his chief, to whom he owed fealty. Not in the face of the priests who studied and kept the law. Yet—

How did a man surrender all he was, and all he might be? A dire punishment indeed.

Mayhap death would have been easier.

He did not expect what happened next. His mother, a quiet, retiring sort of woman, should not step out there before them all, putting herself forward. And yet she walked quietly to face Conall's mother, to look her in the eye.

"Beath MacAert," Mam called. "Will ye no' put a stop to this madness? Ye alone can refuse the priests' decree."

Was that true? Could anyone halt what Aodh declared came from the gods?

With raw heartache in her eyes, Mistress MacAert said, "I cannot."

Mam raised her voice, a thing she did but seldom. She raised it so it echoed round the chamber. "If ye accept this, I will lose my son."

"As I ha' lost mine, Maeve MacCormac."

Conall's little sister sobbed. Her elder sister caught her in clinging arms. Ardahl's gaze slipped over them and fastened upon his mother, who seemed to droop where she stood.

Defeated. Abandoned.

All because of him.

And a deed he had never intended to occur.

CHAPTER SIX

T HE WIND BLEW hard up on the height, making the whole world glitter with shards of brightness. A glorious sort of day, far too lovely for laying one's adored older brother to rest.

As Liadan stood there buffeted by that breeze, she told herself not to think of that. To close her mind upon the fact that her brother would go into the stony ground and be covered over. An abomination. Rocks would be piled atop him, and though the view from here was far-reaching and very bonny, he would not be able to see. The hills in the distance. A pair of lochs, all a-gleam. Far to the east, the sea.

All in motion. The very air in motion.

Liadan, standing with one arm around Flanna and the other around her mother, told herself Conall was no longer an inhabitant of the flesh that went into the earth. Not if she believed what the priests and the shanachies said. For he had winged away to the land for the ever young. With Da.

Her gaze moved to her father's grave, not an actual stone's throw away, alongside her grand-da and countless others of the valiant.

Did she believe the priests? The same who had lumbered them with an intruder in their midst.

He who had slain her brother.

Her gaze moved to Ardahl MacCormac and narrowed. She still could not believe what the high priest had said. Her mind would not comprehend it. There he stood with the stain of her brother's blood still upon his hands—for she'd seen that when they followed him and his guards up the rise.

Were they to accept this dreadful serpent into their lives? Welcome him to their tiny home?

She could not.

He stood now, tall and slender on the far side of the grave that the men had come up and prepared ahead of time. The sunlight lit his auburn hair, worn loose down his back, to fire— something she might once have admired, in another time and place.

No more.

He had absolutely no expression on his face, features closed tight. Hazel eyes wide and blank.

An odd thought occurred to her. Mayhap he could no more accept what happened than she.

Chief Fearghal stood at the head of the grave. The three priests surrounded it. Liadan had seen these burials before. Speeches would be made. Honor paid.

No sooner did Fearghal draw breath to speak than an interruption occurred. A young woman darted forward from the crowd of onlookers and gave a cry.

A beauty she was, and no mistake, with long brown hair and the face of a goddess. Liadan had watched her brother pursue Brasha for nearly a year before winning her attention. She felt certain Conall had been in love with the young woman, though he'd never come out and told her so.

Ardahl would know. Her gaze returned to her brother's friend. Conall had told him everything.

Liadan had not seen Brasha at the sentencing, though, to be sure, she must have been there. Now, apparently unable to contain her grief, she stumbled forward and cast herself upon Conall's shrouded form.

Mam had given her best blanket, the one that had covered Conall's sleeping place, for his shroud. Never to be seen again.

Those gathered in the crowd cried out as one when the beauty cast herself upon her deceased lover. Liadan knew the folk of her tribe. Loyal and valiant to the heart, they loved a good tale, loved a gossip and scandal, and such a display. This would be talked of for days. Years.

Lamenting, Brasha lay upon the sun-warmed ground. The men standing round preparing to lower Conall into his grave, the same who had prepared it, reached to lift her, at which she cried out and struggled to free herself.

So she could cast her body upon Conall's yet again.

The onlookers gave a collective sigh. Mam sobbed brokenly. Flanna stared aghast, and the high priest, Aodh, withdrew from Brasha fastidiously.

Brasha's parents stepped forward and gently took hold of her. They melted back into the circle of onlookers.

Aodh began to speak. Liadan could not deny his words were beautiful. With the rhythm of song, they seemed to spiral up, up through that bright air. To take wing as Conall's soul must have, and fly far. Away from the pain, the ache, the strife.

Conall went into the ground. It seemed like such a simple thing but was not. Mam broke then and ran forward in her turn, falling to her knees beside her son. She wailed, and the women in the gathering wept with her in sympathy and understanding.

This was no new thing. Since the commencement of the battles with the tribes to the west, such scenes occurred far too often.

But those men had died by an enemy's hand. Not that of a friend.

She went forward to embrace her mother. Draw her to her feet. That brought her all too close to Ardahl MacCormac, on the other side of the grave. He stood as if carved of stone, expression unchanging, not taking Conall's place at all. For Conall would have stooped to Mam's side, sought to comfort her, swung her up in his arms protectively.

Instead, it was Cathair who hurried forward and lifted Mam with ridiculous ease.

"Thank ye," Liadan murmured.

He nodded, his fair hair bright in the sun. He stood with them while the grave was filled and never let go of Mam until the three of them—Mam, Flanna, and Liadan together—stepped forward hand in hand to place their stones.

There was singing then, soaring laments that pierced Liadan to the heart and reduced most of the onlookers to tears.

Finally Chief Fearghal spoke. "Here lie our honored dead. Another bright warrior has joined their ranks, this day. All honor to him!"

With nothing more to be said, they turned to walk back down the stony slope.

"Would you like help getting your mother home, mistress?" Cathair asked Liadan politely.

That was for Ardahl to do. But he was somewhere behind her. Glancing back, she saw that Fearghal spoke to him fiercely. She wished she could catch the words.

She turned and looked full in Cathair's eyes. "You are certain Ardahl MacCormac did this terrible thing? Killed my brother?"

Did something flicker in the bright blue of those eyes? It might have been regret. "Aye, mistress. I saw."

She drew a breath that made her chest hurt. "'Twould be a kindness for you to help us home."

They went slowly, Cathair supporting Mam even as Conall might. When they reached their door, tribesfolk came flooding in, giving their condolences and embracing Mam.

When Liadan looked around again, Cathair had gone.

But Ardahl approached. His two guards flanked him still, and Liadan wondered madly if her family was to be lumbered with all three of them. But both guards, after deep nods at Mam, peeled off, leaving Ardahl standing alone.

The mourners avoided him as if he caused a sickness, stepping around him so he stood very much isolated. Alone and quiet. Did he feel no sorrow? None of this wild grief that tore at Liadan inside?

He was a serpent indeed. Never had Liadan been so mistaken as in once fancying she admired him.

Not until many moments had passed and the mourners cleared from the door did Liadan realize Ardahl's mother had followed them. She looked small and very much stricken when she stepped up to embrace her son.

"Mam, I must stay here now."

"But ye have to return home for your belongings. Your clothing. Your sword."

A muscle jumped in Ardahl's cheek. "Chief Fearghal says none of those things are mine any longer. Conall's belongings are now mine."

"But—"

"Mam, ye must trade my belongings as ye can for the things ye will need."

"Not your sword."

"Even my sword."

"It was your father's before ye. I will not lose it as well as—as well as ye." Her voice broke.

"Ye may need to trade for food and the like."

Liadan's mother pushed up, her face ravaged by grief. "Be gone from my door, Maeve MacCormac. Your son has stolen the life o' mine. So ye have a son no more. The priests say this is justice."

Maeve flinched as if she'd been struck. Ardahl bent swiftly and kissed her cheek. "I love ye, Mam. I assure ye—I did not do this thing."

With a sob, Liadan's mam fled into their hut. Flanna followed. Even as Ardahl's mam walked away, Liadan and Ardahl stood looking at one another.

Vile serpent, she thought again. She did not feel sympathy for him. She did *not*.

But for his mam, just a bit.

CHAPTER SEVEN

ARDAHL, ADRIFT IN spirit and shut into the small confines of Mistress MacAert's hut, wondered how much farther he could fall. Just two days ago he'd been upon a height. Secure in his world, among the best of Chief Fearghal's warriors, and working hard to secure the place of foremost. At liberty to spend time with his best friend, to laugh, and train, and drink. To look after his mam.

He had never dreamed, nay, never dreamed how things could change.

He stood just inside the door of Mistress MacAert's hut, struggling to force his mind into acceptance of his fate. He had been here before, to be sure, more times than he could count. When they were young, he had followed Conall home for meals as often as Conall had followed him. He'd even slept here a few times.

Now he must sleep here for good. No going home. The way the druids had explained it, by dictate of Brehon law he must *become* Conall in every way. Be son to his mother, brother to his sisters. Take up his duties. His place. Fulfill his destiny.

He, as Ardahl MacCormac, existed no more.

Despair churned in his gut as he stood there surveying the small, gloomy room. Just a roundhouse it was, with a central hearth fire and a few partitioned areas around the outer walls. Similar as could be to his own home.

Where Mam would now be alone. Och, she had friends who

might help her, unless they did not want the stain of disgrace to transfer upon them.

He had failed her. He had failed his mam, even though after Da's death he'd sworn to protect her in all things. The dearest vow he could give.

His da had been a charioteer, and his father before him. He had died when his chariot overturned on stony ground during a battle. Flung far from the cart. An enemy warrior had taken his head.

Ardahl remembered his mam's face that day when Da was brought home. Bone white and seared by grief.

Much the way she'd looked parting from him today.

Aye, so, the druids' decree had been given and here he stood—unwelcome. He could feel the hostility filling the tiny hut.

Conall's mam still wept. She wept as she breathed, and the younger of Conall's sisters sat by the fire hiding her face in her hands. Weeping also?

Liadan—when had she grown up into a young woman? Ardahl must have missed it while battling his way through his days. A young woman she surely was now, and a bonny one. But he could feel the antagonism filling her. Hate directed straight at him. She had a wall up, but behind it she stored enough hate to flay him alive.

How was he to endure this? And what to do with his own grief, the pit of emptiness at the center of his chest?

He wanted Conall to walk in behind him and give one of his laughs, make one of his quips. Declare that all this had been a wild, misguided prank. Make the world come right.

It did not happen. To be sure, not. Conall lay up in the ground under the cold stones. Had he himself not watched him go in?

Mistress MacAert took herself off into what had been Conall's sleeping place, directly back from the hearth. Wee Flanna still sat as if frozen.

Liadan turned to him.

"You had best come in."

He already was in, but he knew what she meant. Closer to the fire. Into the bosom of her family. The one place she did not want him.

"Mistress Liadan." His voice sounded hoarse. "I but wish to say, I did not mean to harm Conall. I would never have harmed—"

"Do not speak his name." Mistress MacAert flew from Conall's sleeping place and across at Ardahl, nearly setting her skirts aflame from the embers of the fire. "Ye be not worthy to speak his name."

She slapped Ardahl in the face, all the force of her grief behind the blow. He, who had withstood far worse in battle, turned aside from the pain of it.

The woman collapsed into sobs and wails. Both her daughters helped her up.

"Come, Mam, awa' to your bed," Liadan crooned to her.

"Nay. I will not. How can I rest when my boy is lost?"

"Come lie upon Conall's bed, then. The healer has left a draught. I will mix it for ye."

Both lasses led their mother away to the inner chamber, where Liadan drew the curtain. Ardahl stood where he was.

Aching.

A thought occurred to him. It would indeed have been easier had they just taken his life.

"MAM CANNOT ABIDE having ye here." Mistress Liadan stood in front of Ardahl like a living barrier. Her eyes, as blue as Conall's, made two bright shields raised against him. She jerked her head at the sleeping place behind her. "I have managed to quiet her now wi' the help of a draught. When she wakes and sees ye still here—"

"I am not allowed to leave." He said it with sorrow. His entire being wanted to flee this place. Wanted to return to his mam.

Emotions chased one another across Liadan's face. Like Co-nall again, those emotions seemed easy to glean. Ardahl had always been able to tell what his friend was thinking.

Except these past few weeks.

Now he saw dismay, regret, raw pain, and a level of frustration that matched his own.

"I fear what may happen if she wakes to see ye again."

Ardahl repeated with patience he did not feel, "I am no' allowed to leave."

Iron entered her eyes. "'Tis unbearable, this. By the gods, I cannot imagine what the druids were thinking."

Ardahl said nothing. The lass Flanna had disappeared into Conall's sleeping cubby. With their mother incapacitated, it seemed he and Liadan must find a path through this dreadful situation.

Not until she began to turn away from him did he say, "What d'ye wish me to do?"

"Go away." She bit out the words in a fierce whisper, turning to face him again. "Far away where I have to see ye nevermore. Go back to your mam. Or better yet, take yoursel' off and forever wander the face o' the world."

"I would if I could."

Her lips turned down. For an instant Ardahl thought she would weep. Too strong, perhaps. How old was she now? He tried to calculate it in his head. She'd been a mere toddler when he and Conall started playing together. A slim girl by the time they'd taken the field for the first time. A pest, sometimes, whom he had ignored.

Since he had a score and three winters, she must herself be approaching a full score. How was it that a young woman so lovely as this had not been taken to wife by anyone?

"Then"—she waved a hand wildly—"take yoursel' and sit outside the door. I do no' want her seeing ye first thing if she wakes."

"Outside the door. Like a hound?"

Conall had a hound once. It had, to be sure, lain either outside or inside the door depending on the weather, unless it could sneak into Conall's sleeping place to lie with him.

He fished for the name. "Like Blooney?"

She gave a stiff nod. "Till we can come to grips wi' this."

Outside the door. Where he would be prey to the gaze of every passerby. Stares of condemnation. Sympathy. Scorn. There, he would be beneath contempt.

He might have said he was meant to take Conall's place, and that was not outside the door. Instead he gazed into Liadan's eyes and said nothing.

He was meant to claim Conall's sword as well. If he were to guard the door, he needed a weapon. Instead he had nothing except his empty hands, still rimmed with his best friend's blood.

He nodded and slipped outside. The afternoon had just begun to fade, its brightness seeping away over the hills to the west. He stood and breathed deep, unthinkingly taking in the scents of this place he loved. Wood smoke and animals at a distance, and food cooking.

His stomach rumbled. How could he be hungry? Surely he felt far too sick inside to contemplate food. Yet he could scarce remember the last time he had taken anything to eat.

One mercy—Conall's hut lay at the far side of the settlement, away from the chief's hall and the training field. Not many were about. The few who did pass stared at him as if he had six arms and three heads.

No one spoke to him.

But he—and his sentence—would be the talk of the tribe for weeks. Aye, the druids—whom, he had to admit, he had mostly disregarded in the past save for their prayers ahead of a battle— did deal in reparation. Seldom did they impose such a sentence as this.

He walked around the side of the hut where most folk kept a wash pan, bucket, and pot of soap. Conall's family being no exception, he found what he needed and availed himself of it.

He scrubbed till his skin was raw, till the last of Conall's blood came away and only new trickles, from abraded skin, were his own.

Then he returned to the front door, hunkered down on his heels beside it, and waited.

CHAPTER EIGHT

S NATCHES OF SLEEP were all Liadan had that night. She made
sure Mam lay comfortably upon her bed, and saw Flanna into
her own small sleeping place before seizing a blanket and lying on
the floor beside Mam.

Her mind too full, her body aching, she listened as Flanna
cried herself to sleep. Counted Mam's deep breaths. The draught
must have been a strong one. It sent her well under and, thank all
the gods, stopped her weeping.

The hut grew quiet, and yet—it did not. Liadan could feel
him there, Ardahl MacCormac, just outside the door. Feel him
even though she could not see him, as if he shouted his presence
aloud.

How could she ever have been so mistaken in anyone? For
she had admired him, to be sure she had. Even begun to desire
him, after she grew old enough to understand what might exist
between a man and a woman.

He had no woman among the tribe. Looked to no woman,
though other young lasses of the clan spoke of him. He remained
set upon working his way to the foremost of the tribe's warriors,
and on caring for his mother, both things she had admired.

Some whispered that only when he achieved the place he
wanted, at the head of Fearghal's men, would he consider taking
a wife. Choosing a woman and handfasting with her.

Whether he was looking or not, he had never so much as
glanced in Liadan's direction. She told herself now how glad she

was of it.

The serpent.

Knowing what he was and how mistaken she'd been in him, how was it she could still feel him outside the door?

She tried to comfort herself with the fact that Conall too had been mistaken in Ardahl. It did not help.

Conall. Her glorious older brother with the sunny smile, the dancing eyes, and the teasing tongue. He could brighten any day and lighten any mood.

How could it be that he was gone from the world?

Mam stirred and muttered fitfully, but did not wake. Liadan thought about taking some of the draught the healer had mixed, for he had left extra. Perhaps that would quiet her mind.

But what if Mam awakened and needed her?

Night settled around the hut with its accompanying quiet. What if, during this silent time, Conall arose from his cold bed on the hill and came walking down? Came home to the hut, seeking admittance. Seeking his place back from Ardahl, whom she could feel—

Breathing.

Och, but she had to get hold of herself. Find some rest, some peace. Tomorrow was likely to be terribly difficult. Mayhap not so difficult as today—for naught could be, but—

Mam stirred again and whispered a name in her sleep. *Conall.* Liadan squeezed her eyes shut and held on tight.

MORNING CAME WITH livid red light bleeding through the sky, a dire omen. To Ardahl, who had done no more that doze against the wall of the hut beside the door, it looked like the blood that had spread across Conall's tunic when he tried to remove the knife. Straight from his heart.

He did not want to face this day. Did not know how to alter

the fact that he must.

He got to his feet, stretching his back and his legs, feeling three score years of age.

Staring at that sky, he knew to his bones something bad would occur this day. Just like yesterday. Mayhap every day for the rest of his life.

What would be expected of him? He struggled to think. Should he attend training as he and Conall always did?

He and Conall.

Folk would come by here to commiserate with Mistress MacAert, bring her comfort, and pour sympathy upon her.

None would spare a thought for him, though he'd lost something as vital to him as his right arm.

He blinked and again struggled to remember what had happened. How it had happened. As he had five score times already, he relived the argument with Conall there at the edge of the training field.

They rarely argued. Och, there had been annoyances, small things. He'd sometimes become aggravated with Conall's teasing. Conall sometimes seemed to mind that he, Ardahl, gained higher honors than him on the field.

Nothing they could not shrug off.

This time—

For days, Conall had been needling him, and not in a friendly way. Voice sharper than usual, jibes just a bit sharper. There on the field, when they worked together, he had suddenly accused Ardahl of wanting him out of the way.

"What are ye saying?" Ardahl spat at him. "Do no' be a fool. I would lay down my life for ye, as well ye know."

"Would ye? Would ye?" Real anger had flared in Conall's eyes. "Let us see, then."

He threw down his sword and drew the dagger from his boot. For one mad moment, Ardahl had thought it a joke. Then he saw—felt—that it was not.

His own sword fell from his hand. When Conall flew at him,

the two of them grappled together. It had been like wrestling a fury, unrestrained.

The black-handled knife with which Conall attacked him had ended up in Conall's own breast.

Ardahl still did not know quite how.

If he could relive it in truth instead of in his mind... If he could go back and live those moments over again...

He would stand and let Conall do as he would to him. Make no move that could harm his best friend.

So deep was his regret.

A figure appeared out of the grim morning and approached the place where he stood. That of a young man it was, and someone Ardahl knew right well.

Muirin MacGradh had been friend to both Ardahl and Conall a long while. Someone with whom they trained. Laughed and drank.

Now the young man with the dark-brown mane of hair bore no smile, nor any hint of one. He walked up to the front of the hut and stood eyeing Ardahl gravely.

For the span of many heartbeats he failed to speak. At last he said, "Tell me it is no' true."

"'Tis not. I would never have harmed Conall. Ye know that."

"I know that, aye. 'Tis why I came. I spent the night trying to make myself believe ye did this thing. I could not, quite."

A wave of profound relief hit Ardahl. So strong was it, it swayed him where he stood.

"What happened?" Muirin asked.

"I ha' been sitting here the night long trying to answer that question."

Muirin's dark eyes glinted. "Ye had his blood on your hands."

"Aye." No denying it.

"He lies dead."

"Aye. Ye know I would never meaningly harm a hair of him."

"An accident, then?"

Had it been an accident? Given the struggle and Conall's clear intent to attack him, he had to believe its opposite.

He shook his head. "No matter. He is dead and I ha' my sentence to live out."

"'Tis a hard fate, Ardahl. Ye were first among us."

"Not quite. Cathair is still first." He had very nearly made it there, though. "That does not matter either. Muirin, if ye would do one thing for me—"

"Name it."

"Look after my mam. Make sure she is safe and does not go wanting. Without me there to look after her…"

Muirin's gaze softened. "Aye, I will."

"She does no' deserve to pay for this misdeed."

"I am no' certain ye do either. But the druids have spoken."

The door at Ardahl's back swung open a crack. Liadan peered out, lit by the garish red morning.

She took in Ardahl and Muirin. "I wondered who was speaking."

Muirin gave a short bow. "My condolences, mistress. Conall was among my closest friends, and I was ever so fond o' him."

"Thank ye."

Ardahl and Liadan both watched the young man walk away. Easier that than for Ardahl to face the deep wound in Liadan's eyes.

"I am certain," he said slowly, "he is but the first of your visitors this morning."

Liadan said nothing in response to that. Instead, she swept the door open farther and thrust a pot at him.

"Conall always fetched our water first thing."

Ardahl accepted the pot but did not move. "How is your mam this morning?"

Her face clouded, proving its rosiness a mere reflection from the horizon.

"She is sick and groggy from the draught. And just look at that red sky!" She tossed her hands in the air. "I suppose ye will expect breakfast."

"Do no' worry for me."

She swore bitterly, a curse Ardahl could not mistake, since it had been so often on Conall's lips, and shut the door.

With the ewer in hand, he trudged off to meet his fate.

CHAPTER NINE

I N THE PAST, Ardahl had marched out to meet his fate more times than he could number. Gone on foot or horseback into a battle, not knowing if he would return. That had been easier in some ways than what now had to do.

At the well, it being a common place, he found half the tribe gathered. Women with bairns in their arms. Aged warriors no longer fit for much beyond helping with household chores. Children who had slipped beyond their mothers' reach.

He walked into a storm of condemnation. Aye, he knew the people of his tribe, knew how they loved to talk about one another, to whisper. To rate a warrior or a shanachie and the way a woman kept her home.

Respect was the highest coin that could be offered, or obtained. And respect was earned through deeds and appearances.

He had now fallen among the lowest of the low. The slaves, the disabled who could fight no more. The disgraced and condemned.

He did not suppose his appearance helped any. He'd gone straight from the practice field to a cell and thence to his sentencing. He had spent a night outdoors, all without access to clean clothing or an opportunity to groom, beyond the violent scrubbing he'd done.

Yet he went with his head high. Not because of who he was but because of who Conall was. He had taken Conall's place, had he not? He would not then creep like someone dishonored.

Much would be revealed by the way his fellow tribesfolk received him. Teasing and clever mockery were considered a form of liking. Hard anger might be marked by shouting and accusations.

The folk at the well met him with silence. Indeed, it unfolded before him as he approached, like the dark of night. Even the small babes in their mothers' arms stopped peeping like birds and stared with wide eyes.

People shied from him. They peeled away from the well and moved off as if they did not want to breathe his air.

Stooping to the stone-lined spring, where the water bubbled up into a shallow trough surrounded by a low wall, he filled the ewer.

The tribe had settled here because of this spring. A holy place, it was said to be, with healing properties. The first of their ancestors, wanderers with no more than a few beasts to their names, had found the place and stayed.

No one, especially greedy chieftains from the west, should drive them from here. He, like many others, had determined that. Yet the pressure from the west grew intense.

He straightened, turned slowly, and surveyed those who surrounded him. He had fought for them in every battle. Now, so swiftly, they turned on him.

He did not speak a word, yet the bitterness lodged hard like a stone beneath his heart. He wanted to go home to his mother. He could not.

He could not.

LIADAN DREW A breath and fought to quiet her heartbeat, which ran ahead of her like a maddened pony. It had started to gallop when she opened the door and saw Ardahl standing there lit by the red sunrise.

She did not know how to handle the emotions he raised. She did not know how to handle anything that had happened since Conall's death.

Why had she never realized until now how much she'd relied on her older brother in times of difficulty and strife? The extent to which he lifted worries from her, worries about Mam, worries about far more trivial things and more terrifying things too, such as the threat from the west.

Always with a smile. Always so calm. Though her brother was not a quiet man withal, since he did love to tease and tussle, she now saw he had taken her troubles from her without fuss, and usually solved them.

Upon whom was she to rely now?

Mam had awoken sick and grieving. She had retched into the night pot, ill from the draught. And yet the draught was all Liadan had to help quiet her. Even now, Mam lay once more upon Conall's bed and wept.

Poor Flanna had a face like a ghost. She too would be ill before Liadan knew it. She needed food, which meant Liadan had to prepare some sort of breakfast.

She would need to feed the serpent.

That thought, among the teeming others, stopped her cold. Aye, she'd sent him away to fetch water, a few moments' respite. Yet he would return.

Here, where she did not want him.

"Flanna, darling, bring me some kindling that I might light the fire."

Fire was always first. That done, she would beat her thoughts into a line if she had to.

Flanna slipped outside and came back with arms full of dry sticks. Without being asked, she set about arranging them upon the hearth.

What if Ardahl did not return? What was Liadan to do then? Go the chief? Would Ardahl then be punished? Further humiliated?

For he had to be feeling humiliated, aye. Though how he should be, at taking her wonderful brother's place—

The door opened. He came in with the ewer, bringing shadows.

Liadan glanced at him and away. "Place it here. Please." Was one required to treat a serpent with courtesy?

He did as asked, his movements neat and quiet, and stood.

"I will be making some breakfast. Sit by the door." She did not want for him to come any farther in to their place. Her place.

"Mistress, I will need weapons."

"So?"

"I cannot fetch my own. Were Conall's returned here?"

That made her glance up sharply. Should he touch her brother's things? Those most precious to him?

"His weapons were brought here, aye. After the burial." Her lips curled savagely. "All but his black knife."

He flinched as if she'd struck him. Good. She wanted him to hurt the way she did. The way Mam, whom she could still hear weeping, did.

He went and sat by the door even as her thoughts moved furiously.

Ordered to take Conall's place, he would presumably need to train and fight among the other warriors. She tried to imagine what that would be like after having slain one so dear to those ranks, and then tried not to. She did not care.

But aye, he would need weapons. Her brother's sword that had also been her father's.

An abomination to see it in his hand.

His hands, stained red. Aye, she had seen the remnants of Conall's blood there.

Suddenly she wanted to vomit, retch into the night pot as Mam had. She choked back the sickness and set about preparing the breakfast, never once glancing at the shadow that sat beside the door.

When the barley cakes were ready, she passed him a portion,

still not looking at him, which he accepted. The three of them ate in silence, save for the sound of Mam's soft sobs. After, Liadan entered Conall's sleeping place and gently asked her mother if she would take something to eat.

She quietly gathered up Conall's belongings. The cherished sword and the small knife—another besides the black one—he usually wore in his belt. A clean tunic, one she'd washed with her own hands. A spare kilt and a pair of leggings.

All still smelling of Conall.

These she carried out and thrust into Ardahl's hands. For an instant he looked repulsed. His expression shut down—all but for his eyes. She could still see what lay in his eyes.

Flanna, silent as the spirit she now resembled, slipped away to Mam.

Liadan faced Ardahl and asked, "What is to happen now?"

He shook his head. "I cannot say. I ha' never before been in this position."

She wanted rid of him. She imagined he wanted rid of this duty even more. They were caught, the two of them. Bound together in a terrible way, by the druids' decree.

She said, merely because she was used to speaking to Conall, and Conall was not there, "I shall have to persuade Mam to accept this. I do not know how." Or how to accept it herself.

"I am sorry. Mistress Liadan, pray, look at me."

She forced herself to do so. There he stood, slim and tall with her brother's belongings in his arms.

"I did no' mean to harm him." He said it slowly and deliberately with emphasis, as if by doing so he could convince her. "I never would."

"And yet," she returned, everything within her rejecting him, "he lies dead. And ye do not."

He bowed his head. Once again, Liadan's sympathetic heart tried to imagine what he felt. She thrust the consideration from her also, violently.

"If ye would do something for me—for us," she told him

bitterly, "ye will get out of my sight."

He went out in silence, leaving naught behind him but a glimpse, through the leather door, into the red morning.

❖

CHAPTER TEN

ARDAHL WENT TO the training field as he had nearly every day of his life for the past half-score years. In all weather. In times of victory and relative peace, or under threat of war. When tired, when wounded, when eager. A place he belonged—the wide, wide field surrounded by low drystone walls had always welcomed him.

Till now.

Never had it been harder to go there than this morning. Conall did not walk at his side.

Conall did not walk at his side.

But he wore Conall's clothing, his own being foul with dirt and blood. And he carried Conall's sword in his hand.

That made for an odd juxtaposition. So often had he seen the weapon clutched in Conall's fingers; so often had he plucked it up out of the turf to return to his friend, it felt familiar. But och, so wrong in his hand.

The red of the sky had bled away, but clouds hung heavy on the western horizon, promising rain. The light felt stark, and it lit the scene—the green, green turf with the young men all gathered, the glittering weapons and a pony or two off to the side—too sharply.

Just as at the spring, he was met with silence, this one as sharp-edged as the swords. A broad sea of antagonism.

Yet when the first of the men gave a wild cry and came at him, he was not prepared.

A young man named Neil, he was, whom Ardahl knew right well. He and Conall had often sat and drunk with him in the warriors' hall.

Now he came with his brown hair flying and his sword raised, whirling about his head.

Ardahl barely raised Conall's sword in time.

The two blades met, one with maddened rage behind it, the other sheer trained reflex. Ardahl's mind struggled and stuttered, seeing what filled the face behind the weapon. The anger. The hate.

Just like Conall had looked at him in the moment before he'd attacked. Too much like.

He could not allow what had happened then to happen again.

For good reason was he considered among the best of Chief Fearghal's warriors. He had a good eye with a surfeit of strength behind it, and, as Dornach often said, he reacted before he thought. His da, aye, had been a charioteer, and a fine one. But Ardahl had always known he wanted to be a warrior.

To earn a place among the first of them.

He had never thought to slay his friends.

So despite the quickness of his blade, he met Neil with cautious care. Even though the man came at him howling bloody murder, he did not push back but merely met him blow for blow.

His relief, when he managed to knock Neil's blade from his hand, was short-lived. No sooner had Neil fallen back, no sooner had Ardahl drawn a breath, than another of his friends rushed at him in turn.

He began to worry then. As his muscles screamed at him and his mind protested, he stepped back and back, now ringed by his fellow warriors. When he tripped his opponent, whose name was Dalen, and landed him on the sod, a third man came for him from behind.

He turned, barely in time.

He missed his own sword, which, when fighting, felt like an extension of his arm. Conall's was balanced differently and made him clumsy, but he must make it serve. Sweat began gathering on his brow and trickling down into his eyes. He tossed his hair out of the way again and again.

Perhaps one of the strangest aspects of the scene was that, save for the grunts and cries of his challengers and the clangs of the weapons, it was silent. As if the whole world held its breath to await the outcome.

He could not fight like this forever. That thought appeared suddenly in his mind. Defending and not pressing, he would soon grow so spent that one of the crashing blows would break through.

Take his head.

These men, his friends, wanted his head.

Then a voice called out, "Enough. Enough!"

A fierce voice it was, and one accustomed to command. All young men there had trained beneath it and were used to obeying it.

Ardahl's opponent, Craen, lowered his sword. Ardahl followed, even as Dornach strode up to stand between them.

The war chief, a big man, towered over even Ardahl, who possessed more height and quickness than bulk. He had a wild head of black hair and skin tanned like hide from the sun, with tattoos twining over it. His eyes, also dark and furious, stabbed at each of them before sweeping across those gathered.

"What is this?" he bellowed. "What happens here, that one o' us should raise a blade against another?"

Neil spoke up. "Ask him that! He raised a blade to Conall. And killed him. Conall, who was a brother to us. How should we let him walk back here and take a place among us?"

"A place." Dornach swept Ardahl with a look, down his body and up again. Ardahl stood trying to quiet his breath and his heart, which threatened to beat out of his chest. "A place, aye, but what place? Is it no' Conall's? Is that no' what the druids decreed? Would ye treat Conall so?"

"He is no' Conall." It was Cathair who stepped out now from

among the others, hair plaited for fighting and his sword in his hand. "He slew Conall."

Dornach faced the young man, nearly as large as he. "Ye ha' told the priests so. And they have made their decision. Would ye go back and sneer in their faces?"

Cathair said nothing, though his jaw grew tight.

"He *is* Conall," Dornach declared, pointing at Ardahl, "to all purposes. Hard as it may be, ye must treat him as such."

Cathair shifted on his feet. "Then he must take Conall's place in the ranking."

Behind ye, ye mean, Ardahl thought but did not say.

"To be sure," Dornach barked, turning those burning eyes now on Cathair. "And so he shall. Let us get to work. And the first man I see o' ye lifting a blade to his fellow will answer to me."

That did not mean things henceforth got easier for Ardahl. His fellows continued to glare at him from the corners of their eyes. To whisper. Those he faced while sparring held nothing back and, save for Muirin, had nary a good word for him.

When the session ended, when the promised rain moved in, proving the omen of the red morning, and Dornach called it, Ardahl found himself covered with bruises, scrapes, and not a few bloody wounds.

His fellows, clearing off quickly, would now repair to the warriors' hall, where they would shelter amid an atmosphere of camaraderie. Ardahl had no doubt as to what their subject of conversation would be.

He had nowhere to go, save back to the hut, where Conall's mother wailed and his sisters could not hide their hatred for him.

As he moved to leave the field, Dornach called him back. "Ardahl, a moment."

Ardahl stood with the cold rain sluicing down him while the war chief approached. Once again, the canny, dark eyes examined him.

"Are ye much hurt?"

"Nay."

"They were rough on ye."

Ardahl lifted his head and said nothing. He stung from the wounds, and the slights—mayhap the second more than the first.

Dornach's gaze narrowed. "Lad, I have known ye from a young age, when ye came running here and asked to train well before your time. I know ye like a son o' my own. What happened?"

Ardahl's only answer was a shake of his head.

Dornach swore softly. "I believe full well ye would never ha' hurt that lad. He was dear to ye as your own blood."

"Dearer." Ardahl choked. It helped—it helped that this man whom he had respected for so long did not think the worst of him. It solved nothing, yet it did assuage some of the pain.

He looked the war chief in the eye. "I do not know what happened. Believe me when I say so. We were sparring. He—he turned on me. Turned on me like a rabid hound. I saw such rage in his eyes." Ardahl swallowed hard. "I believe he would ha' killed me in that moment. We struggled. The knife ended up in his chest. I began to draw it out again, but there was so much blood—"

"Is that all?"

"All, master."

Dornach stood there regarding him with the rain running down his face. Unflinching. At last one of his big hands came up to clap Ardahl's shoulder.

"Aye, well, there will be more to it, ye may be sure. More may be discovered. Meanwhile, ye must bear your punishment."

"'Tis still harder to bear his absence."

"His absence wounds all o' us. A bright light, was Conall MacAert."

"Master Dornach, why would he turn on me that way?"

Slowly, Dornach shook his head. "I cannot say. I cannot fathom. My advice to ye is, accept your punishment. Fill his place well. Work hard. Trust in the gods that all will come clear in time."

Trust in the gods? Dornach rarely spoke such words, and they startled Ardahl now. Apart from a prayer muttered before a battle, under the duress of the priests, the gods had little to do with him.

Why should they now step forward and take an interest in his life?

Unless—the startling thought occurred to him—they already had. Perhaps they already had.

CHAPTER ELEVEN

T HE RAIN BEGAN late in the afternoon and added to the gloom that filled the small hut. Liadan, trying desperately to keep her mam calm without dosing her to oblivion, at last sent Flanna off the visit her good friend, Lasair, only to give the lass a measure of peace she could not afford herself.

The two lasses were good friends and spent much of their time together at one home or the other. Liadan hoped Lasair's mam would see fit to keep Flanna for a time.

As soon as the young girl left, she ran for the healer and brought him back with her.

"I cannot keep her quiet," she confessed in a hush, just inside the door.

"Not even with the draught?"

"Save with the draught."

Dathi lifted a brow at her.

"I do no' wish to keep her dosed all the time. The draught sends her to a deep sleep."

"Where she needs to be. She is grieving." Dathi gave a sigh. "Let me speak with her."

He entered Conall's sleeping place, which Mam refused to leave. Liadan stood wringing her hands, hearing his soft, patient voice interrupt Mam's weary sobs.

She wished she could be that patient, but she did not have it in her. She felt burned to the bone and had not had a chance herself to weep for her brother, to throw herself down and sob for the sheer hurt of it till she could weep no more.

Even Dathi's quiet words, however, did not succeed in soothing Mam. He soon slipped back out, a concerned frown furrowing his brow.

"She is, aye, distraught. I suggest dosing her until her grief eases, as it will do in sleep."

Aye, and mayhap the healer knew best. Perhaps sleep was the refuge Mam needed.

But with Conall gone, with Mam lost to sleep and Flanna taking comfort elsewhere, whom did Liadan have?

The answer came soon enough after the healer, having administered his dose, left.

He called softly from outside the door, his voice deeper than the pelt of the rain, and when she went there, he asked, "Mistress, might I come in?"

She could scarcely leave him outside in such a downpour even if she wanted to.

"Aye."

He came with his head bent, shedding water, and with Conall's sword in his hand. She saw right off he had a number of scrapes and abrasions, and that his tunic had torn. She did not comment.

"How is your lady mother?"

She did not want to answer him. The serpent, pretending concern. Her words came bitter. "I have just had the healer. She will no' stop with grieving. I have sent Flanna away—for some relief."

"I am sorry."

So he should be.

He lowered himself to the floor just inside the door. As near to outside as he could get.

Liadan cast him a look. "Come closer to the fire. Warm yourself. I do not need an ailing man on top of a grieving woman."

He came and sat beside the hearth, still saying nothing. Stretched his hands out to the warmth. She saw that they trembled ever so slightly.

What must this be like for him? She did not care. *Serpent.*

Silence reigned for many long moments. The draught having taken swift effect, Mam at last eased to silence on Conall's bed.

"What happened to ye?" Liadan asked at length, and nodded at the scrapes.

His lips twisted, and when he spoke, he sounded as bitter as she. "Hard training session."

"I suppose ye will want those hurts tended." She'd often cared so for Conall's simple cuts and strains, him never wanting to trouble the healers.

"Nay, mistress."

"But—" She saw now that he was bleeding from a cut on one forearm and what looked like a nasty slice to his right hand.

"Nay, mistress. Leave it be."

"Then I suppose ye will want to eat."

Again, silence met her statement.

She began to ramble, the words spilling from her aching heart. "Conall always came home from training gey ravenous. Well, he was eager to eat most times, but after working hard he swore he could eat a whole boar on his own. And when he returned from a battle, well… But"—she caught herself—"I expect ye would know that."

"Aye."

"Since I would ha' fed Conall, I suppose I should feed ye instead. Such a simple thing, is it not? Feeding someone. Someone who is hungry. Yet it means a great deal. I used to enjoy seeing Conall eat hearty. Whether Mam fed him or I—"

She paused because her voice broke under the weight of her tears. She could not—would not—weep in front of him. Not in front of him.

"I need naught, mistress."

Well, that had to be a lie. He needed feeding and a change of clothing, and those hurts tended, without doubt. But he was a liar, was he not? He'd lied about killing her brother.

A question screamed in her head. Why? Why, by all the gods, would he hurt the friend he loved? It made no sense.

She set about preparing a hasty meal, mixing the grain for cakes to lay on the hot stone, stirring a pot of meat. She filled a mug with ale, laid the whole of it aside, and lifted the vat of warm water from the fire.

"Now then, let us have a look at ye before we eat."

ARDAHL STOLE A look at Liadan from between his lashes as she tended the cuts on first his one arm and then the other.

She hated him. He could feel that in the stiffness of her touch as well as the antagonism streaming off her. Her eyes remained cool and distant as she swabbed the ugly injuries, smeared on some kind of salve, and wrapped them in clean cloth.

Never had he been so close to her. Indeed, until two days ago he had still thought of her as a child, if he'd thought of her at all.

Could he have been more mistaken?

A child no longer, she had a lovely bosom that pushed against the inside of her bodice, of which he could catch the merest glimpse when she leaned forward to him. Graceful hands and long, narrow limbs. Her honey-colored hair, all plaited, fell over one shoulder. Her eyelashes, the color of autumn barley, were sinfully long, and she had a scattering of tender freckles on her nose. More dusted across the tops of her breasts.

She made it difficult for Ardahl to breathe, and for more than one reason.

He uttered no sound as she tended him. Occasionally she glanced up as if measuring his response to her touch, and their eyes met. Held.

She had beautiful eyes, did Liadan. Blue like Conall's, like the sea on a clear day when it turned still and depthless. A beauty withal, was Conall's sister.

But she was Conall's sister. And she hated him.

When she finished her work, she sat back on her heels, still only a hand's reach away.

"Did they do this to ye on the training field, batter ye this way?"

"Do no' worry for me."

"'Tis difficult to break the habit o' worrying for someone once ye've begun."

To Ardahl's surprise, he smiled. "Ye be like my mam—one who cares for others. She is the finest woman I know."

Her gaze clung to his. She tipped her head to one side. "Ye will be missing her."

Ardahl had to clench himself tight against that thought. "I bade ye no' to worry for me."

"Nay. I should not. But—they are your own friends who battered ye on the training field."

"They are Conall's friends."

"I see."

Did she? Could she glimpse how he was feeling? Far more battered in spirit than in body. Sick with missing Conall. With missing his mam. His own fire, his own bed. The ease he used to know. The ability to hold his head up, having proved his worth.

All of that, gone. And those who had been his lifelong companions turned on him.

"I wish," he said suddenly, speaking to her because there was no one else, "I could have him back even if for just a few moments, that I might ask him why. Why he raised a weapon to me. He, with whom I had scarcely so much as quarreled."

Again Liadan's gaze met his, this time with a hint of surprise. Her lips parted as if she would speak.

Instead she got to her feet, turned away. Ardahl felt the loss of her nearness like a cold wind.

"Eat your supper," she told him, a faint quiver in her voice. "You may sleep there by the fire tonight."

"My place is beside the door."

"Aye, so it is. But not this night."

They sat there, one of them on either side of the hearth, while he ate, listening to the rain crashing down. Liadan took nothing for herself, nor did she speak to him, but he could feel her in an odd way, as if the faint stirrings of the connection forged between them while she tended him still clung to their spirits.

Not a sound came from outside, besides the rain. It felt oddly isolating, as if, with the grieving woman asleep, they two were alone in the world.

It took Ardahl a long while to speak. In truth, he finished picking at his meal before he did.

"Mistress, I have no right to ask ye for anything more. But if ye would grant an act o' charity—not for me, but for another who I know must be hurting—"

She started when he spoke, as if he'd interrupted some private reverie. Of grief, no doubt. Through the leaping flames she looked at him.

"Your mam?"

"Aye. I care naught for myself." He could not allow that. Dornach was right—he must accept his fate however the gods bestowed it, and go on. "She will be desperate in her grief. If ye could find it in your heart to stop by her hut on the morrow. Make sure she is all right. She has no one now."

He stopped abruptly. This woman who hated him would not care for his mother's heart, would she?

Yet she had offered him care.

Roughly he said, "I have no right to ask it of ye."

She did not speak. There was no sound but the rain pelting ever harder and the crackling of the flames. Despair touched Ardahl's heart.

At last, Liadan sighed. "'Tis no' easy for me to get away. To leave Mam."

"To be sure."

"Wi' Flanna gone, I have no one to mind her."

"I understand."

"If I can—" She left it hanging, a mere whisper in the air between them.

"If ye may, 'twould be an act o' great kindness, and I would be gey grateful. And if ye may—" Again he caught himself.

"What?"

"Tell her I love her."

CHAPTER TWELVE

FOLK STARED WHEN Liadan made her way through the settlement. Some stole furtive, curious glances. Some shot her sympathetic ones. A few stepped forward and delayed her to express their shock and grief at Conall's passing.

She wondered how long it would take for his killing to cease being the center of every conversation. A long while, she should think. For now it would be on every lip, the topic of discussion in the council chamber and the warriors' hall.

That her brother's death should become a matter of gossip!

But that was the way of their folk. They spoke of status and standing. They reached for it and they lived by it. Chief Fearghal's bards, for he had two of them, both aged, sang of it and told stories in his hall of his ancestors. How great they had been. How high.

How never had they brought shame upon their blood.

That made her think again of Ardahl MacCormac. The way he'd looked at her in the firelight last night when she tended him. The wound in his eyes.

She hated him, aye. But she was not an unfeeling woman. The gods knew, she often felt too much.

She'd seen pain in Ardahl's eyes, aye. Pain that brought her out on this damp, cloudy morning after Flanna had stopped by to collect a few of her belongings.

"Stay wi' Mam, will ye?" she had bidden her sister. "I have an errand to run."

When Flanna, clearly reluctant, gazed into Conall's sleeping place, Liadan had assured her, "Mam still sleeps. I dare not leave her alone, is all."

So she could not take long over this errand. She dared not.

Last night's rain had ceased but the air struck chill, and mist rose from the sodden ground. Maeve's hut sat on the far side of the settlement and at a distance.

When Liadan arrived, the place looked deserted, the door tight shut, not so much as a glimmer of light showing from within.

She very nearly turned and went back home. Something stopped her. With a look over her shoulder for the staring faces, she stepped up and rapped the doorframe.

No answer.

"Mistress MacCormac?" she called.

The leather curtain wiggled as it was untied and swept aside.

Maeve MacCormac did not appear well. For as long as Liadan had known her—near all her life—she'd been a well-kept woman, quiet and unassuming yet always neat. She had a look of her son, Liadan decided, standing there facing her. The same red-brown hair and eyes that nearly matched. She might have been a beauty once.

Now her hair, loosely bundled, billowed around her pale face. Her clothing appeared to have been slept in, and a frown of pain hovered between her eyes.

"Mistress MacCormac? Be ye well?"

The woman said nothing. Hastily, Liadan eased her back from the doorway and into the hut.

Her heart fell at the state of the place. Ash choked the hearth, and no flame showed there. Items lay strewn about, dishes and pots. A ewer lay on its side. The air had a musty smell.

"Liadan?" Maeve MacCormac's gaze clung to her. "What is amiss? Is it my son?"

"He sent me, aye. He worries for ye." And with good reason, so it seemed. A death might as well have occurred here, from appearances.

It struck Liadan that must be the weight of loss Maeve Mac-Cormac now bore.

"Has aught happened to him?"

"Nay." Save his life had fallen to pieces. Liadan did not want to entertain that thought either. She did not want to sympathize with Ardahl or his mother.

Her brother lay dead.

But who could fail to feel something for this woman? She looked as lost as Liadan felt.

"Here, sit down." Liadan coaxed Maeve onto a rug beside the cold hearth. "Are ye unwell? Shall I fetch Master Dathi?"

Maeve shook her head violently. "Nay. I wish to see no one. No one but my son. And that is forbidden." Her eyes flooded with tears. "He is my son no more."

A hard fate, and no mistake. It seemed cruel to punish this woman for her son's misdeeds. But did they not all suffer?

"When is the last time ye took something to eat?"

"I do not remember."

"Mistress MacCormac, 'twill do no good whatever for ye to neglect yourself."

"Good?" The hazel eyes sought hers. "There is naught of good anymore. Not since—"

"Aye, but—"

"I have no reason left to live. Once I lived for my husband. He was braw and strong. So, so handsome. He was the first charioteer of the tribe when we wed."

"Indeed." Liadan searched around the untidy hearth for a pot of water, or ale, but found naught that had not been spilled or contaminated with ash.

"It did no' take long for us to have a wee daughter. In fact, she came early because we had no' waited to be handfasted—she lived but thirty days. My Cormac said there would be many others. There were, but I lost them one after t'other. Did ye know Ardahl had an older brother?"

Liadan stood now watching the woman. "I did not."

"He had just five years when he died. As bonny a lad as ye could find. He took sick in the winter and was gone before we knew it. That was just before Ardahl was born. Ardahl thrived." Maeve began to weep. "I should ha' known I would lose him too."

Liadan cursed under her breath. Another weeping mother! Another broken heart.

"Whist, now." She hunkered down in front of the woman, who wept into her hands. She did not want to sympathize, nay. Yet she would need to be made of stone did she not. "Ye have no' lost your son. He is alive and well." Unlike Conall.

"As good as dead," Maeve sobbed bitterly. "I have held so many bairns in my arms, only to lose them."

"No' as good as dead," Liadan told her forcefully. "He still walks. He still breathes. He still possesses a beating heart."

Maeve disregarded this. "After I lost my Cormac, him brought home from battle in his own chariot, Ardahl became my reason for living."

"And he is, still. Listen to me. 'Tis Ardahl who sent me here. Worrying for ye, he is. How might I go back and tell him I found ye in this state? Come, let us wash your face and hands. I will make up the fire. Have ye any clean clothing?"

Laying her own grief aside for the moment, Liadan tended Ardahl's mother as she might a child. Raked out the fire. Found the ingredients for a sparse meal. Moved about the hut tidying the mess.

Och, but what was she to tell Ardahl when he returned from training? That his fears had been proved true and his mam coped no better than hers?

Could she place such an additional burden on him? Aye, she should. He had killed Conall, taken his brightness from them.

He deserved this and more.

She should walk away out of here. Leave Maeve to her hard fate.

Her mind more than half made up to it, she wound her shawl about her head and prepared to leave. As she turned away from the fire, Maeve reached out and snagged her arm.

"He would not do such a thing, ye know. This terrible deed."

"Eh?"

Maeve's gaze—now clear of tears as if burned dry—met Liadan's. "My Ardahl would no' have harmed a hair on Conall's head. He loved him like a brother."

"Yet Conall lies dead."

"There must be more to it. The truth lies in it somewhere. Ye must discover it."

"Me? Why me?"

"Because he is yours now. Ardahl is yours. Would ye not know the truth o' him?"

CHAPTER THIRTEEN

ARDAHL RETURNED TO the hut at the end of that day's training carrying a number of new abrasions that caused Liadan to narrow her eyes. Another hard day he had passed with his fellow warriors, and no mistake. It made her wonder.

Were the young warriors with whom he drilled not supposed to be his friends, men who had known him life long? Were they so quick to turn on him?

Aye, and had she not known him most of her life also? He had spent as much of his time here in her mam's hut as his own. Taken his meals here often. Fallen asleep by the fire.

She had been attracted to him then. Considered him the bonniest man to walk the face of the world. Had conspired to make him see her as more than a child. More than Conall's wee sister.

As a woman.

She still considered him braw and handsome. As he quietly entered the hut with his hair hanging down his back in an auburn mane, moving with that quiet competence, and set his weapons just inside the door, her pulse quickened. Against her will, it did. She could no longer feel attracted to this man. Could not allow it.

He shot her one swift look from assessing eyes before glancing away.

"Mistress Liadan. How fares your lady mother?"

"Sleeping. Quiet, for now." Dosed by Dathi's draught. Liadan did not like that, but it was better than the endless weeping.

Weapons laid aside, Ardahl looked at his hands. "I am filthy. I will go wash."

Liadan did not intend to follow him. She but remembered there was no clean cloth there at the washing place around the side of the hut, so she caught one up from those she'd washed earlier and headed out.

She caught Ardahl at his ablutions with his back to her, bent over the wooden basin. He'd had time already to strip off his tunic, so she had a clear view of him, the auburn waves of hair swept to one side. Broad shoulders narrowing to lean hips, clad in rough leggings that failed to disguise the play of muscles. A rash of abrasions. He'd been put down onto the turf a number of times this day.

He'd presumably fought his way up again.

Liadan froze as if an iron grip had seized her by the heart—or lower down.

Hearing something—surely not Liadan's quiet step—he turned. Caught her standing there eyeing him.

The view from the front was even better than the other.

"A cloth. For drying." She flung it at him and fled for the hut.

She must be mad to think of him that way. *Still* think of him that way. After he'd killed her brother.

Maeve's words returned to her mind. *My Ardahl would not have harmed a hair of Conall's head.* There must be some truth in it.

When she reentered the hut, her mam was stirring, whimpering in her sleep. Liadan went to soothe and provide comfort, and soon heard Ardahl come in behind her, nearly silent.

He would need to be fed. Might once more need his hurts tended. Suddenly, she wanted to weep.

She still hadn't had a chance to do that. To weep properly for her brother. To throw herself down and sob as Mam had done.

She could not afford to give way. If she did, she might break entirely.

Mam subsided back into sleep and Liadan tiptoed out to find Ardahl seated beside the door. His place. That of a hound.

Her heart twisted in her breast.

"Come. Sit where ye can get warm. I have made supper."

Just the two of them, with Flanna still at Lasair's house and Mam lost to sleep. A terrible silence fell between them as Liadan filled his bowl.

To break it more than anything else, she spoke. "It appears ye have had another rough day at training."

He shrugged. "They will keep knocking me down until they tire of it. Or I cannot get up again."

"I can scarce believe they have all turned on ye—those who were your good friends."

He gave her a long look. *She* had turned on him. "Not all. There are a few who hold their tongues and their opinions."

"Have ye hurts that need tending?" She could see that he had. An ugly abrasion covered one side of his jaw and the tattoo on one arm had been bisected by a scrape.

He shook his head. "Leave it be."

"But—"

"Leave it be, mistress."

They ate in silence for several moments, Liadan picking at her food. "I went to see your mam."

That captured his attention. He laid his food aside and studied her intently. "How did ye find her?"

What to say? Would he want the truth? If she were him, she would want the truth.

"She suffers the loss. I do not doubt she longs to see ye. But she has faith in ye also—that you did not do this deed." Liadan stumbled over those words.

He nodded somberly. His hair fell forward, half screening his face. "I worry for her alone. No one to do for her."

In Liadan's opinion, he should worry. She did not say so.

He raised his eyes to meet hers. "'Twas kind in ye to go to her, mistress. I appreciate it."

"Whatever happened between ye and Conall, whatever quarrel took place, 'twas none of her doing."

"We never truly quarreled. Never in all the years we were friends."

"Then how? How did the knife end up in his heart?"

"Will ye believe me if I say again I do not know?"

"I cannot."

"Then—there is no more to be said."

Another silence fell, this one fraught. She did not need to defend herself. Not to him. He had been caught in the act, and her brother slain. Cathair had seen—

Her thoughts stumbled there. And who was Cathair? What did she think of him?

Foremost among the warriors, the great war chief Dornach's assistant, and a force to be reckoned with. There had ever been something she could not like about him, though. A braggart, he was. Well, many of the clan's warriors boasted of their deeds or paid Chief Fearghal's bards to do so.

Except Ardahl. He had ever been humble despite the fact that he must by now rival Cathair for the place of first among Fearghal's warriors.

That struck her forcefully. Cathair's rival.

Nay.

It could not be. No one, not even Cathair with all his arrogance, would do anything so treacherous.

She had it all wrong. Her heart did. Ardahl MacCormac was a serpent.

She needed to keep that in mind.

ARDAHL SLEPT BESIDE the door that night. The cold came in under the leather curtain and all his wounds stung. None of that bothered him so much as his thoughts.

His near-crazed thoughts.

He had never wanted much from life. At least, he didn't believe so. Just to work hard to rise among Fearghal's warriors. To prove he'd been right to take a different path from his father and turn his back on the chariots. To take care of his mother following Da's death. To spend time with Conall.

All of that, now gone. He'd become a pariah among his fellow warriors. Forbidden to care for Mam.

Conall, gone from him.

Lying there as the night dragged past, he relived it over and over again. Conall turning upon him, there on the training field. The sheer rage and—aye—betrayal in his eyes. The knife blade coming at him.

He had reacted with pure instinct. Had he directed that blade into Conall's heart?

If so—if so, it had not been by intention.

Why had Conall been so angry? Why had he turned upon Ardahl that way? Ardahl would have bet his life such a thing could never happen.

He had near lost his life.

Mayhap 'twould have been better if he had. Better than what he now endured. For he had no way to defend himself. No way to make it right. He had to live with the scorn of all who knew him.

The hate and despair in Mistress Liadan's eyes.

Near morning, her mother came awake there on Conall's bed and began again with her sobbing. Weeping and lamenting anew. Ardahl had to lie and listen while Liadan rose and sought to comfort the woman. The lass was patient and caring, he would give her that. But he could hear the weariness in her voice. The tears that threatened.

She did not want to dose her mam again. As well she had sent her young sister away from this, to seek some peace elsewhere.

He lay till he could bear it no longer before rising, taking up his weapons, and going out to await the dawn.

<hr>

CHAPTER FOURTEEN

NO SOONER WERE the warriors at practice that morning than a runner came pelting in. One of the younger lads, it was, sent by the guard to Dornach's ear.

"Master Dornach!"

Some frantic quality in the boy's voice caused everyone to stop work and turn. Face red and sweaty, the lad fairly slid to a halt in front of the war chief.

"They come! Aldur, of the guard, sent me to tell ye!" He gulped air. "Our patrol spotted them at first light. Movin' in under cover o' darkness, they were. Dacha's men."

Dornach's gaze turned hard as iron, and he uttered the kind of curse that could curl a man's hair. "Dacha's men, ye say?"

Not their neighbor directly to the west. He was a man named Brihan who had long been on good terms with Fearghal, and acted as a sort of buffer between Fearghal's tribe and that of the ambitious Dacha, who had been steadily conquering the lands around him. It was rumored he'd left Brihan's lands alone only because he considered him so weak, he might seize them whenever he decided to bother.

And because Brihan allowed him freedom to cross his lands and attack Fearghal any time he chose.

Blood had flowed on that border many times, but not that of Brihan's men, who held back from any fray.

Now, at the beginning of the fighting season, Dacha might well be expected to strike. No doubt Fearghal and Dornach had expected it. They had left a strong and canny guard on that border, and drilled the men well.

"How many?" Dornach snapped at the messenger. "Could our men tell?"

"A large force, they say."

"How close?"

"Approaching the border. Aldur wants to know, should he engage them?"

Dornach hesitated. The border must be held, aye. It would take him precious time to organize his warriors and reach the place. For the guards there to engage a large force, however, would mean certain death.

"Send a runner. Tell them to fall back. Tell them we are on the way. Someone run to the chief. The rest o' ye—to arms!"

At those words, a familiar sensation flooded Ardahl. Part dread, part anticipation, part determination. It would be a large encounter, this. A fierce one. It could well mean his death.

He had never before faced such a battle without Conall at his side.

That thought struck through the dread and the determination both, and left him hollow.

How could he do this?

Dornach called orders for the chariots to be readied, and he wondered again.

How to go to battle without Conall in the cart with him? Who would drive their chariot now?

Men scrambled. There was little time to prepare. Some might hurry home under the guise of fetching their weapons, only to impart a frantic kiss on the lips of a wife or the heads of their children. No opportunity for proper farewells.

Some lovers might never see one another again.

For some reason, his thoughts flew to Liadan.

She would not care if he lived or died.

As at some inaudible signal, women came running. Always it was so. Perhaps it was as simple as one of the young lads who haunted the training field running to tell. It seemed far more magical than that.

For several moments, what had been an ordinary training field fell into chaos. Then Dornach, with Chief Fearghal now at his side, began hollering again.

"To order, men! To weapons, and take your places."

What was his place now? Conall's, aye, but Conall had been his driver first, and his defender second.

Chariots drawn by men and lads rattled out over the green turf. Other men led out the ponies.

Ardahl must take himself to Dornach. Tell him—remind him—he no longer had a partner.

He turned and saw someone approaching him.

She came across the grass softly despite her burden, face chalk white, eyes grave. Fixed upon him, she hurried faster when their gazes met.

"Mistress Liadan? What is all this?"

"I heard. Ye go at once?"

"Aye."

"Ye must have Conall's armor."

"But—"

"Ye canna go without." Again her gaze met his, the contact searing. "Ye have taken his place, have ye no'? Then this should be yours."

She tossed the items down in a heap, helped him into the padded hide over-tunic. The hammered metal wrist bands.

Those had touched Conall's skin. Protected him.

"Ye have his sword? Your own things are at your mother's. Ye canna go without."

He stood there washed over by gratitude and shame. He did not know what to say.

A cart rattled up beside him. The driver called down, "Ye be wi'me. Dornach's orders."

His name was Cullan, and Ardahl recalled his partner had been killed at a skirmish near the end of winter. The man did not look pleased to be partnered with Ardahl.

Naught to be done for it. He leaped aboard the chariot, steadied himself with one hand on the front rail.

He had time for only a single look at Liadan, who stood perfectly still in the green turf while they rattled away.

"Just so ye know," Cullan said as they took a place in the line of marching men and chariots. Not where they should be, but back a goodly way. "I am only partnering wi' ye because Dornach ordered it. Me, I want naught to do wi' ye."

"Understood."

"Ye be a betrayer of the worst kind, and a false friend so far as I am concerned. Conall was a finer man than ye'll ever be."

"I agree."

Cullan looked surprised at that. "If ye think so, then why did ye kill him?"

"I did not kill him."

"Och, so it happened by magic, did it? Enchantment, maybe?"

As the chariots rattled along, clansfolk darted forward to speak hasty farewells. To sons, to husbands, to brothers, to lovers. Those they might never see again.

Ahead, in the second chariot—for the first belonged to Dornach and his driver—rode Cathair, pale head high and proud. A figure darted forward to his side—a woman it was, with her skirts caught up high. She reached out a hand to Cathair, and he reached back. Their fingers touched before she fell away.

Her long, wavy brown hair marked her identity. Brasha.

Conall's love.

There was something in it. Ardahl felt certain of that. He had no time for such thoughts now. But it bit at him.

A force awaited them on the border. And a man who allowed his thoughts to stray from battle paid the price, swift and hard.

A broad stream marked their boundary with Brihan's lands. It flowed over the breast of the hill and glittered beneath the rising sun. They rattled on a goodly distance, silent but for the clatter of their weapons and the hooves of the ponies. Each man contemplating the thoughts in his own mind.

A glorious day to do battle. Blue sky with a few fair-weather clouds sailing back eastward. The scent of wild thyme on the breeze. What looked like ten score men spread out on the other side, awaiting them.

Dornach drew them up with a raised hand on the high ground above the water. Accustomed every man to obeying him, they rattled to a halt, the ponies tossing their heads. The warm breeze ruffled their manes, and the hair of the men.

Fairghal's forces had the advantage, aye, of higher ground, yet that force Ardahl saw facing them was a strong one, so strong it felt like a punch to the gut.

Brihan of Brioc must be a fool, to let so many warriors cross his land and do battle with Fearghal. Aye, he might have an agreement with Dacha that he thought would keep him safe. But should Dacha conquer Fearghal's lands, what was to keep him from helping himself to the weaker holding that lay between?

Mayhap he had already done so. That could be why the army arrayed here looked so vast.

They could not allow Dacha a victory.

That realization seemed to spread through Fearghal's forces. It traveled from man to man by whispers and mutters.

Even Cullan, who by his own word detested Ardahl, spoke bitter and low. "By the holy goddess, will ye look at that?"

Before Ardahl could answer, Dornach turned and addressed them from his chariot.

"That boundary protects our lands! Aye, there are twice as many o' them. We must be twice as fierce! Ye will no' let them set a toe out o' that water."

For an instant he touched them all with his gaze. Man by man. "Fight ye well. And any o' ye who meets wi' death, this day, fly well and truly to *Tír na nÓg*."

Perhaps that is what the gods intend for me, Ardahl thought. *The meaning of it all. I will follow Conall so swiftly to the land of the ever-young where we will again sit together. He will tell to me then what happened, and how the knife ended in his breast.*

His life counted for naught. He would not go home from this, and 'twas how it should be.

CHAPTER FIFTEEN

UPON ENTERING BATTLE, a man's mind switched to a single line of thought and a narrow vision. At least, so Ardahl's mind tended to do. He saw only what was before him—opponent by opponent, obstacle by obstacle—and all his being flowed to it. No thought for aught else, save his partner aboard the chariot.

Conall was not with him now. But aye, mayhap he would see him soon.

Before that, he could not let a man of Dacha's clan set foot on their land.

Dornach gave the signal—a mighty cry and a wave of his sword—and they went in down the slope to the stream, the cart crashing into the water. Ardahl could feel in his bones that Cullan was not the driver Conall had been. The cart nearly overturned at the outset, spilling them both.

"There. There!" he shouted, gesturing wildly with Conall's sword. Conall usually knew by some instinct where he wanted to go.

Cullan turned the cart and they headed for the thick of their opponents. A chariot, driven correctly, could be a weapon. A chariot carrying a man flashing a sword could do twice the damage.

So it did now, despite Cullan's clumsy handling. The ponies, fearless, splashed through the water, and Ardahl, focusing on one face at a time, laid to. On their left, he heard men hollering and screaming, the crash of arms. Strangled cries that denoted death.

He heard Cullan cursing in a steady stream. He saw intent in the eyes of an opponent. Blue eyes they were, with death in them.

Conall's sword took the man's head.

A good sword, was Conall's, though not as good as Ardahl's own. He ached then for his own blade, as he might for a part of his arm. As he ached to have Conall there with him.

No time for lamenting, any more than thought. Their chariot, surrounded, rocked as they were swarmed by enemy warriors. Cullan dropped the reins and drew his own sword to defend the ponies.

Their opponents fell to Conall's sword. One, two, three. Swiftly were they replaced, but they had to tread upon their fellows to get close.

Without thought for himself, Ardahl leaped down.

He heard Cullan call to him, what sounded like protest or warning. The din of battle grew so loud then, he could hear naught else. He saw only faces, one after the other coming at him. Felt nothing of wounds. Disregarded the protest of his muscles and swung again and again until—

No new faces appeared before him.

Someone was screaming nearby, as the pace of the battle fell away. Cullan it was, calling to him.

"By the goddess, get aboard!"

Moving by instinct, Ardahl obeyed. The cart, no longer marooned amid corpses—Cullan must have leaped down and dragged them away—turned. Rattled to the left. Toward a knot of their warriors, still fighting.

A part of Ardahl's mind—that narrow part—accepted the new challenge. They waded in, and the new fight surrounded them until it penetrated to his mind that they had turned the flank, there in the water. A good thing.

When they were once more surrounded by dead bodies, when the ponies trod upon flesh instead of stone, Cullan stopped and hollered into Ardahl's face.

"Be ye hurt?"

"Eh?"

"Hurt? Be ye—"

Disregarding the question, Ardahl leaped down and ran to rejoin the fray further along the stream.

He was not meant to survive this fight. Somewhere beyond the western horizon, Conall waited for him. The important thing was to stop the enemy before he died.

Someone attacked him from behind, a slice of a blade in the shoulder of the padded leather armor Liadan had helped him don.

Liadan.

He whirled and took the man's head without looking into his eyes. Someone shouted over and over, a hoarse, repetitive sound.

It was him.

Conall! Conall!

His heart called to his friend. His throat rendered the sound senseless. The enemy fell away before him.

He heard Dornach shouting, shouting.

They pursued the enemy to the far edge of the stream and beyond. Dacha's warriors fled away over the green turf, and Fearghal's men chased them down. On foot. By chariot.

Suddenly Cullan was there again beside Ardahl. Staring. Staring. "Come aboard!"

They pursued the men in flight. Cut them down. Cullan's handling of the ponies was erratic. They nearly overturned again and at last came to a rocking halt.

Dornach called to them. Called them back.

Cullan turned in the cart and stared at Ardahl.

"Are ye hurt, man?" Not the first time he had asked.

"Nay."

"You're bleeding."

Was he? Ardahl looked down at himself. He felt nothing. But aye, blood ran down his arms, and the armor bore deep slices. Conall's sword ran with blood.

Cullan blinked at him. The hostility had left his eyes. "We

must go back. Dornach calls."

Ardahl nodded. Not till the cart turned and rattled back did he wonder, *Why am I still alive? Why am I not flying to join Conall at Tír na nÓg?*

Their forces, and a mountain of dead men, awaited them on the other side of the stream. Fearghal's land. Many of the dead were the enemy, and far too many their own.

Dornach stood among his remaining warriors. The big man towered over the rest and had still the remembrance of killing in his eyes.

As Cullan drew up, his gaze touched Ardahl. It lingered a heavy moment before moving on to the others. Counting. He was counting his surviving men.

An odd silence fell, broken only by the groans of the wounded. The dying. The chuckling of the stream that now ran red in places. The breeze had picked up and the scent of the far hills warred against that of blood.

"A battle well fought!" Dornach called into the eerie silence. "Ye ha' well demonstrated Fearghal's might this day. Not a man among ye of whom I am no' proud!"

Did Dornach's gaze touch Ardahl again? He could not tell. Reaction had caught up with him. Exhaustion. His whole body throbbed like one great wound. His sword arm had gone limp.

"Cathair, Ardan, set a guard. The rest o' ye, locate our wounded. And our dead. Any living members o' the enemy—ye know what to do."

Leave no enemy warrior living. It was an ancient edict.

"Come on," Ardahl said to Cullan, forgetting for the moment he was not Conall.

"Ye need tending."

"What?"

"Man, ye're running wi' blood!"

"There's work to be done."

Cullan stepped closer. "I ha' never seen anyone fight so. How many did ye kill?"

Ardahl shook his head. It was a blur. He did not remember.

"Come, let the healer look at ye." The healer's apprentice, it was, no more than a young lad. The tribe's healers were far too valuable to risk in battle.

"Not now. Mayhap later."

Dornach appeared beside them. It seemed to happen almost magically—not there one moment, there the next. He eyed Ardahl with a measuring stare.

"Did ye see him, master?" Cullan asked. "Did ye see him?"

"I did. Ardahl, go get your wounds tended."

"I am no' bad hurt. There's still the dead and wounded—"

"Will ye offer me disobedience?"

"Nay, Master Dornach."

Cathair appeared beside them. His pale-blue gaze flicked over Ardahl with disdain before he turned to Dornach.

"Master Dornach, we have located a wounded man—Chief Dacha's brother, so we think. D'ye want him slain?"

"No' yet. Bring him back wi' us. And Cathair—ye fought well."

Cathair's gaze flickered over Ardahl again. He nodded.

Numb to the bone now, Conall's sword still dangling from his hand, Ardahl stood where he was.

As it had back on the training field, Dornach's hand descended on his shoulder.

"As for ye—I will speak wi' ye anon, back at the dun."

"Ha' I done somewhat wrong?"

"Ye? Only turned the battle. Ye're the blessed hero, ye are."

CHAPTER SIXTEEN

As their warriors fought at the border, Liadan warred within her own heart.

She did her best to keep busy at her fireside. To tidy the hut and look after Mam, who once more stirred before falling into what seemed a more peaceful sleep.

Flanna came home, pale-faced and worried. They were used to fretting for Conall at such times as these. They did not need to fear for him now, but the habit died hard.

Liadan would not worry for Ardahl MacCormac. *She would not.* But watching him wheel away in the cart had tugged at her heart. Only because he wore Conall's armor and carried his sword.

Habit.

"Come," Flanna bade her. "Let us see what the women are saying."

"The women know nothing. And Mam—"

"She is safe asleep."

"Och, very well." If Liadan stayed here in the hut, she would likely go mad.

The settlement felt completely different with the warriors gone. The women came out, left off their tasks and chores. They stood in groups of two or three speaking in low voices. The old men emerged likewise and told their tales to any who would listen of old battles, the horrors faced. Of wounds and death and blood.

Children, picking up on the peculiar energy, ran about making a din, not knowing why.

A fact of life that all the men who went away, either on foot or rattling in the chariots, would not return. A battle lost could be a devastating thing, costing them dear. The border, though, must be held.

There would, aye, be a cost.

Whose son, brother, husband, lover would come back over the hill?

Whose would not, save on his shield or on the bottom of a chariot?

Liadan might never see Ardahl MacCormac again.

And so what? He was a serpent, was he not? He had taken Conall from them.

Only, he swore he had not.

And was that not just what he would do, the traitor? The betrayer?

Chief Fearghal stood outside his hall with his wife, Bridie, at his side and their two young children running about. During anything save outright attack, Fearghal always stayed back to defend the settlement and hold strong if the very worst happened.

The very worst could right well happen. A crowd of enemy warriors could come screaming over that hill.

For now it was quiet, save for the muttering of the women and the old men holding forth. Fearghal spoke reassuringly to a knot of women.

"Let us hear what the chief has to say." Flanna dashed off. Liadan did not follow. What could the chief say? He knew no more than they what was happening at the border.

One woman stood alone with her shawl raised over her head, half shadowing her face. Shunned by the others.

Liadan took the place at her side. "Mistress MacCormac."

"I did not get a chance to speak a farewell to him." Tears ran down Maeve's face. "I may no' see him again."

"I bade him farewell and gave him Conall's armor. He went

bravely."

Maeve turned and stared into Liadan's face with what might be astonishment.

"Ye did him that kindness?"

"Not a kindness. He has taken Conall's place and has a right to his belongings."

"Och, I was so afraid. His armor is all at my house. I thought—"

Liadan put her arm around the weeping woman. "Courage. My mam always says we who wait back must be twice as brave as those who go."

"'Tis the not knowing that hurts so."

"Aye."

Maeve adored her son. Whatever he had done, whether he be the serpent Liadan thought him or not.

It could take days for word to reach them from the border, even though it was not far. The battle itself could take that long. The agony of waiting might well continue.

But as they stood, she saw Fearghal summon a lad to him.

"Let us see what the chief is about," she bade Maeve.

"Nay, I will no' approach him." Maeve turned and went off away, back home.

Liadan joined the group near the door of the hall, where Flanna already stood.

"The chief is sending runners to see what is happening," Flanna told her.

"Good." Aye, it could be good. Or it could be woeful and terrible. Such runners had been slain before now. Or they had returned with the very worst news.

Better than not knowing? She was not sure. At least now they had this small bubble of time.

And hope.

IN THE STATE of half-dazed awareness that enfolded him, Ardahl could not understand why he had become the focus of so many stares and so much whispering. Did they speak yet, these fellow warriors, of his guilt, of what they believed he had done? Of Conall's death. Och, aye, it would take far longer than this for that anger to lie down.

And he must bear it. Somehow, amidst all the other pain, he must find a way to hold up his head and endure.

"Ardahl!" Dornach stood before him, speaking directly into his face.

"Aye, master?"

Dornach's dark eyes performed a rapid inspection. "Did I no' tell ye to get your wounds tended?"

Cullan spoke, repeating himself to all who were nearby. "Did ye see him? In the fight. I ha' never seen a man, any man, battle so."

Dornach jerked his head at Cullan. "Take him to the healer. Then we are for home."

Men—some already wearing bandages and some with open wounds—moved out of the way as Cullan led Ardahl along. The healer's apprentice himself had brought an assistant, no more than a lad who hurried to fetch and carry. This was rough care indeed, given out in the open. Not what some of the horrific wounds deserved. But the men could be seen by Dathi and his fellows when they reached home.

A string of men waited to be seen. They all stared as Cullan led Ardahl up. Some of them shuffled aside, as if offering up their places.

Ardahl waved a hand. "Nay, I will wait my turn."

"But, man," one of them said, "ye be running with blood."

Was he? Ardahl once more looked down at himself. Only then did he begin to feel the pain.

Cullan embarked on his familiar tale. "Did ye see the man? Did ye see him in the battle? I was his charioteer in Conall's place. Ne'er have I seen a man fight so. He turned the flank, he did.

Single handed. That let us move in upon them."

In Conall's place. In truth, that was all Ardahl heard.

The healer's apprentice gestured to him. The others waiting in line had moved aside.

"Nay," Ardahl protested.

Earnestly, the apprentice said, "We are treating in order of need. Come along."

The healer had eyes of two different colors, one green and one brown. He assessed Ardahl's condition much as Dornach had and pushed him down on a rock they'd been using as a seat.

"This may hurt a wee bit."

An understatement. It was rough treatment indeed, the healer more clumsy than skilled. Perhaps he was merely overwhelmed at the magnitude of Ardahl's injuries. A dire cut to the left arm—that which streamed with so much blood—one to a leg, and one to his shoulder that the healer informed him would have killed him, but for his armor.

Conall's armor.

A long slice to one side of his face, ending at the jaw.

He sat throughout, stoic and unmoving. The other men awaiting care watched. He could feel their eyes on him. Cullan flapped his gums while the soft afternoon air flowed over them, down from the hills, warring with the stench of death.

At last Ardahl stirred and looked at Cullan.

"Leave off, will ye?

Cullan looked surprised, but he went silent. Ardahl wondered how long he would remain so.

He barely remembered the trip home. Cullan drove him in their chariot, one of the long line carrying wounded and dead. A stout guard had been set, manned by those least injured. Dornach, himself heavily bandaged, rode the lead chariot.

By the time their settlement came into view, Ardahl clutched the front rail in order to keep himself upright. He had nothing left but his self-respect. He would not let his fellows, or those waiting at home, see him fall.

A near thing, though. A crowd of clansfolk awaited them. The pony minders ran forward to take the animals. Ardahl leaned down and spoke to one of them.

"This pony on the left—he's taken a cut to the chest."

The lad nodded.

Ardahl's da, among the finest of all charioteers, had always put the beasts ahead of himself. Ardahl could hear him now, in his head, saying to do so.

Just as he could hear Conall saying what he always had when they reached home after a sharp battle.

We ha' done well, my lad. We ha' done well.

$$\begin{array}{c}\text{\textbf{CHAPTER SEVENTEEN}}\end{array}$$

CHAPTER SEVENTEEN

"FLANNA, RUN AND fetch Mistress MacCormac."

Liadan gave the order in a hushed voice, unwilling to wake either of her patients. Two of them now, for her to tend. And what misdeed might she have committed to earn this? Bad enough looking after Mam, whom she loved, without being lumbered with the serpent.

He was not a serpent, though. At least, not at the moment.

He'd been led home by a fellow warrior who would not shut up about the battle—the last thing Liadan wanted to hear—and who told her he'd been seen by a healer in the field and then by another here when they reached home.

Liadan scarcely listened to the man. She could see that Ardahl MacCormac barely kept his feet, and that by sheer determination.

She'd put him in her own bed, there being nowhere else. He'd fallen into an almost immediate sleep, and she'd fretted.

What if he died? His injuries looked grave enough. And she didn't like the expression in his eyes. Half dazed. Half burned to the very spirit.

At first she begged Flanna to stay with her, for she did not want to be alone with these two. But Flanna went outside to vomit, then went and sat beside Mam as if she, no more than Liadan, could bear to be near Ardahl.

Why must I stay and care for him? Liadan wondered as she tended the fire, as she fussed over bandages and salves, as she made sure Ardahl was still alive.

His wounds were extensive, as she could clearly see. No doubt he had lost much blood. But, as she told herself repeatedly, he was a strong man in the prime of his life. So long as none of the wounds took poisoning, he would recover.

For now, exhaustion claimed him. He breathed deep, and naught she did or said roused him. Not until the middle of the night, when she drowsed by the fire, did he part his lips in a plaintive moan.

"Mam. Mam?"

It raised the hairs all over Liadan's body, coming out of the silence that way. When she checked on him, she found him still senseless. Calling for his mother in his sleep.

Hardhearted she might be, at least when it came to this man. Or she might not. Either way, she could not withstand such a plea.

Were there any strictures against her inviting his mother here to help care for him? She did not know.

She would not ask.

When Flanna woke at first light, she bade her go to fetch Maeve.

"I will no'. I do no' like to. Lasair says Ardahl no longer belongs to her." Flanna wrinkled her nose. "He is ours now."

"The woman will want to see him, sore hurt as he is. She will be going out of her mind wi' worry. Think if it were Conall."

"He is no' Conall. He killed Conall."

"Just go."

Flanna went out. Whether she would obey or run back away to her friend, Liadan could not say.

Time passed. A scuttle came at the doorpost.

Maeve stood there, her shawl held up over her hair, face drawn. Her eyes searched Liadan's face piteously.

"He is here? How bad is he?"

"'Tis hard to tell." Liadan hesitated. "He called for ye. In his sleep."

Maeve clasped Liadan's wrist. "'Tis kind of ye to bring me."

"No kindness. I ha' my mam to care for. If ye tend him—"

"Aye, to be sure."

Maeve went away into Liadan's sleeping place. She had brought a basket of bandages, and began at once speaking to her son. Crooning to him. "I am here, lamb. Rest easy now."

Lamb? If Liadan could believe the little bit she'd absorbed of Cullan's blather, the man had turned the battle single-handed.

But, ah, did she care what his mother said to him? With Maeve here, the burden was lifted from her own shoulders.

Mam surfaced from the doze, focused on Liadan, and asked where she was. She seemed so much more clearheaded that hope stirred in Liadan's heart. If Mam recovered, she would not be alone in this misery.

Soon Mam fell into what seemed a restful sleep. Not long after, Liadan heard the rumble of a male voice next door. She went and hovered at the doorway. Aye, Ardahl had come awake. He half sat up, his mam bent over him. Both of them turned eyes identical in color toward Liadan.

"Ah, ye be better." Not waiting for an answer from Ardahl, Liadan hurried on, "Mistress MacCormac, is there aught ye need?"

"Nay. I ha' all I need."

Liadan quickly moved away and set about preparing a meal. Maeve would want to eat. So, presumably, would the recovering warrior.

When the *aran* sat browned on the stone beside the fire, she called Maeve.

"Will ye take your son something to eat? There is broth and bread."

"Thank ye."

"How is he?" Liadan did not want to ask. Then again, she wanted to know.

Maeve pushed tumbled hair away from a face white with strain. "My son is strong. If none o' the wounds take poisoning, he will recover."

Just as she had thought. Was it good news, or bad? Not able to decide, Liadan just nodded.

"Thank you for sending for me. I needed to see him."

"Aye."

"I should go soon."

"Nay, do not." Liadan did not wish to be alone with her two patients.

"I do not know if I am allowed to be here."

"I allow it. With Mam ailing, I am in charge." For better, for worse.

Maeve glanced into Conall's sleeping place, where Mam lay. "What ails your mother?"

"Grief. I can restore your son to ye. I cannot bring hers back to her."

ARDAHL DREAMED OF Conall, the aftermath of one of the battles they'd fought together out on the border. Conall's spirits always rose sky high following a fight—because they'd triumphed, a fearless team, as he liked to say. He'd brag a little while they sat with their mugs of ale after having their wounds tended, but only to Ardahl. He was not a man to talk himself up in the warriors' hall.

In this dream, though, Conall turned to Ardahl, fixed him with a knowing blue eye, and said, "I need to tell you something."

It felt so good sitting with him once more that way, so at ease bumping shoulders companionably as they so often had, that Ardahl nearly did not want to listen.

"'Tis important," Conall insisted.

"Tell me, then."

"Cathair—"

He awoke abruptly and lay stinging in half a score of places. He told himself to disregard the pain. He'd been injured before.

Both he and Conall had.

But he had not Conall to lean upon now. To encourage him. To laugh with about their daring, and their hurts.

He wanted to go back into the dream. To say, "I would never in a thousand lives have believed ye would turn on me in anger. Why?"

His mother's face swam into place above him. "Mam? Ye, here? How?"

"Mistress Liadan sent for me. A kindness."

Liadan. A vision of her danced in his mind. Honey-gold hair. Wary blue eyes.

As if he'd summoned her, she appeared at the opening in the sleeping place. *Her* sleeping place, as he realized.

"Is all well? Shall I call the healer?"

Mam looked at him. "D'ye want the healer?"

"By all the gods, no." The last thing he wanted was another person poking and prodding at him. "They will be needed elsewhere."

Mistress Liadan disappeared from view.

Mam took Ardahl's hand. "Ye must eat. Grow stronger. They are saying out there"—she jerked her head toward the outer door—"ye be a hero."

His lips twisted. "*They* are—the same who hate and despise me?"

She leaned close. "Ye will show them of what ye be made. Ye must grow strong so ye can show them."

Madness. Even his own mam took part in it.

"I must get up."

"Son, nay."

"I need to relieve myself."

"I will fetch the pot."

"Mam, no."

It astonished him, when he fought his way upright, just how weak he felt. Dizzy in the head. No man—no warrior, whatever his disgrace—should be reduced so low.

No man of his years should have to relieve himself into an accursed pot.

Yet the midden sat at a distance. Could he make it there on his own?

"Come." His mam supporting him, they went out into the air. Dark had fallen and the breeze felt kind against his cheek. The night made a fine cover as they went.

By the time they reached the place, he tottered. He went the last few steps on his own, knowing he would need to call on all his strength to make it back again.

Folk stared as he and Mam returned to Mistress Liadan's hut. No one spoke; no one protested his mam's presence at his side.

They parted at the door of the hut. Mam pulled his head down and kissed him on the face. "Ye have grown so tall from when I used to kiss ye. I scarce know ye. But och, I still love ye just the same."

"Take care, Mam. Will I see ye tomorrow?"

"Aye. Och, aye."

He watched her away through the dark till he could see her no more.

CHAPTER EIGHTEEN

S CREAMS WOKE LIADAN from the first good sleep she'd known in days. She'd curled up beside the fire, since Flanna—who'd stayed home—had gone to lie beside Mam.

Ardahl had tried to take the place at the door, surrendering her own bed back to her, but she'd insisted he keep it one more night.

All was quiet before the screaming started. Harsh yells, bellows, shrieks. A distant, discordant clashing.

She opened her eyes, thinking the sounds followed her from whatever dream she'd been having. They did not.

A shadow shifted inside the hut. Ardahl came forward from her sleeping place, only half dressed.

She sat up and, across the fire, their eyes met.

"What—?"

"There is fighting. We are under attack."

"Nay! We cannot be—"

"Get your mother and sister up. Swiftly now."

He moved through the spill of moonlight coming through the smoke hole, and Liadan got a good look at him. Clad only in his leggings. Strong and quiet, but covered with wounds, the wild hair streaming loose down his back.

Conall's sword already in his hand.

"Move!" he bade her.

The sounds outside grew louder. Terror ignited in Liadan's heart. Aye, if this be an attack, she must get Mam and Flanna away.

She moved clumsily. When she reached Conall's sleeping place, Flanna was already on her feet. "Liadan, what is it?"

"Attack, so Ardahl says."

"Who—"

"Dacha." Ardahl stood right behind them. "Get your mam up. The three o' ye, creep out round the back. Do your best to reach the hills. Wait there till others come."

"But—"

"They are burning the settlement. Can ye no' hear?"

"By all the gods! What about you?"

"I will stay and fight."

But when they tried to wake her mam, she would not rouse. And without being on her feet, she could not flee.

Liadan could hear the fighting now, sword on sword and sword on shield. Cries from hoarse throats, women's shrieks, the wails of children.

Ardahl scooped Mam up in his arms and said to her and Flanna, "Come."

As soon as they stepped outside, Liadan could see the flames. They came from the west side of the settlement, as did most the screams, and leaped garishly into the quiet night. Thatch aflame. Was that the chief's hall?

Other people moved through the half-lit dark around them. A woman, their neighbor Mistress MacCade, asked, "What is happening?"

"Attack."

Ardahl led them, a small band of would-be refugees, in absolute silence through the edge of the settlement. So terrified was Liadan, she could barely breathe.

Flanna clutched her hand and Ardahl carried Mam, and not till they were well away from the hut did she realize she'd brought nothing else away with her. Just those she loved.

They headed for the midden, backed by a stand of trees that led away up the hill. Ardahl cradled Mam like a child, his sword—

Conall's sword—in one hand. Every time another shadowy form joined them, he turned until he determined it was one of their own. Ready to fight for them.

"What is happening?" asked everyone who joined them. Several old men. A knot of women.

"Hush," Ardahl told them all. "On your life!"

They slipped like so many shadows through the dark. Behind them, a nightmare raged. Fire. Blood. Terror.

The terror accompanied Liadan. Had she ever been more frightened?

When the ground began to slant upward beneath their feet, Ardahl paused. He passed Mam to two of the older men and told them, "Go on up the hill. Hide yourselves there, understand?"

"Aye."

One of them asked, "Wha' happened to the guard?"

"Dead, no doubt."

"Our defenses?"

"Broken."

Och, by all the gods, what had this night wrought?

Liadan stepped forward and seized both Ardahl's forearms, one heavily bandaged. "Ye mean to go back?"

"Aye."

"To fetch your own mam?"

He hesitated. She could not see his eyes in the dark, but by all that was holy, she could feel him.

"To fight."

"But your mam—"

She was back there. Amid the death and the burning.

"My duty is to your family, no' my own," he said shortly.

So, would he let his mam die? Without him.

Leaning closer, she said, "Go find her if ye can."

He lifted Conall's sword and left them. Like a whisper, he melted into the night, there one moment, gone the next.

Liadan wanted to sob. She wanted to wail and weep. She could not. Dacha's warriors could even now be hunting the perimeters of the settlement. Silence might save them.

Yet she might never see Ardahl MacCormac again.

The serpent. Her enemy. Yet she ached for him. Missed his presence. The night felt colder without him.

Such strength, such courage to go back into that horror. She could not. She absolutely could not.

Turning, she looked down the slope, trying to peer through the trees. Fully half the settlement burned. Against the flames, dark figures, unidentifiable, ran.

Drawing a breath that smelled of smoke, she turned. "Ye heard Master Ardahl. Let us go."

ARDAHL RAN. HE forgot his wounds as he went, forgot his battered body. He very nearly forgot those he'd left behind. *By the gods, let them keep safe.* The terrible scene in front of him claimed all his attention.

The great hall was ablaze, making a towering bonfire that spat sparks and dense smoke. The main body of the fighting seemed to be located not far from there, a dark knot of men all clustered together.

He ran in.

As he went, he wondered if the chief and his family had escaped the flames. No one left inside could survive. Other buildings near the hall were well aflame, and his mind tried to put it together.

A raid. The hall set on fire. Other buildings caught from that. There was no wind, but it did not take much to put spark to thatch.

A man appeared before him, taking form like a demon from out of the smoke. Someone he did not know. He raised Conall's sword.

At once, he felt the pull on his body, the product of torn

muscle and flesh.

If I am to die here, he said to Conall in his mind, *await me. I got your family away safe.*

Not his own. *Och, Mam. Och, Mam!*

I will keep her safe for ye also, said a voice in his ear. Conall's voice.

He threw himself into the fray.

The man in front of him went down to Conall's blade. He stepped over the body, over several others—friend or foe, he did not pause to see. Ahead of him, a grim band of men faced off against the invaders. He saw Dornach there, face set and teeth bared.

Dornach and Cathair and—aye, that was Chief Fearghal, with a sword in his hands.

Instinct took Ardahl around to attack their opponents from the side. The heat here, so close to the fiercest of the burning, was intense enough that he expected his hair to take flame. Sweat poured from him.

He would not let himself heed the pull of exhaustion, the protest of wounded flesh. He held and slashed until the enemy stood no more and he found himself looking into the faces of his fellow tribesmen.

"Come!" Fearghal bellowed. "Away out o' this!"

They fled the flames, stumbling over corpses. Ardahl's legs faltered beneath him and his whole body screamed for relief. He followed Dornach's broad back and they searched for other enemies, but all had flown.

At the edge of the burning, they paused. Other clansfolk hovered here, mostly men and some women. A few children shaking with terror.

Ardahl stared into the faces that surrounded him, black with soot, streaked by sweat and tears. He did not see his mam.

"A raid!" Chief Fearghal cried. Only when he spoke did Ardahl realize he was livid with rage. "They came to take back the chief's brother that we held prisoner."

"And got him," Dornach announced. "All who guarded the man, dead."

"Then they fired the hall and battled to provide a distraction, and get him away."

"How many dead?" a breathless Cathair asked, and corrected himself. "How many o' ours dead?"

Fearghal shook his head. "Too soon to tell. We will take count when the sun comes up."

"They will be back," Dornach said in a growl. "Ye know that, d'ye, my chief? They ha' hurt us, and will return wi' a larger force."

The chief grunted. "Let them but try. We will be more than ready for them."

CHAPTER NINETEEN

THE SOUND OF weeping filled the stand of trees where Liadan and her party had come to rest. They were supposed to keep silent, yet Liadan did not suppose a group of displaced women, many with children and guarded only by old men who shared but a few weapons, could hold their tears.

They had bunched up in small groups high on the flank of the hill. Up any higher, they would lose the cover of the trees. Terror gripped them all, and as the sun came up it was joined by grief.

Below them, the settlement lay in ruins, great gouts of smoke trailing up like desperate prayers. Here and there flames still leaped. Liadan could see distant figures rushing about. Trying to put the fires out?

She did not know who remained alive down there. Who lay dead. Indeed, the women around her spoke of nothing else. Whispers of "My man." "My son." The old men spoke instead of the attack, pondering how and why it had come about.

Liadan, having the two most dear to her in all the world at her side, was fortunate. She had only to worry for friends. For cousins.

For Ardahl MacCormac.

She should not worry for him, the serpent. But her last sight of him, Conall's sword in hand, covered in wounds and racing into the fray, had burned into her mind.

He might even now lie dead. What would it mean to her, and hers, if he did?

They would be free of him. Free of his presence in the hut. In their lives.

With no one to look out for them. Stand for them.

He it was who had got them safe away, neglecting his own mother to do so.

She looked at her mam, who had come awake and sat miraculously quiet at Flanna's side. No draughts here. Liadan did not know if the healers had survived. If the druids had. The chief and his family.

"'Tis no' over, this," said one of the old men who stood in a group near Liadan, Flanna, and their mother. "Dacha will have come to take back his brother. If he has not got him, he will come again. If he has taken him, they will return to destroy us."

Destroy?

Liadan tipped up her head and regarded the beautiful morning. The clear blue sky. The sparkling stream below them—the same that meandered around the foot of the hill and eventually formed the boundary of their lands. The sweet light flowing over the hills.

She had never known any place but this, and she loved it dearly. How might it be destroyed?

Yet she'd learned, had she not, that the things one loved most could be lost. Her da. And Conall.

Och, Conall. I wish ye were here.

Flanna put her arm around Mam and drew her closer. It seemed as strange for Mam to be quiet as had her endless lamenting, and she had a hollow look in her eyes. One shared by the other women.

Liadan learned toward the both of them. "Mam, are ye—"

"Someone is coming," one of the lads, no more than thirteen or so, called out.

Everyone stared down the slope. A party of three men had broken from the edge of the settlement and jogged toward them.

"Should we hide?" one of the women asked.

"Nay. They are our own," declared an aged man, and he

started down through the trees to meet the approaching men.

Three members of the guard, they were. Liadan knew one of them—Marc, who had been friendly with Conall. Streaked with dirt, soot, and blood, they climbed the slope and addressed the crowd.

"Ye can come home," said Marc. "The invaders are gone and the fires almost out. The chief wishes to talk wi' us all."

"How many dead?" a woman cried, and Marc shook his head.

"No way to number them yet."

A woman with a tear-streaked face and two small children appealed, "My husband—"

"I do no' know, mistress."

They started off in an untidy chain, stumbling and stopping. The guards flanked them. Liadan, with Mam leaning heavily upon her, found Marc at her side.

She knew she shouldn't ask, but couldn't help it. "Ha' ye seen Ardahl MacCormac?"

"Him?" The man raised his eyebrows at her.

What was that supposed to mean?

"Is he alive, d'ye know?"

"I do not, but he's hard to kill, that one. Though none would argue wi' trying."

Liadan withdrew from him hastily. Aye, Ardahl might be a serpent. Responsible for Conall's death, though he claimed otherwise. Yet such hate, at such a time, seemed to dim the very air.

"Our house," Mam whispered in a quivering voice. "Is it still standing?"

It was, and in much the state they'd left it. They stopped there first, and Flanna wept to see all their things. Grateful as Liadan was, she felt guilty about it. Many had not been so fortunate.

The events of the night seemed to have startled Mam out of her deep grief. She sat silent beside the fire where they put her, hands hanging beside her knees. The last draught had worn off.

Liadan tried to persuade Mam and Flanna to stay at the hut while she went to the clan meeting. "I will hear all the chief has to say."

But they insisted on coming, so the three of them, with Mam supported in the middle, went off.

The clan—what was left of it—gathered near the well at the center of the settlement, the hall being no more than a pillar of dark smoke. The spring was said to be a holy one and had existed here long before the first of them had built a round house. A good place for the distraught clan members to ground themselves.

They gathered in silence, save for the crying bairns. Some folk still filtered down from the hills to which they'd fled. The rest, in small family groups or alone, stood with the shock showing in their eyes.

Scanning the crowd, Liadan saw no glimpse of Ardahl. But his mam stood there on the far side, her shawl up over her hair as if she hid beneath it.

She stood alone.

Liadan's heart began to pound in big, heavy beats. Had Ardahl indeed lost his life? Had he marched back into the fray only to die there, fighting while wounded?

For an instant, the bright morning broke up into dots all around her, and she swayed on her feet. Then a figure stepped up at Maeve's side.

A tall figure, spare of build, wide of shoulder with a mop of wild auburn hair and blood showing at arm and chest.

Again she swayed on her feet. She tried to catch Ardahl's eye and failed.

Chief Fearghal began to speak. The chief himself showed wounds, proving he had been in the thick of the fighting. A bright bloom of red on his arm. Split knuckles on one hand. Face blackened with soot.

He spoke loudly and clearly, in measured tones. Told them the attack had come from their enemies to the west, that Chief Dacha, armed with surprise, had taken back his brother after firing the great hall.

There had been deaths on both sides. "Many of our valiant gave their lives to defend us," as he put it. "We will honor each one of them. And I vow to ye—Dacha will feel the sting of our swords in revenge."

He went on to say the warriors' hall, which had escaped the flames, would be used to house those whose huts had burned, until they could be rebuilt. And he urged those who still had houses to open them to friends and relations.

"What one o' us has," he said gravely, putting an arm around his wife, "belongs to us all."

Liadan's gaze moved again to Maeve, who looked so isolated even though her son stood beside her. Had she lost her hut? If so, should Liadan offer to house her?

Who else would?

"Mam," she began. The decision should by rights belong to her mother. But Mam's eyes still looked vacant, empty of understanding.

The chief's speech done, Liadan crossed to the group on the other side. Ardahl watched her come, the expression in his hazel eyes guarded and intent.

Exchanging a glance with him, she felt…wary. Awkward. So glad to see him still alive, she had no words for it.

"Mistress MacCormac." She reached out and took Maeve's hands. "Your house—did it survive the fire?"

The woman shook her head, her eyes on the ground. "Nay. I was able to save some things, but—"

Liadan squeezed her fingers. "Then ye must come and stay wi' us. Just until—until things can be made right."

Maeve's gaze came up and met hers. "Your mother will no' want me there."

"Your son is already with us. I feel it is only right."

Maeve shook her head. "I have lost my son."

"He stands here beside ye."

"He is Beith MacAert's son now."

Liadan shot a look at Ardahl. His face appeared drawn with weariness or pain, smudged with dirt and ash.

"Persuade her," she bade him. "Where else will she go?"

He said nothing. Liadan turned and walked away back to her charges, not quite able to dismiss the gladness lodged in her heart. He lived. He would be returning to the hut.

She should not rejoice in that, yet she did.

※

CHAPTER TWENTY

A MAN, AS Ardahl well knew, could sometimes become so weary he grew numb and stupid with it. If he kept pushing through, he came right out the other side. He had been here in the past. After a hard battle, he and Conall had joked about it, turned silly with it. Laughed.

He could not imagine laughing now. His body screamed at him, each movement a protest. Every part of him demanded relief. He had driven his muscles and his nerves beyond endurance. He saw no rest in sight.

The settlement lay in shambles, and Chief Fearghal had done little more than promise them further battles. As if that was what his people needed now. They needed comfort and reassurance, the impossible hope that all would come right.

But for folk such as theirs, the promise of vengeance could be a comfort. Vengeance for the dead. Fearghal knew that. On some level, so did Ardahl.

The thought of further battles provided a blow to his heart. They did not yet know who had survived this one. He'd seen some of his fellow warriors—including Cathair—but a number were so far missing.

Did they lie dead like Conall?

The dead would need burying. The settlement guarding. Homes rebuilt.

He felt tired enough to die.

He turned to his mother. "Will ye go to stay wi' Mistress

MacAert?"

"Not there. She hates me, with good reason."

"Without reason."

"Even so."

"Then where will ye go?" He could not spare the worry for her, with so much else gone wrong.

Mam said nothing.

"Will any o' your friends take ye in?"

"They have turned against me."

Ardahl cursed all of them under his breath.

Dornach appeared. The war chief looked a mess, covered in soot and filthy wounds. But he had survived, which seemed a minor miracle.

He eyed Ardahl gravely. "Ye need your wounds tended. Ye should no' be on your feet."

"I am well enough."

"Liar! Mistress, see your son is tended."

Desperate, Ardahl said, "I must return to my post at Mistress MacAert's hut. Master Dornach, my mother refuses to go there with me."

The big man turned to the woman. "Mistress, my good wife and I would be pleased to house ye, for the time."

"Will ye?" Relief poured through Ardahl.

"To be sure. Our hut did no' burn, and save for the smoke, we are whole. We have the room. My wife is taking others in."

"I would be most grateful," Ardahl said.

"And ye"—Dornach eyed Ardahl again—"get back to Mistress MacAert, if ye will but first get ye to the healers and have them tend ye."

Ah, but if he went straight to Mistress MacAert's, might he not get care there? Mistress Liadan's hands upon him as before. The thought sent him dizzy in the head.

"I will be available for guard duty or patrol—"

Dornach touched his arm. "Ye will no', for the time. My orders. Mistress MacCormac, if ye will come along o' me..."

Kindness, Ardahl thought as Dornach led Mam away. Who would have thought it of the gruff war chief?

He met a number of blank stares as he walked back through the settlement. Women wept. Children were silent. Warriors stood in hard knots, talking fiercely.

Of revenge, no doubt.

Someone ran past him, crying out to all who would listen, "Aodh is dead! The high priest is slain!"

Was it so? A staggering loss.

He approached Conall's hut and stood for a moment, unwilling to enter. The door, pinned open to admit the air, emitted not a sound.

Were the women in?

Aye, so he discovered when he ducked his head and entered. He left his weapons beside the door and took a moment to absorb the scene.

Mistress MacAert, well awake, sat beside the hearth place, the expression on her face as blank as if she still slept. Her eyes found him and he expected some reaction, an outcry. But she made none.

Flanna, who sat beside her, had been weeping. Liadan bustled around, trying to keep her hands and thoughts busy, he did not doubt.

She whirled and looked at him. "Och, Ardahl. Ye should no' be on your feet."

"That is what Dornach said." Yet he was on his feet, if barely.

"Sit ye down."

When he stood where he was, unwilling to intrude, she came to him, clutched his arm, and pushed him down with ridiculous ease.

"I just heard Aodh is dead."

All three of them looked at him. Flanna and Liadan with horror, Mistress MacAert still blankly.

"Nay," Liadan breathed.

"Would not the gods protect him?" Flanna wondered. "Such

a holy man."

Ardahl pressed his lips together so he would not say what burned behind them. That he'd heard more prayers for protection on the brink of a battle than upon any holy day, and they seldom meant aught. That the gods rarely stirred to protect those who deserved it.

Like his da. And Conall.

"Whisht now," Liadan said. "'Tis not our place to question the acts o' the gods." She looked at Ardahl. "How did he die?"

"I do not know—I merely heard his death cried out."

"Aye, well, 'tis a dire loss, but we will ha' to go on without him. Just like all the rest who lost their lives this day."

"How many?" Flanna asked with tears in her eyes. "How many have died?"

"Impossible to say before the bodies are gathered," Ardahl told her.

"But," she appealed to him, "it is over, is it not? We will no' be attacked again."

Should he lie to these three women who watched him so fearfully? What good would any lie do?

"Dacha has taken back his brother whom we held prisoner. He may be satisfied wi' that. Or he may decide to strike again while he believes we are weak." He hesitated. "Finish wi' it."

"Finish us, ye mean? Och." Liadan comprehended the threat if her sister did not, if her mother stared uncomprehendingly. They balanced on a knife's edge of danger.

She shook her head and said no more, then hurried to pull together a meal, which they shared without further discussion.

Afterward, Flanna sat with her head on her mother's shoulder. Quietly, Liadan came to Ardahl and said, "D'ye think they will attack tonight? While—while all remains in confusion?"

He looked at her from beneath his lashes. He didn't like to admit that was what *he* would do, were he Dacha. Strike while the iron was hot. Deliver the killing blow. Then walk in and take the territory he'd been chasing so long. Kill whomever he chose.

Chase the others off or make slaves of them.

"Do no' worry," he told Liadan. "I will be here. In Conall's place. I shall sleep beside the door wi' his sword. None shall touch nor harm ye."

Her gaze held his. "Even should it cost your life?"

"Even so."

"Come, then. Let me tend your wounds, that ye will be fit for the task."

It proved a lengthy process, and not without hurt, though she made her hands as gentle as she could. First she brought a basin and washed him down, which felt...almost unimaginably pleasurable. But nay, *pleasurable* was not the proper word. For despite his bone-deep weariness, her act of wiping away the soot and the blood, stroking the cloth over his arms and down his chest, aroused him.

He turned his face away. Conall's sister. His sister, now, by the order of the druids. He could not possibly desire her.

But she was a grown woman, and a beautiful one.

She despised him. Thought the very worst of him.

Yet that did not tell in her touch. Indeed, it must be his maddened imagination that made it seem she touched him with something other than hate.

By the time she finished, both her mother and sister slept there beside the fire. Liadan went and gently roused them, sent them off to their beds. When she came back, she brought Ardahl a blanket.

He looked up at her, questioning the action.

"At least ye will no' be cold," she explained.

Another kindness. He barely dared breathe for his surprise. Even more so when she sat down beside him, leaning her back against the outer wall next to his.

"Mistress, ye will be better off in your bed."

"I cannot possibly sleep, waiting for another attack."

So she meant to sit here with him? Keep him company as a friend might?

"It is quiet out there."

It was, save for a few calls between the guards at a distance. Dornach would have a heavy presence around the settlement this night. One of which he should be a part.

But nay. His place was here. Defending Liadan.

"I am worried for my mam," she whispered.

"She no longer weeps."

"Nay. But such a sudden change—"

"Perhaps the fright shook her."

"I do no' doubt that. But there is an emptiness. One I do no' like."

Not only did she keep him company, she confided in him. What had altered between them?

"Try no' to worry for it now," he bade her. "Let us merely get through the night."

"Aye." She stirred and moved just a little closer. For warmth, he told himself. "Aye."

They fell silent, listening hard to the night.

CHAPTER TWENTY-ONE

L IADAN DOZED, AND when she dozed, she dreamed. Mere flickers of scenes, those dreams were. Like glimpses from the past. Memories both distant and closer at hand.

The group of them up on the hillside, watching the settlement burn. The chief speaking to his people, trying so hard to be strong and reassuring. Conall, speaking to her on a warm day, the sun lighting his hair to gold.

She could not hear what he had to say, because every time a sound reached her from outside, she came awake again, all her senses alert, fear pounding up through her with every heartbeat.

If another attack came, could she get her mam and sister away in time? It all depended on her. On her, and the man beside her.

He did not sleep—at least, she did not think he did. Whenever she roused in fear, his voice was there to soothe her.

"All right. That is but the guard calling. It is only a stag in the hills. A dog barking."

He held Conall's sword in his right hand. She could see the gleam of light that rode its keen edge, reflected from the dying fire.

The knowledge that he was there let her go back to sleep, time after time.

At last she came awake to find that she lay against his shoulder. That she clutched his left hand in her own.

His hand—the same that had slain Conall? That had performed an act of unendurable evil and harm? But, broad palmed and heavily calloused, it felt warm in the night, somehow battling against the cold that seized her and penetrated to the bone.

She lay there, eyes open to the dark hut, unwilling to surrender that warmth, that narrow grasp upon comfort. He breathed quietly and evenly. Did he sleep at last? But nay. As soon as she stirred, he whispered, "Hush, now. All is still well."

His hand squeezed hers more tightly. Their fingers had become interwoven, palm to palm, skin to skin. She should free herself and move away from him.

She did not want to.

"How long till dawn?"

"Not long. The night is near done."

"Sometimes the enemy strikes just at dawn when all lies most vulnerable." Conall had told her that.

"'Tis so. No matter, I am here."

And could he defend them? One man covered in wounds. Spent and exhausted.

She believed it. There in the dark of the night, she believed he would.

"I am almost afraid for the sun to come up," she confessed. "To see how many lie dead. They will all be gathered together by now."

"They will."

"We will have so many burials. Without Aodh—"

"He will be first among them, I do not doubt."

"Aye."

He stirred and very gently released her hand. Before she could protest, he tucked his arm around her and drew her more securely against him. "Rest while ye can. Sleep if ye be able."

With her face tucked into the crook of his neck, his hair like a cloud against her cheek, she absorbed the comfort that flowed from him. This serpent. And it felt so right, she never wanted to move away.

She should, aye, do as he suggested and rest while she could.

How to do so, when her pulse pounded in her ears? When she could catch his scent, a tantalizing fragrance that seemed to curl through her and lodge down low in her belly?

She wondered how it would feel to kiss him. How he'd taste. And then she flagellated herself for the thought.

Holding his hand and even absorbing his warmth through the night was one thing. She absolutely could not have feelings for the man who'd killed Conall.

RAIN MOVED IN soon after sunrise, which put out the rest of the fires and made a mess of everything else. Mud and ash and sodden, half-burned belongings lay everywhere. The trees dripped moisture and the ground became a morass.

Soon after breakfast, Ardahl reported to Dornach for orders. He had the reward of seeing his mam there. In fact, she opened the door to him and they had a moment to embrace before he went in.

"So many hurts!" she noted, performing a swift inspection. "Are ye fit to be up on your feet?"

Ardahl was not at all certain. He hurt as if he'd been thrashed from head to foot, and several of his wounds stung enough to make him grit his teeth.

But he answered the worry in her eyes. "I am well enough. And ye? Are ye treated kindly here?"

"Aye, so, and I am able to help with the children. They do no' judge me, and I feel—well, useful."

He would owe Dornach for this, Ardahl thought. An unending debt of gratitude.

He found the man beside his fire, taking breakfast. The war chief lumbered to his feet, moving very much as if he too hurt.

"Join us, Ardahl, and break your fast."

"Nay, thank ye. I have eaten." A hasty meal provided by

Liadan.

Liadan. The very thought of her made it hard to breathe. She'd slept beside him last night, what little she had slept. Soft and vulnerable. Trusting him to protect her, even though she did not truly trust him.

A sacred debt, she had become. Was that what the druids had intended? That he would fulfill Conall's duty at the prodding not of duty, but love?

Nay, but it had been meant as a punishment. Had it not? He could never ask Aodh now.

He lifted his head and met Dornach's gaze. "I am here reporting for duty. Fit for standing guard or a patrol, whatever ye ask o' me."

Dornach glanced at his wife, pale and shattered, and at Ardahl's mam, who had followed him in and stood listening.

"There is much to be done," he admitted. "And all hands will be needed."

"Aye, Master Dornach. How many dead?"

"More than a score. No' all o' them warriors."

His wife began to weep.

"There are three bairns," Dornach said, "and some women."

"I would volunteer for the burials."

Swiftly, Dornach ran his gaze over Ardahl. "I am no' certain ye are yet fit."

"I say that I am."

"I hear wha' ye say, lad. And while I admire ye for offering, I must differ." He clasped Ardahl by the shoulder. "Come ye with me."

Together they went outside into the morning. Here in the watery light, the weariness and pain showed clearly in Dornach's face.

"Listen to me, Ardahl. I do no' want the women to hear this, but I wish ye to know the truth. Dacha will be back. Sooner rather than later, if I do not mistake it. The season has just begun, and he has shown his intentions."

"Aye, so."

"Listen." Dornach's hand tightened on Ardahl's shoulder. "We shall have to meet him here, or on the border. When that happens, I will need every warrior. No' every gravedigger, understand? No' every guard."

"I am no' certain I—"

Dornach gazed into Ardahl's eyes. "I saw how ye fought in the battle at the border. Saw what ye did there. I also saw the wounds ye took. Despite what happened wi' Conall, I believe ye belong at the head o' the men."

Shock ripped through Ardahl. "But—Cathair. He is already your assistant and wants to stand at the head o' the men."

"I know he does. And he is a fine warrior, is Cathair. Valuable to me. I believe"—Dornach's gaze did not waver—"he would do anything to gain first place among Fearghal's men."

Ardahl's eyes narrowed. What was Dornach saying, exactly? "Ye think—"

"Whisht, lad. Such suspicions are no' to be spoken aloud. Keep your eyes peeled, and so will I. The long and the short o' it is, I need ye healed and at your best when the next battle comes. No' still suffering wounds torn open while buryin' the dead."

"I see," said Ardahl, who didn't, not entirely.

"Go home. Rest. Think on wha' I have said. And *not* said."

"Aye."

"Be ready with your sword when I call ye."

"Aye, master." Home. Had Conall's hut become that? Not truly. Not yet.

Liadan, though, was there. His heart insisted that counted for something.

He raised his eyes and studied the expression in Dornach's. "I will be ready to fight, Master Dornach, whenever ye summon me."

"See that ye are."

He walked back to Conall's hut slowly through the rain, not certain what he would find there. The folk he passed still stared at him, but a large measure of their animosity had flown, consumed by a wider misery.

Would he find acceptance in time, for this thing he had not done? Forgiveness? Dornach, at least, believed in him. That meant much.

But this thing Dornach expected him to do, take first place among the warriors and without Conall at his side, seemed equally impossible.

What had he implied about Cathair? That what Ardahl had considered a friendly rivalry had turned into something else?

Something deadly.

He'd never liked Cathair, braggart and bully that he was. And aye, they had competed against one another for some time. But Cathair would never go so far as to harm Conall just to ruin Ardahl.

And if he had—how? It had been Conall who'd turned on Ardahl in anger, there in the sunny field. Cathair who'd been close enough to bear witness.

A cold chill chased its way down Ardahl's spine, one not caused by the rain.

✦

CHAPTER TWENTY-TWO

LIFE, AS LIADAN knew it, had flown. She thought it had changed irreparably with Conall's death, as it had. With Ardahl's presence among them and Mam's grief. Hard enough to bear, with all the feelings tumbling through her, and her need to make things right.

Now the entire settlement had been turned on its head, everything altered again. What had been personal grief became widespread and consuming. The hurt and terror touched everyone.

And she learned something about herself. She liked order and a quiet life. She liked knowing what was going to happen, and when. She could handle difficulties if she saw them coming.

This kind of unexpected, disastrous change felt harder. It threw her off her stride.

And then there was Ardahl.

Och, what to do about him?

The long night they had spent together and its accompanying terror had also brought a change. She might wish to deny that, but in all honesty could not. She had clung to him for comfort, and he had provided it.

She found it harder and harder to believe him a serpent.

And her heart—her treacherous heart began to react on its own. Whenever she saw him, when he came back from the war chief's hut or some warriors' meeting, it leaped without her permission. Her eyes flew to him as if she needed to touch gazes

124

with him for reassurance.

If only he were not such a handsome man. She liked every-thing about him, from the mane of red-brown hair to the way he moved. Living close to him as she now did, the desire—for she could not in honesty name it as aught else—rendered her helpless.

His presence lifted her. Intoxicated her. Threw her into des-pair.

Following the attack that Chief Fearghal insisted on calling a raid, there was a string of burials and so much grief it was hard to bear. The chief, who had himself lost his home, called frequent meetings, during which he spoke from the heart about recovery and revenge.

A good chief, was Fearghal. But rebuilding would be difficult and recovery long. Especially with the chief druid, Aodh, gone. Tamald, second in rank, had taken over for him, but as Liadan heard whispered when she went to the spring or elsewhere among the women, if such a holy man could be taken from them, had the gods themselves turned on the tribe?

Waiting for another raid, day by day, kept everyone on edge. Women wept for very little reason, and men lost their tempers without warning.

At least Mam was better, if Liadan could call it better. She had ceased with her endless grieving since the night of the raid and the flight up the hillside. Now she stayed quiet all the time. She sat in Conall's sleeping place or beside the fire with idle hands and empty eyes, and had to be persuaded to eat. It was difficult to get so much as a word out of her.

Gone was the mam who had chattered endlessly over her work, showered affection on her son and two daughters, laughed easily.

It felt as if Liadan had lost someone else she loved, just a shell left behind.

She set herself to care for that shell and prayed Mam would come back to herself. She worked hard to do all she could around the hut and out in the settlement, volunteering to do laundry for others or help drag away the ruined rubble from the huts. She waited, like everyone else, for attack. At night she longed to sit once more holding Ardahl's hand.

She never did, and kept well clear of him.

Ardahl healed. Since she'd watched Conall recover from similar injuries more than once, she knew what to look for. She treated Ardahl's wounds when they looked dirty and he did not wish to trouble the healers.

It frightened her how much she enjoyed touching him during those moments, smoothing her fingers over freckled skin. Sitting near enough to catch his scent. To glance up and encounter the expression in his eyes.

What did that expression mean? So guarded was it, she never could quite tell.

He could not possibly desire her. He had given no real sign, and anyway, he was as good as her brother, and that made it forbidden. Did it not?

When he returned to training, she made excuses to pass by the field just so she could stand and watch him at work. Shameful, aye, but she owned it. She was never the only young woman who so indulged herself for a glimpse of some particular man. She encountered friends there.

She encountered Brasha.

A tall and very beautiful lass, Brasha was. When they encountered each other there beside the wall, Liadan expected Brasha to say something about Conall. She had been seeing him for the last half year of his life—on and off at first, and then so frequently that Liadan had begun to wonder if they would marry. She remembered being a little uneasy about it, for though Brasha was popular, Liadan had never taken to her. The lass had an edge. She talked about people, even her friends, behind their backs and sometimes had a sly look in her eyes. She had never once come by the hut to commiserate with them after Conall's death. She'd shown little enough grief, apart from that terrible scene when she'd thrown herself on Conall's body at his graveside, despite how long the two had been seeing each other.

And she said nothing of it now. Instead, with her two particular friends, she hung about the training field, gossiping and giggling. As if naught was wrong in her world.

It was not difficult to determine whom she watched, either. That was why Liadan had to be so careful with her own interest—people saw and talked of where a woman's eyes turned. What a piece of crack it would be to report that Liadan MacAert lusted after her brother's killer.

Even if she did.

She could see that Brasha watched one especially tall, fairhaired figure move about the field. Cathair. And although the warrior in question rarely spared any attention for the women at the wall of the field, acting as if they were beneath him, he did flick a glance once or twice toward Brasha.

It made Liadan uneasy enough that she brought it up with Ardahl the next time she had an opportunity.

She had given Flanna permission to go and visit with Lasair, and Mam sat quiet on Conall's bed when Ardahl arrived home, which as good as left the two of them alone.

When Ardahl ducked into the hut and laid his weapons beside the door, Liadan said, "Come sit wi' me. I have the supper ready."

He shot her a look and as quickly glanced away. "Aye, mistress. I am filthy. Let me go wash first."

She didn't mind him filthy, she decided, with his hair half come loose from the plait he wore for practice and a gleam on his skin. She liked him clean also, when he came back in with his hair wet and smelling of the soap she made. When he sat down by the fire, she experienced a flash of rare satisfaction. She liked him here with her, whatever his condition.

"How goes the practice?" she began.

"Better. I am nearly recovered, so I believe."

She'd been able to see that when she watched him, though she did not say so. Had he noticed her there by the wall? Had he thought her there only to speak with her friends?

He shook his head. "I cannot manage to convince Master Dornach. He refuses to let me expend myself. 'Tis almost as if he is saving me."

For the next battle, no doubt. The next raid. "D'ye believe Dacha will strike again?"

"Unless Fearghal decides to strike first, it seems inevitable."

"Waiting is an agony."

"'Tis hard, indeed."

He ate in silence a few moments while she marshaled her thoughts.

"Tell me, Master Ardahl, what d'ye think o' Brasha Mac-Gowd?"

Surprised, he lifted his gaze back to her. He took his time answering. "She and Conall were seeing each other, there before the end."

"Aye, so."

"I had no say in whom your brother saw."

"To be sure. But what did ye think o' the association?"

He must wonder why she asked, for he directed another long look at her. "I did no' like it much. But in that instance, Conall did no' welcome my opinions. He got swept up in her. They—" Abruptly he silenced.

"Master Ardahl, ye need not fear to speak plainly wi' me."

"You are his sister."

"And no longer a child. I know fine what happens between a man and a woman—even if that man be my brother."

He shifted his shoulders in a twitch of discomfort and glanced at Conall's sleeping place, where Mam sat.

"She is no' paying attention." Liadan leaned closer to him. "They were—"

He made a face. "She was tumbling him. Regular." The hazel eyes met hers, steady. "Ye know what that means?"

"Of course I know what it means." Her cheeks heated. "She was taking him to her bed."

"Naught so formal as that. They met wherever they could. In corners. In the pony sheds. At her house, if no one was to home."

"The pony sheds!"

Another steady gaze. "He got right caught up in it."

"As any young man might."

"He told me he wanted to marry her. I told him to take his time and be sure about it."

"Good advice."

"There is somewhat I cannot like about her. But ye canna tell that to a man, even your best friend, about the woman wi' whom he is enamored."

"I suppose not."

"He kept the whole thing close to his chest, but all the warriors knew. When I expressed doubts about her, he did no' like it. Grew annoyed wi' me. Even asked if I were jealous." He snorted. "As if I would be jealous o' that—" He caught himself abruptly.

"I see." Did Liadan begin to?

"We rarely argued. Ye know that. But," Ardahl paused and a new look came to his eyes, "that was when he began growing edgy wi' me. Turned right prickly about it."

"Could—could that be what he was so angry about that last day, when—"

Ardahl shook his head. "I do not know what he was so angry about that day. I have racked my brains over it. That was not mere anger, but rage." Again, he studied her. "Ye believe me?"

"I find that I do."

He puffed out a breath.

"Not," she added, "that it matters what I believe."

"It matters. To be sure, it does."

"Brasha—she does not seem as grieved at Conall's death as she was at first, or as a young woman hoping for marriage should."

"One who'd taken him so often on her thighs."

"She laughs with her friends and stands to gossip by the wall of the training field."

"So I ha' noticed."

"It does not seem right."

Their gazes met again.

"Have ye noticed whom it is she watches during her time there?" she asked.

"I have."

Liadan leaned still closer. "Is there something in it?"

Again, Ardahl took several moments before answering. "I cannot imagine how. Unless…"

"What?" Liadan settled close beside him and drew up her knees. Now they sat close to one another indeed, making the conversation intimate.

"It cannot be," he murmured. "No one would—"

"What?" Liadan repeated.

He gazed once more into her eyes. A stare of connection, this was.

At last he whispered, "Master Dornach seems to feel Cathair resents me. That we are—were—in competition for the place of first among the warriors."

"Ah." First among the warriors denoted much honor, including one's place in the great hall during feasts—the great hall that no longer existed.

"Me, I have never competed wi' anyone. It was enough for me to fight my best and wi' Conall at my side." Ardahl swallowed hard. "But aye, this last year I was declared foremost a few times above Cathair."

Puzzled, Liadan waited for him to say more.

"What if…" he whispered. "What if Cathair used Brasha to turn Conall against me?"

"How so?"

"I am no' sure. 'Tis a feeling more than aught else. The way Cathair looks at me. The way Brasha looks at him."

"And he was the one, was he not, who spoke out to say you killed Conall?"

"Aye."

They were both silent for a few moments.

"Ye think," Liadan asked then, "they were together in it, trying to stir trouble between ye and Conall?"

"Mayhap."

"But no woman, not even Brasha—whom, I must admit, I do no' much respect—would lie wi' a man just to turn his loyalty." A woman lay with a man because she loved him. Because she desired him beyond reason. Because she wanted a life with him.

"I cannot claim to know what lies in the mind or the heart o' a woman."

"If this be true—" Liadan widened her eyes at him. "The treachery o' it! The sheer evil. If those two have schemed in such a way to hurt ye—to hurt us—they must be exposed. Cathair is no' worthy of the honors he collects. And ye... Ye do no' deserve the disgrace ye ha' received."

Now his gaze burned on hers. "Aye, yet I canna figure how—even if she seduced Conall for the purpose—she could have turned him so against me. Caused such anger as I saw in his eyes that day."

Liadan laid her hand on his arm. "Perhaps I can help to discover that part o' it. I am able to go among the women as ye are not. I can get close to Brasha. Ask and listen."

"Ye would do that?"

"I would."

"I would be that grateful, mistress." For the briefest moment only, he laid his hand over hers.

"Together," she told him, "we may yet arrive at the truth."

CHAPTER TWENTY-THREE

I T MADE A difference, feeling that Conall's sister believed in him. That she accepted he'd meant no harm to her brother. That she did not, perhaps, hate him.

She, among all women.

He went out to practice or to other work about the settlement with a lighter heart. It did not sting so much when others slighted him or he heard the grumbles and the whispers. Some among the warriors did not believe he belonged in their ranks, let alone at the foremost of them. When they gathered and especially when they drank, they became vocal about it.

Now, he began to notice most of them were close cronies of Cathair's.

Cathair himself did not say much to Ardahl, but his hard glances relayed all that needed to be said. That, and the way he came at Ardahl when they faced one another in practice, with no regard for past injuries and no mercy.

Dornach did his best at such times to keep them separated and to keep them focused on the true enemy.

Dacha. Though they waited day by day for it, and night by night, he had not attacked again. Ardahl almost wished he would. Waiting for the blow to fall was agony.

But each day made him stronger. And he did have one or two who would speak to him—Muirin, who remained friendly, and Cullan, who had been assigned the permanent place as his charioteer.

Conall's place.

He noticed now when Liadan came by the training field to stand among the other women. Noticed for a number of reasons. The way the sun caught her hair. The way she moved, and her smile. He saw her approach Brasha several times and speak to her in a quiet fashion, and ached to know what was said.

Always, he looked away quickly. Many an association had been made here at the training field. Indeed, Brasha had begun paying attention to Conall here, and their relationship had followed.

Whatever that relationship may have been.

Now in her coy fashion, Brasha followed no one but Cathair, and he strutted all the more when her eyes rested upon him.

One day after practice, Dornach came to Ardahl and placed a hand on his shoulder. In a low voice he said, "I want ye to know, we will be going into battle soon."

Ardahl's gaze flew to him. "Eh?"

"Aye. Do no' spread that around, lad. The chief has been meeting wi' mysel' and his other advisors, including the druids. No one wants to sit and wait for another attack."

"Nay."

"Dacha haunts the border we share wi' Brihan. Fearghal would like to chase him awa' out o' there while the season affords, and then try for a binding treaty wi' Brihan, which would give us time to rebuild."

Why was Dornach telling Ardahl all this? Privileged information.

"Ye will no' speak o' that to anyone, aye?"

"Aye, master."

"I want to know if ye will be ready to fight when we roll out."

"Aye, so, master. For certain."

Dornach's canny gaze moved over him. "Those hurts are not quite healed."

"Well enough. I am nearly in top form."

"I can see that, aye, but would no' wish to undo the good ye have gained." Emotions flickered in Dornach's eyes. "I wanted ye to know, I would like to send ye out at the head o' the men, Ardahl. Ye have earned it, in my estimation. But 'twill have to be Cathair this time."

"I understand."

"There is still much talk against ye."

"I have heard it."

Dornach's lips twisted. "Much o' it coming from Cathair himself. No one will yet countenance yourself at the head o' the men."

"It does no' matter, Master Dornach."

"I believe it does. There is such a thing as justice."

"No' for me."

Dornach grunted. "Are ye content wi' Cullan for a partner?"

Content was not the proper word. Ardahl ached for Conall back at his side.

Dornach added, "He is eager for the place."

"Is he?" And should Ardahl expect treachery there also? Would he have to keep a watch, with Cullan beside him, for a knife in the ribs?

Or in the heart.

"Aye, so. Ye will have a care, lad. Keep clear o' Cathair as much as ye can."

Ardahl thought about Dornach's words as he walked home, relived for the hundredth time that last scene between him and Conall, when his best friend would have taken his life.

He entered the hut to find all in confusion. Flanna pestered her sister, since she would no longer approach her mother with her wants. Mistress MacAert sat beside the hearth, silent as always, and Liadan bustled about trying to prepare a meal.

He wanted to duck out again. In fact, he did, leaving his weapons and going around the side of the hut to wash.

Liadan found him there not long after. He had his hair wet and his head in the basin when she joined him, and when he straightened, he caught a look in her eyes.

A look no man could mistake, however oblivious.

Well, well! He found himself attracted to her also, however inappropriate that might be. But the way she seemed to notice him while pretending not to only proved Conall's sister was no longer a child.

"Mistress, what is it?"

Her gaze flicked over his shoulders, his damp, bare chest, and away.

"Flanna has begged a night with Lasair and Mam—well, ye ken fine how Mam is. Come have your supper. I have somewhat to tell ye."

"Very well, so. Just let me finish here."

She did not walk away as she should, but stood with her hands wrapped in her smock, watching as he dried off. Not till then did she turn, and he followed her inside.

Flanna was on her way out, and he pressed against the wall to allow her room. The lass had now come mostly to ignore him like part of the furnishings.

When he turned to the fire, though, he found Mistress MacAert gazing vacantly at him. Something in that stare sent a chill down his spine, and he as swiftly turned away again.

Even if Liadan began to accept him, he feared her mother did not. Would never.

He would have taken his customary place by the door, but Liadan waved him forward. The three of them sat, Liadan between Ardahl and her mother, and she spoke mostly to her mam, urging her to eat though the woman did no more than pick at her portion with skeletal fingers.

She dwindled away to naught, did Conall's mam, and that caused a pain in Ardahl's heart.

After they finished the meal, Liadan helped her mam away to her sleeping place before returning, bustling around briefly and settling on the rug beside Ardahl.

Leaning close, she asked, "What news from the training field this day? Any signs of possible attack?"

He could not tell her that with which Dornach had entrusted him, so he shook his head.

She refilled his cup with heather ale.

"I ha' some word for ye. I ha' been feeling my way around the settlement, talking—well, let me admit, *gossiping* as the others tend to do, finding out about Brasha."

He searched her face. A reluctant smile tugged at his lips. "And, Liadan, d'ye no' usually, like the others, gossip?"

She shook her head and wrinkled her nose. "Nay. I despise such chatter. I am making an exception for the sake o' truth."

A rare woman, indeed.

"One can discover much through gossip. And the folk of this tribe do love to speak o' one another. Above all things, I think. Of course, one must then decide what, of all that's heard, is true."

"What ha' ye determined?"

"Much. Some of it"—she hesitated—"painful. Some o' it, to be honest, hurts my heart. I have a good friend, Soni, whose sister is close wi' Brasha. She told me Brasha was seeing Cathair before ever she took up wi' Conall last year."

That, in itself, was not surprising. The young folk of the tribe, living in essence within a closed society, tended to make and form relationships many times before settling and handfasting. And Brasha, being quite beautiful even if she did have a waspish tongue, was much sought after.

Conall had scarce believed his luck when she turned her attention to him. Even though Conall, like all his family, had been well favored.

Liadan leaned still closer. Her blue eyes, so like Conall's, sought Ardahl's. "She has apparently returned to seeing Cathair now."

Ardahl remembered Brasha running forward to touch Cathair's hand when they'd headed out to the battle on the border. "Aye, so." It made him uncomfortable then; it did still.

"The true heart o' the gossip, though, is that Brasha was still seeing Cathair *while* she was wi' my brother."

"Are ye certain o' that?"

"As certain as I can be wi' gossip. No one wanted to talk about it. 'Tis one of those ugly things that are shoved into the shadows. Conall was well liked. And no one wishes to get on the wrong side o' Brasha."

Slow anger stirred in Ardahl's heart, ramping up the doubt and rage already there. Conall had been happy with Brasha. At least, he had until shortly before his death, when something had changed.

"She was cuckolding him? All the while?"

Liadan shook her head. "Or cheating on Cathair. 'Tis difficult to know how to view it."

Ardahl said nothing, letting his anger burn.

"Whatever the case," Liadan whispered, "you will admit there is something wrong in it. Much wrong."

"Aye."

"Add to that the fact that I have been haunting the places Brasha likes to linger, at the spring and the training field, in order to insinuate myself and catch a word wi' her. Here and there, ye see, so she will no' get suspicious. There is a sharp mind behind those sly eyes of hers."

And a clever one, so it seemed, in the head of Mistress Liadan.

"I began by being all sympathetic toward her, saying how much she must miss Conall and be grieving for him. How much she must ha' loved him. How much we all loved him. I looked for"—Liadan hesitated and drew a breath—"I looked for a mite of genuine feeling when she spoke of him." Now anger showed in her eyes. "I found none. Naught but indifference. As if she had never cared for Conall at all."

Ardahl absorbed that as best he could. "Yet," he said unsteadily, "she lay wi' him. More than once." Conall had been ecstatic about it.

I will ask her to handfast wi' me, Ardahl, just as soon as I can.

His eyes met Liadan's again. "It meant much to him."

"Aye. We were taught"—she fumbled a little—"one does no'

lie down wi' a partner wi'out first giving one's heart."

Suddenly Ardahl felt sick. Conall had given his heart to Brasha. And all the while—

"What d'ye think she was about?" he demanded of Liadan. "I ha' a mind to ask her."

"As do I. Indeed, I had to bite my tongue to keep from challenging her on it. Yet folk handle grief in different ways, and all I have with which to accuse her is rumor."

Ardahl snarled. "Rumor I well believe."

"As do I." Just like she had before, Liadan laid her fingers on Ardahl's forearm, as if to calm him. "I will keep talking and gossiping and digging. 'Tis far easier for me to do than ye. We will find the truth."

We. Ardahl took a rare comfort from the word. He had felt so alone since losing Conall and being sentenced to take his place.

He covered Liadan's hand, still resting on his forearm, with his own. "I canna help thinking—"

"What?"

"Whether all this business wi' Brasha had any bearing on what happened there at the training field, that last day. Conall's anger wi' me."

Acknowledgment filled her eyes. "As do I. But would Conall no' rather have been angry wi' Brasha? With Cathair, if he found out."

"Aye, so. And he did not confide in me as he so often had."

"Or in me."

Ardahl looked at her gravely. They two were left. He could only be grateful he had Liadan on his side.

⸻ ◈ ⸻

CHAPTER TWENTY-FOUR

A RARE EARLY summer's day it was when Fearghal called them all together the next morning. The sun shone golden across the land, setting the river to sparkling, and fair-weather clouds sailed like white curraghs across the sea of blue. A soft, gentle breeze brushed Ardahl's cheek as he joined the crowd of mostly men and a few women near the spring.

Indeed, Liadan stood beside him. He had just been leaving for training when the call came, and she'd come along with him, leaving her mam behind.

This, since the hall had burned, had become the unofficial meeting place for the clan. Fearghal, with Dornach and the two druids flanking him, stood to one side, awaiting his people as they filtered in.

His gaze roamed from face to face as he allowed them to still before speaking.

"My people! This is a call to arms. Since the last raid, Dacha's men have been haunting our western border, where Brihan Brioc allows him to be. Naught we have done has succeeded in chasing him from there. I have consulted with my advisors and our holy men. Indeed, we were up all the night. We will ride out in force and chase Dacha from our border. Not only that, we will pursue him through Brihan's lands. If our closest neighbor has chosen to side wi' our enemy, we will show him no mercy."

A thrill went through Ardahl, followed swiftly by a feeling of sick dread. To choose such a course—an attack as opposed to defense—Fearghal must be very certain Brihan had indeed turned against him.

That meant war against not one tribe, but two.

The crowd stirred and muttered with what Ardahl took as approval. Many among the warriors had been arguing in private for such a campaign, wondering why Fearghal did not call them up.

They had their answer now.

Yet Fearghal looked wary and, to Ardahl's eyes, not entirely confident. Dornach's gaze, which roamed the crowd made up mostly of his warriors, looked hard.

And the holy men? It seemed very strange seeing just the two of them standing there without Aodh. Aodh, who had always led them. Who rarely allowed any uncertainty to show.

Who had sentenced Ardahl to his current fate.

Before he could contemplate that further, Liadan grabbed his arm. He'd grown accustomed now to her touch when she treated his hurts, or when she reached out impulsively while they spoke together.

She touched him casually, so he told himself, as a sister might a brother. Now, though, the touch seemed to ground him, and to unite them.

"We will ride out with a full complement of chariots and as many men as we can spare." For the count of ten heartbeats, Fearghal gazed at his people, hard-eyed. "Make your farewells and settle your households. No' all o' ye will be coming back."

The air trembled as it received those words. Someone called, "Chief Fearghal, when do we leave?"

"Before dawn tomorrow."

He left then, turning his back smartly and walking away. Leaving his people with unanswered questions.

But truly, there was only one answer, was there not? They went to fight. Nothing more.

Liadan turned to Ardahl, her gaze clinging to his, both her hands clutching his forearms.

"It is dreadful news!"

It was, and the kind of bold move Fearghal made but rarely. "He must be very certain o' the threat, to take such a step."

"Aye, but—but—" Liadan shook herself. "I cannot like it. So many to go."

"He wants to be certain we will prove victorious."

She leaned close to him. "I have a terrible, bad feeling about it."

"Do ye?" That made Ardahl's spine tingle. There were feelings, and then there were *feelings*, some merely the product of fear, and some indicating truth.

Persistently, her gaze clung to his. "What if ye do no' come back again?"

It was a terrible thing to ask a man, a warrior on his way to fight. A curse, almost. Many among the clan believed it was doom to express such fears aloud.

Ardahl did not take it that way, not in this case.

It meant she cared. It meant she wanted him to come back to her.

And that fair stole his breath away.

"Liadan—"

"We cannot talk here. Come."

They were surrounded by others questioning one another, protesting, exclaiming. She seized him by the hand and towed him away from the throng, not toward her mother's hut but a stand of rowan trees that marked the edge of the wood.

There he tried to halt her. "Liadan. Liadan—"

But she hurried him on. Not until they were quite alone, save for the no doubt distant guards, did she pause and turned again to face him.

"Ardahl." She spoke only his name. But a thousand words warred in her eyes. He stood and watched her fight her way through them till she fair trembled with emotion. "I thought ye a serpent," she said at last. "A vile *nathrach*, I did, when I believed ye had killed our Conall."

His heart clenched in his chest. He had to lick his lips before he could say, "Ye believe that no more?"

"I believe that no more."

"Och, Liadan, lass—"

She threw herself into his arms. She did it so violently, his weapons rattled. He didn't care. He gathered her in, close and then closer, arms folded across her slender back.

He'd seen the tears in her eyes a moment before she landed.

"Och, lass. Och, do no' weep."

Face half buried in his neck, she moaned, "What if I lose ye? What if I lose ye just like Conall?"

That made him tingle from head to toe. He mattered to her, in some way he could not fairly define. As a substitute for her brother?

As something more?

"I canna bear it."

Aye, so she was frightened. At being left once more with no one to care for her, her young sister, and her ailing mother.

But her arms, clutching him so hard, argued there might be something else behind it.

Their relationship had changed since the long night she'd sat and held his hand beside the door. Since she'd decided to help him discover the truth.

"Here now," he crooned to her, speaking the words soft into her mane of golden hair. "I will return."

"That is no' certain. A big battle, this will be."

A series of them, no doubt.

"Much hard fighting. And ye are no' yet fully recovered."

"I am as recovered as I need be."

"What if Chief Brihan joins his forces with Dacha?"

Aye, what if?

"Ye will be facing twice as many men. And I will not know— all that while, I will not know."

Aye, an agony. If she cared.

He said the only thing he could. "I will come back."

"How can ye say—"

"Liadan, I will come back. To ye."

She raised her head at that and looked into his face. Her eyes swam in tears, luminous with her emotions and what lay in her heart. Fear. Hope. Unmistakable desire.

Ah, by all the gods! Despite his wild attraction to her, he'd dared hope for no more than forgiveness and perhaps friendship. Indeed, a tentative friendship had grown between them. Was there more?

"Do no' fret for me, lass."

"I canna help it. I—"

"I will return to ye." He said it for the third time, a charm. "So I do promise."

She did not say what an impossible promise it was to keep. That in the heat of battle—battle after battle—a man could not dodge every sword and every blow. That death would surround him. That he might well end sprawled on his back in the green turf, staring at a sky as blue as the one that now arched over them.

The promise was what she needed to hear, impossible or not.

Her lips parted with words she did not speak, and she trembled in his arms.

He kissed her, because he could do nothing else.

Ever since he'd moved into her house, since he'd seen her anew, the desire had simmered inside him. As he claimed her parted lips there alone in the grove, tasted of her for the first time, it roused into flame. What began as an attempt to comfort became a rush of pure want.

Strong and bright and victorious, with a life of its own.

A sob sounded in her throat as she wound her arms around his neck, fingers digging into his hair. He made a corresponding sound—inquiry and demand—and she opened for him, allowing him in. Tongue finding tongue. Reaching, reaching—heart finding heart.

He strained her to him, and she clung, she clung, trembling

with need equal to his own. From two separate beings, they became one.

How long that kiss lasted, Ardahl would never know. He forgot to breathe. Forgot the tribe and the world around it. Forgot anything existed, save this.

"Ardahl. Ardahl." They must have stopped kissing, because she spoke his name. In a broken way, she did. She wept, the tears running down her face. "I canna bear it if ye do no' return to me."

"Here, now." He thumbed the tears away, following them with his lips. Salt and sweetness. "Have I no' said I will?"

"Aye. Aye."

"List to me. Liadan, listen." He raised her chin so her gaze met his again. "Ye ha' the courage o' a she-wolf in your heart. Rarely ha' I seen a stronger woman. Ye will carry on while I am awa', for the sake o' your mam. For your sister."

"I will." Her gaze steadied from what she saw in his. "I will. But ye will be sent in at the head o' the men—"

He gave a wry smile. "No' at the head. Cathair claims that place still."

"And should Cathair fall?"

"Then it rests in the hands o' the gods. All of it."

"The gods have no' been good to us of late."

"Have they no'?" They had brought him this. Out of a wealth of heartache, pain, and sorrow. This bright and priceless feeling of belonging, as if he had found the one person in all the world who carried a missing piece of him.

Of his heart.

"Aye, so." She blushed, and her gaze fell from his. "Ardahl, I do no' understand what this is I feel for ye—"

"Nor do I, in truth."

"But it is strong. *Strong.* I will let it be my strength."

"I ken fine ye have it in ye. Now, ye must get back to your mam, and I must away to the field."

Still she did not release him, clutching hard. At last she nodded, drew her hands from him reluctantly. "I will see ye later at home."

"Ye will."

"Go carefully. Ardahl. Ardahl?"

"Aye?"

"Go carefully," she repeated. He walked away knowing that was not what she'd meant to say.

What, he wondered, as he reached the field and joined the other men, made up friendship? When did it deepen to love? What fired up such a sense of belonging?

Fragile, but strong. That was Liadan. He set to practice with a will.

CHAPTER TWENTY-FIVE

THAT DAY PROVED endless for Liadan, even though it was broken up by a number of visitors, all wanting to talk about the chief's announcement and the prospective campaign. These included a friend of Liadan's called Niam, Flanna's friend Lasair, and her mam. Several acquaintances of Mam's. All wished to talk, to speculate, to express their fears.

Liadan, who got precious little actual work done besides grinding the day's grain, could not make herself care. With each visitor, her own fear increased as if it caught flame from theirs. She could think only of Ardahl. Of that kiss they'd shared.

Och, she'd never dreamed any kiss could be like that. It had been akin to tearing asunder a weir holding back a mighty river.

No hope now of stemming the torrent.

How much of that crashing surge of emotion was desire? How much something else? She could not tell. Only that she needed him on a heretofore unprecedented level.

She needed that man, whom she'd once considered a traitorous serpent.

Vital as the need seemed to be, she knew it must go unanswered. Even if she did believe he had not harmed Conall, could never have done so deliberately, the rest of their world did. Including Mam.

And with the way things were, she might never get the chance. Many men went away to fight. Many did not return, at least breathing.

One of the greatest certainties, aye—that life was uncertain.

Late in the afternoon, Maeve arrived. Ardahl's mother wore a look on her face that all too closely matched what lay in Liadan's heart.

She scratched humbly at the doorframe and stood.

"Mistress MacCormac, come in."

"I do no' wish to intrude." Only Maeve's gaze moved past Liadan into the hut. "Is Ardahl no' here?"

"Still at the training. He should be home soon, though I do no' doubt—I do no' doubt they train extra hard and long this day."

"It is true, then—they go to fight?"

"Aye. Were ye no' at the spring for Chief Fearghal's meeting?"

The woman shook her head. "I merely heard after. They leave in the morn?"

"Before first light."

"I hoped to see him."

She surely must. "Come, wait within."

"I dare no'. Your mother—she has lost her son."

"Both o' ye have." Pray to all the gods this woman would not, in truth. Liadan would make an offering to Brigid at nightfall. To Lugh with the sunrise.

Before Maeve could make up her mind to stay or go, a soft step sounded behind her. Liadan whirled to see Ardahl, his weapons on his shoulder.

"Mam?"

He quickly laid his weapons aside, handing the shield to Liadan, and his mother fell into his arms.

Liadan ducked back inside, taking the shield with her, affording them what privacy she could. Tears filled her eyes.

When Ardahl came in moments later, looking weary and grim, Liadan performed a swift inspection. No new injuries she could see, other than grazed knuckles. His hair had worked its way out of its plait and his skin shone from his exertions.

"Ye've worked hard," she observed, saying nothing of the agonized scene with his mother. She handed him a pot of soap and a cloth, at the same time taking the rest of his weapons. He liked to go and wash as soon as he reached home.

With a nod, he went back out. He took a goodly while, likely struggling to get hold of his emotions as much as wash. Striving to seem as strong as he thought he should.

She told him as soon as he came in, "Sit and eat."

Only one night—one very short night—lay between them and parting. All day long, her need for him had been an open wound.

Let me have this. Only this.

With Flanna gone off and Mam lying as she tended to do on Conall's bed, they were as good as alone.

"What is the word?" she asked as he sat down.

"Naught of change. We muster at the training field before dawn."

She took it like a blow. All day long, she'd hoped the plan might alter. That one of the druids would cast his stones, declare the signs said they should not make the venture.

"I see." Her hands shook when she gave him his bread.

"If we can put an end to the fighting, set Dacha in his place, 'twill be all to the good."

"One thing I have learned in nearly a score o' winters is there is never an end to the fighting."

His food served, she sat down beside him. Close. He shot her an inquiring look before beginning to eat.

"Chief Fearghal goes wi' us this time," he told her between draughts of broth. "He wants to direct the fighting, to be seen at our head. To let Dacha know he has a strong hand on the reins."

Liadan experienced a stab of uneasiness. "Is that wise?" Not appropriate, perhaps, to question the decisions of one's chief. Yet she spoke only to Ardahl, after all. Though the chief remained a youthful man, he rarely went to fight, keeping back to direct the defenses of the settlement with so many of the men gone.

Ardahl shrugged. "He will leave a stout guard. So"—he gave a wry smile—"Cathair will no' claim the place o' honor after all."

Aye, so Fearghal wanted the might of the clan on full display when they reached the border. It made sense, at least in the way men tended to think.

"How long d'ye guess ye will be gone?"

Their gazes met, held, full of emotions that could not be spoken. "Impossible to say. A day and a night? Longer if the campaign pushes forward."

Forever, if he fell.

"Ardahl." She caught her breath. "Ardahl, I cannot bear it."

"Liadan." He laid aside his supper, raised a hand to her cheek. Caressed it gently. "We have spoken of this."

"The fear will not leave me. I have naught but bad feelings about your going."

"By all the gods, do no' let anyone hear ye say it. Tamald, he who has taken Aodh's place as head druid, spent many precious moments when I would ha' rather been here, telling us we must go with high hearts and only triumph on our lips, if we are to prove victorious."

"Ye would have rather been here?" She searched his eyes.

"Aye."

Liadan leaned forward and kissed him. She did not mean to do it, did not truly understand the impulse. Nor could she hold it back.

Only their lips touched, their lips and his finger, fleeting, on her cheek. But the day's long agony inside Liadan eased for one blessed instant before they flew apart and glanced quickly at the opening to Conall's sleeping place.

Had she gone mad? They weren't alone, though the curtain, half drawn, surely limited what her mam could see.

"Ye best get some rest," she told Ardahl then, knowing it might be his last respite for days untold.

"Aye."

"Do no' sleep by the door tonight. Keep warm here beside

the fire."

"But that is my place."

His place, so she began to suspect, was anywhere she was. Where she drew breath. Where her heart beat.

"If ye rest by the door, I do also."

"Liadan—"

"Nay, do no' tell me what I may or may not do. This might be the last—" She caught those words hastily. He was right. She should speak only hopeful words.

She tidied away the supper things and went to check on her mam, who slept soundly. When she left the sleeping place, she drew the curtain all the way across.

Ardahl, so she discovered, had made up the fire and spread his blanket beside it. She made sure the outer door was fastened shut before going to lie down beside him.

She half expected him to protest her presence. He did not, but reached out through the firelit air to take her hand in his. Palm to palm. Fingers intertwined.

"The chief will send a caller when we are to rise," he said in a soft rumble. "I canna be late."

Liadan slid closer to him so their shoulders met, warmth against warmth. She watched the smoke from the fire rise toward the rafters through narrowed eyes.

"Liadan, I cannot tell ye what it means that ye believe in me. If I never have another chance to say—"

"Hush. I should have believed ye from the first. Conall could never have been so mistaken in his friend. Forgive me?"

"There is naught, lass, to forgive."

She moved so her head found his shoulder. Snuggled in against him. Satisfaction and longing arose in equal measures, a staggering wave.

"Sleep," she bade him.

But he did not. Neither of them did. Instead they dozed and roused again separately or together. Sometimes they kissed. Soft, tender kisses that said more than words ever could.

When Liadan next became fully aware, it was still dark and she lay with Ardahl's arms wrapped around her, her body half draped over his.

Outside, someone shouted. A searing cry that raced past the hut. Liadan could not catch the words. She did not need to.

Ardahl arose immediately with a groan. She lit a rush light and he gathered his weapons. The fire had died to orange embers and the hut felt cold.

"I am coming with ye." She took up her shawl.

"Liadan, nay."

"'Twill afford us a few more moments together."

"Best we speak our farewells here."

She moved into his arms. In the dim light of the hut, she could barely see his face. But she felt the emotions that roared through him, akin to her own.

"I do not know what to say to ye," she whispered.

"There is naught to be said."

"If I could trade my life for your protection, I would."

"And I for yours." In fact, was that not what he went to do?

A vow of sorts.

She leaned up and kissed him again. One single, searing kiss to seal that unspoken vow.

Before she could blink the tears from her eyes, he was gone.

CHAPTER TWENTY-SIX

C ULLAN WAS ANXIOUS, worked up, and far too ready to
chatter. In the dead of the morning before first light, Ardahl
found it immeasurably annoying.

He was used to having Conall at his side at such a moment as
this. Conall might have high spirits, aye, or a measure of fear and
uncertainty. But he knew when to hold his tongue about it. After
fighting together so long, they needed only to exchange a glance.

His heart gave a throb. Conall no longer entered battle at his
side. And from where he stood now, up in the chariot, Cullan
made a poor substitute.

"I ha' rarely been so far forward in the line," Cullan confessed, unhampered by any lack of reply from his companion.
"No' first, no. Nor even second, wi' the chief after leading us. But
up there. Can ye believe the chief is wi' us?"

"Hush, by all the gods, that we can hear Dornach's direc-
tions."

"Aye, so. To be sure, we must listen." Over the rattling of the
cart, Cullan raised his voice. "Wha' d'ye think of the team I got
for us? I think they are fine ones. Among the best."

"'Tis a grand team, aye."

"I waited at the pony sheds half the night to get the team I
wanted. I had no' first choice, nay. But I was able to claim those
upon which I'd set my eye."

Ardahl nodded, hoping his silence would invite his companion's. Ahead of them, Dornach shot a displeased look over his

shoulder.

"And a fine cart also," Cullan went on, oblivious. "Was this no' the one ye always shared wi' Conall?"

Ardahl was going to strangle Cullan before they ever got to the battle, at this rate.

"Whisht," he advised. "Master Dornach does no' like chatter."

"Right ye be. D'ye think when we get there, Master Dornach will assign us to the flank, like before?"

"I do not know."

At the head of the column of chariots and the men afoot, Chief Fearghal raised his hand. They broke into a trot. The men behind the chariots took up a jog.

"I think—" Cullan began.

Ardahl lost whatever he said in the rattle of the carts, the passage of the cool air against his cheeks. The beating of his own heart.

He thought of Liadan. How could he do aught but think of her when she'd spent the night in his arms? Something fragile and immeasurably strong had been born between them.

He fought for her, if no one else.

As good a cause as any, said a voice at his side. His right side, away from Cullan.

He turned to find that Conall stood there. At least, it looked like Conall, in a dim, light-rimmed guise. He had his fair hair all braided up and his sword at his side. Ready for battle.

Nay, it was but a glint of his sword. For had not Ardahl himself claimed that?

A glint. A shade.

There should not be room for him in the small wicker cart, yet there he stood, as ever.

He's a half-decent driver, Conall said, jerking his head at Cullen, *but I do no' doubt he will drive ye mad.*

Not knowing how to reply, and so astonished he had to clutch the wooden bar across the front of the vehicle, Ardahl said nothing.

But he thought words at his ghostly companion. *Wha' are yet doing here?*

I could no' let ye go into a battle wi'out me, could I? Especially such a battle as this.

Will it be bad?

Aye, so. Though there will be bright spots o' courage and valor. There usually are.

Desperate to disbelieve what he was hearing and seeing, Ardahl clutched the crossbar all the harder. In his left ear, Cullan still chattered, unaware of any extra passenger.

Ye must tell someone, Conall.

I just did.

Nay, I mean tell Dornach. Or the chief. Go and tell them this battle will be hard. Treacherous.

Conall—or his shade—shot him a look from the corners of his eyes, a look so typical it made Ardahl ache. *Ye think they would believe what they canna see?*

Aye— Ardahl paused in his thoughts. *Nay.*

Only ye can see me. We ha' a bond. I must tell ye—

"Are ye listening?" Cullan demanded, and poked Ardahl in the arm. Conall disappeared faster than an eye could wink.

"Can ye no' hush, for the sake o' the gods?" Ardahl turned on Cullan and drew his sword. "Or must I silence ye?"

Cullan fell silent.

THEY REACHED THEIR border to find no massed defenders, no warriors, no enemy guards at all, though watchers there must surely be. The stream ran clean under a cloudy sky, the face of the land seemingly innocent of danger.

The whole train stopped and the men in the first two chariots conferred. Cullan began to push their chariot in, but Ardahl halted him with a growl.

"Hang back."

"But—"

A fierce glare once more silenced Ardahl's companion. They waited while a breeze shivered over the land. Clouds boiled and towered on the horizon. The hairs stood up all over Ardahl's body.

"Somewhat is no' right," he said.

Cullan stared at him. "But wha—"

A signal came and the chariots spread out. The chief had decided to press on. They rumbled and splashed through the stream and onto the turf beyond.

Ardahl wondered if the others felt as uneasy as he did.

"Be ready," he said. He spoke to Conall, who was no longer there, rather than to Cullan. To Conall, as he always had at such time.

Strange, how the bond endured.

Would he die here this day? Was that what Conall had wanted to tell him? Had his friend come for him, to escort him to *Tír na nÓg?*

All too possible, if they met with any enemy, rather than open country.

More slowly now, for the ponies as well as the men behind them began to tire, they traveled on. The land spread out, empty to the eye, and the clouds streamed overhead. Ardahl could smell rain on the wind.

At length, Fearghal drew up again. This time when he turned in his chariot, Ardahl heard him say, "Where is Dacha? Or Brihan's guards, at the very least."

"My chief." Dornach scowled. "Should we turn back?"

Fearghal considered it. In the distance, away toward the west, thunder rumbled. A chill chased its way through Ardahl's bones.

"'Tis a trap!" he called. He did not know why he said it, had no intention of doing so. The words just came.

Everyone in the lead chariots, including Cathair, stared at him

With a look of disdain, Cathair said, "What makes ye say so?"

Ardahl could only shake his head.

Cathair sneered.

"Brihan is no' guarding his border," Chief Fearghal called out. "Moreover, neither is Dacha."

"Mayhap, chief," said Dornach with a sideways glance at Ardahl, "they are luring us in so they may—"

"Attack!" someone called from the rear.

The enemy warriors appeared as if by magic, half materializing out of the rocks, the turf, the land itself. In truth, they came from the hills and the copses of trees, but they streamed in so swiftly, Fearghal's men had barely time to react. And they came from all sides.

Fearghal's warriors, caught in a knot, found the enemy all around them, Ardahl, Cullan and their chariot confined near one end.

"Spread out. Spread out!" Dornach bellowed over the instant crash of metal on metal.

"Go. Go!" Ardahl hollered at Cullan. Conall would already have been moving. "There!" He waved to an empty space past Fearghal's chariot.

The ponies tangled, wheels hit wheels, and their cart rocked violently before it broke free.

Cullan managed to wheel around to face the enemy. Ardahl found himself in the thick of battle.

No time to think, no time to do aught but react, to rely on instinct and the strength of bone and muscle. Opponent after opponent rushed their chariot. It rocked and swayed beneath Ardahl, but he had the advantage, striking down at men afoot.

Face after face, they fell to his blade. He could hear the clang of battle all round him, and Cullan swearing continually as he tried to maneuver the ponies in the tight space.

No matter how many Ardahl felled, others replaced them. Men died everywhere around him. He did not count them.

Suddenly their ponies reared as the chariot went over. Ardahl heard Cullan cry out even as he leaped clear—again by instinct—

and found his feet. A man loomed to the right of him, sword raised. He got his blade up in time to meet the one swooping toward him, stopped that blow, another and another. Got in behind his enemy's weapon with a slash to the man's throat.

The man fell.

Before Ardahl could draw a breath, another opponent attacked him from the left. He heard Cullan call something from the overturned cart.

Nay, that was Conall's voice. His friend was still with him.

Have at him, man!

I am going to die.

Nay, no' ye!

He paused as his opponent fell, miraculously, at his feet. He could no longer feel his sword arm, though it still obeyed his unconscious command. He could not truly feel his body either, nor the rain that crashed down.

It was raining.

The water rinsed the blood from his blade.

He whirled. The battle had spread out from where he stood, some of the chariots trundled away. Men fought in a seething heap. Overhead, thunder boomed and the day had gone dark as night.

A bolt of lightning split the sky and lit the scene garishly. He saw—

Dornach's chariot far down the line, crushed by enemy warriors, both the war chief and his driver fighting for their lives. Closer at hand, Chief Fearghal, with his face fixed in an agonized rictus, his blade whirling. Not far off from him, Cathair also battled hard against a tide of enemy warriors.

Instinct moved Ardahl again. He was sworn to his chief, and his chief needed his sword. He ran forward and threw himself into the fray.

The rain fell so hard, it was difficult to see. But Fearghal did see him and seemed to take renewed heart.

Cathair sent them a wild, burning look. He'd taken a slash

down one cheek, from which the blood ran freely, chased by the rain. So close did they fight, Ardahl could see the desperation in Cathair's eyes.

But when the chief faltered, when his boot slipped in the sodden grass and he went down, followed by his enemy's sword, it was Ardahl's blade that moved fast enough. Ardahl who leaped and interposed his body to guard his chief's. His blade that took off the head of the enemy.

He hauled Fearghal to his feet. The chief, badly wounded, gave him a hard nod. Shouted something.

Ardahl needed to get him from the field. Where was Cullan? Cursing, he tried to search for his driver and their chariot, forgetting it had been turned over. No sight of them.

"Turning!" Fearghal screamed at him.

Was the battle turning? On his life, he could not tell. But aye, there seemed to be fewer opponents, though the rain still made it hard to see. If the battle had not yet turned, it *could* be turned.

"My chief, get ye behind me. I will be your shield!"

After that, he fought. He did not remember the blows or how many opponents went down before his sword. He felt neither weariness nor pain. They went through Dacha's men and out the other side.

When the rain slackened, the enemy had gone save for a raft of dead lying on the ground. They had vacated the way they had come.

Ardahl looked around for Conall, remembered, and searched for Cullan instead. He spied the chariot still on its side. Bodies lay heaped around it, and the ponies stood with their heads hanging down.

He headed there, only to be stopped by someone who stepped directly in front of him. Chief Fearghal, it was. He seized Ardahl by the shoulders.

"Ardahl MacCormac—ye saved my life."

"Eh?" After the clamor of the battle and the rain, Ardahl's ears felt muffled.

"Ye saved my life."

Dornach stepped up. Like the rest of them, he stood liberally slashed and wounded, but he stood.

"Ye saved your chief, man. I saw it." He gestured around at the men behind them, which included Cathair. "We all saw."

Ardahl returned his gaze to Fearghal. He did not know what to say except, "My chief, I swore fealty."

"Aye, so." Approval shone in Fearghal's blue eyes.

"Excuse me, my chief. I must check on my driver."

When he got to the place, the ponies raised their heads wearily and looked at him. Behind them, half covered by the cart, Cullan lay dead.

CHAPTER TWENTY-SEVEN

T HE ATTACK CAME without warning in the middle of the afternoon. The weather had been brooding all day, with clouds streaming in from the west, and sometime before supper it grew dark as night.

Mam began to fret, mumbling and pulling at Liadan's hands when she tried to soothe her. She spoke so seldom now that Liadan found the agitated state alarming.

She'd been unable to think clearly all day, unable to focus on anything but Ardahl and the other men, now well to the west. She'd prayed to Brigid for his welfare. Prayed to Lugh at dawn. The worry would not leave go of her.

Was it raining where he was? Did he battle? Had he fallen beneath some blade?

If he had, och, however would she bear it?

When she could not comfort her mother, she made the dire mistake of leaving her alone to go fetch the healer. Flanna was away, and Liadan tucked Mam up beside the fire with many soft entreaties for her to be still and wait until she returned.

Mam reached out and seized her by the wrist, staring into Liadan's eyes. "They come."

"Who comes, Mam? Our men?" Could they possibly return so swiftly? "How do ye know?"

Mam moaned as the hysteria deepened. Liadan freed herself from her mother's grip and ran out.

Nay, she was not thinking clearly, had not for some time, or she could never have left such a fraught woman alone.

The healers' hut was not far. She imagined one of the men might have gone with their warriors, since they anticipated such a mighty battle.

She had the healers' hut in sight when the screams sounded. At first she thought it was Mam, having followed her. Then she realized the truth. Voices raised, cries of alarm, the crashing of arms.

"Attack! Attack!"

For several precious moments, her mind stuttered. She froze, not knowing which way to run. Her own home lay behind her. Flanna—Flanna had spent the night at her friend's hut.

She ducked back and saw strangers rushing toward her through the settlement. Enemy warriors. The truth hit her, hit her like a boulder off the hillside. The enemy had but waited, waited till their own men were gone.

Fearghal had left a guard, aye, but from the numbers of enemy warriors she saw flooding the settlement, they would not be enough.

"Mam? Mam!"

She hollered the name as she ran. In truth, her hut was not far, but sudden danger lay everywhere. Men with swords, with torches.

They would burn the settlement to the ground.

Weaving between huts, nearly colliding with fleeing neighbors, she strove for home. She must reach there before the enemy did.

Someone careened into her, knocking her to her knees. It was a woman.

Ardahl's mother.

"Here." Like something out of a dream, Maeve loomed over her, holding a sword. She helped Liadan to her feet and thrust the weapon into her hands. "Take it!"

Instinctively, Liadan did. For years she had handled Conall's weapons, though she'd certainly never trained with them.

Any weapon was better than none.

A man rushed at them, screaming. One of the strangers.

"Get behind me!"

She did not wait to see if Maeve obeyed. She swung clumsily at the stranger, who, taken aback by the sight of a woman with a great sword, failed to react in time. The blade took him in the side of the neck. A vulnerable place, as Liadan had heard Conall say many a time.

The man stumbled to his knees. There was blood. So much blood.

"Run!" she told Ardahl's mother. She did not see the woman stoop and take up the fallen man's sword.

Lightning flashed as they went, and thunder shook the ground. People ran everywhere, pursued by the attackers. Liadan saw two women cut down, one with a babe in her arms.

Maeve ran and snatched up the child in the face of the attacker. Waved a sword at his chin.

He veered away.

Liadan's hut sat only steps off. She had to fight her way to it. When an attacker bore down on her—an ugly brute of a man with a sneer on his face—Maeve attacked him from behind.

Screaming now filled the settlement. Invaders were everywhere. Those who encountered Liadan and Maeve ran on. Two women with swords did not interest them when there was much weaker prey.

Flames soared up, defiant of the rain.

"They are burning the settlement!" Maeve cried.

Finishing the job they'd started last time. Liadan had to reach Mam.

Her hut had not been set alight, but the door stood open—not the way she'd left it. The opening seemed to gape at her like a dark, ugly mouth.

She hesitated one terrible moment before stepping inside. Maeve, with the second sword in her hand and the baby on her shoulder, followed.

The small main room of the round house had been wrecked, belongings overturned. Mam lay beside the fire—just where she'd been when Liadan left her.

For an instant, Liadan could not comprehend what she saw. The body—her mother's body—sprawled. So still. Too still.

"Mam?"

Behind her, Maeve gasped. The babe in her arms set up a wail. The rain crashed so hard on the roof, it nearly drowned out the other, more terrible sounds outside.

"Come away," Maeve said in a harsh breath. "Away out o' this!"

"But my mam—"

"There is naught ye can do for her, lass."

Later, Liadan wondered if it was the rain that saved them. Back outside, it fell like spears thrown from the sky. They dodged and ran the gauntlet of it, Maeve now leading the way with the child clutched to her chest.

Faces appeared out of the confusion. Those they knew turned and followed them. Enemies they fought. Liadan's mind, too burned and blasted to function aright, saw only obstacles and dealt with them.

They made their way into the trees. Hushed voices sounded around them. Gasps. Soft sobs. The babe had fallen silent.

Liadan's mind stuttered. It sought to shut down.

Mam.

They made their way through the trees and up the brae. Behind them—

Nay, but she could not look behind.

No one pursued them here. The clamor from the settlement died away, but the rain accompanied them, thunder rolling overhead like the voice of an angry god.

At last they stopped. Someone touched Liadan's arm. Maeve, it was. Liadan blinked at her. She would not have recognized the woman had she not still the sword in her hand and the babe in her arms. Soaked to the skin, she had turned paler than milk, a haunted look in her eyes.

"Are ye hurt?"

"Eh?"

"Ha' ye any wounds, lass?"

Liadan could not comprehend the words. She saw only her mam sprawled beside the fire.

An old man—Liadan knew him, though she could not find his name—came up and took the sword from Maeve's hold, gave Liadan a doubtful look. She realized they were surrounded by others, elders of the clan mostly, men and women. A child or two. The young ones were weeping.

Liadan drew away from the man. She did not want him to take her sword.

"Brihan's men," the old man said bitterly. His voice seemed to come from far away. "Those were not Dacha's, but Brihan's men. He is in it with Dacha. Must have made an alliance with him."

Did it matter? Did it matter who wielded the swords? They had brought death.

"A scheme!" cried someone else. "They waited for our warriors to go away."

"At least they cannot burn us out," came another voice, filled with hard irony. "The rain has defeated those efforts."

Sluggishly, Liadan's brain tried to comprehend it. She stepped away from Ardahl's mother and peered down the hillside.

Great gouts of black smoke rolled up from the settlement like curses, trapped by the rain. Here and there, flames still licked up. Impossible to see what else happened there. How much death.

She said something even she could not hear.

"What?" Maeve came up beside her. Someone had taken the child.

Liadan repeated, "Are we the only survivors?"

"No," answered the old man. Aye, Ferghan was his name. It came floating up from the deep pit of Liadan's mind. "There will be others, fled away to the hills."

And many who could not flee. The small. The weak. Those with no one to defend them.

Like Mam. She had left her mam.

Ferghan said, "We will wait for nightfall and climb higher, search out the others. Aye, there will be others."

Liadan wondered if he lied to himself.

CHAPTER TWENTY-EIGHT

L IADAN'S GROUP DID encounter other survivors, shadowy figures that materialized out of the trees in small bands of two, three, or more. They came with their own terrible stories, tears, and hushed lamenting.

Ferghan gathered them in. Some of the other old men sought to soothe them, an impossible task. The rain passed, and far to the west, the sky brightened though ugly clouds still hung overhead.

West. Where Ardahl was. In battle.

Had he survived?

Wet to the skin, they shivered. The children wept until they cried themselves to sleep. Maeve remained near Liadan, always close at hand.

"Has anyone seen the chief's wife?" someone asked. She spoke in a whisper. Sound carried, and they were mice hiding from an eagle.

No one had.

"There will be more groups o' us," Ferghan reiterated. "She and his wains may be there."

Time passed. Liadan found herself sitting on a fallen tree, shivering so her teeth rattled, with Maeve still beside her.

"Come," Ardahl's mother said. "Ye can leave go of that sword now. Let's see if you are hurt."

"I canna." Liadan's hand remained fused to the hilt. Spots of blood, too thick to be chased by the rain, clung to the blade.

"Ye can. Here now, gi' it to me." Maeve attempted to pry the weapon from Liadan's hand. Liadan would not release it. "Now, lamb," Ardahl's mother crooned. "At least lay it across your knees."

Liadan did. It balanced there, winking at her in the glimmers of western light.

"Ye gave this sword to me."

"I did," Maeve confirmed.

"Whose is it?"

"That is Ardahl's. He fights wi' your brother's, as ye know. That was left with me. I brought it awa' when my hut burned. And when I heard—when I heard the screaming begin, I drew it out."

Staring at the sword, Liadan said nothing. He had carried this at his side. His hand, like hers, had grasped the hilt.

Her heart tried to stir within her. Had he survived? Had he fallen? Did he exist yet beneath this same sky? She shut the thoughts down tight.

She could not let herself feel.

"Come now, let us see if you are hurt."

"I am all right."

"Ye are no'. There is blood on your clothing."

Liadan looked down at herself in surprise. "Not mine. I do not think."

"Aye, it is. Ferghan?" Maeve called softly. "Where is the healer?"

"Is she hurt bad?"

"Aye."

"But I feel naught."

She *felt* naught.

A darkness came into her head. Voices, hushed, surrounded her. When she returned to herself, one of the healers appeared miraculously and knelt before her, his basket set on the sodden ground.

"How did ye come here?"

He gave her a grim look. "Hush."

Disobedient, she stared at the wound he treated on her arm. "I do not remember getting that wound."

"Warriors rarely do."

"I am not—" She stopped. Ardahl's sword still lay across her knees. Did that make her a warrior?

When the healer finished his work, Maeve came and sat close beside Liadan, put an arm around her, and drew her in.

"My mam…" Liadan began.

"I know, bairn. I know. I saw. Cry it out, if ye must."

But Liadan could not cry.

"I do not know where my sister may be."

"'Tis a torture, not knowing."

This woman did not know where her son was. Just like Liadan. She did not know if Ardahl be living or lost.

An agony.

"Rest." Maeve tucked Liadan's head into the crook of her shoulder. "All we can do is wait."

THEY WAITED TILL dawn, none of them sleeping save the children, the adults too chilled to find slumber. At first light, scouts went stealing out to read the lay of the land.

They came back at length to report the enemy had gone, having destroyed whatever they could and slain whomever they'd encountered. Their plan to burn down the rest of the settlement had been mostly thwarted by the rain.

"There be other groups like us," one of the men reported, "who flew and hid. One has already gone back down. Others will follow."

"Is it safe for us to return?" asked a woman cradling two children.

"So far as we can tell." The scout—a rare surviving member

of the guard who had found them during the night—shrugged.

Said an older woman, "What if they return?"

That question went unanswered. Another member of the scouting group who'd ventured farther afield came hurrying.

"Our men return! They are far to the west yet but on our land. Donnacht has taken them the news."

Is Ardahl among them? Liadan wanted to ask, but her tongue cleaved to the roof of her mouth.

"The chief comes!" the man cried as if in answer.

Those gathered exchanged glances. The chief's wife and young children had not yet been found. Mayhap they were with one of the other groups of fugitives.

Maeve tightened her arm around Liadan. "They return," she murmured, "and will defend us. Let us go home. Bring the sword."

The air reeked of smoke, so thick and heavy that Liadan could scarcely draw a breath without choking. When they reached the settlement, they found others there before them. With no one in charge, folk wandered around looking lost, many of the woman weeping.

Liadan could not go home. Her mam lay there—and not for a fortune in gold could she have made herself walk in. The hut of Maeve—who seemed to have set herself to look after Liadan— had burned long since. So had that of Dornach, where she'd been staying.

Like so many others, they fetched up near the spring, lost souls at sea. One of the older men took charge, sent out others to patrol the perimeter and send word when their men drew close.

More and more folk drifted in from the hills. That was when Flanna, still with Lasair and Lasair's mother, found Liadan. Flanna flew into her sister's arms, weeping with relief.

"Liadan! Sister! Is Mam all right? Where is she?"

Clinging to her sister, Liadan could not speak.

"Liadan? Why are ye all bandaged? Are ye sore hurt?"

"Flanna." Liadan drew away just far enough to look into her

sister's face. It was smudged with dirt and soot, streaked by tears. "Mistress MacCormac and I made it awa' out o' the fighting. Mam—Mam did not."

"What?" Flanna's blue eyes widened impossibly. "I do not understand."

"I left her at the hut."

"Ye—what?"

"I left her to go and fetch the healer, ye see. I was on my way there when—"

"She is at the hut? Let us go." Flanna started away, pulling Liadan's hand.

"Flanna, nay. Nay, ye do no' want to see."

"If she is there—"

"They killed her. They killed her, Flanna."

Suddenly, Liadan dissolved into tears. Her legs gave way and she crumpled to her knees, covered her face with her hands. Hiding. Hiding from what had happened.

"Ye left her?" Was that shock or accusation Liadan heard in Flanna's voice? "An ailing woman? Alone?"

"Here now," Maeve said softly. "'Tis no' your sister's fault."

Flanna turned on the woman. "Ye get away from me. Your son killed our Conall. Now we have naught left."

Lasair's mother, still standing by, took Flanna in her arms. "Here now, here now."

Liadan remained where she was on the ground. She wanted to fall through it. She wanted to disappear from the world. The hardest thing of all, to stay and face the truth.

The chief's wife and young children returned to the settlement not long before their men arrived from the west. Like everyone else, Mistress Bridie looked pale with shock and strain, but she set to right away giving instructions, asking whoever was able to begin gathering the dead that they might be numbered, identified, and buried.

Still, Liadan could not make herself return to her hut. Flanna had moved away from her. Liadan and Maeve sat isolated amid all the confusion, one thought only obsessing Liadan's mind.

Had Ardahl survived?

If he had fallen in battle, she would have nothing—nothing left. Conall gone. Mam gone. Flanna having disowned her. She would have no reason to go on.

The clouds broke and watery sunlight flooded the settlement, making it more terrible somehow. Suddenly, women began exclaiming. Calling out. Crying and running.

Their returning menfolk had arrived. A much-reduced fighting force. Limping chariots.

Liadan got to her feet, there beside the spring, and waited, trembling in every limb.

✦

CHAPTER TWENTY-NINE

WHEN THE MESSENGERS intercepted Fearghal's returning forces, Ardahl could scarce believe it. He himself drove his chariot, which had survived being overturned, the traces feeling familiar in his hands. His da had taught him to drive not long after he could walk, hoping Ardahl would follow him and become a charioteer.

Ardahl, though, had wanted to be among the clan's best warriors.

Cullen's body lay on the floor at his feet. They had brought whatever of the dead they could transport away from that terrible place at the border and home with them.

Ardahl's chariot rode third in line behind the chief's and Dornach's. Cathair rode behind him in a fellow warrior's chariot. His own had been wrecked.

If Ardahl had energy to spare for it, he might have felt the ire Cathair no doubt directed at him. He had not. The battle ended, he now felt every wound, and weariness weighed upon him.

The whole train shuddered to a halt when their tribesman appeared out of the damp and foggy air. Men carrying burdens—corpses on shields—put them down.

"Chief Fearghal! The settlement has fallen under attack! They came yesterday afternoon. Many dead and injured. The settlement—"

"What—?" Fearghal faltered. Rarely had Ardahl seen him do that, and his men stared.

"The settlement! Attacked!" Winded from hurrying, the messenger could say no more.

"But we had Dacha's men engaged!" Fearghal seemed dazed. "We bested them."

"No' Dacha's men." The messenger, an old man well wearied, shook his head. "These carried Brihan's colors."

Ardahl, not in a position to see Fearghal's face, watched him stiffen. "Betrayed! Brihan has allied with Dacha to destroy us!"

Aye, so, Ardahl thought. Had they waited for Fearghal's men to roll out and engage Dacha's? No wonder they'd met no resistance while crossing Brihan's land. They'd been lured on, leaving their own lands exposed to an unsuspected enemy.

By all the merciful gods, was this what Conall had wanted to tell him?

Unbidden, he called out to the man, "How many o' our people survive?"

Chief Fearghal did not object to the question.

"We can no' tell. Some fled. They were still coming down from the hills when I left."

His mam? Liadan.

Chief Fearghal swore bitterly and exchanged a look with Dornach before turning in his chariot and calling back to his men.

"Let those o' us driving go forward with all due haste. The rest o' ye afoot, come as quick as ye can."

The weary ponies quickened their pace. A half-score or so chariots—all that remained—leaped forward and into the morning.

If ever anything could quicken the steps of the rest of them, Ardahl thought grimly, it was the desire to discover whether or not their loved ones lived still.

They saw—and smelled—the smoke long before they entered the settlement. It hung like a dark pall, refusing to dissipate. They were met by members of their own guard, which seemed to consist of old men. Fearghal halted repeatedly as they imparted information.

"Chief, your wife and family have been found safe. They are back in the settlement."

"Thanks be to Lugh," Fearghal replied.

"The dead are being gathered to the east o' the settlement."

The dead.

Ardahl began to feel ill, and his hands trembled on the traces. The ponies grew uneasy, pulling up in alarm.

If ye keep calm, your team will also. How many times had his da told him that? But Da was—

Dead.

The next thing to reach Ardahl was the sound. Weeping. Grieving. Like the heavy clouds of smoke, it seemed to rise from the very stones of the place. Distress most profound.

They rumbled in, and the chief dismounted. He gave no orders. What were there to give? Each man would go searching through the horror that lay before him.

Ardahl was no different. He spared pats for the ponies as he passed them by, but abandoned Cullan's corpse, hoping someone would look after the charioteer, and the ponies, and started through the rubble that had been the settlement.

Each man who returned had someone for whom he cared. That was the reason they'd been fighting.

If *Tír na nÓg* be a paradise, this must be its opposite. His step faltered as he went. His nostrils quivered at the scents of burning and blood. Death overlay all.

Many of the living, aye, were on their feet. They appeared dazed and stared at him with empty eyes like those of Liadan's mother.

Liadan.

Ahead lay her hut, the door open as a gaping wound. It had once more escaped burning, and his heart leaped with hope. Inside, though, all lay in disorder as if an ill wind had scoured every item from its place. Empty.

He went on and heard someone call his name.

"Ardahl!"

"Mam?"

She ran at him as a girl might, and was suddenly in his arms. She did not weep—it came to him that his mam was too strong for that, and pride twisted his heart. She had endured so much.

She squeezed him impossibly tight before seizing his face between her hands. "Be ye hurt?"

"Some." No one returning did not carry wounds. "My…charioteer is dead."

Dark horror invaded her eyes. "Many are dead. They are saying it was Chief Brihan's men."

"We heard. Liadan…?"

"Here." Mam looked over her shoulder. "Here!"

This time Ardahl's heart near convulsed.

"But her mam—"

"Och, nay."

Mam moved out of his arms. Liadan stood behind her, though Ardahl would scarce have recognized her as the same lass he'd left behind. Clothing in rags and stained with blood. Damp hair hanging down. Eyes overly large in a pricked white face.

But alive. *Alive.*

He did not remember moving, nor did he see her move. Suddenly she was in his arms, smashed against him as if she would become one with him, flesh for flesh. He felt her trembling. Felt her shock and fear. Her need.

She hid her face in the crook of his neck, arms clenching at him fiercely.

"She is dead. My mam. My mam. It is my fault."

"Hush—nay, lass, it is not. Hush now. How could it be?"

He could smell blood on her and smoke and sweat. She was the best thing he'd ever touched.

"Lass, be ye hurt?"

"She is." Mam stepped forward, since Liadan did not reply. Over Liadan's shoulder, her eyes met her son's. "We had to fight our way free."

"Flanna blames me." Liadan spoke from his neck. Mam's eyes

filled with tears that she still did not shed.

"Liadan." He tried to disengage her from him, without success. "We will make it right. We will."

"Ye came back. Ye came back alive. Had ye no', I could not have gone on."

A sharp thrill went through Ardahl, despite his weariness, his immense distress, the grief and the pain. He tangled a hand in her hair and pressed her closer.

"Had ye no' been here, I do not think I could have gone on either."

Mam gave a muffled sniff and covered her face with her hands. Aye, so, mayhap she did weep after all, but only out of love.

"Liadan, have your hurts all been tended?"

"Aye," Mam answered, "but there was only the one healer, and him in much demand. She needs to be seen again. And ye?"

"The same." Ardahl let his gaze drift over the terrible scene before him. "We will worry about that later."

"Aye. Come to the spring. It is where—where most are meeting."

"Conall's hut—" he began.

Liadan stirred in his arms. "I canna go there. I canna go there again."

NAUSEA TOOK ARDAHL in a hard grip as they moved through the settlement. The sickness came backed by anger—that such a thing could have happened while they were away fighting to prevent it. That Brihan, long a neutral neighbor between them and Dacha, could have turned against them this way.

He felt worry and concern for his mam, who appeared ready to fall down. Liadan refused to leave go of him, and they moved in a bonded pair, not speaking but for one exchange when she picked up a weapon from the ground.

"Is that my sword?"

"Aye."

An odd thought circulated in his head thereafter, more or less independent and disconnected from the horror. If a woman possessed a man's sword, did that mean she also owned his heart? He did not know, but figured he'd better leave it in her hands.

At the spring, where the chief did find and reunite with his family, Fearghal made a speech. Or tried to. The chief, clearly broken, stumbled over his words and struggled with his emotions.

He promised revenge. Rebuilding. Reparation. Ardahl barely listened, busy numbering heads in the crowd. Those here. Those missing.

How many dead?

The chief's voice caught his ear when he heard his own name.

"At the border, we were victorious. And this man, Ardahl MacCormac, saved the life of his chief. I declare him now first among our valiant warriors."

━━━━◦━❮❮❯❯━◦━━━━

CHAPTER THIRTY

AND SO, ARDAHL wondered, how did a man, in the span of one day, go from being despised to among the most honored? It scarcely made sense, and amid all the grief and confusion, he could barely grasp it. He did not feel honored. He had far too many dire troubles occupying his mind.

Life as they'd known it when they rode off in more than a score of bright chariots had ended. A hundred terrible discoveries came at him that day, slamming against him like tree limbs tossed in a gale. Loss upon loss and horror upon horror. Pain and exhaustion. Hunger that simmered beneath the nausea.

Liadan would not part from him, and he did not want to part from her. He had no name for what had been born between them and needed none. It was strong. Quite possibly unbreakable.

She needed him, as did Mam. The three of them, together. As a trio, they were eventually seen by a healer—the same that had accompanied the warriors westward. He and only one of his fellows remained. The third of their number, Dathi, had died defending a group of children.

Such stories abounded. The mass horror did not lessen the individual losses. Ardahl could not imagine how they would recover from this.

When night fell, they built a great bonfire there beside the spring. It being a mild night, they would all stay together. Only they were not all together. Flanna, whom Ardahl saw across the way with Lasair and her mother, refused to come near Liadan.

Dornach, with an ugly cut to his face and a great, bloody wound at one shoulder, approached.

"We are organizing a watch." He flicked a glance at Liadan, who clung to Ardahl. "Ye may take the last turn, toward morning. I am that sorry—everyone is needed."

"I understand."

He would have to reason with Liadan. Comfort her somehow. But he had no words of comfort.

"Son?"

From somewhere, Mam had obtained food. She knelt before Ardahl and Liadan, offering up the bowl full of choice morsels.

Ardahl's stomach felt sick, but his hunger remained nonetheless. Raising his gaze to his mam's, he asked, "Where did ye get all this?"

"Over there." She jerked her head. "The women are cooking. Chief Fearghal himsel' insisted ye should have all this. Is it true, son, what he said? Ye saved his life?"

That made Liadan stir also, and pull away to look at him.

He grimaced. "Aye, but I am no hero. Men save one another all the time in battle." And he had not been able to save Cullan.

It was not right, was it, for him to have more than others around them? Still and all, it was how their clan functioned. In the hall, the foremost warrior sat in the highest place and received the choice portions.

He did not want to be first. Not without Conall, and mayhap not at all. Once, mayhap—but that was no longer why he fought.

Though the food might tempt Liadan and Mam.

"Here," he told the girl beside him. "Take somewhat to eat."

"I cannot possibly."

"Do it for me. Lest later, when I go to my turn at guard, I will no' be easy in my mind about ye. Ye too, Mam. Let us share this."

They did, Liadan taking but a few bites and Mam little more. Ardahl finished the rest, unable to deny that he was ravenous.

The others around them ate and settled to attempt sleep. Children wept and women also, invisible in the night. Some folk wandered. Ardahl's wounds made themselves felt, and the sting kept him awake, throbbing in time with his heartbeat.

Liadan dozed against his shoulder, and Mam slept at his side. Once, Liadan roused to say, "I keep seeing her. Lying there. Every time I close my eyes."

"Aye." He often saw Conall also, lying at his feet with the dirk in his chest. And Cullan slumped in the grass beside the chariot. Was there no end to it? "Whisht, now."

When one of the men came and called him to take his place at watch, he had to set Liadan aside. Half asleep, she murmured a protest, and he tucked the hilt of his sword into her hands.

Out in the dark at the edge of the settlement, the night felt perilous. They formed a chain, each man just out of sight from the next and within call.

He could see the light from the bonfire, still burning. He could make out the line of the hills above and hear the rushing stream.

Beyond that could lurk anything. A hundred warriors creeping. Death come to finish them all.

When a thread of light appeared and spread in the east, he breathed a sigh of relief. That light appeared divine, as if brought by the god Lugh himself, riding in his golden chariot.

He stayed where he was till a man came to relieve him, saying the chief had decided to keep a watch in daylight also. The fellow was elderly, but he had a determined look in his eyes.

"Go on down, Master Ardahl. The women are making breakfast."

THE ENDLESS NIGHT came to a finish with a rush of golden light and sickness in the pit of Liadan's stomach. She woke feeling cold to her bones, her hands wrapped around the hilt of Ardahl's sword, which he had left with her when he rose to go on guard.

She sat up and, fumbling, laid the weapon on the ground beside her, drew up her knees, and pressed her forehead against them.

Where was her sister? Flanna had to be nearby, as were all the surviving members of the clan. But Flanna blamed Liadan for Mam's death.

What could she have done differently? She'd had no idea when she left Mam that they would fall under attack. The healers' hut had been only steps away.

Fateful steps.

Could she have defended Mam against intruders, had she stayed? Could she, without a weapon? They might both have died.

It came to her then in a rush, how precious was her life. How precious the lives of all who had survived—and how fragile. The gods had spared them, and there must be a reason.

She lifted her head, thinking about it. Could she repay such mercy by huddling here, weak and broken? If she had a life still, she must do something with it.

"Liadan, *alanna*, how d'ye feel?" Maeve laid a hand on Liadan's back, and she looked into a pair of kind hazel eyes, so much like Ardahl's that it shook her. Aye, Maeve was a good woman, and a strong one.

"Better. I am better this morning."

"Good. The men are coming back from their places at guard. Ardahl will be here soon."

"Aye." And Liadan would meet him on her feet. "Is there anywhere to wash?"

"I will see."

Maeve hurried off. Liadan did her best to straighten her clothing, but it hung on her in tatters, beyond saving. Like one seeing them for the first time, she surveyed her injuries—a long gash up her left arm, a wound at one shoulder that did not seem terribly deep but had bled much, a nick to one ear. Bruises everywhere. She would no doubt be black and blue when she stripped down.

She had other clothing, but it would be at the hut. Her every instinct flinched from the thought of the place, even though she supposed they were fortunate to still possess a roof when so many did not.

She struggled to imagine what would happen this day, and failed. It helped a woman to know. But her mind merely stuttered over it. Dead to bury. Wounds to tend. Children to care for and many to feed.

She must make herself useful.

She had survived for a reason.

Maeve reappeared at her side. "Come. There is hot water."

A kind of communal washing place had been set up halfway to the midden. Numb-looking women, elders, girls, and children all lined up to use it, many with wounds far worse than Liadan's. No one spoke much. Children wailed; mothers tried to comfort them in hushed voices.

When they returned to their sleeping place, Ardahl was there before them. Liadan wanted once more to rush into his arms, but did not. Yesterday had gone, and a hundred eyes watched. Tongues would soon wag if she clung to him.

Her brother's killer. The *nathrach*.

Only he was not that.

He looked like a stranger, tall and battered and wounded, his hair long having escaped from its battle plaits and hanging in a tangle. How badly was he hurt? She'd scarcely asked yesterday. But aye, bandaging stood out against his tanned skin as well as unbandaged scrapes and gashes, only the worst of which had been wrapped.

Their gazes met and spoke a thousand words, though Ardahl uttered none upon seeing her. Nor did she speak.

"Come and wash," his mam told him, and towed him away. A woman came by, handing out breakfast. Liadan claimed three portions, even though the sight and smell of the food still made her ill.

She caught no sight of Flanna before Ardahl and his mam

returned. The three of them sat together on their blankets, which smelled of smoke.

At last Maeve spoke. Looking at her son, she asked, "What will happen today?"

He shook his head. "Burials, no doubt."

"Burials, aye. The chief will make a speech." He usually did. He might speak of healing.

Could they heal from this?

"I do no' doubt," Ardahl said softly, "he will try to set up some kind of structure. Those who are hurt must be seen. Food. Shelter if it rains. Defense."

Liadan eyed him. He would have to go from her, to take his turns in the guard over and over again. She would have to manage without his presence—over and over again.

She let her fingers whisper over the length of his sword, which she'd kept beside her in the grass. Smooth. Strong. Reassuring. In an odd way, it grounded her.

Even if she was not touching him, the connection between them held.

CHAPTER THIRTY-ONE

L IADAN FACED THE dark doorway of the hut, which yawned in front of her. She'd come with the best possible intentions. To see what remained inside. To find what might be used by herself or others. To lay aside fears, if she could.

But now her feet froze to the ground. She could not take a single step forward.

Six days—and six endless, uncomfortable nights—had passed since the attack. Ardahl had been proven right in his assumption. Chief Fearghal had made a speech. In truth, he had made several of them.

So also had the druid priests, the two of them who remained. Tamald, who had been second to Aodh, had stepped up to support the chief, declaring that as a clan they now had a divine purpose. Insisting that their gods were with them and would help them answer the treachery with which they'd been met, as it deserved.

Thereafter, the two priests had circulated among the members of the tribe advising any who required it. Liadan had herself met with Tamald at Maeve's insistence. Kindly and with exhaustion in his deep blue eyes, he had assured her Mam's death was not her fault, and he prayed with her that she might find peace.

Hesitantly, she'd told him, "Master Tamald, I feel as if I must now have a purpose."

"To be sure, my dear." The kindness in his eyes deepened.

"Each and every one of us has a purpose. Do we not return here to this world of sorrows time after time only to discover and achieve that purpose?"

She'd whispered, "We have lived before?"

"Indeed. What use would one life be? We come to live out the lessons we have learned before. To meet those we have known before. Discover your purpose, lass, and ye will find your courage and your meaning. One life"—he smiled at her ruefully—"is not all."

That had comforted her in an odd way, the more she thought about it. She found hope in the belief that she would meet her da and Conall again—if not in *Tír na nÓg* then in some future, unimagined existence. And Mam. Would she have the chance to ask Mam's forgiveness? It came to her that if she had not the courage to face one empty hut, how could she ever face a future life?

Now that she stood here though, her resolve wavered. Mayhap she should have brought Maeve with her and not come alone. But Maeve was busy helping the mothers with young children, and those about to deliver amid all this madness. Liadan had come to rely on her too much.

Just as she'd come to rely on Ardahl.

Ardahl. She scarcely knew what to make of him. She scarcely understood her feelings for him, what he meant to her.

A strong man, unflinching in the face of the sentence the druids had placed upon him. Steadfastly carrying the weight of his wounds. Surely she could be as strong as him.

The hut, so she assured herself, was empty. Mam's body no longer lay sprawled there. Many burials had taken place, including hers.

Liadan took a step forward. Another. She ducked through the doorway and went in.

Dust motes danced in the light coming through the smoke hole. No body lay on the floor. Or upon Conall's sleeping bench, which she could see straight back from the door. Belongings lay strewn everywhere, though, the reeds scuffed into drifts on the floor.

Beneath the scents of smoke and disuse, it smelled like home.

They could come back here—she, Maeve, and Ardahl could, even if Flanna refused. Many people who still had huts standing had returned to them. It would get them out of the weather and free up space desperately needed by others.

Had she the courage?

She heard a sound behind her and whirled, the breath catching in her throat. Ardahl ducked in through the door, his gaze fastened to her.

Some of his injuries, the most superficial, had healed. Most had not. He appeared thinner than he had been, and strained. But as he moved, the sun turned his auburn hair to fire. She'd rarely seen a better sight.

He wore his weapons with his shield on his shoulder and must be on the way to practice, which Fearghal had reinstated long since, despite all the injuries.

Their lives currently hung upon a strong defense.

Ardahl's gaze met hers, burning with emotions she could not name.

"All right?"

"Aye. She is not here." Liadan gusted out a breath. "Not here." Only she was, if but in spirit. This had been Mam's hearth. Where she cared for her family.

For the first time it occurred to Liadan—it was best, perhaps, Mam had ended that life here, of all places.

Ardahl came forward, and she went into his arms. Just as simply as that. He wore his leather armor, which made a rough padding against her cheek, but she did not mind and merely clutched him harder.

"Och, lass," he whispered against her hair. "I am sorry. I am that sorry for all o' it."

With her face against his shoulder, she said, "The druids teach that we live not one life, but many. Do ye think that is true? D'ye think we will see them again? Be once more in their company?"

"I hope so."

And might she meet this man again, be with him time after time? Safe and at home in his presence? But he was not hers. He was not hers yet.

She lifted her face and gazed into his eyes. At what she saw there, all the breath left her body.

The kiss, as inevitable as her heartbeat, breathed new life into her body. Born like a flame, it unfurled deep in her belly and rose, spreading warmth to every limb, melting the numbness that had held her tight. Her lips, as she knew from that moment, belonged to this man. Her heart to him. Her life.

"Liadan. Och, Liadan." He breathed her name before drawing her to him with such power, her feet left the floor. The second kiss begged entry, and she granted that to him, opened and let him in, tongue on tongue, soul to soul. At that moment she thought she caught a glimpse of her destiny.

When the kiss broke, they were both breathless. She caught his face between her palms and gazed into his eyes. She sought words. Found none.

He rested his forehead against hers and they clung, clung while their hearts settled within, while their beings aligned.

"If we return here," she said at last, fumbling for the words as if for a foreign tongue, "can we be together?"

"Together?"

"Man and woman."

"Is that what ye want? Liadan, is that what—"

"It is all I want."

He drew a breath, and she saw his thoughts move in his eyes. He had killed her brother, or so their society claimed. He was here in her brother's place, as blood to her. She did not know if they would ever be given permission to handfast.

As impossible as the rest of their world.

But he nodded. "I will make it happen."

"Then we will return here." She stepped away from him and

looked around the hut. "I will clear the place out. Ch-change it."
If she could. So many memories here. It would be a hard task.

For him, she could do anything.

He drew her back to him for one more precious moment. Kissed the palm of each hand, dropped small, soft kisses on the corners of her mouth, her cheeks, her forehead.

"I must go to practice."

"So ye must."

He did not want to leave her. She could feel that in him. He did not need to say.

"I will see ye after," she promised. But when she watched him duck back out through the door, it brought a pang to her heart.

She had learned that each and every parting could be final. Attack and separation could occur at any moment.

Only the love remained.

Did she love Ardahl MacCormac? She asked herself that question as she worked in the hut, tore it apart inside even more thoroughly than had the invaders. Dragged all the furnishings outside. Swept and shook and purged.

She decided what she felt could not be mere love. Not as she understood that emotion. Love could be strong, aye, but it was also soft. Reassuring. This that she felt for Ardahl reassured her, true, as did nothing else. It also terrified her with its depth of need and its power, a power that had taken the man from a serpent in her eyes to—

But that was where she stuttered and her understanding failed.

She stood with the blanket from Conall's sleeping place in her hands, arrested by the intensity of what she felt and could not name.

Brigid, she prayed to the goddess as she stood there beside the cold fire, the very place where her mam had died. *Look after him for me. Please, above all things.*

CHAPTER THIRTY-TWO

DORNACH SHOULD NOT be working. That much appeared obvious when Ardahl arrived at the practice field, that wide, green-turfed expanse surrounded by a wall of stone. The man bore a number of desperate wounds, not the least of which was a great, bloody gash to his face that, as he moved, refused to stay closed. Beneath the man's stoical expression, Ardahl saw pain.

But the same was true of nearly all of them, himself included. In the past, in ordinary times, none of them would be considered fit to drill as yet. These were not ordinary times.

Take the fact that when Ardahl reached the field following his encounter with Liadan, his marvelous encounter with Liadan, the chief was there before him, and at work.

Though Fearghal—who had less than two score winters—was in essence a warrior, and though he'd gone to fight with them in the last battle, he did not ordinarily train with the rest of the men. Ardahl knew that Dornach sometimes worked with him in private. Now he had stripped down to his kilt and leggings like the rest of them, displaying the wounds he carried.

Ardahl's own wounds stung as he walked across the turf to join the others. But inside—inside he still carried the great joy that had unfurled inside him, born of having Liadan in his arms. A warmth, it was. A precious, living thing birthed between them. Come to him like some secret power, a gift of the gods.

One that just might keep him alive.

He could still feel her in his arms, taste her on his tongue. He carried her scent. What was mere pain or weariness compared to that?

On an ordinary day, the training field was a noisy place. Men shouting to one another, contesting in mock battle. Weapons rattling. Challenges issued. Today it brooded beneath a sky that promised rain. The gathering clouds cast shadows across the green. But the silence, more than aught else, told Ardahl how much had changed.

He meant to join a group of men working together near the center of the field, but as he went, Dornach looked up, caught his eye, and gestured him over to where he and the chief stood.

"Master Dornach. Chief Fearghal." Ardahl bent his head.

"Ardahl." The chief held a weight of grief, exhaustion, and what might be anger in his eyes. Aye, so, they were all angry. But the emotion had been thrust away beneath the others.

For now.

Dornach spoke. "Chief Fearghal asks that ye train wi' him, Ardahl."

"Me?"

"I request it," Fearghal said. "I would be honored by it."

That stole all Ardahl's breath. A day, this, of astonishments.

Taking in his expression, Fearghal smiled ruefully. "Did ye no' save my life there on the border?"

"'Tis my place and my duty to save your life."

"'Tis the proof o' a loyal man, to say so."

"But, my laird, I am dishonored."

"So ye do be. And I am no' certain I can lift that from ye, what our priests have imposed. Under law, a sentence is a sentence, aye?"

"Aye."

"But ye be also a lion o' a warrior, and I owe ye a debt o' gratitude. Not that I deem mysel' so very important as a man. But as a chief?" Fearghal grimaced. "That be something else again. The only thing that could make our situation worse would be the loss of the clan's chief at this place and time."

"Aye, so."

Fearghal's brother had been slain in battle some two years back, and his son had but seven winters or so, far too young to lead.

Ardahl eyed his chief candidly. "Yet ye plan to return to battle, should we go? Ye would continue to risk yourself?"

Fearghal spread his arms and gestured widely. "As ye can see, we are woefully short-handed. Every warrior counts. And I was that—a warrior before ever I was chief."

One could not fault the man for courage.

Again, Ardahl bowed his head. "I will be honored to practice wi' ye, since ye ask it."

"I do. Have I no' declared ye foremost among our warriors? No' formally, perhaps. There should be a declaration in the hall." Starkly, Fearghal concluded, "There is no hall."

"'Tis no' necessary, my chief."

"It is quite necessary, especially given the circumstances. I know fine ye stand disparaged in the eyes of many. But I want ye to stand anyway at my side."

He nodded at Dornach, who stood by silent, his eyes watchful. "Though he will no' freely admit it, my war chief is sore injured. Ye may be injured also. That did not keep ye from preserving my life."

"My laird, the other men—they will protest if ye name me first among them." Cathair would, though Cathair too bore livid wounds, including one that coursed across his forehead and fair disfigured him. "They will no' want to yield a place o' such honor to one they consider disgraced."

"Mayhap not," Fearghal admitted.

"Cathair—he will believe the place should be his."

"Ardahl." The chief's clear blue eyes met Ardahl's. "I do not know what happened between ye and Conall. He was a high-hearted, valiant young man, and I liked him right well. He is dead, and his blood was on your hands. But I saw ye fight in this last battle, and had Dornach's account of the one before that. These being dire times, I want ye at my side."

Emotion fair choked Ardahl's throat. "May I speak plainly, chief?"

"Please do."

"I am no' at all certain either what happened between me and Conall. How he came to have a dirk in his heart. I would have sworn blind he could not turn on me in anger as he did, but 'tis what occurred. And the dirk did end in his breast.

"I now carry his sword, no' my own. I fight—and live—in his place. If ye want Conall's sword at your side, 'tis at your command."

"Good man." Briefly, Fearghal gripped Ardahl's shoulder. "When again we roll out to fight, your chariot will be second only to mine. In any battle, you will fight at my right hand."

"Ye think, chief, we will enter battle again?"

"Och, aye."

"Soon?"

"I hope to deal wi' Brihan first. He is supposed to be my ally, at least nominally. Instead, he came onto my land and slew innocents while I was away fighting another enemy. He needs to be challenged for that. If he has turned his cheek, we indeed have a great problem on our hands."

Fearghal let his eyes wander over the field. "I must, aye, challenge Brihan. But I would stall it as long as possible. We need to heal. And mourn."

"Aye, chief."

"To be sure, if Dacha decides to return and attack us at our weakest—perhaps wi' Brihan's help—we will no' be able to choose the time o' our battles. We will be fighting here." His eyes met Ardahl's. "For our lives."

"I understand."

Only, Ardahl would not be fighting for his own life, or even Fearghal's. For his mam. And for the woman who had so inexplicably taken possession of his heart.

They drilled for the rest of the day, even after the clouds lowered and the threatened rain began to pour down. Ardahl did his best to ignore the stares of the other men who watched him drill with their chief. And the glares from Cathair, whose ugly expression might well have felled him.

Trouble there, Ardahl thought as he at last left the field. But aye, they had nothing but trouble.

Fearghal had worked hard, no one could deny it. So had Ardahl and his wounds stung as he started away. He longed for nothing—not even food or drink—so much as to see Liadan.

He would walk past the hut to see if she was still there— better perhaps to spend the night there than in the open, given the rain, even if she felt uneasy in the place.

The door of the hut was tied shut—against the rain?—and firelight flickered around the edges of the leather door. He knocked at the doorframe, and Liadan swept the curtain aside.

"Mistress? Might I come in?"

"Please."

Her eyes met his, conveying so much more than the simple word. Inside, almost nothing looked the same. The floor had been swept, the furnishings dragged about and rearranged. The curtains at the sleeping benches had all been tied open and a good fire burned at the hearth.

"Put your weapons here." She took them from him and laid them beside the door. "Come near the fire. Ye be wet to the skin."

"Aye." But he did not move from where he stood. "Liadan, be there ghosts here?"

She gazed around the place and bit at her lip. "I suppose there are. But we have come to an understanding."

"Ye wish to stay here, then?"

"I wish to stay here tonight. Wi' ye."

CHAPTER THIRTY-THREE

THE ACHE THAT had dogged Liadan all the day long eased only when Ardahl came through the door. A persistent sort of hunger it had been, gnawing at her despite all her other worries and preoccupations, without stopping.

When she saw him standing there with his hair and clothing dripping wet, the relentless worrying—like a dog at its bone—at last ceased. He was here. From that moment, nothing else mattered.

She'd done her best this day to cleanse the hut. To fashion it anew as her own. She did not know if she'd succeeded, but the fire burned low and bright. She had food set aside—for Ardahl, only for him. Everything from now on would be for him.

"Is my mam no' here?"

"She has gone to help at a birthing. A difficult one. Imagine, a babe choosing such a time to be born, and backward, so she said when she stopped on her way." Liadan caught Ardahl's gaze. "She will no' be back tonight."

"Ah." He said no more, but she caught the flicker of the thoughts, light and dark, in his eyes. Just the two of them here alone. Them and the ghosts.

The ghosts had better turn their eyes away, given what Liadan had in mind.

"Come. Get those wet things off. I will fetch a cloth."

When she returned with one, he had taken a few steps closer to the fire but had not otherwise complied with her instructions.

He stood, hands dangling at his sides, only his gaze following her.

She tugged off his hood—sodden—and began untying the bindings of the leather armor beneath. She stripped away the armor. Took the cloth and dried his face. His arms. Moved around to his back. His hair hung past his shoulder blades. She gathered it into the cloth before returning to the front and beginning to unfasten his belt.

"Liadan—"

"Aye?" She kept her tone light even though her fingers trembled. Not with fear, or even honest nerves. With desire.

She had wanted this man a long time. Much had come between her and her desire. Now it had become so much more than a physical want.

When she went down on her knees before him to unfasten the bindings over his leggings, he stiffened and seized her shoulders.

"Liadan—"

"What?" She gazed up at him, met his eyes. "Did I no' tell ye earlier what I wanted?"

"Ye did. but I am here in your brother's stead. To all purposes, I *am* your brother."

She got to her feet. "Ye could no' be less my brother had ye descended from the moon. Now, d'ye have any hurts ye need tending? Before I finish removing your clothing, I would know."

Stricken silent, he shook his head.

She had an excuse to strip him down, him being wet from the rain. No such excuse to remove her own clothing, though she shed it anyway, not quite daring to meet his eyes. Though she had never experienced the act she wished to perform this night, it required little or no covering on either of their parts.

She'd seen her brother naked while growing up. Living in such close quarters, glimpses in passing proved unavoidable. She'd never thought much of it. Men and women were, aye, different. There was a purpose in it, planned by the gods.

No unintended glimpse she'd ever caught of any man approached this.

He was beautiful, her Ardahl. So beautiful, despite the wounds, scrapes, and bruises that fair covered him, it stole her breath away. Made her heart pound. Made her fingers quiver.

Broad, strong shoulders aglow in the light from the fire. A finely molded chest patterned with auburn hair. Strong legs without bulk, and hips whipcord slim.

Her mind failed her there. Her mouth went dry. *Och, holy Brigid! He was made for me. Only for me.*

He said nothing as she met his gaze at last, not aloud. His lips did move, though no words came, and his eyes sang her a song. One so ancient and holy it did not need to sound in the air.

She heard it instead in her mind. In her heart.

"Ardahl," she whispered when they were both stripped naked. She moved into his arms. Och, and she could feel him, every part of him as he wrapped her in his arms and drew her in, natural and wonderful as breathing. As being alive.

They kissed. And kissed.

She gave herself to him, fairly and freely she did. Arms wound around his neck. Fingers twined into his hair. Legs around his hips.

He boosted her up without effort, his palms at her bottom, and breathed into her. "Where?"

Not in Conall's sleeping place, nor here beside the fire where her mam had died.

"There." Her parents' sleeping place, which her mam had abandoned after Conall's death. Unused now.

He deposited her there gently, as if she were something precious. She pulled him down on top of her.

"Wait, Liadan." He said no more as he stood and looked at her by the light filtering in from the fire. She'd never been self-conscious about her body, never been conceited about it either, or given it much thought. But now she wondered what he might think.

She wanted to be beautiful for him. No one else.

She reached up for him, pressed her mouth to his, and he came down atop her. All other thoughts flew as sensation—blinding in its intensity—seared her mind.

Desire rose in a staggering wave even before he put his tongue into her mouth, deep. She understood it then. She had been created to open herself and accept him. Give to him on a rush as strong as a flowing river.

He began to run his hands over her, gently and carefully, palms abraded and rough with callouses. They smoothed the skin at her sides, cupped a breast, traveled over her belly and downward. All the while Ardahl and she continued to kiss as if fused mouth to mouth, unceasing.

So easy was this, so natural, and at the same time utterly transforming. She teetered on the edge of becoming someone she'd never imagined.

Ardahl's woman.

"Ardahl, please." She broke the kiss to gust the plea, breathless, into his mouth.

"Ye be certain o' this, lass?"

"I need—"

"Aye." He gusted a half laugh. He lay upon her, and she could feel the hot hardness of him resting on her belly.

Greatly daring, she reached between their bodies and wrapped her fingers around him. His whole being jerked in response.

"Please," she begged again.

Instead, he bent his head. His mouth found her breast, and though she would not have thought it possible, her mind shattered again. The rest of her was primed to follow. If she did not have him soon, deep inside her, she would dic.

Leaving go of him below, she buried her hands in his hair and drew him to her, fingers urging. The closer he got, the closer *they* got. She held him to her breast and rocked him. With a kind of sigh, he stopped suckling, lifted his face, and studied her in the dim, filtered light.

Gazed straight into her eyes. Repositioned himself.

And slid inside her.

It felt so right, she nearly missed the sudden pinch of pain. That did not matter, for he was suddenly where she wanted him, where he was meant to be. In this moment she belonged to this man—nothing before and nothing after, one being, with one heart and one flesh.

She rose through the sensation and expanded, taking him with her. Her blood beat for him, like the beating of wings, and his blood beat through her. Mouths still fused, she tasted nothing but him as she shattered.

His arms guided her as they tumbled back down to earth onto her parents' sleeping bench. She lay there, her body still singing, striving to think. There were no words for trust such as this. For bonding such as this.

Without words, she lay quiet. He touched her face, her neck, her collarbone.

"I am sorry."

"Sorry?" she echoed, barely comprehending the word. "Why?"

"I spilled myself. On your belly."

Had he? Indeed, she felt wet there, and warm.

He whispered, "I did no' want to give ye my babe."

Oh. Aye. The result of such an act, such joining. She experienced a rush of tenderness at the thought and touched his face in turn. "Did ye think I would no' want your bairn?" She wanted every part of him.

"I thought, given our situation, 'twould not be wise."

Their situation. She crashed down to earth far harder than before.

"I do no' care."

"Ye should, Liadan. Ye must. This is not meant to be."

"There could be naught more meant to be than ye and me together, Ardahl. There could be naught more right than this." Did he not feel that? She'd just given herself to him. Her life and her being. All that she was.

Should she tell him she loved him? Nay, love did not even touch what she felt.

"Bonny lass, beautiful girl," he crooned, "ye must see 'tis impossible."

"It canna be impossible. For I am here and so are ye. 'Tis the gods have sent us this, Ardahl. Amid all the loss and the pain and the ugliness."

He buried his face in her neck and held on tight.

CHAPTER THIRTY-FOUR

R AIN POUNDED ON the roof of the hut, no harder than Ardahl's own heartbeat. He should arise from the sleeping bench and leave. Some madness had come into his head, and it lingered there yet, though a few strands of sense still threaded their way through.

Enough to assure he'd withdrawn from the warm haven of Liadan's body before he gave her what he should not. Enough to know he could not hurt or harm her in any way.

He should remove his weight from her now. Young and tender, bearing the wounds got during the attack, she was not accustomed to accommodating him.

She might well want him gone.

Yet he remained where he was with his face buried in her neck, breathing her scent, groping for those strands of good sense. He felt changed by what had just happened.

Everything had changed.

Who would have thought it? Conall's wee sister. But out of a terrible darkness had come a precious flame.

Surely he might warm himself at it for a few blessed moments before tearing himself away.

"Ardahl." He liked the way she spoke his name. It echoed through him like a song, an ancient and beautiful one. He liked the scent of her and even more the way she tasted. He liked the feel of her when he was inside, the way she gripped him with her whole being.

She had begged for him inside.

Nay, he could not move away from her just yet.

Did her arms not clutch at him? Hold him tight? Her palms ran over his back as if she would memorize the feel of him. She did not seem to mind that he had spilled himself on her skin.

"Liadan." Still half dazed, he sought words.

"Um?" She kissed the side of his face and his ear, through his hair.

"I am meant to protect ye. To guard and defend ye. In your brother's place. Not—not—"

"And do ye no' defend me? Wi' your very body."

"Not what Aodh intended."

"Aodh is dead. So many are dead—we are no'."

Indeed, they were not. They had risen together on one set of wings, strong wings that had bound them together.

Yet it could not be.

"I am commanded to serve ye."

"Then serve me." She stirred beneath him, moved with a wisdom beyond her experience, a woman's wisdom. He settled once more between her thighs.

"Liadan, I must arise."

"Arise." She breathed it in his ear, and he did.

"If we are discovered, 'twill mean terrible disgrace. Ruination."

"How might we be discovered? No one is here save, perhaps, a few ghosts."

Ghosts.

"Should my mam return—"

"She will not yet. And if she did, can ye imagine she would betray us?"

She would be shocked. She would not betray him, though.

"Ardahl, I do no' care what the druids say. What anyone else says. We have been given this—this wondrous thing. Given it out o' a world of darkness. Can we deny it?"

He could not.

"Please," she breathed in his ear, and guided his mouth to her breast.

THE RAIN ENDED late the next morning. Ardahl had drowsed for a time in Liadan's arms before gathering his wits and enough of his intentions to leave her. He'd washed outside, the taste of her still on his tongue, before heading off with his weapons for the training field.

He would go through his day, perform his duties, and meet his obligations while pretending—pretending nothing had changed.

Yet everything had. He was not the man he'd been when he lay down with Liadan last evening. Indeed, he might appear the same, seek to behave the same.

He was a different man, indeed. He now carried a part of Liadan—a large and significant part—inside him. She filled him, clung to him, whispered to him. No longer alone, he must harbor her like a precious secret.

No one could know.

Physically, last night had been like nothing he'd ever experienced. From the moment she'd stripped away his wet clothing and touched him, he'd been claimed entirely. And the moment he'd entered her, he'd claimed her also—flesh no longer just flesh, but something that made one of them part of the other.

Who would imagine coupling could be like that? A thing of spirit as much as flesh and blood.

Not to say the physical part had not mattered. It had. Her breasts were a soft haven, her thighs a place of sweet welcome. She was perfection. But his desire for her reached beyond that, so strong it terrified him.

Once known, how might he live without her?

His mam had not come home by the time he left. No one

knew what they had done. Liadan had straightened up the sleeping place, built the fire. Given him breakfast.

Kissed him goodbye.

He might never have the chance to lie with her so again. If he did not, it would hurt like a constant, open wound.

Better to carry that wound than not to have had her at all.

At the training field, Dornach set them to drilling upon the sodden ground. Ardahl once more trained with Fearghal, and he felt the glances of the other men, curious and resentful. Cathair, as he could not help but notice, watched him and Fearghal from the corner of his eye, and he was unusually hard on his designated companion.

Cathair, angry, made a daunting proposition.

At midday, the women brought food. The rain had ceased by then, and a watery sun appeared. Ardahl half hoped Liadan would come, half hoped she would not. He dreaded seeing her, for he did not know how he might hope to behave toward her, as he had before.

She did not come. He and Fearghal were served by one of the women from the chief's household.

They sat on the wall and ate together as if they were of the same station.

"My wife is gey worried," Fearghal said as he consumed his barley cakes. "She greatly fears my going off to fight again. Tries to tell me 'tis not my place as chief.

"I tell her it is my place as chief. That if I will no' stand strong at the head o' my men, I can no' expect them to lay down their lives in my absence."

"Aye." Ardahl could only agree, and stole a look at the man. He still appeared weary beneath the high color earned by working hard, and blue flags flew beneath his eyes.

Ardahl experienced a flare of worry. What would happen to them if Fearghal fell?

He would have to make certain that did not happen.

Fearghal gave him a brief grin and, as if hearing his thoughts, said, "I tell her I will have the best warrior our clan can boast at my side—ye."

With calm he did not feel, Ardahl repeated, "I am disgraced."

"Aye, so." Fearghal frowned.

"The druids have declared it so and put me in Conall's place."

Fearghal stopped eating. "I have said I do not know what happened between ye and Conall." He fixed Ardagh with a cool eye. "Tell me again what you say occurred."

"Conall turned on me for no reason I could tell." Should Ardahl speak to the chief of his other suspicions, about Cathair? But he had no proof beyond Cathair's association with a young woman. "There was a flurry and he lay dead."

"And that is the truth?"

"That is the truth."

Fearghal sighed.

Summoning all his strength, Ardahl said, "My chief, I do no' see how ye can put me first among the warriors. The others will no' stand for it." Deliberately he added, "Cathair will not."

"I put ye there because ye have earned the place. 'Twas ye and no' Cathair who saved my life."

"Even so."

"Dornach believes in ye."

"I am humbled by his regard. And yours."

Fearghal smiled wryly. "Among our warriors, *humble* is no' a common thing to be. Aodh, who imposed your sentence, is dead. I canna say I have the power to lift what he laid upon ye. I do not. Ye will have to stay and serve Conall's family as sentenced."

"As his surviving sisters' brother."

"Aye. But these are no' ordinary times, and I need ye at my side. Soon—very soon—I will have to go and deal wi' Brihan. Charge him for turning against me."

"A dangerous mission."

"Aye, so. And I will need ye with me, Ardahl."

Ah, by all the gods! What would Liadan say if he went from her for such a perilous course, perchance not to return?

"My chief, my fealty is yours, as is my sword." Conall's sword. Liadan still had his.

"Good man. Ordinarily I would take Dornach. He does no' want to admit it, but he is no' fit. I will tell him he is needed here to keep a strong defense. 'Tis all too true, given what happened last time."

Ardahl said nothing. He wondered what Fearghal could possibly say to Brihan, who had already turned his cloak and sided with Dacha. Whether Fearghal could trust the man if he got the assurances he wanted. If Brihan would speak only lies.

And what he could say to Liadan, when the time came.

※ ⬥ ※

CHAPTER THIRTY-FIVE

THOUGH LIADAN DID her best to keep busy all that day, it did not help her state of mind. Her longing for Ardahl and her tendency to relive all they'd shared remained alive within her. She swept the hut out again, shook out the blankets from her parents' bed—not before inhaling from them the last of Ardahl's scent—and fought the desire to walk past the training field, where he worked.

Like some green girl.

She was no longer a girl but a woman. He had made her so.

Maeve came home around noon, mentioned the hard fight she and others of the women had staged to save Seona's babe, and went off at once to sleep. Left alone, Liadan fell prey to her thoughts once again.

Relentless thoughts and desires.

She had supposed—hoped—that having Ardahl once would be the cure. Would render her satisfied. But she would need to have him again. Once touched, constantly desired.

Whether that would happen—whether she would ever again lie in his arms—she could not say. It did not seem likely. They had so few opportunities to be alone. And the future—

Well, try as she might, she could not quite see a future for them.

At last, unable to bear the hut any longer, she went out. The sun had emerged, and a stiff wind chased the lingering clouds eastward.

Welcome as the sunlight was, it exposed the widespread ruination of the settlement. The great hall, no more than a pile of charred timbers. The dwellings that had once clustered around it, likewise. The armory, the pony sheds—thanks be to Brigid that whatever ponies not away with the chariots had been in the field that night, and so saved.

Other structures half ruined in the second attack, roofs collapsed, belongings strewn far and wide.

Some women worked at sorting through those belongings while children wailed and pulled at their skirts. Anger reigned here, and despair.

Across the way, near the spring, Liadan spied Flanna in company with Lasair. When Flanna saw Liadan approaching, she turned her face away.

"Sister?" Liadan beseeched her.

"I do no' wish to speak wi' ye." Ready tears began to flow from Flanna's eyes.

"We need to speak, do ye no' think? To heal this misunderstanding that lies between us."

"'Tis no misunderstanding. Ye left Mam alone. To die."

"I did not know—"

"Abandoned her, a woman who was ill, on her own. Wi' no protection."

"'Tis because she was ill that I went. 'Twas but a few steps."

"Enough! Enough for her to be alone when they came."

And where were ye? Liadan wanted to ask. *Off taking your own comfort with your friend. Leaving the hard task to me.*

But she could not say that. Flanna was but a child. And it would only widen the rift between them.

So she bit back the words and said instead, "Ye will ha' to forgive me. We have only each other left. Da, Mam, Conall, all gone."

Flanna turned on her, face flushed and eyes awash with tears. Folk stared now, the women swiveling where they stood. "I do no' have to forgive ye."

"At least come home so we can talk together."

Lasair's mother, close by, stepped forward. "Flanna, my dear, mayhap ye should go wi' your sister. Are there not enough wounds that we should no' heal those we may?"

Flanna began to tremble. "Mistress MacDragh, If ye no longer want me with ye—"

"I did not say that." Mistress MacDragh's gaze met Liadan's with regret and a measure of understanding. "To be sure, ye are welcome wi' us. Perhaps in time—"

Liadan did not stay to hear her sister's further reproaches, or to be pushed further away. Instead she turned and went home, a heaviness on her heart.

Maeve was at the hut and needed but one look at Liadan's face before sitting her down beside the fire.

"Lass, what has happened?"

Liadan put her head in her hands.

"'Tis never Ardahl?"

"Nay. I ha' not seen him."

"Then what?"

"Forgive me. I canna speak of it."

Silence fell between them, but it was an easy silence, one that let Liadan think and breathe. The hut quieted as Maeve prepared a meal, and some of the tension fled from Liadan's body.

"Ardahl should be home from the practice field soon," Maeve remarked softly, at length. "He will be hungry with the working. He always is."

It struck Liadan that Maeve had, in a curious way, got her lost son back again. But only because their world had shifted so completely that nothing was as it had been.

"Mistress MacCormac"—Liadan lowered her hands from her face—"what has become o' our lives?"

Maeve made a soft sound in her throat. "Life has been spun on its head, I do not doubt. The floor pulled out from beneath our feet, and the roof open to the sky."

"I must admit, I canna see my way forward."

"Nay. Mayhap not now. But ye will."

"Every touchstone I had is gone." Should she tell this woman Ardahl had become not so much a touchstone as the rock at the center of her life? That even the word *love* did not describe what she felt for him?

Neither she nor Ardahl had pledged that one thing to each other, *love*.

"We ha' lost much," Maeve agreed. "But let me tell ye somewhat. I thought the worst day o' my life had come when I lost Ardahl." She paused in her work and looked at Liadan. "When he was given to ye and your Mam and taken from me. Now I am with him again. There is always hope. We have lost much, but not hope."

"Aye, so. I did not ask—did Seona's babe survive the ordeal?"

A beautiful smile spread across Maeve's face. "She did. It was, as I said, a hard fight, but Seona has a bonny wee girl at the end."

Sudden longing pierced Liadan's heart. Would she ever have a child of her own? Ardahl's child. It did not seem so.

Yet her heart would cling to him. Even if it meant she must forsake having a husband and a family, a home of her own. She belonged to him, lifelong.

He did not return until late, the practice in the field having stretched long. When he did come, he looked weary, shoulders slumped and skin streaked with sweat.

As was his custom, he deposited his weapons inside the door.

"Mam," he said. But it was at Liadan he looked, and she saw the change come over him as their gazes met, the weariness lifting from him and light seeping in.

He went out to wash. She waited but a moment before snatching up a cloth and a pot of soap and following him.

Around the side of the hut she stood, her back pressed against the wall, and watched him. Watched as he stripped off his tunic and bent over the basin.

He was filthy, and new bruises and scrapes showed on the skin thus revealed. It did not matter. She held out what she'd brought and let her eyes touch him, as her fingers had the night before. There, and there, and *there*.

"A new pot o' soap. Go carefully wi' it. There is not much to spare."

He took the pot and the cloth from her, their hands brushing. She relived the feel of his hand at her breast, the thumb sliding over her before his mouth followed.

"I missed ye," she said. Simple words, but they caused him to stop washing and raise his head, caused the light in his hazel eyes to flare.

"I missed ye also, full well."

Not much of an exchange—it was all she was permitted. Just to have him near her this evening, to watch him wash and eat and smile and speak. It would have to be enough.

To last the rest of her life.

CHAPTER THIRTY-SIX

FEARGHAL DID NOT make any announcement about the planned venture to Brioc. Though it had always been his way to gather his folk and make speeches concerning clan affairs, this time he avoided it, saying, "Our folk ha' endured enough wi'out suffering more uncertainty."

He gathered Dornach and Ardahl and made his plans with them in private. He meant to send a lone messenger to Brihan of Brioc so that Brihan would be expecting him, then journey with but a small party.

As he told Dornach and Ardahl, with a rueful sort of smile, "We do no' want to be mistaken for an attacking force."

Be that as it may, the prospect made Ardahl uneasy. Since Fearghal had assigned Dornach the task of keeping the settlement safe in his absence—also unenviable—only four of them were to make up the party to Brioc. Fearghal himself, an older warrior named Tierney who often advised Fearghal, Ardahl, and Cathair.

The very idea of having Cathair watching his back made the hairs stand up all over Ardahl's body.

Yet Fearghal's mind was set. Moreover, he did not want to waste time, and at the last meeting between the three of them said, "We leave come the morn. I have spoken about it at length wi' Tamald, as well as with my wife. Tamald says the portents are not bad. He has cast the stones thrice. My wife"—he made a face—"is far less happy."

Dornach spoke in a grumble. "Nor, my laird chief, am I. I

would ye might spare yoursel' and let me go in your stead."

"Ye be no' yet healed enough to travel, and ye know it. Besides, if Brihan is to be persuaded, 'twill only be by me. 'Tis I who have forged past agreements wi' the man."

"Aye, Chief Fearghal, but he has already broken one o' those agreements. If somewhat goes wrong and ye fail to return—"

"I ha' discussed that also with the druids and my wife. If I am slain, she and Tamald together will lead the clan until my son, Rhaod, is of an age to assume the place." He gave Ardahl a dour smile. "But Ardahl will be there to assure I am no' slain. Aye, Ardahl?"

"I will do my best." But they might all be slain, the four of them. Dornach was right—Brihan had already offered them treachery. Might he not look on this as an opportunity to offer more?

Dornach gave Ardahl a long and burning glare. He knew how heavy was what Fearghal asked of him.

Ardahl walked home from that meeting slowly, trying to marshal his words. Dark had already fallen. He would not have long to gather his belongings. To make his explanations.

When he entered the hut, Liadan stood bent over the fire, its light washing over her, and he was struck still for a moment, taking her in. The graceful line of chin, throat, and breast. The golden hair hanging down her back and the feeling that reached out to him from her.

Belonging.

She glanced up, and a smile of welcome transfigured her face. "Ye be late."

"I had a meeting wi' the chief." Ardahl laid aside his weapons and ducked back out to wash. She would follow. She usually did.

In the soft dark around the side of the hut, he could barely see the basin. He could barely see Liadan when she joined him, but he could well feel her there.

"I missed ye."

It had become their customary, if private, form of greeting.

This time, though, she moved into his arms.

"Liadan, nay."

"No one can see. Hold me. For a moment. Just hold me."

He did, the need within him arising in answer to her own. Like something precious, he gathered her to him, her head to his heart.

"Liadan." He said it hoarsely. "We must no'—"

"'Tis too dark, I tell ye, to give us away. And I need, I need—"

She kissed him, a simple press of lips to lips with nothing simple in it. And aye, desire came leaping on the heels of that more fundamental wanting, pure and powerful, enough to shake him to his toes.

Such a need as this—what did it mean? How might it be answered?

The kiss lasted forever, and not long enough. He moved away from her, backing off like a man on the edge of a cliff.

She pressed her back once more to the side of the hut. "How was your day?" she asked on a note of teasing, mocking herself for asking something so ordinary after that searing embrace.

"Interesting." He stripped off his tunic and splashed water over himself. He did not want to tell her what he must.

Yet he must.

"I—we—leave in the morning for Brioc, that Chief Fearghal might talk wi' Chief Brihan concerning his betrayal."

She went dead still. No need for her to speak. Ardahl could feel her emotions all too clearly.

"I do not know how long we will be gone. Two days. More. Ye will look after Mam while I am gone?"

"Why ye?" It came as no more than a whisper in the dark.

"The chief has requested it. Because I saved his life on the field, he wishes me at his side. Master Tierney and Cathair come also."

"Cathair! But I do no' trust him."

"Nor do I. 'Tis no' myself, though, doing the choosing."

"Can ye no' persuade Chief Fearghal ye would be better

here?"

"I canna." He said it flatly so she would not hope. She needed to accept his duty.

"Come morning," she whispered.

"Come morning," he answered.

"Should somewhat go wrong there among strangers—"

He laid aside the cloth. "I shall have to lay down my life for my chief. So I am sworn."

When she said nothing, still pressed there against the wall, he stepped up and took her shoulders between his hands.

"Liadan, I want ye to know… An honor it has been to be here wi' ye, in Conall's place. Ye have changed my life. Changed me."

Silent, she went forward into his arms. Clutched him hard.

"Come, we must go inside. I need to tell my mam."

They went in, walking separate, yet not separate. Ardahl sat down beside the fire, and his mam gave him a smile of welcome.

"Ye'll be hungry," she remarked.

He was, and he was not.

"Mam, I ha' something to tell ye, hard news. Come morning, I will accompany the chief on a journey to Brioc. Just a small group o' us, it will be. Fearghal goes to speak wi' Chief Brihan about the future."

"The future," Mam repeated softly.

"Aye. Ye—ye will look after each other, ye and Liadan, while I am gone."

And forever, if need be.

LATER, WHEN MAM went to bed, they pretended they could not hear her weeping. Mam, whom Ardahl had believed never cried. He and Liadan spoke in murmurs, if at all, and at last he made to bed down there by the fire.

"I will stay here with ye," Liadan said.

"Eh?"

"Here, by the fire. As we have in the past, by the door."

He did not argue it. A short span of time they had, before parting.

He lay stretched upon a rug with her beside him, holding his hand. A clasp in the dark that meant so much more than the press of flesh to flesh.

Should he tell her he loved her? Should he, before he went off and perhaps never after had the chance to say so?

What he felt for her was so much more than love.

Before he could make up his mind, she fell asleep with her head against his shoulder and he left her to that peace.

Morning came, and he roused to find her still there beside him. Warm and soft, and smelling of woman. The scent of belonging.

It took all his strength to rise and gather his weapons, and prepare to leave.

He stepped into his mam's sleeping place. "I must go."

She arose and embraced him. "I want ye to know, ye are the best son. The best any woman could hope to have."

"Aye." It was all he could manage.

When he turned for the door, Liadan was on her feet, the morning sun coming in the opening behind her.

"I will walk wi' ye."

"Liadan, I do not think—"

"I will come."

"Best, perhaps, to say farewell here."

Though his mam watched, Ardahl drew Liadan to him. Kissed the palms of her hands, the corners of her mouth, both cheeks, and her forehead.

"Be safe," she implored, and he went out into the morning leaving the better part of his heart behind.

⬥

CHAPTER THIRTY-SEVEN

THEY WENT IN two chariots, Ardahl himself driving the chief's fine cart and Cathair piloting the other with Tiernan aboard. Since there had been no announcement, not many saw them go, but folk who realized what was happening were quick to spread the word.

Some of them ran alongside, asking questions till Dornach came out and called them back.

Save for the rattle of the carts, silence ensued. No one spoke. It was a beautiful morning, and the new sun rising behind them lit the world to gray and green and gold, a pale-washed blue lighter than the color of Liadan's eyes.

A reminder of everything for which they fought. As if he needed it.

They headed for the stream where the last battles had been fought and they would no doubt encounter Brihan's guard, who would either challenge them or let them pass. From there, the gods alone knew what would befall them.

Ardahl needed to be prepared at any moment to lay down his life. Until then, he need only drive, a skill his da had taught to him at knee height. Da had wanted so for him to follow him as a charioteer. If he had, would he be where he stood now?

All warriors should be able to drive, so Da had insisted. A man's driver could well fall in battle and he would need to step in, get himself and perhaps an injured companion safe away.

Da had himself fallen in battle. As had Cullan.

In this world, it seemed there was no safe place to be. But surely Ardahl did not dwell on the question of death as they went, glaring as the possibility was. He thought instead of Liadan. Of seeing her again. Her fair face like a flower, the color coming and going in it like light. Her wide eyes and trembling lips.

In his mind he swore a vow. *I will return to ye. I will always return to ye.*

Should he have repeated that to her before he left? His heart argued so. Yet as a promise, it seemed near impossible to keep. Feeling for her even as he did, what promise could hope to hold across distance and death?

Fearghal murmured something beside him, and Ardahl glanced at the chief. Anchored with both hands clutching the crossbar, he looked tense.

"The border," he said in response to Ardahl's glance.

So it was—the broad swath of earth at the foot of the rise with the stream cutting along it, the water glinting silver. The area, churned and scarred and torn, still showed signs of their battle.

No dead remained. All those had been collected.

Instinctively, Ardahl slowed the ponies. Cathair's cart rattled behind them.

"Where's the guard?"

"I do not know." Fearghal's eyes narrowed. He scanned as far as the eye could see. Brihan's dun was farther on, out of sight.

"Somewhat is amiss." Ardahl's whole body told him so, the very blood beating through his veins. No matter how long the border, Brihan should keep a presence.

"Aye," Fearghal agreed.

Cathair called, "My chief? Do we go on?"

"Aye."

They splashed through the stream, broad and shallow enough here to serve as a ford. A rough track led across the turf beyond, and on up a slope covered with rowan and hazel trees.

An army could wait beyond that rise. Was Ardahl about to

die?

But nay, why would Brihan or even Dacha root an army here? Neither knew their party was on the way.

Not until they'd scaled the hill did Ardahl breathe again. Beyond the rise, they saw—

"Here they come," Fearghal called over his shoulder. "Hands off weapons."

A difficult order to follow, even though the men advancing on them did not at once appear aggressive. They too were aboard a chariot—a patrol, as Ardahl realized. Far more mobile than men afoot.

He drew up again. This time Cathair pulled up beside him, their two chariots abreast. They watched the others come. Brihan's or Dacha's men?

They were Brihan's. Two young warriors wearing his colors. One was fair, one red-haired. Neither looked friendly.

"Halt!" called the fair-headed man, though they had already done so. "Ye be on Chief Brihan's land."

"I am Fearghal MacErst," Fearghal called boldly, "Chief o' the Marren. And I come to speak with Brihan."

The two men exchanged startled glances. The one on the left, who had half drawn his sword, thrust it back into the loop at his belt.

"Did Chief Brihan call for ye?" the other asked.

"Nay. I come to speak o' the alliance between us."

That alliance, informal as it may have been, surely lay shattered now, broken by Brihan's attack upon the settlement. Yet neither of these young men was versed in such matters.

"Will ye give us safe passage to his dun?" Fearghal requested.

They conferred with one another, low, fierce tones before the first said, "Aye. Follow us."

"Hands off weapons," Fearghal said again to Cathair, and they rolled out.

In all his life, Ardahl had never been to the heart of Brihan's holdings. He'd fought in many a battle on the perimeter—he and

Conall had—but that had been against Dacha's rather than Brihan's own men.

He'd imagined one holding must be much like another and that the folk here lived as he did, more or less. But as they rattled their way in past dwellings, enclosures, and other structures beneath the warm sun, he saw signs of lack and want that surprised him.

The people turned and stared as they passed. Some looked ragged. The children had hungry looks in their eyes.

Why? The land gave much in game. There should be no reason for such want.

A further presence of a guard showed here—warriors came running. Their train halted as the escort consulted with them. A man ran ahead. Informing Brihan of their arrival, no doubt.

They drew up at length before a hall, a good, stout one. By the time they reached it, a crowd followed, and Brihan himself stood out front, surrounded by his men.

Ah, and would the battle take place here, then? The one in which Ardahl spent his life? If so, it would be fight and die. No getting away out of here safely.

Brihan did not appear pleased to see them. A man of early middle years, he had reddish hair already beginning to gray and a broad build, not much above ordinary height. He had come out in his house clothes—no armor—though he did wear a sword.

"Chief Fearghal!" he called without any welcome. "Did I send for ye?" A hint of irony hung in the words.

Fearghal grimaced in answer. "Chief Brihan." If Fearghal felt great anger over this man's treachery, he did not show it. "We need to speak together. I request safe conduct that we may do so."

Brihan exchanged a look with the man at his shoulder, an advisor, no doubt. Much hung on what he would next say. If he rejected Fearghal's request and called up his warriors, a battle would ensure. A short, sharp battle.

He did not reply with words. Instead he swept his arm out in a gesture inviting them in.

CHAPTER THIRTY-EIGHT

THE INTERIOR OF Brihan's hall bustled with people, so Ardahl saw when they went in. Some must be extended family. He saw several women, a few with children. A number of servants. Warriors. Advisors? It seemed more a meeting place than a fine dwelling.

Ah, but who were they to judge? Their own hall lay blackened and burned.

"Abban," Brihan called to a servant. "Bring drink. Clear us a place at the fire."

Clear us a place apparently meant chasing those already there away. A couple of old men. Two children and three women, one of whom cast a horrified look at Ardahl's group before stepping up to Brihan and beginning an intent conversation.

The four of them waited, Ardahl's spine tingling at the threat of attack from behind. It seemed Brihan was willing to talk, but anything could happen. It could end very badly indeed.

Ardahl did not want to die in this foreign, slightly squalid place out of sight of the sky.

Brihan reassured the woman—his wife?—and she left. The other occupants of the hall trickled out also.

Brihan turned to his visitors, hard eyed. "Will ye sit?"

They did so, Fearghal and Brihan together, Ardahl, Cathair, and Tiernan slightly behind, like guards. Though how they could hope to safely guard their charge, Ardahl could not tell.

A hundred things might happen. A charge. A rush. Poisoned

fare, he thought as a servant stepped up with a flask. Their ponies might be slain so they could not get away.

Nearly impossible for him to keep his hand from his weapon in such circumstances, but he managed. No need to appear threatening.

"Chief Fearghal," Brihan said when they were all seated, "ye ha' surprised me wi' your arrival here today. I must admit, ye ha' balls—or a surfeit o' foolish temerity."

"Have I?" Fearghal peered into his cup, clearly wondering whether or not to drink.

"Och, aye."

"At one time," Fearghal said slowly and clearly, "I would have been certain of my welcome in your hall. That was before ye turned against me and mine."

Brihan gave a grunt at that, nothing more.

"We had an alliance," Fearghal began.

"We never had an alliance."

"No' a formal one, mayhap. But 'twas understood between us we would live in peace aside one another, whatever happened around us."

"Circumstances change."

"Indeed, they do. Now ye send your men to attack and murder innocents while our warriors are otherwise engaged."

Brihan's face grew carefully blank, but a muscle jumped in his cheek. He said nothing.

"It is a betrayal," Fearghal declared. "Of trust, if naught more."

"I regret this, but we had no formal alliance."

"'Twas given that I would no' attack yours and ye would no' attack mine. Brihan"—Fearghal leaned forward slightly—"wha' happened?"

Brihan raised brown eyes to Fearghal's face in a level stare. He did not speak.

"Ha' ye made an alliance wi' Chief Dacha that supersedes our own?"

"Nay." Violently, Brihan shook his head. "I ha' no alliance wi' him either. No' as such. I stand alone."

"'As such'?" Fearghal asked.

"Dacha is a strong neighbor. A dangerous one. This season, he has grown more so."

Ardahl, watching Fearghal carefully, saw his eyes narrow. Brihan's position—pinned between Dacha, who wanted Fearghal's lands, and Fearghal, who refused to give up those lands—had, aye, long been a perilous one. Yet he had managed to balance there.

What had changed?

Fearghal clearly wondered. "Chief Brihan, had your neighbor become so strong as to threaten ye and your tribe, I should hope ye would turn to me."

"Would ye? Would ye, so?"

"Aye."

"Well, ye would be wrong."

"Why?" Fearghal lowered his voice. "Brihan, ye should ha' known I would aid ye. 'Tis in my best interest."

"No' perchance in mine."

What does that mean? Ardahl pondered as a servant came in, offering food and more drink. Brihan waved him away.

Ardahl's back twitched. He felt sure they were being watched.

"Dacha," Fearghal pressed, "makes a gey dangerous neighbor."

"Ye can see that, can ye?"

"Aye, I can see that. Yet long ha' ye held that place and no' raised a hand against us. Now ye come spilling blood. Ye must know I ha' to retaliate."

That brought Brihan's gaze to Fearghal's face.

"We, who were once friends," Fearghal pushed, "are now enemies. I wished for the sake o' old understandings to talk wi' ye first."

Emotions moved suddenly in Brihan's stern face, as if it

would crack. Grief filled his eyes.

In a voice so low Ardahl could barely hear it, he said, "He has my young son. Dacha does. Taken wi' a number of other lads at the beginning o' spring. Out larking, they were, on our own lands. He has but ten winters."

A deadly silence fell.

Savagely now, Brihan said, "The other lads, three o' them, ha' all been sent back one by one. Slain. No' just slain but killed in—in the cruelest o' ways. They suffered before they died."

Children.

"Ah," Fearghal said.

Brihan's gaze once more came up to meet Fearghal's. "The message was clear. 'Tis no' an alliance I ha' wi' Dacha but a kind o' *geis.*"

"Have ye tried to get your lad back?"

"How? He is at the heart o' Dacha's stronghold. One wrong move on my part—he will be dead afore we reach him."

"Aye."

"Ye must see, Fearghal, that while I did no' want to raise a weapon against ye, and while there is nay honor in it—"

"I do see, aye." Fearghal also had young children.

"My wife—" For an instant, Brihan's voice failed him. "She is distraught. Ill wi' it. She saw the bodies o' the lads returned."

"As any good mother would be."

"He is my only son. We ha' a crop o' daughters, but—"

"I am certain that despite his torment o' the others, Dacha is treating him well. 'Tis in his best interest to do so, aye? If your son dies, Dacha loses his hold over ye."

"I do try to believe that."

Fearghal scowled. A hostage made for a perilous situation.

"Dacha," said Brihan abruptly, "has made up his mind to conquer all of Armagh. From his own lands to the sea. He has ambitions about which he is no' shy of boasting—to rival the *Ard Ri* himself. His druids and mine have cast stones in his favor. What am I to do?"

"If he conquers my lands, Brihan, he will take yours also."

"He will leave me to the last, until I am o' no' more use to him. Then he will no' only cut my son's throat, but mine."

"Will ye sit still for it?"

"What choice have I?"

"Ye should ha' come to me. Come in secret if need be. We might—"

Brihan shook his head. "He is too powerful. He has eyes. Some o' my own men, I do no' doubt, have been bought or threatened. He will know ye ha' been here. I only hope it does no' cost Donen's life."

Fearghal clapped the man on the shoulder. "Chief Brihan, I do no' wish to be at war wi' ye."

"Nor I wi' ye."

"But it, aye, does seem the way the stones are cast."

Brihan said nothing. An agony lay in his eyes.

"Will ye at least gi' us safe conduct from your lands?"

"Aye, I will. Go home, Fearghal. Set your defenses. Set them well."

The meeting at an end, they arose and made their way from the hall, past all the staring faces that waited outside.

It seemed they would get away alive after all.

No one spoke until they had mounted their chariots and ridden off, when Fearghal turned to Ardahl and said, "Who can blame a man for loving his son?"

Who, indeed?

Not until they reached home, when the two chariots rolled into the settlement and they disembarked, did Ardahl find Cathair at his shoulder.

He turned, half startled, to face Cathair's fierce blue eyes.

"I suppose ye think yoursel' somewhat to brag of, Ardahl MacCormac, wi' your place at the chief's side. But I am here to warn ye. Ye would do well all the same to watch your back."

CHAPTER THIRTY-NINE

D ARK HAD BEGUN to gather on the backs of the hills before Fearghal's party returned. Liadan, who had found excuses to roam around the settlement throughout the day, was near the spring when the first cries came. Despite the chief's desire for a measure of secrecy, members of the guard had been watching all day. They passed the word ahead of the arriving party, into the settlement.

Though Liadan ran forward, she was not the only one and could not get close—not close enough. Did they come whole, injured, or on their shields? Would she see both chariots?

Aye. When she glimpsed the heads of all four ponies and the men in the carts, she near fell down with the power of her relief.

The chief was there, already giving orders. And aye—Ardahl beside him. She could not glimpse him easily with so many in the way, but he moved briskly. She caught sight of him leaping down, then pausing as a tall man with very fair hair spoke to him.

Cathair.

Despite her glorious happiness at having Ardahl back, a chill went through her.

"They ha' returned, then?"

Maeve stood beside her, composed and quiet, only the light in her eyes betraying her happiness.

"Aye."

"We will let him finish wi' his chief and come to us, eh?"

"Cathair is there. I do no' trust Cathair."

Maeve looked at her.

As soon as Cathair stepped away, a woman bulled her way forward and greeted him. Even from a distance she looked haughty and beautiful.

Brasha.

Liadan lost sight of the pair when Ardahl stepped through the crowd, Conall's sword in his hand, eyes searching. Searching. He found them and came directly to join them.

"Mam. Mistress Liadan." Calm words with nothing calm about them.

"Son, I am happy to see ye returned. Ye will be hungry."

"Aye."

"Come ye home wi' us."

Liadan ached to touch him, longed to press herself into his arms, but could not. Not even his mam embraced him here in front of so many onlookers.

So she paced sedately at his side, just absorbing his presence. The scent of him in the soft gloaming. Each and every breath he took.

"How went the talk at Brioc?" Maeve asked.

"I will explain anon."

No other words passed among them. When they reached the hut, Liadan turned to him at last.

"Gi' me your weapons. Go and wash."

He nodded and unburdened himself into her hands. Maeve ducked inside. Liadan followed, but only long enough to lay the weapons aside.

"Go," Maeve told her then.

Liadan caught up with Ardahl round the side of the hut, where she helped him remove his tunic. And there, in the soft dark, she moved into his arms.

"I was so afraid."

"Aye."

They kissed, every other consideration flown before the urgency of it. The terrible, unceasing longing inside her eased.

"Liadan." He trapped her face between his hands. Too dark to see one another clearly, but she did not need to see what she could feel. "I should ha' told ye before I left—"

That he loved her? Would he speak that word?

"'Tis well, Ardahl. I know."

"Do ye?" He kissed one side of her mouth in that way he had, then the other. Her forehead, her eyes, as if the kisses were blessings. "Do ye?"

"I believe my heart knows. Here—wash yoursel', come in, and take your rest."

She stood there while he scrubbed down, unable to pull herself away.

"Was the meeting most terrible?"

"Aye. The news is no' mine to tell."

"Your mam will say naught. Nor will I. Are we in trouble?"

He straightened from the basin and used the cloth she handed him to dry off. "Deep trouble, aye."

She puffed out a breath. What had become of her world? What, since Conall's death?

No matter. Ardahl remained in her world. She could endure anything.

THEY ATE BESIDE the fire, the three of them together, and Ardahl told them in a low, even voice what had taken place at Brioc.

As might be expected, the first thing Mam said when Ardahl finished was, "And who would blame the man? His son."

"Still and all, it does naught to help our position."

"What will Chief Fearghal do?"

"Set a strong guard, I imagine, even as Brihan suggested. But"—Ardahl hesitated—"'tis summer. I believe Dacha will make best use o' the season. He will try to finish his task while the weather does hold."

"Conquer us, ye mean?" Liadan stared at him, her beautiful eyes wide.

"We are in peril indeed," Mam whispered, and shot Ardahl a look that spoke of her love for him. "But at least ye ha' returned to us safely, aye? Let us look no further than that now."

Difficult not to look farther, though. In Ardahl's head, he could see Dacha's warriors arrayed, ready to cross Brihan's lands and swoop in upon them. Countless chariots. Many, many fighting men. Could they withstand it?

When they finished their meal, Mam tidied away the remains before getting to her feet. "I ha' just remembered," she announced abruptly, "I promised to call in upon Mistress Maehan, who does not feel well." She eyed the couple beside the fire kindly. "I'd best go to her. And I do no' doubt she will want me to sit wi' her all the night."

Ardahl did his best not to look at Liadan.

"But Mistress MacCormac," Liadan half babbled, "are ye certain?"

"Aye, I am that. I am sorry to say ye will no' see me before morning."

She knew, Ardahl thought. She knew how he felt for Liadan. Guessed what they would do here alone tonight. A staggering wave of gratitude hit him.

Mam bent and embraced him. "Son, I am so glad to have ye home."

She gathered a few things into a basket and went out softly. Liadan arose from the fireside and tied the door curtain shut behind her. When she turned back to Ardahl, her face was alight.

"That was kind of her."

"Aye."

"D'ye think she knows—"

"I hope not but—aye, I expect so."

"D'ye think anyone else will come looking for ye this night? Asking about the meeting, or guard duty, perhaps."

"I expect they would sooner go to the chief."

"Then"—she came and knelt beside him—"'tis a gift she has given us."

"Aye. Liadan, I want—"

"As do I. I have been famished, Ardahl, for the taste o' ye. Hungry for the feel. Do no' say nay."

He would not. He could not. But first…

He caught her shoulders between his hands. "After I left this morning, I regretted no' saying all I wished to ye."

She leaned forward so her lips were but a breath from his, so her eyes gazed deep into his eyes.

"Wha' is there to say?"

"That whatever happens now or in the future, whether I live or die—I will return to ye, Liadan. Somehow, I will find ye. Even if I have to search this world and the other world."

She made a gusty sound in her throat. "That sounds like a promise."

"It is. A promise. A vow. One the gods themselves will help me to keep."

"Och, Ardahl, I will wait for ye—forever if I must. This also do I promise."

"Aye, then, lass. Aye."

His relief at the words given was overwhelmed when she moved into his arms, when her mouth met his. He went over backward with her atop him, a wondrous armful of warmth.

"But for now, Ardahl, we are together. And we have all the night long."

CHAPTER FORTY

T HE NIGHT DID not prove long enough, at least not in Liadan's estimation. Even though she had her mouth all over Ardahl, kissed him from head to toe. Even though she begged him— begged—to give all of himself to her, that she might keep part of him. Even when she had him more than once inside her, filling her in a way she could not begin to understand, satisfying spirit as well as flesh.

Even though the scent of him became part of her. Morning would come. It was not enough. Especially if—

If this were to be their last night ever. For Liadan did not know what would happen. And she had learned that terrible things might come at any time.

They lay twined together, naked beside the hearth, when dawn came creeping under the door curtain, for they had never made it any distance from the fire. Ardahl dozed with her cradled against his chest, and she lay listening to his heart while the morning stole in.

Such a strong and yet fragile thing to keep a man alive, a heartbeat. So easy to stop. His, so essential to her world.

"Ardahl." She spoke just to say his name.

"Um?"

"Your mam will be coming home soon. We should arise."

"Aye. And I do not doubt I will be assigned to a place in the guard."

"Away from me."

"Away." He ran his fingers through her hair. "Yet no' away."

She raised her head and looked into his face. His beloved face. His glorious face, so perfect, so dear to her with its sculpted planes and the sad, sweet smile hovering in his eyes.

"Tell me, how am I to behave when I meet ye beyond these walls? As if ye do not matter? As if I canna still taste ye on my lips? As if ye be no more than a brother to me?"

"Och, lass." He brushed her cheek with his thumb. "Ye will because ye must."

"If I act indifferent to ye, if I turn away and behave coldly, 'tis only because I am afraid that if I look at ye, what I feel will show."

"I understand." A rueful smile quirked his lips. "I will remember."

"Remember," she urged. "Remember every part of this night."

"Until I am dead, and beyond."

"Do no' speak that word."

"Forgive me, lass. Death and a final parting do not exist between us."

"So they do not! We have agreed. I belong to ye, Ardahl MacCormac, in a way I never imagined belonging to any man. My body does, as ye ha' been assured this night. My life. My very spirit."

"Och, Liadan, lass." He closed his eyes for an instant as if absorbing the beauty of it. "Then wha' have we to fear?"

Plenty, as Liadan discovered when she was up on her feet. When they were washed and dressed and she had braided his hair for him, her fingers lingering over the task. When she tied back the leather door curtain and the world came rushing back in.

Voices, calls across the settlement, the whinny of a pony, the wail of a small child. Soon, aye, Maeve would come. Her presence would change everything, dispel the magic woven last night.

"Cathair went with us yesterday," Ardahl said in a low voice as he drank the broth she gave him.

"Aye?"

"When we reached home again, he made a threat. I should rather say, he warned me. To watch my back." He lifted his gaze to Liadan's face. "Liadan, I am convinced, more than ever, he had somewhat to do wi' Conall's death."

"As am I. Him and Brasha."

"Aye, but how?"

"I do not know. Brasha had been working her wiles on Conall."

"Had him in the palm o' her hand."

"Aye. D'ye think—" Liadan hesitated, tentative in her words and her thoughts. "D'ye think she somehow turned Conall against ye? Spoke in his ear, perhaps. Whispered—I do not know. Lies."

Ardahl's eyes—clear hazel in the morning light—met hers. "'Tis possible, aye. The same has been in the back o' my mind. But why—"

"Cathair. If Brasha is under his thumb even as my brother was under hers—and if Cathair wanted rid o' ye…"

Ardahl drew himself up. Before he could speak to accept or refute the idea, his mother appeared outside the door, her basket over her arm. She shot a quick look from one to the other of them, bright and perceptive, before sweeping the inside of the hut with a glance.

"Is all well here?"

"Aye, Mam." Quickly, Ardahl gathered up his weapons. "I must off to the practice or whatever other duty Dornach assigns me."

"Ye ha' had no breakfast but that broth," Liadan protested.

"I ha' all I need." For an instant his gaze seared her, blessed her, before he ducked away into the morning.

A marked silence fell once he'd gone. Maeve put down her basket and unwound the shawl from her head.

"Liadan, I am thinking ye and I need to speak together."

"Och, aye?"

Maeve, avoiding Liadan's gaze, gave a frown. "Ye are without a mother o' your own, and as I ha' more or less stepped into the place—well. Ardahl is my son and I adore him, but when a young lass begins lying down wi' a man, there are things that should be said."

"Are there?"

"Yes."

Liadan turned to face her. "Ye adore him. As do I. I do no' believe there is more to be said."

Maeve's expression softened. "But Liadan, the situation—"

"The situation is, aye, unfortunate. Dire and desperate. Each time he walks away from me, I canna be sure I will see him again. If an attack will come. If Fearghal will take it into his head to ride out and beard Dacha once more. If he will come back in the bottom o' his chariot."

"Aye, so. That is why I left the two o' ye alone last night, exactly why. That ye might ha' some time, at least."

"Precious time."

"But then while away, I got to thinking. I should no' ha' left ye. What if there is a child? What would ye do then?"

"There will not be." Liadan flushed scarlet. "He was careful."

Maeve gusted out a breath. "Aye, so, for I can scarcely think o' a worse disaster."

Liadan could. Quite easily, she could. Truth be known, she ached to bear Ardahl's child, a miraculous and physical proof of the ties that existed between them. It would be the most natural of things.

Bitterly, she said, "In the old days before—before Conall's death, it would have been well accepted for me to wed with my brother's closest friend. Accepted and approved. Ardahl did no' so much as look at me then."

"I do no' doubt he thought o' ye as a wee girl. Growing up around ye as he did."

"I never thought o' him as a brother. I admired him always and thought him the best man this clan had to offer. Is that not a cruel thing? For now he is my brother. And forbidden to me."

"He is the best this clan has to offer," Maeve insisted quietly. "He shall prove himself so, the first among Fearghal's warriors despite any disgrace heaped upon him."

Aye, and Cathair had not counted on that. Liadan had no doubt that Cathair and Brasha together had schemed to bring Ardahl down.

She had only to prove it.

If Ardahl gave his life for this clan—and well he might—if the unbearable happened and she lost him for good, it should not be in disgrace.

There could be no child. Theirs was not a world, by any means, into which a babe should be born. She'd just better accept that fact and be done.

CHAPTER FORTY-ONE

"**I** WOULD LIKE a word wi' ye."

Brasha started when Liadan spoke in her ear, and swung around in surprise. Her eyes, a glorious gray blue, widened with surprise before narrowing in a guarded expression, and she tossed a head full of thick brown curls.

As usual, Brasha haunted the wall at the practice field in the company of her particular friends, watching the men at work. In Liadan's opinion, the lot of them could do something far more useful, mind some of the children or help with the ongoing clearing of the settlement.

That did not matter now.

Liadan herself had stopped by the field at noontime with a bite of food for Ardahl, only to set eyes on him for a moment. To catch the reflection of his smile, if he gave her one in gratitude.

He had not been there, though—the gods alone knew where he was. Impulse took her to Brasha's side.

"Aye, so?" Brasha said. "Ye wish to speak to me?"

"If ye can spare a moment or two."

Thoughts moved quickly in Brasha's eyes as she wondered what Liadan might have to say. "Aye, so," she said again with a glance for her companions. "What is it?"

"Let us walk."

Liadan did not want any of the other girls hearing. They squawked like birds and had even less discretion.

Brasha made a sound of protest but moved away at Liadan's

side. Liadan saw her cast a glance at Cathair, who worked at the far end of the field.

"How long ha' ye been seeing Cathair?" Liadan asked once they were clear away. "Since before ye were with my brother?"

Brasha gave her a swift glance, hesitated but a moment before she said, "What is it to ye?"

"I loved Conall very much. I suppose I still feel protective o' his interests. Did he know ye were no' true to him?"

"True to him? To Conall?" Brasha said with astonishment. "Who said I ever was?"

"He thought so. He believed it. He was in love wi' ye."

Brasha gave Liadan a look from the corners of her catlike eyes. "Any number o' young men are in love wi' me."

The flash of anger that shot up through Liadan shocked her. "Conall thought ye were his alone."

"I never told him so."

"Nay?"

"To be sure, no. Can I help what thoughts get in a man's head once he lies wi' a woman?"

That caused another sort of pang. Had Conall—sunny, even-tempered Conall—felt toward this woman what she felt for Ardahl after being with him, touching him, tasting him? Her heart convulsed in pity.

"So," she said weightily, "ye did lie wi' my brother. Why? Why, if ye did no' love him?"

Another look, sharper this time. "Och, Liadan, ye cannot be such an innocent as all that. D'ye think a woman has to feel love before she lifts her skirt for a man? There are plenty o' other reasons."

"Like what?"

"Your brother was a nice lad. A sweet lad. And I am a generous woman."

Was that what she called it? "He wanted to handfast wi' ye."

"Did he? And how d'ye know that? Did he tell ye so?"

"He did not need to. I knew my brother, the kind o' man he

was. Honorable. I could see by the way he spoke o' ye that he had given his heart."

Brasha snorted. "Honor! 'Tis overrated."

"Ye might well say so, if ye have none."

Brasha stopped walking and turned to face Liadan. "Your brother is dead and gone—killed by his closest friend. So what does it matter now, what he felt for me?" She tipped her head to one side. "It must be terrible for ye, having the very monster who killed Conall living wi' ye, taking his place. How ever d'ye bear it?"

Liadan could not speak, her anger too bright.

Brasha shrugged and answered herself. "I suppose we bear what we must."

"How long ha' ye been seeing Cathair, Brasha? I want to know."

Thoughts again moved in Brasha's eyes like light on water. "I can see whomever I wish. Stop seeing whomever I wish and go back to him after. What did ye expect me to do once your brother died? Grieve forever? Go to my grave as an old woman alone?"

"So far as I can see, ye did no' grieve at all."

Brasha shrugged. "Ye must have seen me, at his grave."

"I saw somewhat." It might have been a braw show.

"Your brother was a sweet lad, as I say. 'Tis a pity he had to die."

Had to die? What did she mean by that?

"Would ye ha' married him, if he'd lived?"

An amused smile danced over Brasha's lips. "Probably not. The ties that bind also tie a woman down, do they no'?"

And besides, then how could she have gone back to Cathair?

Liadan felt sure Brasha had used her brother. To damage Ardahl, no doubt. But how?

"I pray," she told Brasha viciously, "your misdeeds come back upon ye and that ye pay for them."

Carelessly, Brasha tossed her head. "Do we no' all pay for our misdeeds, in the end?"

"WHERE WERE YE this day?" Liadan asked as soon as Ardahl entered the hut at nightfall. "I came to the training field at noontime hoping for—well, hoping. Ye were no' there."

He slid his gaze over her, head to toe, intimate as a touch. If he ever looked at her that way out in the open, they would be undone. "I met wi' the chief and Dornach for a time. Then I was assigned to the border."

"The border? Which one?"

"The west."

The west. From whence trouble might well come at any time.

Ardahl set his weapons beside the door. "Where is my mam?"

"Here." Mam stuck her head out from one of the sleeping places. "I ha' saved your supper."

"I will go and wash."

Liadan followed him because she could do nothing else. She stood up against the wall of the hut with her hands tucked behind her so she could not touch. Just to be near him.

Her gaze followed his every movement as he stripped down. She had kissed him there. And *there*. And—

The taste of him flooded her tongue, and her heart beat so hard, it shook her whole body.

"Ye sat in wi' the chief?" she asked, in an effort to distract herself.

"And his advisors."

"Are ye one o' his advisors now?"

He stopped splashing long enough to look up at her. "I am no' certain what I am."

"Fearghal holds ye in some esteem, despite—despite everything."

"He is trying to decide how to handle the present situation wi' Dacha and Brihan."

"Aye, so. Will ye go to war?"

"'Tis possible."

"Ardahl. How will I bear it?"

He shook his head, and his plaits—the same she had fastened that morning—beat upon his broad back like the traces on a pony.

"I spoke wi' Brasha today."

"Ye what?"

"I challenged her about her feelings for Conall. The woman is a—Well, I know but one word for that, and I will no' speak it."

Ardahl gave a harsh laugh. "I did try to warn him—Conall. He would hear none o' it. She besotted him."

"I believe she had a reason. That she and Cathair are indeed in it together. I just canna tell how."

Ardahl said nothing.

"If they had some scheme to ruin ye, it must be driving them half wild to see ye so close to the chief now. D'ye think that is why Cathair told ye to watch your back?"

"I have little doubt." He began to dry off.

Liadan stepped forward and took the cloth from him, then finished the task tenderly, running it over his bare chest and arms.

In a whisper she said, "I must be wi' ye again. Somehow. All day long I ha' been hard put to think o' anything else."

"As have I." His hands chased hers, but only to take away the cloth. "Liadan, we cannot."

"But—"

"We cannot."

He spoke the words with great regret. Unmovable. Everything she desired there in the half dark.

"Best accept it, *alanna*," he whispered. "Best accept it."

CHAPTER FORTY-TWO

ARDAHL STOOD IN the dark amid a stand of hazel trees with his sword—Conall's sword—in his hand. It had to be past midnight. Beyond the twisted branches of the trees, stars glittered in a field of deep blue, the vault of sky suggesting eternity. There was no moon.

A good night for attack.

Two days had passed since he'd warned Liadan off, there outside the hut, and he'd barely seen her since. Dornach had switched him to night guard, the post he now filled. During the day he slept and kept busy on the training field or sat in meetings with the chief.

Though he ached to see Liadan, at the same time he could not bear seeing her. If he saw her, he would want to touch.

Besides, if anyone observed them together, their secret would be out. The lass was not good at hiding her feelings. Each time he looked at her, he could see everything they had shared together. Every touch. Every kiss, each quiver of flesh. He wanted her unceasingly, but not so much as he missed her. The simple comfort of being in her presence. Catching the smile in her eyes…

He snatched his attention back to the present when he heard a rustle, not far off. Just a fox. No gleam of starlight on weapons. If invaders did come—

He spared a thought for his mam and Liadan, there alone in the hut. He should be there to protect them. Lay his life down for them if need be. As Conall would have done. He had taken Conall's place, had he not? Could he do any less? Any more? Meanwhile, Liadan had his sword. Some manner of protection…

As for his love for Liadan—could this be called love? It seemed so much more. Deeper. And higher. He carried her within him now, which, curiously, did not assuage the longing.

After this night's duty, if the morning came without an attack, he would be able to see her, at least for a short while. She might come out with him while he washed. Sit with him while he ate.

The promise of it would be enough to keep him alive.

Another rustle and he turned toward it. A movement amid the trees had his sword up hard.

"All quiet?" Cieran, his neighbor on the picket.

"By the gods, Cieran, I near took your head off."

"Sorry. I am jumpy tonight. What a night for an attack, eh? But I can hear nothing."

Ardahl nodded. Much easier to hear than see in the dark.

"D'ye think Dacha will be coming?" Cieran asked.

"Aye. 'Tis but a question o' when."

A bit diffidently—for he was among those who had denounced Ardahl after Conall's death—Cieran asked, "Ye are close to the chief, are ye no'? D'ye think he will send us to war?"

Ardahl did not know. He did not think Fearghal had yet made up his mind. Was marching out to the attack better than sitting and waiting to be attacked?

"Either way," he said heavily, "'twill be this season. Dacha is no' a patient man."

"Aye."

"Best get off, lest someone hears us talking." A sword in the dark could end a life quite easily.

Cieran left. Another rustle had Ardahl spinning the other way. If Cathair wanted to put a knife in his back, here was as good an opportunity as any.

Watch your back.

He imagined he heard those words again there in the dark,

and spun to find himself alone. Aye, like Cieran, he was jumpy tonight.

He stood, feet spread, and forced himself to breathe quietly and evenly the way he and Conall had practiced before a battle when waiting to begin the fight. Moments when uncertainty could lay hold of a man and ruin him, if he let it.

He tried to see ahead into the future, but it was like peering through the murk at the bottom of a tarn.

Fearghal was a good chief, a strong man in his own right. Ardahl liked him. Trusted him. Dornach quickly healed from his dire injuries and would soon be back to practice adding his strength to their number, which Ardahl found vastly reassuring. Was that what Fearghal awaited before making any plans? Or did he merely await the clan's partial recovery from the past attacks?

On the other side of the scale from Dacha's ill intent was Cathair's. Bad enough to fear the blade of the enemy without that of a fellow clansman.

For Cathair was no friend.

Only one thing for certain. There would be blood. There would be blood in the end.

WHEN HE WALKED home through the morning light, having been relieved of his duty, he still felt uncertain. His spirits lifted when he saw Liadan waiting for him outside the door. Och, she pretended to be sweeping out the hut, but her eyes were watchful, and when she caught sight of him, her whole demeanor changed.

His step quickened. His heart lifted. When he reached her, she ceased plying the broom and regarded him.

Och, and she should not look at him so. The whole world would see.

"All quiet?" she asked.

"Aye, for the moment. Liadan, ye should not—"

"Keep the hut clean?" Her gaze challenged him. "Here, give me your weapons and go wash. Your mam is not here at the moment."

His pulse leaped. Might they have the gift of a short time alone? But it was daylight. Anyone might come to the door. Anyway, he'd told her they dare not be together again.

Meekly, he handed over his weapons. Went around the side of the hut.

She did not join him, and he drowned his disappointment in the cool water. When he entered the hut, still damp, she waited beside the fire and stepped past him to tie shut the door curtain.

"Liadan, we cannot—"

"Let me have this. Please, only let me have this."

She came forward, stepping into his arms, and clutched him hard. His heartbeat accelerated alarmingly, and yet it was pure bliss. All the ache, all the longing drained from him, to be replaced by a searing physical desire.

For time unmeasured they stood so, her cheek pressed to his shoulder, arms wound around him, his arms wrapping her tight.

At last she murmured, "Each and every time ye go from me, I wonder if I will see ye again. Be wi' ye again."

"Aye." He drew her still closer, wanting to feel her against him. "Life is full o' comings and goings. We never know when."

"Your mam will no' be back till—"

"Liadan, we cannot." But he wanted her. He wanted her naked here beside the fire, or anywhere else in the hut. Longed to be inside her and so end the fierce ache that plagued him.

She lifted her face and kissed him. The sweetness of it flooded his senses, eroded his caution. The taste of her filled him, both a gift and a temptation.

"I need ye inside me."

He needed that too.

"Each time may be our last."

"If we should be discovered—"

"They'll think ye sleeping after night duty. Ye often do sleep in the mornings."

"With ye at my side?"

"Ardahl." She gazed into his eyes, speaking now without words, a second language so magical he heard it with his heart.

If his mam came—well, Mam knew how they felt about each other. Had she not given them an opportunity to be alone? Anyone else…

"Liadan." He caught her face between his palms. "'Tis a terrible risk."

"I do not care."

"If one o' Cathair's cronies should be watching us—"

"I do not care!"

"*Alanna*, ye must." He did not want to deny her or himself. But they existed on the edge of a knife's blade. "'Tis dangerous."

"'Tis dangerous each and every time ye step outside that door," she told him. "Every time I watch ye walk away from me to go on guard. Take up your sword to fight for the clan once again. Each time ye stand in the dark, prey to Cathair's blade. Ardahl, Ardahl, gift me this."

Unable to deny her, he took her hand and led her to her parents' sleeping place.

CHAPTER FORTY-THREE

L IADAN LAY WITH her cheek on Ardahl's bare chest, limp with contentment. How long had they been here this way? She needed to get up and dress herself. Leave the sleeping bench so he might rest after his long night. Go about her day.

But for the life of her, she could not move. Could not deny this precious feeling of stunning rightness. Of completion. Her world falling from chaos to a place she could understand.

All she could hear was Ardahl's heartbeat. All she knew was him.

She'd unbraided his hair when first they lay down on the bench together. After they'd removed their clothing. Before she'd kissed him all over with a ravenous hunger that shocked her. She wanted the scent of him. The salt and taste of soap on his skin. The pearls of moisture her tongue found when she took him in her mouth.

She'd half wanted to end it there, to steal the wild, transforming taste of him. But she needed him inside her still more.

Now she could feel the softness of his hair beneath her fingers, and the hairs of his chest. Could smell him, a scent both satisfying and arousing.

This man. This one above all others. No man would ever exist for her besides him. Not even if she were born and died a thousand times.

"Liadan?" He cradled her head, but strained beneath her. "We had best—"

"One more moment."

"Ah, darling—"

Despite the uncertainty, the fear and dread, she smiled. "Call me that again."

"Darling. *Alanna.* Love."

Her breath caught impossibly in her chest. Tipping up her face, she looked at him. He lay on his back like a man slain. Had she killed him? His uncertainty, his doubt? Had she, even though it was he who had pierced her to the very spirit?

"Am I?" His love.

"Ye know that ye are. Now and forever."

She let out a sigh and put her cheek back against his warm skin.

"But if I am to look after ye—we must arise."

"Go back to behaving as if we mean naught to one another."

"Aye."

"Mayhap ye should talk about how annoying I am, when ye be with the other men."

"What makes ye think I do no'?" He ran his hands through her hair. "Ah, no. No one could ever believe ye annoying."

"Ardahl, I have something to ask ye."

"Then ask me when we are up and dressed, while ye give me my breakfast."

"Aye." She rolled atop him and scooted up his body even as he framed her face between his palms. "But first gi' me my blessing."

"Eh?"

"Ye know how ye do it. Kiss me."

A smile appeared in his eyes, twin sparks of light. He bestowed the kisses, one in each palm, at each corner of her mouth, each cheek, the center of her forehead. "There."

"Now I may live. Till next time."

They dressed, and she opened the door curtain so that anyone passing could see they but sat by the fire. That she gave him breakfast. As a sister might.

"What did ye wish to ask o' me?" he inquired.

"First, promise ye will no' say nay."

He laughed, a sound so rare it sent a spur of delight up her spine. "How can I do that?"

"By trusting me. Ye do trust me?"

Their eyes met in a long look. "Wi' my life. And beyond."

"Well, then." She drew a breath. "I want ye to teach me to fight. I ha' your sword. I need to know how to use it. Should another attack come—"

"Ye did use my sword last time."

"Not properly. Might I ha' been able to save Mam, had I been trained? Ardahl, I never want to feel that helpless again."

"Liadan—no one can know whether you might ha' saved her."

"But my heart wonders over it, time after time."

He eyed her with compassion and caution. "It takes years to train wi' the sword, as well ye do know. Conall and I started by the age o' thirteen."

"Aye, but ye be the best among Fearghal's warriors. Deny it if ye will," she challenged him when he began to sputter. "Why d'ye think he keeps ye near to him? And ye and I have—a special connection, aye?"

"Aye."

"Who better to teach me than ye?"

"'Twill cause a stir. Ye know fine it will."

"Ye can drill me in secret."

"Lass, there is no place in the settlement to keep that a secret. Everything is under a watchful eye."

"Well, but—we will tak' it out o' the way. Ye think about it while ye sleep. Ye do need some sleep." She added in a whisper, "Alone."

He nodded.

"When ye wake, I'll braid your hair again." It would give her another chance to touch him. She would take any chance that came her way.

Pure pleasure for her fingers. Pure joy for her heart.

ARDAHL DID THINK about Liadan's request between bouts of fitful sleep. He rarely slept well anymore, having always one ear open. Listening for Liadan's voice if she were in the hut and speaking with Mam.

Imagining what might lie ahead for them.

Another attack would come. No one could say when, which did not make for good sleep. He supposed he would feel better if he thought Liadan knew how to react when it happened.

He could not train her properly in but a few days, nay. But he might be able to impart a measure of guidance, a skill or two.

He arose around noon to find the hut empty, the door curtain tied wide open. He gathered his weapons and went out to the training field, but aye, he had made up his mind.

He ducked back to the hut early that evening before reporting for guard duty, while Mam and Liadan were at their supper.

"Aye," he said into Liadan's ear as he passed her by.

"Eh?" She turned up her face to him, almost close enough to kiss.

"I will gi' ye some training. We will start about this time tomorrow, before I report to the guard."

Her face lit up.

"What's all this, then?" Mam asked.

"Ardahl is going to teach me to fight. Properly, I mean. So if—if there is another attack, I will no' be caught out again. I have his sword," Liadan added tightly, while Mam stared. "His own. So there alone, is that no' like magical protection?"

Mam did not look certain. But Ardahl understood what Liadan meant. A part of him with her even when he could not be.

If naught else, training would give him a few more moments with her before—

Before, for better or worse, their world came apart around them.

CHAPTER FORTY-FOUR

"KEEP YOUR HEAD up. And your blade. I could ha' killed ye then."

Liadan jerked the blade of Ardahl's sword higher. Sweat ran down between her shoulder blades and stung her eyes. She smarted in other places also, where Ardahl had given her gentle swats from his sword. Conall's sword. Each had been accompanied by the words *I could ha' killed ye then.*

Her first training ever and she'd have been dead half a score times already.

Ardahl's sword seemed much heavier than when she'd used it before. Of course, she'd had terror on her side then. And a surge of determination.

Now she faced the man she adored, him circling in a half crouch, his hazel eyes bright on her face.

Even she—a stranger to such skills—could tell why he was such a good warrior. He reacted with uncanny swiftness, his movements like controlled lightning. She had less than a chance of getting any blow in upon him.

He also possessed a casual strength honed, aye, by years of training, that she doubted he even applied consciously. It just came to him without thought.

She, however, had to think about every move. Worst of all, they'd acquired an audience.

After supper, when the light began to soften, they'd gone off beyond the huts to the open space where the trees began. No one there at all, and the guards at a goodly distance. Now they stood surrounded by a curious crowd of folks who had drifted up and stayed to stare. Mostly women. A few members of the guard who'd moved in closer to watch.

Enough to make Liadan's humiliation complete.

She flattened her lips as Ardahl tapped her on the left shoulder with Conall's blade. Light as the blow was, it hurt. She would likely have a bruise there.

Bruises everywhere.

It wasn't as if he hadn't warned her. "I do no' wish to hurt ye, Liadan. But training does hurt."

It did. *It did.*

They circled. One of the first things he'd told her: keep moving. It made a more difficult target. The second thing: *Whatever ye do, never let the enemy disarm ye. Disarmed, ye are likely finished.*

Since the beginning he'd sought to do just that—disarm her. Taps with Conall's blade upon his. Swoops and clangs, harder. So far she'd managed to hold on, though the blade felt progressively heavier and heavier.

"What are ye doing?"

The bellow halted both of them. Dornach came striding up, an incredulous look on his face. Gratefully, Liadan let her blade sink to the turf.

Dornach swept Liadan with one disbelieving glance before focusing on Ardahl. "What is this, then?"

Ardahl flung his braided hair behind him. Another lesson—Liadan should have braided her own hair as well as his. It kept getting in her eyes.

Next time.

And aye, though she hurt, there would be a next time.

She stepped up to face Dornach. "I wanted to learn how to fight. I asked Ardahl to show me."

Dornach turned on her. He sought visibly for words to say. "Ye? Ye're naught but a slip o' a thing."

"My brother was a fine warrior, aye? And my father. Generations back. Why should I no' fight?"

Instead of answering, Dornach eyed the weapon in her hands. "Ardahl, is that no' your sword?"

"It used to be," Ardahl replied somberly, "before I took up another. Now 'tis hers."

Dornach gave him a long look, and Liadan wondered what he saw. "And d'ye expect her to face an enemy?"

"Enemies will come," Ardahl told him. "She will face them one way or t'other, with or without a sword in her hands.

"Madness," Dornach breathed.

The crowd of onlookers had stilled. Now one woman, a bit older than Liadan and with a child at her side, called out, "Aye, Master Dornach—and what are we women to do when an enemy appears at the door? How to defend our wee ones? I would fight also if I had a sword."

Murmurs from other women supported her words.

Dornach shook his head. "Do your men no' step out to defend ye? 'Tis the way o' it!"

"'Tis the way it used to be, aye," Liadan heard herself say. "Now we are here and vulnerable while our men are away. The fight comes to us."

Dornach's hard expression softened just a mite. "I understand these are difficult times. But we canna have this sort o' thing. Ardahl, ye will cease wi' this nonsense at once." He reached out for Ardahl's sword. "And I will tak' this for safekeeping. Before," he added deliberately, "someone loses her head."

Liadan snatched the sword away. "Nay."

Dornach's dark eyes narrowed. "What did ye say to me, woman?"

"'Tis no' yours to take. It was Ardahl's. It is now mine."

Dornach looked taken aback. He actually stumbled a step away from her.

"Aye," called another of the women, "'tis hers. Are we now to lose our possessions as well as our lives?"

Still another, older woman: "Will ye, great war chief, also

come to our doors and steal our cots and cook pots?"

"To be sure, nay!" Dornach bellowed. "Those are things ye are meant to have."

"And who can say," demanded an aged man in the crowd, "what a woman is meant to have? When I leave my daughter in order to take my place at guard, I do no' like thinking on her being defenseless."

"No' defenseless! We are her defense. Ye and me."

Everyone there stared at Dornach. The number of new graves attested to the success of that argument. The number of hearts broken.

"Look," he said, "'tis this way. Wha' if I leave Mistress Liadan that fine sword and she tries to use it during an attack? Wha' if she fails? Her opponent will take the weapon from her. Then Dacha will ha' a fine sword to use against us."

"Or," another aged woman proposed, "she may learn to defend hersel' and kill one or two o' the invading bastards."

Dornach shook his head. "I will ha' to speak wi' Chief Fearghal about it. Meanwhile, Mistress Liadan, give me the sword."

"I will not."

"Then gi' it to Master Ardahl. 'Twas first his."

"It was. Mine now."

Clearly frustrated, Dornach turned on Ardahl. "Wha' kind o' fool gives a sword to a woman?"

"Mayhap one," said a younger man, a member of the guard, "who hopes she will survive."

Dornach tossed his hands in the air. "We will see about this."

He marched off. Everyone there eyed one another.

The guard called, "I am surprised, Ardahl, he did no' order ye off to your post."

Ardahl said, "I expect he did no' think of it. Liadan"—he eyed her—"d'ye want to carry on while we ha' the time?"

Did she want more bruises? Further embarrassment?

If anyone could teach her, it was this man.

"Aye." She lifted her chin and the sword. "Let us carry on."

Murmurs of approval sounded all around. Surprisingly, their audience moved off.

"There now." Ardahl's hazel eyes met Liadan's. "First hurdle crossed. There will be others. Come."

She set herself for endurance.

ARDAHL HAD NO doubt that Dornach had gone straight to the chief with his complaint, and after he'd sent home a visibly wilting Liadan—with the sword—he awaited chastisement. He waited while he paced the boundary of the settlement, through the night, but not so much as a stray fox disturbed him.

Not till morning when he headed home beneath the first threads of morning light did a lad run up to him.

"Chief Fearghal wishes to see ye."

His stomach tightened. He did not want to fall out with Fearghal, one of the few men who approved of him. He'd already stood in opposition with the other man who approved of him—Dornach—over the matter.

"Aye, so," he told the lad, and redirected his steps.

The chief and his family had moved into what had been the warriors' meeting hall, after the great hall was burned. In the way of such things, the warriors still congregated there, hanging about the door of the place.

They stared when Ardahl came up, and stared when the chief's wife invited him in.

The chief's wife did not look happy. Visibly with child, she carried an expression that denoted strain, as if she had not slept.

The chief had two children, both young, and the fireside proved chaotic. Fearghal sat there trying to eat his breakfast.

He cast a look at Ardahl and waved a hand at one of the unoccupied rugs. "Sit down. Will ye ha' breakfast?"

"Nay, thank ye." Ardahl wanted to go home. To spend those

precious few moments with Liadan outside the hut while he washed himself. To let her say the things she could not, with her eyes.

He sat, and Fearghal eyed him. "All quiet last night?"

"Aye, chief. A bit too quiet, if ye know what I mean."

"I do. There is a quiet that feels like eyes in the dark, watching."

"Just so."

"Dornach has been to me. Complaining about ye drilling the women."

"I ha' no' been drilling the women. Naught but trying to teach a single lass to protect herself while holding a sword. My foster sister," he added deliberately.

The chief's wife stopped bustling around the fire and directed a sidelong look at Ardahl.

"That is no' the way Dornach tells it. He declares that furnishing our women wi' weapons is admitting we cannot defend them."

"Forgive me, and meaning no disrespect, but Master Dornach is wrong."

Both Fearghal's eyebrows flew up.

"The lass is frightened. She fought off some of Brihan's men when they came—when we were no' here to defend the settlement—and lost her mam anyway. I seek only to reassure her, at her own request."

"And is placing a great sword in her hands reassurance?"

"Aye." It was the chief's wife who replied. "It may well be."

Both men stared at her where she stood by the fire.

"Do ye think I ha' not wished for a weapon, Fearghal? A hundred times I ha' while ye were away. Ha' I not armed mysel' with a boning knife? 'Tis no' a welcome feeling, being helpless."

A curious look crossed Fearghal's face. "Are we to arm our women, then?"

She put a fist on her hip. "Would ye rather arm us or come back from some battle to find us dead?"

"Bridie," he whispered.

His wife turned to Ardahl. "I think ye do well, training this lass, if she wants it. Were I no' wi' child, I would ask ye to train me also."

Ardahl said honestly, "I canna turn her into a warrior. But I may be able to still some o' her fears."

She nodded and glanced at her children. "Is a woman who can bear the pain o' childbirth so weak she canna take up a sword?"

Fearghal exchanged a speaking look with Ardahl before saying, "No one would ever call our women weak."

"Well then! Send the young man back about his business." She gestured at Ardahl. "And let him get some sleep."

Ardahl got to his feet. "Have I your leave, my chief, to continue wi' some training?"

"Aye," said Bridie.

"Aye," Fearghal echoed her. "Some. But use your head now. Just a few pointers, mind."

"Aye, chief." Ardahl smiled to himself as he stepped back out into the sunshine, but not so Fearghal could see.

CHAPTER FORTY-FIVE

T HE NEXT EVENING when Ardahl and Liadan ventured out to the same place to train, they found a small gathering of women waiting. Still more filtered in after they arrived, drifting up in ones or twos.

All carried weapons in their hands—if weapons they could be called. Most were makeshift at best. An ordinary household did not run to surplus weapons. Swords and even knives were valuable and hard earned.

So these women came with what they could find. What, indeed, they might snatch up if their homes were attacked. Pokers from the hearth. Hoes and barley hooks. Fishing gaffs and boning knives.

They all brought something. And they all held their weapons tentatively, though, young and old, they stood firm.

Ardahl stared at them in horror. He had not foreseen this, though perhaps he should have. Fearghal had given him permission to train Liadan, not half the women of the settlement.

What to do?

He glanced at Liadan uncertainly. She'd refused to admit this morning how sore she was from yesterday's training. He'd been able to tell, though, by how carefully she moved.

And he'd been *gentle* with her.

Was he to be responsible so for bruising other men's women? Mothers, wives, sisters, daughters. They all gazed at him with similar expressions of hope and desperation.

"Ye had best all go home," he told them. "I ha' permission to train Mistress Liadan. No others."

A woman stepped forward. Of middle years, she clutched for a weapon a length of iron so rusted, it glowed bright orange.

"I was there, master. I am a servant in the chief's house. He did no' deny ye permission to train others o' us."

"Only because he did no' expect all o' ye to come to me." Ardahl waved a hand. "Else he would ha' done."

She lifted her chin. "My mistress sent me. Chief Fearghal's wife. She says someone among us must be ready to fight, if he is awa'."

Ardahl puffed out a great breath. "Master Dornach will no' like it. Nor will your menfolk."

"My man," declared one woman stonily, "is dead."

They all stared at Ardahl, unmoving.

"Very well. Form up ranks, and pay heed."

IT MIGHT HAVE been amusing, had it not been so pitiful. Ardahl was not in the mood to laugh. The assortment of weapons proved less prepossessing than the women who wielded them. The length of bright orange iron snapped at the first pass. Its possessor fought on with the remnant.

By the end of that session, they once again had an audience, silent and grim faced. Apparently none of them ran off to tell Dornach, because he did not arrive puffing flames. The dire little session drew to a halt when the women began to stumble and sway on their feet.

No one was bleeding. Ardahl considered that a victory.

Moreover, all the women gave him grateful glances despite the abuse. As they drifted away, one stepped up to him.

"Same time tomorrow, master?"

If he had not been brought up before Fearghal and chastened

by then. Banished from the clan. "Aye."

When the others had gone, he turned to Liadan. She drooped with exhaustion, sword trailing on the ground, stray hairs stuck to her cheeks and neck with sweat. At least this time she'd thought to braid the bulk of her hair, to keep it out of her eyes.

That thought brought another—her braiding his hair for him, an intimate act. Her fingers weaving the tresses, brushing against his skin. He half closed his eyes in a moment of remembered bliss.

"Ah, and what is that look supposed to mean?" she asked. "Was I truly so bad?"

"No' bad at all." She'd been better than the others. Of course, she had a proper weapon. "I was just thinking—"

"What?" She took a step closer to him.

"How much I want to kiss ye." He should not say it, he truly should not. But there was no one left to hear, and anyway, his whole body longed for her.

A gleam took hold in her eyes. "No' half so much as I wish to kiss ye. I am that surprised I have the strength for it."

He smiled. She had heart, this woman he adored.

"Let us make an agreement, Ardahl—since we are no' at leave to touch one another. When I look at ye—this way—that is as good as a kiss. And when ye wink at me—"

"Wink?"

"Ye know." She gave an overtly emphasized wink. "Ye ha' kissed me back."

"I am no' at all certain I can wink. Both my eyes tend to close at once."

She smiled still more broadly. She stood so near, he could reach out for her. He had to fight the impulse.

"A blink, then."

He blinked at her and laughed. A miracle, that he could still laugh. "Folk will think there is somewhat amiss wi' my eyes, I will be blinking at ye so often."

"The women will no' care. They adore ye. But no' so much,"

she breathed in a whisper, "as I do."

Suddenly their connection became deadly serious. "Liadan—"

"I know. I should no' say it. Ye are as good as my brother."

"Go home and put a poultice on the worst o' your bruises. I am goin' to my post."

"Be safe," she beseeched him as she moved past, not looking at him now. "For ye carry my heart."

THE NEXT MORNING when Ardahl left his guard post and walked home through the misty morning, for it looked like rain, folk sidled up to him—mostly men, many of them aged. A few women. A few younger men, all wearing sheepish expressions.

They handed him weapons. Passed them to him in a secretive fashion with whispered words.

"A sword I do no' use anymore."

"Have this for the women."

"It belonged to my brother, it did."

Ardahl accepted the offerings because he did not know what else to do. When he got home, he placed them in a clattering pile inside the door, beside his own.

Mam and Liadan, who were both there making breakfast, stared in astonishment. He shrugged in response.

"Passed to me by tribesmen, mostly, on my way home."

"Our men worry about their women as much as they worry for themselves, it seems," Mam commented a bit dryly.

As usual, Liadan followed Ardahl out to watch him wash. "All quiet on guard duty?" she asked, touching him with nothing but her gaze.

"Aye. The men are jumpy, though. Every sound sends them scrambling."

"The women too. And I—"

She stopped speaking abruptly, so he looked up at her, hands running with water.

"I have this feeling," she said, "one I cannot dismiss, that somewhat is going to happen. Somewhat terrible."

"Aye, so."

"You have it also?"

"I think everyone has it."

Such was proved the case. By the time Ardahl awoke later in time for training, the pile of weapons inside the door had grown.

"People have been dropping them off all day," said Liadan, busy braiding her hair. "I ha' no idea where they all came from. Most are old and no' very good. But better than what we had, and a far sight better than nothing."

He stepped up to her. When she raised her arms to braid her hair, he saw a spreading bruise on one of them. He touched it softly.

"I hurt ye."

"Nay, 'twas no' ye. Aenodh from the chief's house gave me a mighty swat there."

"Liadan." Emotions fair overwhelmed him, and he drew her to her feet. He had no idea where his mam might be. Not here. "I canna bear the thought o' ye being battered and bashed about."

"Is it no' better than the thought o' returning fro' battle to find me dead?"

Agonized, he whispered, "Do no' even think—"

"Yet 'tis a truth with which we live."

"Och, lass." He drew her into his arms and up against him, closed his eyes against the rampant feelings pounding through him. "I would give my life to defend ye. Ye know that."

"And ye may, yet." She backed off just far enough to gaze into his eyes. "If we have another life after this one, I pray it will be together. I ask Brigid for that every day. Life after life wi' ye, Ardahl."

That made him smile, if sadly. "Plait my hair for me, lass. Help me gather up all these weapons. We will go."

CHAPTER FORTY-SIX

I T RAINED ALL that night. Liadan, curled up in her parents' sleeping place, which had now become her own, could think of naught but Ardahl standing out in the wet. She slept little and opened her ears continually to catch any sounds of attack above the crashing of the rain.

She hurt from head to toe and had more bruises than she could readily count, but they ached less than her heart.

Ardahl. If they could not be together in this life, if that fate were denied to them, would there be another?

Could she grow old finding solace in a future of which she could not be certain?

Before dawn, she rose and dressed. Checked on Maeve, who still slept in Flanna's old place. Stirred up the fire and heated water so that when Ardahl came, he could wash beside the hearth, in out of the rain. Here with her.

He did not come.

Delayed, she thought at first. Perhaps more clansfolk had stopped to give him weapons. But when Maeve arose, when the dawn came struggling through the heavy clouds and eventually the rain ceased, she wrapped herself in her shawl and went out.

The whole world dripped with water. From the roofs of the huts that yet stood, from the branches of the hazel and rowan trees. Smoke hung in a blanket over the settlement, morning fires such as hers struggling to rise in the heavy air. Away over the hills that surrounded this place, the clouds rolled.

She felt a sudden hitch at her heart. She loved this place most deeply—she did, despite all the fear and the pain. Its beauty lay deep within her on days such as this as well as bright, sunny ones.

Home. Belonging. How could it be wrong, to fight for it?

Yet now she sensed something amiss. Men straggled home from watch, Ardahl not among them.

Dread crawled up her spine, making it difficult to breathe. She could not live without him. *She could not.*

Even if she could never lie with him again, hold him to her, or kiss him, sharing this world with him might be just enough. If she lost him from it—

No reason to go on. The man she'd believed a traitorous serpent had become important to her existence.

A member of the guard passed, a man she knew named Muirin, husband to one of her friends. She ran forward.

"Muirin? Ye were on watch, were ye no'? Was all quiet?"

He was wet to the skin and looked at her with a hint of impatience. He must want to get home. "Aye, Liadan. Though—" His gaze became haunted. "There is somewhat—just hanging out in the dark, ye ken? No' being able to hear above the rain made it a bad night."

"Aye, so. Did ye see Ardahl MacCormac there?"

He shook his head. "His post is no' near to mine."

"But did he come in wi' the rest o' ye? He has not reached home."

Muirin's eyes sharpened. "I have not seen him. Have ye reason to worry for him?"

She shook her head, and he went on his way. Liadan stopped others, asking each the same in turn.

At last one man told her, "I think he has gone off to the chief's place."

"Fearghal's? Why?"

"Summoned there, was he no'?"

He hurried off also, and she directed her steps to the former warriors' hall, which lay just beyond the spring. People went in and out, but she did not see Ardahl. She wanted to push her way in, to set eyes on him if he were there—if only to reassure herself he was well. But she dared not make her interest too plain.

One of Conall's former friends stood at the door. He had always shown an interest in her, and smiled when she stepped up to him.

"Good morning, Brecad."

"Mistress Liadan."

"Is Ardahl within?"

His smile faded. "He is. Summoned by the chief. There is a meeting going on."

"A meeting?"

"Aye, so. The chief, some of his advisors, the druids."

The dread in Liadan's stomach stirred and grew claws. "Aye, then. I will wait."

He looked curious but asked nothing. Everyone knew Ardahl had taken Conall's place.

She kicked her heels near the spring, keeping an eye on the hall. The area still served as a gathering place for those with no roofs, though construction went apace. They looked wet and miserable.

At last men began to leave the hall in ones and twos. The two surviving druids together. Other advisors. Cathair.

Another prick went up Liadan's spine. What was he doing there?

Finally, Ardahl and Dornach appeared together. Ardahl with his weapons still on his shoulder. She waited till the two men parted with a few words spoken, before she fell into step with Ardahl.

He shot her an assessing look, and she another right back at him.

"What happened? Ye did no' come home. I thought—well, I do no' know what I thought."

His lips formed a hard line and his eyes were guarded. She knew this man now. *She knew him.*

"What is it? Somewhat is amiss."

"I canna say."

"To be sure, ye can. Has something terrible happened?"

"Liadan, I ha' been ordered to keep silent."

That made her stop walking and face him. "Even wi' me?"

They stood so for several long moments with the bustle all around them, while her heart beat up high in her chest. Alone, but not alone.

"Ye know ye can tell me anything."

"Let us get home, then."

The sick feeling in Liadan's gut did not subside while she helped Ardahl stack his weapons. When he greeted his mother. While Liadan watched him wash there beside the fire, passing him the pot of soap when he needed it.

"Come and tak' your breakfast," his mother bade him then, and Liadan had to discipline herself hard while they all sat together and he ate. "Ye were over late getting home," Maeve observed.

"The chief asked to speak wi' me."

His mam gave him a look but asked nothing more. After shooting a second look at Liadan, she got to her feet. "Aye, well, get some sleep. I ha' a few visits to make."

She went out, and silence settled between Liadan and Ardahl. He shoved the remainder of his breakfast aside.

There on the deerskin beside the hearth, Liadan scooted closer to him. She reached out and took his hand. So strong. Deeply and permanently calloused where he gripped the hilt of his sword.

"Liadan, ye canna breathe a word o' this to anyone. Not my mam. No one."

"Very well, so."

"We are going to mount a raid. A secret one."

The breath caught in Liadan's throat. "On Dacha?"

"Aye."

"And Chief Fearghal wants ye to take part in this?"

He hesitated a moment. "Aye."

"Why is it secret? Why does he no' announce it to all the clan?" As he always did. Fearghal tended to be open with his intentions and to share them with his people.

Ardahl rubbed Liadan's knuckles with his thumb. "'Tis no ordinary raid, this. No one can know about it. Fearghal has been in secret talks by a messenger back and forth, with Brihan Brioc."

"Brihan Brioc—who betrayed us. Who attacked us. His men killed my mam!"

"Aye. Liadan, if ye do no' want to hear the rest o' it—"

"I do. I do." She dropped her head, fighting her emotions. He went on steadily, barely above a whisper.

"Fearghal has negotiated a new alliance between himself and Brihan. I think he believes we cannot withstand both Dacha and Brihan's forces combined. Bad enough when Brihan merely held himself apart and let Dacha cross his lands to move against us.

"But the proposed alliance rests upon Brihan getting the return of his young son, held prisoner by Dacha. The boy is the reason, the only reason Brihan has fallen in wi' Dacha and become our enemy."

Liadan raised her head in sudden horror, searching his face. "This raid—"

"'Tis meant to be a rescue. We are to go in and find the boy. Get him away."

We. Fearghal had, aye, included Ardahl in this terrible plan. Horror stopped Liadan's breath entirely. For an instant, her heart faltered.

"'Tis madness," she whispered when she could. "To go into Dacha's lands. 'Tis certain death."

Ardahl's lips twisted in a wry grimace. "Mayhap not. Brihan has some o' his own men there at Dacha's holding, negotiators. One o' them has been working on this scheme to free the boy. A small force, so he believes, can get in and out wi' the lad, if that force be quick and careful enough. If no one knows we are there."

"Fearghal chose ye to be part o' this because he thinks ye will be quick and careful enough."

"Aye."

"Ye and who else? Will Fearghal go?"

"Nay." Ardahl's lips twisted again. "No' this time."

"Nay! Because he knows it is too risky."

"His people need him, Liadan."

She took a moment, the space of twenty heartbeats, before she said, "I need ye, Ardahl. I *need* ye. Like breath. More than that."

He slid his hands up from her fingers to her shoulders. Seeking to lend comfort.

"'Tis to be a small party that can travel under cover. Dornach claims he is well enough to go."

That was good. Dornach, a fierce fighter, also favored Ardahl.

But against Dacha's whole clan? "Who else?"

"Cathair."

"Cathair! But he—" Once again she momentarily lost the capability for speech. "He threatened ye."

"Aye."

"What better opportunity for him to put a knife in your back? Claim it happened there by an enemy's hand."

Ardahl said nothing.

"Ardahl—" She scuttled still closer, captured his face between her hands. "Ye canna do this. Ye canna risk yourself this way. It is madness."

"I have no choice. No choice, Liadan. I am sworn to Fearghal."

"And does that mean ye must offer yourself up for certain death?"

"Aye. If he asks it, it does."

"Ardahl. My darling." She had never before used such a name to address him. "I admire your loyalty. Your courage."

"'Tis somewhat beyond loyalty, Liadan. It is fealty. A sacred vow."

"And if Cathair does no' hold his duty as sacredly? If he sees this as an opportunity to be rid o' ye? Or if—if this negotiator Brihan has there wi' Dacha betrays him? If Dacha has turned the man either through bribery or threat? If he tells Dacha of the plan, that ye will be coming?"

"Aye. There are a thousand ways it can fail."

"And but a thin chance it will succeed."

She crawled onto his knees, right up against him. Should someone come into the hut unexpectedly, it would cause outrage.

What was that compared with the risk of losing him?

She held him tight, seeking something beyond mere kisses, beyond the physical. She needed the very warmth of his soul. His arms folded around her and drew her in.

"I do no' want ye to go from me. I fear—I fear if ye do, I will never—"

"Hush, *alanna*. Do no' say it."

Nay, she would not give voice—and more power—to this terror that gripped her heart.

"When? When d'ye go?"

"Tomorrow night, when we are thought to be on watch." He bent his head tenderly and peered into her face. "'Twill help me if ye keep faith. Believe this will work. He is but a young lad, and there alone."

"I believe in you." She would, till she died and beyond.

CHAPTER FORTY-SEVEN

I T HAD BEEN a warm, kindly day, the sort men dreamed about when they thought of home. The sort that lived in the memory. Skies washed with blue, a soft, gentle breeze carrying fragrance from the hills. Sunlight sparkling on the waters.

Something for a man to carry with him when he went off to die.

Ardahl recalled countless such days from boyhood, running half wild with Conall and others of their friends, their mams not knowing where they were most the time. Getting a scolding—albeit a mild one—from his da when he got home, for Da was still alive then.

Now the day faded away from him as night set in. A memory of beauty.

Just like the woman he left behind.

Ah, but she was beautiful, his Liadan. More beautiful than a summer's day. It wounded him to cause the grief he had seen in his eyes when he left her.

How, och, *how* would she endure if he did not return?

He'd wanted to hold her at their leave taking. To kiss her. To impart impossible reassurances. He could do none of those things.

They'd practiced with the rest of the women. But after, he had not gone to take up his post.

Now he stood at the edge of the settlement, in the dark, with Dornach, Cathair, Fearghal and three ponies. No one else around.

No chariots this time. Chariots drew notice. They would cross Brihan's land in the dark, unchallenged by his guard. Meet with Brihan's man at his border with Dacha. They would leave their ponies at that place while the fellow guided them in.

If the man in question had not turned his cloak.

"Ye will return the boy to his father," Fearghal told them, there in the new dark. "And the alliance between us will be bound."

Aye, so. Ardahl understood it. He just did not know it could be done.

"Have faith," he whispered to himself now, as he had to Liadan when he left her, denying the terror in her eyes.

Come back to me, she'd beseeched him silently.

I will return to ye. I will find ye. Always.

It might be better, Ardahl thought as the three of them set off, Fearghal remaining behind there in the dusk, if there had been some cloud cover. Even rain. The sky arched over them like a transparent dome, light blue fading to deep cobalt in the east. They could use better cover.

None of them spoke as they went. Dornach had thumped both of them on the shoulders before they set off, his form of reassurance.

They rode in a line, Dornach first, then Cathair, and then Ardahl, who would rather have Cathair ahead than behind him.

The ponies made more noise than they did. Like shadows, they moved across the land. Ardahl did his best to shut away the doubts that threatened his mind.

What if Brihan's guide did not meet them? Worse, what if it was a trap? *Do not think that way.* He had not let Liadan say such things. He could not allow himself to.

Liadan.

His longing for her was a livid wound. Would he die with her name on his lips?

Nay, he would not die. He could not. For he must return to her.

He held that thought and only that thought till they reached the border with Brihan's lands. There, at a place marked by three white boulders, Dornach held up his hand.

Ardahl already knew the plan. They would pass through here, where Fearghal said Brihan had placed no guards.

Or Dacha would have an army waiting, if Brihan had betrayed them.

Dornach nodded. They passed through with no more than a whisper of the air around them.

"We must hasten," Dornach called softly. "All depends on darkness."

They rode more quickly now through country they did not know. The dome of the sky above them turned deep blue and then black, with only the faintest of light hanging in the west like a beacon.

Ardahl's heart rose and fell like his pony's hooves. Brihan had not betrayed them. Not yet. But Dacha might want to lure them onto his own land before taking them prisoner.

Would they be killed outright? Would there be torture first? Could he endure?

Aye, if he clung to the thought of Liadan.

When, some inestimable length of time later, Dornach drew them up again, it was with considerably more caution. A small clearing lay ahead, full of dim light. As they entered it, a man stepped out.

He was cloaked, hooded, unrecognizable. Brihan's man, here under cover? Who could tell? Ardahl tensed, ready to turn his mount and flee if so much as a second shadow stirred. His pony was winded—he would not get far.

"Granan?" Dornach spoke the name of their contact.

"Aye. Leave your ponies here in the shadows. We go the rest o' the way on foot."

Ardahl exchanged glances with Dornach as they dismounted. Dornach once again touched him on the shoulder. Reassurance. But this was the moment when the worst of the nightmare began.

Granan shoved back his hood. He had a thin, tense face and worried eyes. "Ye must be absolutely silent and follow my every move. There are guards everywhere ahead, but I know where they stand. We will need to get into the hut where the lad is held."

"How?" Cathair sounded as edgy as Ardahl felt.

"A section o' the wall has been cut awa'. Put back again."

"Dacha does not know this?" Dornach now.

"Nay. 'Twas done in secret. I bribed the man who watches the lad."

Ah, well, if this man—Granan—did not turn on them, the guard might well. With what might a man be bribed to turn against his chief?

"We canna stand here talking. Come."

With a conviction that he went to his death, Ardahl did.

Though it must by now be past the middle of the night, the settlement did not lie quiet. As soon as their party of four emerged from a small woodland, there was light—a good fire burning somewhere ahead—and bustle, and voices carrying on the clear night air. A man laughed. Another spoke in a rumble.

Granan crept between Ardahl and Dornach. "See that building there? The small hut between the two taller ones. Donen is there."

Donen. Aye, the lad had a name and an identity. Someone's son.

"We will go forward one at a time. I will go first. Pick up your heads and walk like ye belong here."

"'Tis too bright," Cathair protested. "I thought 'twould be darker."

"'Tis darker round the far side where the opening has been fixed."

Possibly. Or a stout band of guards could be waiting there to fall upon them.

Ardahl thought he heard Cathair whisper, "Madness."

Aye, so it was, and Ardahl supposed Cathair wanted to live, just as he did.

Granan walked off, taking his time with it. As Ardahl watched him, his skin crawled. If it was a trap, they would let Granan through. The next man to go—

Dornach swept both him and Cathair with a glance. Touched Ardahl on the shoulder. "Ye next."

His stomach tightened and nearly heaved. He'd long since ceased being this frightened when he entered battle. This was no ordinary battle.

He drew his sword, had it in his hand, hidden beneath his cloak, when he stepped out from cover.

The light washed over him. A torch flared somewhere close by. There must be a warriors' meeting place not far off—he could hear the men laughing and joking. Was that why the lad's prison had been set here?

Around the side of the hut, it was indeed darker. Granan waited for him there and already had a section of the wattle wall set aside.

"In," he told Ardahl. "In."

Ardahl had to get down on all fours and crawl, a poor position to be in if enemy warriors, rather than a young prisoner, waited beyond.

Dim light greeted him—surely no more than a rush light. He sprang to his feet to find a slim youth staring at him with wide eyes.

Dressed only in a kilt and tunic with bare feet, he had fair hair and looked twice as frightened as Ardahl felt.

Just the lad. No sign of any guard, though Ardahl knew very well they must be stationed outside the door that he could see behind the boy.

"Donen?" Granan came through the wall behind Ardahl. "'Tis a rescue. Come. Hush!"

The lad's lips parted. No sound came. Granan leaped forward and dragged him to the wall.

Ardahl turned back, his sword at the ready. No sound from outside the door.

But he could hear Donen whispering a question, and Dornach's voice. Making too much noise. Any guards out front would hear.

A scraping at the outside of the door told Ardahl the bar had been lifted. He dove for the hole in the wattle, scrambled to his feet even as Cathair pulled the lad away and Granan replaced the section of wall.

"Go. *Go!*"

Men poured around both sides of the hut. Armed men.

The group of five ran, Cathair and his charge in the lead followed by Dornach, who, at his age, did not run so well, then Granan, and Ardahl bringing up the rear. Even as the thought occurred to Ardahl that he should stop and fight, Granan turned and ran at the guards, howling.

It gave the rest of them time to reach the trees. And convinced Ardahl that, aye, Granan's heart had been true.

He heard Dacha's guards cut Granan down, though he could not spare a glance for it. His group reached the trees and paused.

"Ye go on," Ardahl said to his companions. "Get the lad away. I will hold back as many as I can." *Before I die.*

Aye, so, he was to die here after all. Here with Conall's sword in his hand.

Liadan, I will find ye. If no' in this life, then in the next.

CHAPTER FORTY-EIGHT

WHEN MORNING CAME and Ardahl did not return from guard duty, Liadan had to begin making excuses. She had several ready—that Ardahl must have gone to another meeting with Fearghal. That he'd been waylaid by Dornach.

Her own worry, though, made it impossible to dissemble. She found it even harder to lie to Maeve. Yet she was not supposed to know what she knew. And she would never betray Ardahl's trust.

So when Maeve eyed her and asked, "Where is he?" she merely shook her head. "Why, lass, have ye no' prepared his water for washing as ye always do?"

Aye, she should have done that.

She said only, "I believe Ardahl will be delayed this morning." *I believe. I believe.*

"Why?"

"That I cannot say. Pray, do not ask me."

Maeve went silent. Too silent. They shared the space but did not speak.

Waiting was a torment. The day crept to life around them, and Liadan's hands trembled at their work.

What was happening with Ardahl now? And now? Had he left the world, been driven from it on a shower of blood? Surely she would know. She would feel the loss, bone deep. Her heart would falter; the sun would dim.

Instead, all remained the same. Birds sang. Morning fires

lifted smoke lazily into the air.

Did that mean he still lived?

Nay, but she had not felt it when Conall died. Nor her da.

Nor mam, for all that.

"Lass, why do ye no' go and fetch some water?"

She went out with her ewer. Early as it was, folk hurried around, and a line of women had formed at the spring. Liadan sent her gaze everywhere.

And when it was her turn at the spring, she prayed.

Glorious Brigid, guard him. Guard him for me. Send him what help ye can.

AT THE EDGE of the wood, there in the dark, Ardahl set his back against the trunk of a tree. It felt like stone at his back. Strong, as he would have to be strong.

Behind him he could hear Cathair and Dornach guiding the lad away. Dacha's guard came at him. It had not taken them long to hack Granan to pieces.

Ardahl's heart pounded up in his chest and his breath came quick. Here would he die. If only he could give the others time enough before he did.

The first of the guard reached him howling. The man had a good sword, which he whirled around his head before crashing it into Ardahl's—Conall's—blade. Not good enough. The force of his charge overbalanced him, and Ardahl slit his throat in a single blow.

The other men came with greater caution. Three of them together. More would be on their way, likely an unending stream of them. Ardahl could hear the voices, the shouts. The alarm given.

If he could take these three before the others arrived, he just might slip away.

He gutted the man on the left without delay, but the other two came at him as a team. A blade laid open his right arm. He felt no pain, but the loss of blood would weaken him.

Two snarling faces. The intent to kill showing in four eyes. His blade was quick, his arm still strong. Mayhap not the best warrior his clan had ever known, but good enough.

The man on the right went down, taken by a slash above the heart. He was holding them, giving the escaping party time.

All that mattered.

He now had a little bulwark of dead at his feet, inhibiting the approach of any enemy. But more men were rushing in even as he fought this last. He could see them, hear them.

He would die here after all.

He stabbed his last remaining opponent in the eye and received a shower of blood. Even as the man fell, he made to step around the tree. No time. The next of Dacha's men came whooping like madmen, all too soon upon him.

So far, no one had got past him into the forest.

Aye, he would die here.

Liadan.

Upon the thought of her, the sounding of her name in Ardahl's mind, something moved beside him. A figure it was, a familiar one glowing all in white.

Conall?

Did ye think I would let ye fight alone?

The shade of Conall held a sword. It must be Ardahl's sword, since he had Conall's in his hand. But he had left his sword with Liadan, along with his heart.

No matter, for the ghostly blade connected with those of their enemies. Struck against their blades. Slashed and wounded flesh.

More will be coming, Conall said even as the last man facing them fell. *Come.*

They ran, ducked between and through the trees, dodging the trunks in the dark. Ardahl could see nothing of the escaping party ahead. Had they got away? Been caught?

He realized suddenly he ran alone, the spirit of Conall so swiftly gone. Dacha's men came after him, a great crowd of them, as it sounded. The breath surged in his lungs. Blood dripped steadily from his arm. From other places also, where he did not remember taking wounds.

He ran on but could feel himself weakening. If the pack behind reached him, they would fall upon him like hounds on a fox.

His steps began to lag. The breath seared his lungs. He caught a toe and nearly stumbled.

Up ahead, through the trees, he saw a light. Heard a rattle. A chariot appeared and rumbled up next to him.

But it was not a real chariot. They had not brought their chariots, and anyway, this one glowed with unearthly light, just like the shade of Conall. To be sure, he could see that Conall was aboard, driving the pair of white ponies. He leaned down and called to Ardahl, *Come up!*

A cry familiar from the battlefield, when a charioteer wanted to get his partner out of danger.

Ardahl leaped for the cart, felt Conall's hand close on the back of his cloak and haul him aboard.

They took off, Conall driving through the trees in a reckless fashion. He had pushed Ardahl to the bottom of the cart, and there he stayed for the moment.

I am dead, he thought quite clearly. *I must have died back there with my back against the tree. This is the afterlife.*

But I thought I'd be flying away to Tír na nÓg. Not riding in a chariot with Conall.

I have somewhat to tell ye, Conall said. *Quick, before my time wi' ye is done.*

Ardahl struggled up, clutched the crossbar with both hands. "Am I dead?"

No' yet. But I am. Conall gave his familiar, crooked grin. Almost ran the chariot into a tree.

"How is it ye are here?"

My sister asked for help. But listen. That day in the practice field, when I died, 'twas no' supposed to happen that way.

Ardahl went still. "How did it happen? Why did ye turn on me in anger?"

For weeks, Brasha had been feeding me lies. Tumbling me senseless. Making me believe what she said. She told me ye were jealous o' me.

"Surely ye never believed that. We were close as brothers. Closer!"

Aye, and were ye no' a better warrior than me? Nay, she said ye were jealous o' my having her. That ye'd pressed yourself upon her. Vowed to have her awa' from me. She kept at it and kept at it till I was half mad.

Conall slowed the chariot. Ahead, Ardahl could see the clearing where the ponies waited.

She was in league wi' Cathair. I see now, she was always his woman. They wanted me angry enough to kill ye. Get ye out o' the way so Cathair could be first among the warriors.

"But—"

It did no' turn out that way, nay. Conall seized Ardahl's wrist. It felt like the kiss of lightning. *At the end, I could no' harm ye. I plunged the dagger instead into my own heart.*

"By all that is holy, Conall—"

But his friend and the chariot were gone. Ardahl found himself standing on his own two feet among the trees. With a whoop that sounded like a sob, he stumbled forward into the clearing.

CHAPTER FORTY-NINE

THREE FACES TURNED toward Ardahl as he entered the clearing. Dornach was in the act of helping Donen up onto one of the ponies. The lad looked stupid with shock. Cathair swung around with his sword in his hand.

Cathair.

Ardahl wanted to rush at him. To put his already-bloodied sword to the bastard's throat.

He had not the opportunity. Dornach's face lit at the sight of him, and he cried, "Ye made it away? By all the gods! Cathair, gi' him the pony. He is winded. Ye can go afoot."

Cathair did not argue it, but the glare he gave Ardahl—bitter with hate—declared he had neither expected nor wanted Ardahl to survive.

With the last of his strength, Ardahl vaulted onto the pony.

"They are still coming," he told Dornach. "Behind me."

"Aye."

Those were the last words spoken for moments beyond counting.

They ran till Cathair was well winded. Then Dornach doubled with the lad, and Cathair took his mount.

The air turned gray around them and grew bright with dawn. Any sounds of pursuit had faded away.

At last, Dornach drew up. "That is your father's land ahead," he told the boy.

They entered Brihan's lands just as the air turned bright

around them. All too swiftly, they met members of Brihan's guard, who exclaimed in amazement and joy to see their chief's son with Fearghal's men. Swiftly, they were escorted to Brihan's hall.

"Chief Brihan, Chief Brihan, your son is returned!"

Brihan rushed out from his hall, stark disbelief on his face. The worry and weariness fell from his features when he saw Donen on the back of the pony. He held out his arms, and the boy half launched himself, half fell into them.

Donen's mother ran from the hall behind him, wailing. She rushed at the pair and enfolded the boy in a frantic grip, weeping.

Leaving the boy to her, Brihan turned and likewise embraced Dornach. "Ye did accomplish the deed! By all the gods. I cannot express my gratitude."

Dornach held him off. "Your man, Granan, is dead. He gave his life to get that lad away."

Grief clouded Brihan's features.

"As for the rest o' it, ye may thank this man." Dornach gestured at Ardahl, who had dismounted and stood by. "He held off the pursuit single-handed so we could get the lad away. This is Ardahl MacCormac, the greatest warrior our clan has ever known."

Ardahl found himself enfolded suddenly in a hard grip. Brihan looked into his eyes. "Thank ye. If ever ye need the last drop o' my heart's blood, 'tis yours."

"Keep him safe, just, Chief Brioc."

"I have set a stout guard and will increase it even now. I ha' no doubt Dacha will be furious. He will come wi' an army."

Dornach nodded. "He will, surely. I do no' doubt 'twill all be battled to an end. But ye will fight wi' us, aye?"

"We will. To the death, if need be."

Dornach grimaced. "Dacha will find us no' so easy to kill."

"AYE, SO," DORNACH said as they rode away. "We ha' won his loyalty, and no mistake."

Cathair said nothing. Ardahl could tell from his glances that the man had not much liked the declaration Dornach had made.

Naming Ardahl the greatest warrior of all their clan.

Aye, well, they had a score to settle, did he and Cathair. For Conall's sake, and Ardahl's own.

They rode into their home settlement well after full light. Fearghal came out instantly, proving he had been keeping watch for them, his expression raw with worry. It eased only marginally when he saw all three of them returned.

He hurried to them and laid a hand on the bridle of Dornach's pony, his eyes searching those of his war chief. "All is well? The deed is accomplished?"

"It is, my chief. Brihan's son is safe wi' his family again."

Fearghal looked so astonished, it was clear he had more than half expected them to fail.

"And," Dornach went on in a low rumble, "Chief Brihan has confirmed his commitment to an alliance. He is setting up his defenses against Dacha and swears he will hold strong."

"By all the gods!" Fearghal's wild gaze moved among them. "Are ye all whole?"

"Brihan's man whom he had there wi' Dacha lost his life. And Ardahl here did a hero's work, hanging back to mount a defense while Cathair and I got the lad clean away. He has a nasty slash to his arm."

Fearghal turned to Ardahl. "Ye must see the healer at once. And ye have my deepest gratitude, along wi' that o' all the clan."

Ardahl nodded. He wanted but one thing, not to see the healer but to go home to the small hut where he'd left his heart. The area where Fearghal had met them was busy, and his eyes searched for her everywhere.

"Aye, my chief. I would go home first—" And then he saw her. Liadan with his mam beside her, cutting a path toward him through the bustle. Mam had tears in her eyes. Liadan's face looked bone white, her eyes full of agonized relief, as she beheld him.

She wanted to run to him, that he knew. And he wanted nothing but to take her in his arms, hold her close for the sheer reassurance of it. He could not. *He could not.*

Even though it would provide all the healing he might need.

Fearghal still spoke to him, going on about the ugliness of the slash to his arm. Cathair stood strangely silent.

He would have to speak with Fearghal about Cathair.

Mam reached him, embraced him. He returned her embrace gently, his eyes meeting those of the lass who stood behind her. Liadan quivered, and so many emotions brimmed in her eyes, he thought the others must see.

"Mistress MacCormac," Fearghal said, "take him home and make sure he sees the healer."

Once more, Dornach's hand came down on Ardahl's shoulder. "No guard duty for ye this night. Get some rest."

"Aye, so."

As the three of them walked away, Mam with her arm still around him, Ardahl heard Dornach say, "He is a hero, Chief Fearghal. Wait till I tell ye all—"

"How badly are ye hurt?" Liadan walked at Ardahl's left side, not touching him though he wished with all his being she would.

He had injuries aplenty. The gash to his arm. One to his shoulder. The skin of his back abraded where he'd anchored himself to the tree.

He looked into her face. "It does no' matter. None o' that matters now."

His mam led him into the hut, relieved him of his weapons, and sat him beside the fire. "Liadan, run and get the basin. We shall clean his wounds here as best we may before I fetch the healer."

Liadan obeyed, looking as if she would burst. Ardahl felt the same way—he would come to pieces if he did not touch her soon. When she brought the basin, Mam waved her to the task, and

Liadan knelt beside Ardahl with her pot of soap.

As soon as she laid hands upon him, her cool fingers on his torn arm, the agony eased. The terrible tension inside Ardahl backed down a few steps. He could breathe more easily.

For Liadan, the tears came. They brimmed up from her eyes and ran unheeded down her face even as her fingers caressed him.

"Och, by all the gods, I did not think I would see ye again."

From the corner of his eye, Ardahl saw his mam go out into the clear light. The moment she did, Liadan came forward into his arms. Settled across his knees and wrapped both arms around him. Held him tight, and tighter.

"I tried to keep believing," she said in a broken voice. "As ye bade me do. I did my best. But the fear—"

"Aye." He wove his fingers into her hair. Absorbed the feel of her, breathed in her scent. "There were times I doubted I would be able to return. But I did. I did."

He gazed into her face. "I ha' so much to tell ye, Liadan. Conall was there."

"What?" Her eyes widened.

"He came to me. Fought beside me. I hung back so Dornach and Cathair could get the lad awa'. I did no' expect to survive. But then—he came. Him, or his spirit. Fought beside me. Fetched me awa' in a ghostly chariot—"

She drew back a little, laid one hand on his cheek, and ran it up to his brow.

"Nay," he told her, "I do no' have fever. It happened, Liadan. And he told me—"

"He spoke to ye, my brother?"

"Aye. He saved me. And he told me what happened the day he died."

CHAPTER FIFTY

L IADAN GAZED INTO the eyes of the man she loved. They appeared over-bright, as if he did in fact harbor a fever. And well he might. He'd returned to her covered in wounds, had Ardahl, more than she could readily count.

He had returned to her.

She could scarcely believe it, still. Her heart sang with wonder, a glorious sort of tune that flowed through her even as she worried for the state of his mind.

"Ardahl, dear one, ye could no' have seen Conall. He is away to *Tír na nÓg.*"

"He is not. At least, not yet." He shook his head decisively. "He has stayed, Liadan, mayhap to help us. And he has told me the truth."

He clutched at her now with both hands, one seeping blood where a slash across his knuckles had broken open.

"Tell me. Tell me, then." Truth or imagining, or fevered, waking dream, he needed to unburden himself.

"'Twas Brasha, as we thought. Brasha and Cathair. She was always Cathair's from the start. She played at wanting Conall. Bedded him, by all the gods. Drew him under. Then she fed him lies—that I had tried to seduce her away from him."

"What? But ye would never—"

"I would never." Absently, he caressed her shoulder. "I did know his manner of late had changed, sharpened. And that morning—well, he grew angry wi' me as never before. I laid it down to the coming battles. The hard work o' training."

"There is anger, and *anger*."

"Aye. They wanted him angry enough to kill me. I believe Brasha would ha' harped at him and harped at him when they were together, until she poisoned his mind so he would strike against me. As he did."

Liadan hissed out her anger. She longed to take up Ardahl's sword, to march out and face the wretched, black-hearted wench who had so betrayed her brother.

But not yet.

"He wanted ye out o' his way," she breathed. "Cathair did. So he could be assured the place of first among Fearghal's warriors. I knew that, on some level I did."

"Aye, as did I. I just could no' reason out how. But it did not work the way they planned. In the end, when Conall and I struggled together, he could no' bring himself to kill me. The dagger ended up in his own heart instead o' mine."

"Despite her lies," Liadan whispered. "He loved ye too well, despite the hate she tried to foster."

"Aye, so. Liadan, I believe—I must believe—that love is always stronger than hate. And I do love ye, my beautiful lass."

He kissed her then, the kind of kiss for which her heart had longed all the while he was away. A long, slow kiss it was, lips parting lips, the one of them drinking from the other. Giving and taking in equal measures as it would always, always be between them.

He kissed her until his breath became her own. Until she could no longer tell where her lips ended and his began. Until their very spirits melded and found depthless peace.

Only then did he withdraw far enough to drop small kisses into the palms of her hands, at each corner of her mouth, her cheeks. Her forehead.

"We must bring this to the druids," she told him then. "Brasha and Cathair must pay for the terrible thing they ha' done."

"Aye, so they must."

"I admit, I would rather exact justice myself."

"As would I," he agreed. "But that will not serve us well. Liadan, I have been thinking all the way home. If we can persuade the druids to withdraw Aodh's sentence upon me—"

"We might be together." She lit up at the very idea, her spirit soaring. "Och, Ardahl, d'ye think we can?"

"I do not know whether the druids will believe such a tale as I ha' to tell."

"If anyone will, it should be men who speak wi' the gods, and interpret their signs."

"Mayhap. If 'tis meant for us."

She gazed once more into his eyes. "It has to be."

"But, Liadan"—he gathered her hands into his—"there will be trouble coming. Battles, fierce ones. Dacha will no' take the rescue of Brihan's lad, nor Brihan turning away from him, lightly. Brihan has vowed to set up a defense, and we will join him on our own border, but—"

"The battle may come here," she finished for him. "Again."

"Aye. Just so ye know, should I fall, I will find ye. Somehow. In the next life."

"Ye have promised it, and I believe it."

He dropped more kisses into the palms of her hands, one after the other.

"And now, let us get your wounds cleaned. Your mam will be coming soon with the healer." And Liadan would have to behave as if he meant no more to her than a foster brother.

She could do so. Surely she was strong enough, for she carried his promise in her heart.

THE HEALER ARRIVED, and a painful session followed. Liadan did not stay for it—it would not be proper for her to see Ardahl stripped down as good as naked, but his mam remained with him. Liadan stood out front of the hut in the thin sunshine and uttered a prayer of gratitude to Brigid.

Thank ye, great goddess, for bringing him back to me.

Far to the west, she could see rain clouds gathering. Aye, it would be from there the trouble came. The heartache. The death.

Away from the direction of the training field, someone shouted what sounded like orders. Dornach, setting the defense? Assigning his men?

Ardahl would have to fight again. He was strong, aye, this man she adored. A fine warrior. But blood and bone and sinew could endure only so much. She had witnessed the death of too many. Seen those she loved die.

If Ardahl was right, and love proved stronger than hate, should it not overcome greed also? The harm that came of a man wanting more and more land. Desiring to lord it over others. To be first among his fellows.

Would ever there come a time when such desires were laid aside and men reached instead for peace?

There in the watery sunlight, she shook her head. Men were men. And men such as Dacha or indeed Cathair cared little for whom they destroyed.

A flame of anger flared within her when she thought on Cathair.

Please, Brigid, great goddess. Help me as ye will. Let Cathair meet justice for the harm he has caused and the harm he would do.

A soft breeze stirred the hair at her cheek. An answer? Another promise?

Ardahl slept away the rest of that day. Liadan checked on him many times where he lay on the sleeping bench they had twice shared. His mam also remained nearby, her worry visible in her eyes. They spoke little, reluctant to disturb his sleep, but they shared their worry silently.

Outside, the settlement bustled with unaccustomed activity. Fearghal understood full well the outcome of what he had wrought. Dacha would exact a price for last night's work—first from Brihan. Then from this clan.

She shivered over it as she stepped out to fetch water. Men hurried everywhere, all of them armed. Women wore fearful, distracted expressions on their faces. When she reached the spring, she beheld a sight. Cathair, who must also have taken his rest, was up on his feet, armed like the other men. In deep conversation with Brasha.

Indeed, so intent was their exchange, they did not notice Liadan across the way. Cathair, his white-blond head bent, held his face just above Brasha's. She had laid her hand upon his wrist in a gesture of claiming.

No one seeing them so could ever deem them anything but lovers. But of what did they speak?

Liadan trembled. With all her being she wanted to approach and confront them. To charge them with what they had done, the shame and dishonor of it, that had cost her beloved brother's life.

She could not. Because they would meet her accusations with feigned hurt and denial. Ardahl was right. They would have to speak first with the druids.

Yet a combination of hate and superstitious fear caused her skin to prickle all over as she passed by them to fill her ewer. An awareness—almost a premonition—of harm to come.

When she straightened from filling her ewer, she caught Brasha looking at her, eyes narrowed as if she too felt the discord between them, approaching like a storm.

CHAPTER FIFTY-ONE

Ardahl woke from his long sleep feeling worse than when he'd gone to his rest. He lay still for a moment with his eyes wide open, mentally prodding each individual wound. Recalling those moments at Dacha when Conall had fought at his side.

Near impossible as it was to believe, he could not find it in his heart to doubt.

He could hear rain pounding on the roof of the hut and hushed voices beyond the sleeping place. He glimpsed firelight leaping.

His mam and Liadan.

Liadan.

At the sounding of her name in his mind, he dissolved into pure longing. Longing for her. The breath in his lungs quickened, and his beating heart. Even his aching body.

What if they could not convince the druids to believe his account, and lift his sentence?

He felt that, aye, he might have been able to convince Aodh. But Aodh lay dead.

If he could never be with Liadan rightly, then he would take no other wife, have no children, and live alone—for a life lived thus, loving her, would be better than anything else he could hope to achieve.

He stretched on his sleeping bench and groaned involuntarily. Liadan's face appeared around the curtain as if she'd been listening for him.

"Ah, so ye have come awake, then. How did ye sleep?"

"Well."

She tiptoed in and sat on the edge of the bench. Reaching out, she touched his jaw, a quick caress before laying her hand on his bare chest.

"The healer left a draught, if ye woke in pain. Shall I bring it?"

"Nay, I need naught more than you here wi' me." He wove his fingers through hers and held tight. His mam still bustled in the next room, else he would have taken Liadan in his arms. Kissed her. "What is happening out there?"

"Fearghal has mobilized the guard. No training this day—'tis all in deadly earnest, the men sent to their assignments despite the rain."

"Aye, so." Attacks would be coming. Where and when remained to be seen.

"I saw Cathair and Brasha." Her eyes clouded. "At the spring, speaking together."

"Aye. Cathair will not be pleased I survived holding off Dacha's men. No doubt he hoped I would fail to come back and will be looking for a way to sink his knife in my back." The rush and confusion of the next battle would make as good an opportunity as Cathair was likely to find.

Liadan shivered. "We cannot allow him that chance. We must go to the druids."

"Aye, but not now. Not when they will be drawn into the defense, looking for signs and portents."

He struggled to sit up, grimacing. Each and every muscle hurt and his wounds pulled tight.

"Rest yet a while yet," Liadan urged.

"Nay, I will be needed. By Dornach, if no' the chief."

"Ye need more time to recover." She added in a whisper, "I need more time wi' ye."

Before he could answer, she pressed her mouth to his. A simple enough gesture, only it sent a current of energy through him, far better than any healer's draught.

"Liadan." The kiss turned into something twice as deep. Not till Ardahl's ears caught a movement from beyond the sleeping place did he come to himself. "Liadan, my mam—"

"I am sure your mam knows or at least guesses some of what lies between us. I confess, I do no' understand the whole o' it."

"Nor do I." Only that he loved her, if such an emotion could be labeled as mere love. He needed her as much as his heartbeat. "Here, help me up. And aye, perhaps I will have that draught. I cannot go out hobbling like an old man."

ARDAHL WENT FIRST to the warriors' hall where the chief was lodged. He felt better once he'd taken something to eat and downed the bitter draught. Better still when he got moving.

At the chief's dwelling he found a meeting already in progress, Fearghal with Dornach and both surviving druids, along with a few of Fearghal's other advisors.

Fearghal waved him in. "Here he is now. Ardahl, I did no' have a proper chance earlier to thank ye as ye deserve." His fierce gaze met Ardahl's head-on. "I wish ye to know, were these ordinary times, ye would be feasted here in this hall. Bards would sing your praises down through the ages to come."

Ardahl smiled reluctantly. A dubious reward. "But"—he inclined his head—"these are not ordinary times."

"They are not. And for ye to be praised as ye deserve, for ye to be named first among my warriors, we shall first have to survive as a clan. I will need your sword for that. Your strength and your courage."

Ardahl nodded again. The other men there, sitting in a rough circle, all watched him. He eyed the two druids, Tamald and Reghan. It was to Tamald, now head druid, he would have to speak. Ardahl did not know what sort of man Tamald might be. His savior, perhaps? And Liadan's.

To Fearghal he said, "My sword is yours, my chief." But his heart's blood—aye, that belonged to Liadan.

"Sit. We are discussing our defenses," Fearghal told him. "Eventualities. What may happen if we and Brihan fight together or if Dacha defeats the Brioc and we make a final stand alone. We will save our lands."

Ardahl took a place in the rough circle of men while Dornach spoke. "Aye, chief. We will spill the last drops o' our blood for this land, and those we love who dwell here."

Fearghal gave a rueful smile. "Always it is the way. Men fight." He spread his hands. "Women mourn. Men fight either for the sake o' increase—because they are greedy to expand their holdings—or, aye, for love of what they hold already to their hearts."

Tamald spoke in a voice barely above a whisper. "Far better, and cherished by the gods, to fight for love."

"Aye, so, Master Tamald," Fearghal said dryly. "But those who do so are no' always triumphant."

Tamald's pale blue eyes met the chief's. "No' in this life, mayhap. Only a fool would believe this life is all."

Ardahl felt those words echo through him, a song so distant he had could barely hear it. For an instant he stared.

But Dornach turned to him and said, "Master Ardahl, since ye be first among the warriors, so declared or no', I would assign ye to defend your chief. Chief Fearghal has decided he will fight, should we march out."

"To be sure I will," Fearghal averred.

"Whether, as the chief says, we fight here in the settlement or at our border, I want ye, Ardahl, at his side. D'ye accept this charge?"

Ardahl well understood what Dornach asked him. He was being requested once again to lay down his life for the man who led his people. And he had no choice. He had sworn fealty, had he not? He and Conall had, in the same ceremony.

That meant Fearghal—and his family—would not die unless

he, their defender, perished first.

But what of his own folk? His mam and Liadan? He wanted to swear his sword to them.

Everyone there watched him. Once more, he inclined his head.

"I accept the charge, Master Dornach. Chief Fearghal, my sword is your own."

"And," said Tamald, his voice still thin, "may our rewards be found in the next life."

CHAPTER FIFTY-TWO

"I HAVE SENT another messenger to Chief Brihan," Fearghal said when the meeting broke up and he, with Ardahl and Dornach, stood at the door. "He will have a runner ready to send us, should Dacha attack him." The chief corrected himself wryly, "*When* Dacha attacks him. We shall then have enough notice to march out. I confess, I would rather make a stand on our border than here. That way our folk can once more move out for the hills. Some o' them, at least, may survive. All o' our blood will no' be lost."

Ardahl eyed the chief, who now bore deep lines in his face. "Permission, Chief Fearghal, to speak plainly."

Dornach eyed him, but Fearghal said, "By all means. Ye ha' earned it."

"Your words make me think ye do no' believe we will win the upcoming fight."

"That is not so. By no means. It all depends upon how matters fall out, and that no man can tell." He gave a wan smile. "Not even the druids, casting their stones. I think ye will agree, Ardahl, Dacha will no' be easy to defeat."

"He will no'."

"And unless we defeat him whole, he will merely lick his wounds and keep coming. Our chances are better wi' Brihan fighting alongside us than with us facing both Dacha and Brihan under Dacha's thumb.

"Should Brioc go down to defeat"—Fearghal stopped speaking abruptly and struggled visibly with his emotions—"then our fate is in the hands of the gods and men such as ye, Ardahl MacCormac. Will we live on, or will we be naught more than a story told in some other chief's hall on a cold winter's night?"

Ardahl had no answer to that. He and Dornach walked out together to find the rain had slackened, but fell still in a fine silver curtain.

"Master Dornach," Ardahl said when they stood as alone as they might amid so many, "I wish to speak to ye about Cathair. He will no' be happy wi' the praise Chief Fearghal has heaped upon me."

"'Tis not up to him to like or dislike it. Ye have earned the praise."

"I do not trust Cathair." Ardahl met the war chief's gaze. "I believe he will no' rest till all such honor goes to him."

He dared say no more. But he saw the spark of comprehension take hold in Dornach's eyes.

"Ye think he means ye harm?"

"I think he has already caused me great harm and would do more still."

Dornach grunted. "I will speak wi' him. Make it clear that ye ha' been elevated by Fearghal, and any man who moves against ye moves against his chief, and so betrays the fealty sworn to that man."

"Aye, so."

Dornach lowered his voice. "'Tis difficult for a man to battle if he must watch his back the whole time."

"Aye, master, it is."

"Go home. Ye are relieved o' assignments this night. Continue healing so ye will be ready to stand for your chief."

"I am ready now. If there be attack—"

"If Brihan falls so swiftly that there is attack by morning, ye shall surely hear o' it. Lad, I ha' seen your wounds. Go home and take what rest ye may."

Go home. That meant but one thing—go to Liadan. He would

not argue having so much as one moment of extra time with her.

Hoisting his weapons, he went.

LIADAN KNELT BESIDE the hearthplace, praying. She did so often, spoke to the great goddess Brigid, who surely understood a woman's lot and the longings of her heart, as to a friend.

Please, Brigid, let him remain safe. I do not know how that is possible, given what we face, and him a warrior who must march out wi' a sword in his hand. But please. Even if he can never in truth be my own, let him live and thrive.

She heard a step behind her and turned. Ardahl stood in the doorway looking like a figure from some old, heroic tale—his weapons on his shoulder, hair and cloak wet from the rain. Eyes all for her.

Had Brigid sent him? No matter. She surged to her feet and went to him, unfastened the pin of his cloak and laid it aside. Glanced into his face and became lost in those hazel eyes.

"I ha' been sent home to regain my strength," he said, not without a hint of irony in his voice.

"Have ye indeed?"

"I would full rather lose it, in ye."

"Would ye?" Her hands began to shake as she reached for the laces of his tunic.

He covered her hands with his own. "Is my mam here?"

"Nay." Liadan went breathless. "Gone to a lying-in. She may be gone all night."

"Liadan—this may well be the last time. Our last time ever. I ha' been assigned to protect the chief when the battles come. Lay down my life for him, if necessary. Given what is coming..." He shook his head.

"Aye." Liadan struggled to accept it, this thing most unacceptable. "Aye, so. If 'tis to be the last time, then we will have to make it count."

He trapped her face between his palms. Kissed each side of her mouth, her cheeks, her forehead. Then kissed her so deeply, with such tenderness and devotion, her heart felt it must break.

Her hands still shook when she tied shut the leather curtain across the door. Shook with desire and with wondering.

If this truly would be the last time they lay together, became one in body as well as spirit, could she bear it?

She turned back to find him standing there watching her. She summoned up a smile and held out her hand.

"Come. Let me treat a hero as he deserves."

In the sleeping place, she undressed him slowly and carefully, followed the removal of each garment with a caress on bare skin. Over bruises. Cuts and bandages. When mere touch failed to be enough, she blessed each place with her mouth. A thousand kisses could not be enough.

She removed his tunic, his kilt, his boots, and the wrapped leggings beneath. Now it was he who trembled like a pony in the traces of a chariot, eager to run. He stood ready for her, and when she fell to her knees and kissed the smooth, heated length of him, he made a sound deep in his throat.

"Liadan—"

"Nay, Ardahl, do no' hinder me. If this is to be our last, I would ha' all o' ye."

He made no further protest, but caught her head between his hands as she wooed him with her lips and tongue, coaxed him into the warm cavern of her mouth and drank what he had to give. The muscles of his stomach rippled as he gave himself to her. And when she'd had every drop of him, he drew her to her feet and babbled her name.

"Liadan. Liadan!"

He undressed her then, with as much care as if she were a high king's bride. Drew her onto the sleeping bench behind them. Gazed into her eyes.

"My turn, wee one. My turn to worship ye."

He began with her breasts, a slow burn of desire that soon spread through her blood and turned her wild. She buried her fingers in his hair and drew him closer, then closer still.

"Liadan," he gasped, his breath whispering over the tender skin of her breast. "May I love ye as I desire?"

"Anything, Ardahl. Aught that I am is yours. Aught that ye ask, I give. My body is yours this night."

And, in truth, for all time.

Leaving her breasts, he kissed his way downward. He was already hard for her again—she could feel the weight of him slide against her skin as he moved. When he reached her thighs, he hooked them with his fingers and eased them apart.

He drank of her even as she had of him. She gave to him fully and completely, without shame, her body convulsing at the persuasion of his lips and tongue. With his man, she would never know shyness or hesitation. Only a sense of rightness so powerful it permitted her to withhold nothing, body nor heart.

When she lay utterly and completely open to him, he rose and slid inside her—into that place so ready for him, deep and deeper. Still, he did not give her his seed, but spilled it on her belly even as she wrapped her arms around him fiercely and held on for dear life.

If this were to be the last time—

He lay quiet except for the seething of his breath, his face in her neck.

She wept.

"Liadan? Ye are never greeting. Why?"

"For the beauty o' it, just."

"Here, now." He lifted his head and kissed the tears away, catching them with his lips.

"If," she said aloud this time, "it is to be our last..."

A slow, bright smile invaded his eyes. "Aye, but surely not the last this night."

❦❦❦

CHAPTER FIFTY-THREE

I N THE MORNING, even before Maeve returned to the hut, Ardahl rose, dressed and went out with his weapons. Many were the fervent kisses exchanged between them first, the desperate, whispered promises and assurances.

But the fact remained. As Liadan watched him step out into the watery sunlight, she acknowledged it.

She might never see him again.

He went off to take the place he'd been assigned, to guard the chief. Attack could come at any time.

For an instant, standing there watching his auburn head disappear between the huts of the settlement, she felt sure she could not bear it. Too much loss, too much pain and uncertainty. A woman could not live with such uncertainty. There must come a time when her life, her heart, could settle.

Yet she'd given her heart to this man, whatever that might entail. And better, she admitted fiercely, a life of uncertainty with him than a dull and secure existence with anyone else.

"Whatever the gods may bring me," she murmured aloud, "I accept for his sake."

When Maeve came home, they worked together sorting out the belongings they would need to take with them if they had to flee, and loading them into packs. These they set beside the door.

Later, when Liadan went out to fetch water, she saw nothing but other women like herself all wearing distracted expressions. Unhappy mothers hurried about tasks and spoke to their children in tense, harsh voices, hoping to keep them close. The very air had a sharp, stifling feel. She looked for Flanna, but could not spot her, so when she had filled her ewer, she stopped by Mistress MacDragh's hut, where her sister had been staying all the while.

She found both girls—Flanna and Lasair—outside the door, sharing duties at the quern stone. When Liadan paused there, Flanna looked up at her with doubt and little sign of welcome.

"Flanna, sister, I've come to ask if ye will come home."

Flanna took a moment before she answered. "Is he still there?"

"He?" Liadan questioned, even though she knew to whom Flanna referred.

"Ardahl MacCormac."

"Aye. Ye know full well he is assigned to stay wi' us. To fight and hunt and otherwise care for us in Conall's place. It is his—"

"Punishment, aye. And ours. I will no' come back if he is there."

"Flanna, there may be more dangers coming. I would like ye with me."

"Nay, not while he serves his punishment. Anyway, the hut is no' the same wi' Mam gone. I can scarce stand to set foot in the place."

Mistress MacDragh stepped out from the hut behind the girls to listen.

"Please, Flanna—it would mean much to me for us to be together once more."

Flanna said nothing. Lasair would not meet Liadan's gaze.

Though she hated to do so before these others, Liadan asked, "Do ye still blame me for Mam's death? Is that it?"

"Nay." The denial was not convincing.

Quickly, Mistress MacDragh said, "Liadan, pray, do not worry. Flanna is very much welcome here and safe wi' me."

"Mistress"—Liadan faced her—"there may be further attacks ahead. If we are forced to flee—"

"I shall make certain she gets clear away."

What could Liadan say? She nodded and went off, feeling more unsettled than before.

When she reached her own hut and set aside the water, she said to Maeve, "I am going past the training field." Ardahl might be there. "Will ye come wi' me?"

Maeve looked torn. "Should we take our packs?"

That made Liadan hesitate. She knew as well as anyone that anything could happen just a few steps from home.

"Aye."

Dragging their packs, they went. Other women stood at the stone enclosure wall ahead of them, yet it was strangely quiet. The men were there, but they did not practice.

Instead, unless she was very much mistaken, they mustered for battle.

The sight terrified her so, she turned sick inside. Aye, she had expected this. But seeing the men with their weapons on their shoulders and the chariots rolling up in a line made it seem immediate and all too real.

She searched for Ardahl and found him on the far side of the field with the chief. As if he felt her gaze, he turned his head and their eyes met. Swiftly, he leaned in and spoke to Fearghal before jogging over to meet Liadan and his mam at the wall.

"Ye be mustering," Liadan burst out.

"Aye. We leave this night. Fearghal wishes to cover the distance to the border in the dark. To be waiting there for Dacha, if—"

"If Chief Brihan goes down," Mam said.

Ardahl looked at her. "Aye. Or if Brihan needs to fall back there, and we have to stand with him."

Before either woman could reply, he reached for Liadan's hands. "Come wi' me."

"What?"

"I ha' Fearghal's permission." He leaped the wall, still holding her hand in his.

"Where?"

"To see Tamald. There is time—just—before we depart."

Liadan searched his eyes, which appeared flinty and determined. She spared one glance for Maeve before allowing Ardahl to tow her away.

"What—" she tried again as they hurried along.

"I am going to tell Tamald what happened when Conall appeared to me. Relate what he said. See if I can get him to lift the sentence upon me. Then when I return from the fighting—if I return—ye and I can be joined as we should be. Handfasted, as is right."

Liadan's heart bounded—a painful surge of perilous joy. She dragged him to a halt. "That is what ye want?" she asked, gazing into his eyes.

"'Tis all I want. Liadan, ye must know that I live and I breathe only for ye." He reached out and touched her hair very gently. "If I know ye may in truth be mine—that will gi' me the strength to fight my way home, if aught can."

"Aye." She could see the power and beauty of it, and hope trembled inside her, enough almost to banish the doubt. "But will Tamald believe ye?"

"If he does no', who will?"

They ran the rest of the way, Ardahl with his weapons and Liadan with her pack over her shoulder, and arrived at the druids' hut breathless.

Tamald was there, the place in disarray, as if he and his companion had also been sorting through belongings to take with them, should they need to flee. The two men spoke in low, terse tones and looked up in annoyance when Liadan and Ardahl darkened their doorway.

"Wha' is it, Master Ardahl?" Tamald asked. "Does the chief call for me?"

"Nay, not yet. We leave at sundown. Are ye coming with us?"

"Aye," Tamald said unhappily. He nodded at his companion. "Master Reghan will stay here with the tribe."

"Master Tamald, I would beg a few moments o' your time. Now, before we leave. I ha' the chief's permission, and it is important."

The look Tamald gave Ardahl was unusually impatient. He drew visibly on his composure before he said, "Is it somewhat that cannot wait? We are going to war."

"'Tis somewhat I would have settled before we go to war."

Tamald sighed. "Come."

They sat knee to knee in the watery sunlight, the three of them. Liadan had rarely been so close to one of the priests, and she felt a measure of awe.

Yet her heart rose on the thin blade of hope. If she knew that Ardahl might be hers then, aye, she could endure anything.

Tamald had clear blue eyes that remained serene in his tense, pale face. "Master Ardahl, what is it?"

"'Tis about the sentence Aodh imposed upon me following Conall's death. I was directed to take his place, to become Conall, for all purposes. Live out the rest o' my life carrying his obligations."

"Aye, so. I was party to Aodh's decision to impose that sentence, as was Reghan. We gave it full and heavy deliberation. According to the Brehon law, it provided for the best justice."

"And I ha' sought to fill my place—that place. I have." For the first time, Ardahl seemed to falter. To lose his determination.

Liadan took it up. "Master Tamald, Ardahl has done all ye asked o' him. Guarded us in Conall's stead. Defended and provided for us. But—he and I ha' fallen in love."

The priest's eyes widened. This, he had not expected.

Ardahl said, "We wish to handfast. I would like to know before I go off to fight that I have permission for it."

"Nay. It is impossible." Tamald bit the words off harshly, if with regret. "Forbidden."

"Even if my sentence was unjust? If I can prove I did no' and would never harm Conall?"

"Unjust?" Tamald sounded offended. "How so?"

Ardahl launched into the story. Conall's appearance beside him at Dacha, helping him to fight. Their journey in the chariot after, when Conall had told him what Cathair and Brasha had done. How they'd schemed against him for Cathair's gain.

Tamald listened, Liadan had to give him that. He forgot his impatience and gave his full attention to the tale. She could not tell what he did or did not believe.

"And so I thought," Ardahl concluded, "if ye could see fit to lift the sentence—"

"Lift it," Tamald repeated.

"As unfounded. Ye can surely see it never should have been imposed."

Tamald hesitated. He looked into Liadan's eyes before searching Ardahl's face. His lips formed a hard line. "Forgive me," he began, and Liadan's heart leaped.

Was he going to express regret for being mistaken? For believing Ardahl could ever harm his closest friend? Was there hope for them?

Tamald went on, "I do no' mean to express doubt for your accounting. 'Tis no' in me to doubt that the departed can return to us, especially in times o' great need. Yet at such times, we can also imagine such visions." He shook his head. "'Tis but a story. Ye ha' no proof."

"Proof!" Anger kindled in Ardahl's eyes. "Am I to summon the shade o' Conall here to stand before ye?"

"Nay, but the law is the law. Ye ask me to lift what has been imposed so that ye may join wi' one who is as good as your sister. The only way I may do so is if Cathair—or at the least Mistress Brasha—might come to me and admit full well what they did."

Ardahl blinked at him. "Ye expect Cathair to confess? Cathair, of all men?"

"Or Mistress Brasha."

"Then," Liadan said, sickness settling once more in her gut, "they would be disgraced. Shamed. Master Tamald, neither o' them is likely to take that on."

"I am sorry," Tamald said. "Truly I am. Whether I believe ye or no', surely ye see I need more than the accounting o' a tale to bring such condemnation down upon them."

"Yet ye took Cathair's word that I slew my dearest friend."

"And so condemned us," Liadan half sobbed, "for all time."

"If Cathair comes to me and admits his fault, I will lift the sentence. I can do no better," Tamald said. He got to his feet. "Now I must go and prepare to leave. Ye must also," he told Ardahl. "Time is short."

He left them. Liadan stumbled to her feet and Ardahl rose after, a hard, bemused look in his eyes.

Liadan seized his hands. "Mayhap there is still hope."

"Cathair will never admit fault. 'Tis the last thing he will do. And should he perish in the fighting—"

Their eyes met. If Cathair perished, he could never speak. The small flame of hope Liadan had cherished went out like a guttered rush light.

"Ardahl, I am frightened."

He gazed into her eyes, his devotion plain to see. "All is no' lost," he whispered. "No yet. We will be together, Liadan. Have I not promised ye?"

If not in this lifetime, then in the next.

CHAPTER FIFTY-FOUR

S ELDOM HAD FEARGHAL set out with such a sizeable force. That evening before sunset, every chariot rolled out. Each and every warrior, including some men well past the accepted age of fighting, who had thought they would never march out again.

The rest—aged, young, wounded, and the women who had trained with Ardahl, stayed back to guard the settlement. They had already seen what could happen in the absence of their men.

Ardahl and Liadan had only one moment of parting at the hut, after leaving Tamald. He drew her around the side where so often she'd remained with him while he washed. And he kissed her for what might be the last time.

The parting from his mam proved equally hard. And he knew both women stood watching while he walked off. He would not let himself look back. He must now become a warrior and nothing more. He must devote himself to protecting his chief, without distractions.

Not even those of the heart.

The first person he saw when he arrived back at the field was Cathair. His height and fair hair made him visible even among the milling men.

Ardahl experienced a tightening in his gut—a flood of anger he could not stem. Fiercely he told himself he could not allow even that to distract him, and he turned his gaze away from Cathair as he went to Fearghal's side.

There, he discovered Dornach had assigned him a new charioteer, a seasoned warrior called Kell who had been laid up with an injury for some time. Ardahl knew him, to be sure, from practice on the field—a big, rawboned man with a crop of dark hair and a beard streaked with gray.

"We are to go first," Kell told Ardahl after Dornach left them. "Even ahead of the chief."

Ardahl nodded without conceit. If he had been designated the head of the spear, he would not argue it. The whole point of this was for him to protect Fearghal in any way he could.

Even if he could not keep his heart from yearning for those he left behind.

"Any word of fighting at Brioc?" he asked as he leaped aboard the chariot and Kell took up the reins.

"No' yet, though I do not doubt they are at it hard. Dacha is no' the man to hold his sword arm, is he, when it comes to revenge?"

"He is not."

Kell hesitated a moment. "I know fine there are rumors and tales about ye, Ardahl MacCormac. That ye murdered your sword brother. That ye've been touched by the gods, for how well ye fight. The greatest warrior ever among the tribe, so it will be declared in the great hall." His lips twisted in a wry smile. "If we ever again can boast a great hall."

"The first, no' true," Ardahl told him. he considered. "Neither is true."

"Aye, well, that does no' concern me now. I do no' doubt we are going to die together. And I wish to say, 'twill be an honor to fight and die in your company."

He thrust out his hand. Ardahl grasped it, forearm to forearm. Some of the terrible tension inside him faded. It felt well, having such a strong man at his side. Not Conall, but a braw man nonetheless.

"We are to be the point o' the spear," he shared with Kell as calmly as he could. "If we are to have one aim beyond protecting our chief, it must be to kill Dacha. For I do not believe this madness will end till he is slain."

Kell nodded. "Let us go to it, then."

Those were the last words they exchanged for some time. The chariots rolled out through the night, not quite silent as the dark deepened all around them. Neither were the men who followed silent. Their booted feet made contact with the earth. They coughed, they breathed, they whispered to one another. Yet the night remained quiet enough that they heard the conflict ahead long before they reached the place.

The clashing of weapons. The cries of men, sounding spectral from the distance. The hairs rose all over Ardahl's body—he had never heard such a sound. Kell's hands faltered on the reins and the team pulled up.

"Master Dornach?" Ardahl called back.

Dornach's driver directed their chariot up alongside. Ardahl could not see the war chief's face clearly in the dark but heard him catch his breath.

"How far ahead, master?" Kell asked.

"No' far. Brihan has fallen back fro' his settlement toward our shared border. The gods only know what has happened to his folk."

"We are well come, then," Fearghal called. "We can throw our might against Dacha."

"Aye."

Fearghal turned in his chariot and addressed his men, all of whom had now heard the din and knew full well what awaited them.

"We go in hard, men, and we spare no one of Dacha's blood. May all o' ye fight well for those ye love."

That was the heart of it, was it not? In the end, they did not fight for land, for revenge, or even for honor. If they could stop Dacha here, they would protect those they loved.

"May the gods go wi' us," Kell said as he took up the reins and urged their team forward. "And if we spend our blood, Ardahl MacCormac, I wish ye a swift journey to *Tír na nÓg*."

The sounds of that battle grew as they wheeled toward it. Ardahl, standing braced on the floor of the cart with his sword in his hand, tried to take it in all at once, to choose a target before one chose him, as Dornach had long ago taught him to do.

Kell took them straight into the heart of the melee. Others of their chariots, so he knew, would spread out to the flanks, but aye, he was the head of the spear.

The battle, fierce as it was, must have been raging for some time. Dead and dying lay everywhere. The hooves of their ponies and the wheels of their chariot bounced over one—Ardahl could only hope already dead. But he could not think of that. He could focus on nothing but fighting. One opponent at a time.

A momentary check in the battle occurred as they came crashing in, attackers and defenders alike taken unawares by their arrival. Ardahl got a single glimpse of Chief Brihan fighting in a knot of his men directly ahead, before the first of the enemy swords engaged him. And then it was all about killing and survival.

Kell proved a good charioteer—not so good as Ardahl's own da, perhaps, but good enough. He kept control of the ponies during the confusion of the battle, got Ardahl in close and away again after an opponent fell.

In a curious way, Ardahl saw everything at once, even while he saw only his opponents and the various blades coming at him. Saw the path he and Kell opened up with their chariot. Saw Fearghal dart in with Dornach's cart close behind, trying to reach Brihan. Saw the whole ebb and flow of the battle from his perch in the wicker cart, which rocked beneath him like a curragh at sea.

He and Kell were in deep. Half Dacha's army lay ahead and before them. He could see the man himself just ahead, fighting on foot, with a crashed cart at his back, face twisted in a rictus of fury and strain.

Dacha knew as well as Ardahl how deadly earnest was this fight. The achievement of all his ambitions, or the end.

"There he is!" he bellowed at Kell. "Take me in farther. Far-ther!"

Kell looked at him with half-crazed eyes. "We go in farther, we will be cut off."

Aye, so they would. Beyond reach, quite likely, of their men.

Which meant they would most certainly die here.

For the briefest instant, grief touched him, a wild, raw long-ing for Liadan and the life they would never have together.

Aye, Kell and he would die. Just so long as they killed Dacha first.

He made a savage slash in the air with his blade, and Kell took them in. The surging, seething bodies closed behind them.

I love ye, lass, Ardahl thought. *I love ye forevermore.*

Then he thought of naught save life and death.

CHAPTER FIFTY-FIVE

T HEIR CHARIOT ROCKED violently as Dacha's men mobbed it. Deep in among the enemy, their only allies now were Brihan's men, who fought here in a desperate knot, making a last stand.

Get down and fight! cried a voice close beside Ardahl. *Out o' the cart now!*

Conall. He once more stood at Ardahl's side, clad for war with a sword in his hand and his fair hair flying.

"Why?"

Conall turned his head and looked into Ardahl's eyes. *If ye do no', ye will die.*

He was going to die anyway, Ardahl thought even as he leaped clear of the chariot, which went over, swarmed by Dacha's warriors. Their ponies screamed. Ardahl did not see what happened to Kell.

Just ahead, Dacha fought amid a group of his warriors, facing Brihan and his desperate defenders. *The head of the spear,* Ardahl thought even as, slashing at attackers to the right and left, he ran straight for the man.

Conall had gone. Ardahl was alone deep in enemy territory. But Brihan, his face running with sweat and blood, looked up and recognized Ardahl as he came in, swinging his sword around his head.

No excuses now. No doubt. No fear. As a warrior, Ardahl existed for this moment. He must take out Dacha before he died.

Brihan cried out and made room for him there in that knot of struggling men, facing Dacha's best warriors. Two of Brihan's men, both badly wounded, fell back leaving Ardahl as—

The point of the spear.

For several moments then he knew nothing but the whirl of swords, blow upon blow from all sides, swearing and hollering, and the sight of Dacha's face, toward which he must fight. Dacha's defenders were fierce, and Ardahl took wounds, though he neither heeded nor felt them.

A man fell before his blade. Another. *Another.* Dacha stood directly in front of him.

The man appeared half maddened, eyes far too wide, face still fixed in that terrible rictus.

He too bled. On his feet. It would be up to Ardahl to take him down.

Then—only then—could he let himself think again.

Conall's sword felt good in his hand, a part of him even as his own sword might. He imagined he could hear Conall again, speaking in his ear.

Right. To the right! Left. Turn! Turn! In upon him there. There!

Ardahl spun, his feet digging into the grass, his blade and every intention aimed for Dacha's head. When his blade met flesh, sinew, and bone, it would end.

A chariot came crashing in upon them from his right. It rocked violently as the ponies dispersed Dacha's defenders.

A man leaped down.

Amid Ardahl's shock and the fighting rage, he recognized a fellow warrior—a man easy to know for his height and the color of his white-blond hair, now marked by blood.

Cathair.

Here.

Ardahl grunted and tried to bump him aside. Dacha and his defenders, still in a knot, recovered from the intrusion and regained their feet.

Ardahl needed room to fight.

But there was no room. The chariot, half tipped and with Cathair's driver still aboard, had him trapped and curtailed his sword arm. A crush of men on his left and others—enemies—at his back.

Cathair leaped forward—a magnificent surge of power that took him directly at Dacha. Ardahl knew the truth then. Cathair wanted the glory of that kill, wanted the privilege of being the man to slay Dacha.

First among warriors.

Yet Dacha saw Cathair coming and raised his sword in time. The two blades met with a furious clang.

Ardahl, well occupied against Dacha's men, had little time to spare for that battle. *Let him have the glory so long as Dacha dies. So long as it ends.*

He took down one of Dacha's two remaining defenders. The man fell in a shower of blood and Ardahl had time to draw a breath. To turn his eyes on Cathair and Dacha.

Yet another man came at him from the right. Without conscious thought, Ardahl drove him down beneath the hooves of Cathair's team, which stood nearly on top of them, trembling, and ran his sword through the man's heart.

A mighty roar snared his attention. He spun in time to see Cathair, trapped between Dacha and the wheel of his own chariot, lose his footing in the slick grass and fall back.

Back, and back.

Ardahl saw it all in an instant. Dacha's sword at the ready, drawn back for a blow that would take Cathair's head. The shocked realization in Cathair's eyes as he grasped that he would die. Die here on a day that barely yet reached for dawn.

Ardahl's sword moved without his direction. A great, whirling sweep it made, cutting through the pale light of the morning. Ending in Dacha's neck.

Dacha's head flew, the intent to kill still in his eyes, and his sword fell from his suddenly flaccid hand before it could complete the blow it had begun, and end Cathair's life.

Cathair fell hard down beside the wheel of his chariot. Dacha's head rolled away with the force of Ardahl's blow.

Ardahl and Cathair stared at one another for a moment suspended amid the screaming, the struggling, and the slaughter.

Cathair began to scrabble up. He still held his sword in one hand. Ardahl reached down swiftly and hauled him up by the other.

Cathair gawked at him, gazed clear into his eyes. "Ye saved my life."

Ardahl had, if not consciously. It had been instinct. No time to worry over it now. Dacha's remaining men, having witnessed the death of their chief, came on.

"Fight!" he bellowed at Cathair. And they did, standing shoulder to shoulder till they were joined by others of their men. Dornach, standing strong. And Fearghal, streaked with blood, moving up beside him.

The enemy fell back and back over the broken ground now lit to gray by the morning. Until, deprived of their chief, they broke and ran, and all that remained was the silent dead and a litter of broken chariots and abandoned weapons.

FOLLOWING THE BATTLE, when the last of Dacha's men had fled, pursued by whatever of Fearghal's chariots remained, Fearghal and Brihan embraced one another. Even though Ardahl stood nearby, he did not hear what was said. Words of gratitude, he supposed, and mayhap fealty.

Dacha's men had recovered his body but not his head. That, Fearghal eventually picked up and used to decorate his chariot, the visage still fixed in the ugly grimace with which he'd faced Cathair.

The sun climbed victoriously into the sky and Ardahl tried to come to terms with the fact that he was still alive. He had not thought to survive this battle.

"Ye can put that down now, I think."

Someone stood in front of him. Hollering at him. After the din of the battle, everything sounded muffled and yet too loud.

He stared at Dornach, who addressed him. The war chief ran with blood and the ugly wound on his cheek had been reopened, but aye, he too had survived.

Ardahl felt glad of it.

Dornach jerked his head at Ardahl's hand. "Ye can put away your sword."

"Oh. Aye."

Ardahl sheathed the weapon and only then realized his hands shook.

"Are ye bad hurt, lad?"

"I—" He did not know. "Nay."

"I saw what ye did. We all saw."

He nodded at the group of men standing together, and Ardahl counted heads as he might treasure. Fearghal had survived, aye. And he saw, miraculously, Kell just beyond. *Cathair.*

"Have we lost many?"

"Too many. But, by the gods, I believe it is done. Wi' Dacha dead and our two tribes united this way, I do no' think any will soon step out against us."

Dornach's hand came down on Ardahl's shoulder. "Ye ha' done well this day. I marked how ye fought—rushing in there without thought for yourself. And your honor, it did no' bend."

Ardahl said nothing.

"Come get your wounds tended. Grand news—the healer also survived. But he will be kept busy this while. Come."

Ardahl did not expect to be tended ahead of the chief or Dornach himself. When he reached the group among which the chief stood, Fearghal embraced him, thumped him hard on the back.

"The hero o' the battle! First among our warriors."

Ardahl did not know what to say. His gaze met that of Cathair, who stood close by. In Cathair's wide, blue eyes he saw—

Not the jealousy he anticipated. Nay, indeed, but something far different. Hesitancy. A marked lack of the usual aggression.

Gratitude?

No time to ponder it, then. The healer took him into care, and he suddenly and painfully remembered just how many wounds he had.

He sat staring at the sky, an expanse of achingly perfect blue, and endured the treatment. He would return to Liadan torn and shredded, a remnant of the man he'd been.

He would return to Liadan.

Suddenly his heart bounded so strong and triumphant, he knew nothing else. He would look into her eyes. Catch the gift of her smile. Even if they never shared anything more than that, it would be enough.

It would be enough.

CHAPTER FIFTY-SIX

LIADAN ONCE MORE knelt on the floor of the hut beside the hearth, praying. She did not remember why she'd got down here in the first place—to blow on the fire, no doubt. Nor did she know how long she'd knelt here—a while, mayhap, for her knees had cramped.

She spoke to Brigid, wise and understanding. Brigid, who had always listened to her. Who knew a woman's heart.

Liadan did not believe she had ever asked too much of life. Just for those she loved to be safe. For a stout roof when the wind blew, and food enough to sustain her, and hers.

But perhaps that had been too much to ask after all. For look what she'd lost. Look what was gone from her. Her da, and Conall of the bright, strong heart, and her mam.

Ardahl.

But—had Ardahl ever been hers? Aye, they had lain together. He'd possessed her body for a time as she'd possessed his. And he owned her heart forever, he did. There would never be another man in her sight.

But what they shared was forbidden. And being so, it seemed to her all too likely he would never return from this dire battle to which he'd gone. That the gods might so resolve their forbidden love. Take him from her, perhaps in punishment.

For he went at the head of the men to defend his chief. First into battle. First to fall?

If he did not return—

A small sound escaped her throat, a wordless entreaty to Brigid. If he did not return, she supposed she would have to live on—there would be no choice. She would live at least until Chief Dacha's forces came and burned the settlement, killed the old men, and made slaves out of the rest of them.

She would fight when they came. Take up Ardahl's sword. Do as he'd taught her. She might and she might not survive.

It would not be living, though, without him.

"Please," she whispered to the goddess. "Please."

Maeve entered the hut behind her. The woman had been wandering the settlement since their warriors rolled out, unable to keep still.

Liadan experienced a stab of pity. Poor Maeve. She had already lost her son once, denied him by Aodh's ruling that turned him into someone else's son instead. Circumstances had so altered their lives that she had come here to live with them. Had him back for a time.

Was she to lose him again now, for good?

"Lass," Maeve gasped, "wha' is it? Has word come?"

"Nay." Moving like an old woman, Liadan got to her feet. "But I fear—"

She and Maeve looked at each other. Liadan saw her own terror reflected in the woman's eyes.

"It does no good to fear," Maeve said. "All we can do is wait." She added softly before Liadan could speak, "And aye, I know what torture it is." Reaching out, she brushed Liadan's cheek. "Just as I know what it is ye feel for my son."

"Forbidden," Liadan whispered.

"We shall see. The good Brigid can accomplish many things. Come—the women are waiting at the spring, hoping a messenger might arrive."

The women were, indeed, located at the spring, a whole throng of them. Some had brought what weapons they could find. The old men and the lads too young to go off to fight stood with them, and all eyes turned westward.

If Dacha's forces did come, if they rolled over Fearghal's and Brihan's men combined and came to pillage and burn, they would find weapons waiting.

Yet no messenger and no enemy warriors came. Old Fergus said a pair of lads had been sent out to watch and had not been heard from again. The group fell unnaturally quiet, so much so that Liadan could hear birds singing in the trees, not far off.

Birds that did not know life and death teetered on what was to come.

Even the bairns in the crowd remained mostly quiet. Women sat down with their backs to the spring and nursed them, rocked them, coaxed them to sleep.

The afternoon dragged on toward evening.

At last, a cry came. A long, undulating cry it was, causing a disturbance of the very air, as if the world suddenly trembled. Those waiting were instantly on their feet. Facing all into the sunset.

One of the two lads who'd been sent out appeared, approaching at a dead run.

"They come. They come!"

"Who comes?" The words appeared on Liadan's lips, and she heard them repeated all around.

"Who?"

Who?

The boy paused, his lungs working like bellows. A member of the guard, an aged fellow called Bran, labored up beside him.

"Our men. They come! Heads upon their chariots. Victorious!"

Victorious.

But was Ardahl among them?

As a body, the women, old men, and children ran. Out through the settlement toward the sunset. Along the track where the road ran through the trees. Until they could hear the jingle of harnesses. The rattle of wheels, and voices, beloved voices.

The two parties met in joy and grief, at the place where the track sloped downward. Women with bairns in their arms threw themselves at their men, gathered in tiny groups, screamed with joy. Wept.

Liadan, desperate to see, tried to peer between bodies, among heads. She could feel Maeve at her side, straining likewise. And then the crowd shifted. Liadan saw Fearghal, with his wife already in his arms. Cathair. Any number of warriors she knew, and—

Their eyes met across the distance, and it felt as if everything else melted away. The noise, the bustle, the cries, and the wondering. Liadan's heart beat so hard in her chest that she could not breathe, and her world brightened around her in a flash of gratitude so strong it translated into wonder.

Beside her, Maeve cried, "He is there!"

Ardahl's mother flew forward, threw herself into her son's arms. Liadan's feet refused to move. If she went to him now, flew to him as she longed to do, the whole world would see the truth.

So she stood rooted as, with his arm around his mother, he came to her. And when he stood before her, the joy became so bright she could no longer feel her feet on the ground.

He was wounded, and sorely. She could see that. Blood stained his clothing, and livid cuts—only some of which had been tended—still wept. But he gazed into her eyes and smiled at her.

Smiled with his eyes. With his heart.

"Master Ardahl. I am that glad to see ye safe returned."

"I am that glad to be here."

Maeve patted her son's face. His arms, as if seeking out the injuries. "Son, be ye whole? Did ye vanquish that serpent? Did ye win?"

"We won. There should be peace for a time."

Peace. Liadan did not know what that meant for her. For them. But he stood here beside her, big and alive and breathing. For the moment, she needed nothing more.

Fearghal called for their attention. There among the joyous and the grieving and the dead, laid in the broken chariots, he spoke to them from his heart.

"There has been a great victory. We and Clan Brioc are now united against all comers. Dacha is dead."

He held aloft the trophy that had decorated the front of his chariot. Silence fell once again.

"We shall rebuild. Endure our grief. Hold these lands we love so well. Many have died for the sake of them. We shall no' forget their sacrifice. To honor them, we will live on. We shall thrive just as they would wish us to."

Were those tears in the chief's eyes? Aye, for he blinked rapid-ly.

Fearghal went on, "Many have displayed great valor this past day and night. But there is one man—Ardahl MacCormac, step here to me."

Ardahl did not move. He stood so close to Liadan, she might have reached out and snagged his hand, but it took his chief repeating the command for him to step forward.

"This man," Fearghal declared when Ardahl stood beside him. "Amid a wealth of valiant deeds during this battle, he emerged as bravest. Strongest. First among our warriors. He it was who took Dacha's head, and delivered us from that dark threat."

A chill ran over Liadan's skin. She watched something mo-mentous. Something that would be told down through the ages. And if Ardahl could never be hers in truth—well, mayhap it was for this he had been destined.

Yet he did not look like a man comfortable with glory. He bowed his head to his chief and to all who cheered for him.

His gaze returned to Liadan—only to Liadan—before he said, "I have done naught but any man here might do. We defend this land and those we love."

"This belongs to ye." With a grand gesture, Fearghal present-ed Ardahl with Dacha's head. Ardahl took it by the hair but did not so much as glance at it, his eyes all for Liadan still.

CHAPTER FIFTY-SEVEN

DACHA'S HEAD HUNG outside their hut, suspended by its hair from a peg Ardahl had hammered there, with absent-minded disregard. Indeed, it dangled from one of the braids Dacha had no doubt put there before going off to maim, maul, and conquer. Which, Ardahl could not help but feel, was only fitting.

He did not want the trophy. He did not want the acclaim. He wanted to be alone with those he loved—with his mam, and most especially with Liadan.

He had not touched her yet, had not so much as brushed his fingers across hers. He still had blood on his hands—on most of him, to be fair. And so as he had done so often since he'd come to take Conall's place, he went around the side of the hut and tried to scrub it off, a task much harder than one might imagine and one that took him back, back to the day he had stood covered in his dearest friend's blood.

Life was made up of circles, he thought. It all came round again and again. Birth, death, and to birth again after a time spent in *Tír na nÓg*. The gods' cauldron of rebirth spat them out and they returned to this beautiful, troubled, treacherous world to—

What? Learn? Love.

Surely it was all about the love.

Liadan followed him around the side of the hut as she had so many times before. As he'd known she would. Their eyes met, and he thought, *If she ever looked at me that way out among the tribe, everyone would know the truth.*

And he thought about circles, and how such a love as theirs must endure. That even if they could not be together now, they would be, someday.

Someday. Because a circle had no beginning and no end. Neither did their love.

"Let me do that for ye." She took the cloth from him, dabbed it into the pot of soap. Just for the chance to touch him, as he knew. And when she did, when her fingers met his, the contact felt so intense, so complete, he knew that, aye, in truth, he needed no more.

"Ye must see the healer."

"I ha' seen him. I would far rather ye tended me, Liadan."

Their eyes met. Memory united them—the slide of skin on naked skin. Lips fused to lips in a storm of effortless belonging.

"That, aye, I will do, though I do not know that I can push your mam aside. Ardahl, I was so afraid."

"Aye, but"—with one scraped hand, he touched her chin gently—"I am here. Liadan, I will always be here."

Her eyes flooded with tears. She nodded. "Still, naught is promised."

"Naught is promised but that I will belong to ye, for eternity."

She caught her breath. "Come inside. I will finish wi' tending ye. And—"

She wanted to kiss him. She wanted it as desperately as he wanted it. Yet Mam was in the hut. So very hard for them to be alone.

Liadan towed him inside to the comforting gloom, and pushed him down beside the fire.

"There is food," Mam said, "and drink. And I—" She gave her son a long look. "I ha' an errand elsewhere."

She did not, not at such a time as this. But Ardahl would not argue it, and silently blessed her as she slipped out through the door.

Liadan came into his arms. The simple motion failed to describe what it lent—an answer to all the longing that had beset him when he was away from her. She kissed him, and the terrible need that had been inside him all the while eased. Something so basic as breathing, he thought as he held her fast in his arms. As the blood rushing through his veins. As simple and as profound as loving.

Loving this one woman.

"Here, do no' weep," he told her, feeling the tears wet her face.

"They are tears o' joy. Ardahl." She drew away far enough to gaze into his eyes. "I discovered somewhat while ye were away, when my fear burned its brightest. Love demands what it demands, and for me that is your presence. If I can ne'er be wi' ye as your wife, at least I can be near ye. I ask only leave to watch the smile come and go on your face, the way the sun pricks red from your hair, the way ye lift a sword. See the thoughts flicker in your eyes. Hear your voice, your laughter. Spend my life near to ye."

"And I to ye. My very soul clamors to be your own."

"It *is* my own."

They kissed again there beside the hearthplace, knowing they might have only moments before life once more intruded. And he told himself it was enough to hold this woman for even a brief time. For was not time a circle also? And might they not have other lifetimes?

When his mam returned, she wore a curious look on her face. They sat apart by then, Ardahl with his eyes half closed, absorbing the fact that Liadan remained beside him.

Mam called them forth. "Ardahl, son, ye must come. The chief has stopped me on my way. He bade me tell ye that he needs to see ye at once."

Ardahl's eyes flew open. "Now? 'Tis no' another attack? Dacha has not the men."

"Nay, no' that. He is outside the warriors' hall, with the druids and some other men."

When Ardahl arose, it was with a groan, and Liadan had to help him, her shoulder beneath his arm. They went forth so with her supporting him as she would a brother. And indeed, Ardahl fancied he caught a glimpse of Conall from the corner of his eye.

Smiling.

Folk stared as they went by. Some followed. And indeed, a good number of people stood out in front of the hall when they reached it.

Dusk had fallen by then, upon this day that had held so much. Too much. The last of the gloaming lit the sky with soft radiance, and Ardahl's heart leaped in his chest with the love he felt for this place.

He turned his gaze on the people awaiting them. The first person he saw was Brasha. She stood to one side with her father, and she was weeping into her hands.

And Chief Fearghal with his wife beside him. Aye, both the surviving druids wearing grave, serious expressions.

What was this? What, on this night when he desired only peace?

"Och, by the goddess Brigid," Liadan whispered in his ear. "What now?"

And then Ardahl saw Cathair stepping out to stand shoulder to shoulder with Fearghal. His heart sank violently. Some new horror, then. Some accusation cooked up between Cathair and Brasha, perhaps.

Some penance he would have to bear.

He and Liadan stepped up with Mam at their side. Ardahl raised his gaze to that of his chief, who stirred suddenly and held up his hand, stilling any murmurs from those gathered.

Into the clear night air, he declared, "It has come to my ears there has been a grave miscarriage of justice. We are gathered here this night to put it right."

Ardahl tensed and felt Liadan go rigid at his side.

"Not long since, we lost one o' our best young men. Conall MacAert perished on the training field, and the blame fell upon this man, Ardahl MacCormac. His closest friend." Fearghal glanced at the two grim-faced druids. "A sentence was imposed, as dictated by the highest of our most sacred laws. Ardahl MacCormac would carry the blame for the death o' his friend and would henceforth take Conall's place and live out the balance o' his life."

Tamald stepped forward, his eyes meeting Ardahl's. "So it is," he declared. "Much has transpired since then, but Ardahl MacCormac has carried this blame."

"Ardahl MacCormac," he called out almost melodiously into the dark, "just recently ye did come to me and ask me to rescind this punishment due to an injustice."

"I did," Ardahl managed to croak.

"I told ye I could no' do so without the main witness to Conall's death confirming the injustice."

"Ye did."

"And so he has done."

What?

Cathair stepped forward from Fearghal's side.

His wounds, too, had been tended. The linen bandages, like his pale hair, reflected the light from the torches at the front of the hall. His face, though, appeared still paler, and might have been carved from stone.

"Ardahl MacCormac," he announced for all to hear, "I stand here to confess I ha' done ye great ill. Both ill thoughts and ill wishes I ha' aimed against ye." He hesitated an instant. "And false accusations.

"In the battle just past, ye saved my life." Cathair's eyes met Ardahl's in the flickering light. "I would no' be standing here to speak if your sword—Conall's sword had no' been so strong. 'Twas I who made sure certain words were poured in Conall's ear before he died, to poison him against ye. To turn his heart to anger. I thought that through jealousy he would remove ye from my path, that I might claim the place o' first among us."

He did not name Brasha or her part in the lies and deception, but her tears said much.

Softly now, Cathair concluded, "'Tis I who should carry the shame ye ha' carried. 'Tis I who caused Conall's death and 'twas his own hand that landed the dirk in his heart. I beg ye, master druids, lift the sentence from this man."

CHAPTER FIFTY-EIGHT

IT GREW SO still there in front of the warriors' hall, the leaping flames of the torches sounded loud in Ardahl's ears. He could feel the tension in Liadan's body, pressed to his side, and sense how this affected her, even as it did him.

He held Cathair's gaze and saw the emotions there also. The sorrow, the regret. The shame.

Tamald stepped up. "Words have been spoken here this night, words o' truth. In light o' them, Ardahl MacCormac, I lift from ye the sentence that had been imposed upon ye. Ye be free to live no' Conall MacAert's life, but your own."

A sob broke from Mam's throat. Ardahl's thoughts raced. Anger, aye, that Cathair's scheming had cost Conall's life. That Liadan and Flanna had lost their brother. That Liadan's mam had died still grieving her son.

But mayhap Conall and Mistress MacAert had heard this truth. He must believe they had.

And aye, as he turned to face Cathair more fully, seeking words to say, he thought he again caught a glimpse of Conall from the corner of his eye.

He could express his anger. He could cry out his grief. But Cathair had done the right thing in the end, and he would now have to carry the shame of his treachery.

Ardahl knew firsthand how hard that would be.

So he said, "I am that grateful to you, Cathair MacBain, for speaking this truth. I would never have raised a hand against

Conall, dear to me as my own life. I am glad to be free o' that blame.

"As for ye—aye, ye ha' a life. I bid ye do good with it. Speak truth. Help others. Live as Conall might ha' done."

Somberly, Cathair nodded. Ardahl's mam began to weep in earnest. Fearghal came forward and embraced Ardahl, which meant Liadan had to leave go the grip she'd taken upon his arm.

Ardahl felt the absence of her touch like another wound.

Yet—a light began to shine ahead of him, a glorious path opening wide. He had regained himself, Ardahl MacCormac. As such he might claim her, his best friend's sister, for his wife.

Naught else mattered to him. Not the victories on the field or the place of first among warriors, or even Fearghal's approval, showing clear in his eyes. Not Cathair's shame.

But that the circle had closed for them here in this life, and Liadan might be his bride.

Tamald waited for Fearghal to embrace Ardahl, for his fellows to congratulate him and mumble apologies. For Dornach to come up and give him an embrace that nearly knocked him off his feet. Not till Liadan had reclaimed her place at his side and tucked her hand in his did the druid priest step up to them.

"I find I can now agree to your request to be made handfast." A quiet smile shone in the man's eyes. "And this rite will I perform wi' a full and happy heart."

Ardahl had to fight down his emotions before he could speak. "No' half so happy as mine." He snaked his arm around Liadan and tucked her closer to his side. Glancing into her face, he said, "I believe we should keep the joining quiet and simple, given all that has passed."

"I disagree," Tamald declared. "I believe it should be a grand and wondrous gathering and needs to take place just as soon as can be. For do we no' now step into the sunlight o' our future? And is no' the tying o' the knot the best way to do just that?"

His eyes twinkled. "Shall no' the handfasting o' the first among our warriors be well celebrated? So say I."

IN CHIEF MACMURTRAY'S Highland hall, a shower of crystal-clear notes trembles through the air as Finlay sets his harp from his shoulder. His tale has garnered the attention of everyone there, from the highest chief, his host, to the lowest of the servants.

He smiles around at them all and concludes, "And so a mere three days later, Ardahl MacCormac and his Liadan were made handfast in a braw ceremony. And were they no' among the ancestors o' this very man we honor here this night?"

He grants a nod to the chief, who smiles in pride and satisfaction.

But it is the lovely daughter of the house whom Finlay seeks with his gaze as the last notes of his song die away. It is one woman—only one.

For an instant he feels the circle of his own fate tighten around him. And he smiles because he knows love has no beginning, and no end.

"Another song!" Chief MacMurtray calls out. "Another, Master Finlay."

Aye, he will sing his songs, and gladly, until his heart comes home.

THE END

ABOUT THE AUTHOR

Laura Strickland delights in time traveling to the past and weaving deliciously romantic stories for her readers. Her first love has always been Scottish Historical Romance, and her work has garnered her several awards including a RONE. At home in Western New York, she's been privileged to mother a number of very special rescue dogs. Her lifelong interest in Celtic history, magic, and music, along with her mantra of *Lore, Legend, Love* are all reflected in her writing.

Visit Laura at www.laurastricklandbooks.com